The African Agenda

To Kevin with thanks and
I look forward to a fruitful
business partnership
CBaezie
23/12/11

Camynta Baezie

GW00778995

You were looking, O king, and lo! there was a great statue. This statue was huge, its brilliance extraordinary; it was standing before you, and its appearance was frightening. The head of that statue was of fine gold, its chest and arms of silver, its middle and thighs of bronze, its legs of iron, its feet partly of iron and partly of clay. As you looked on, a stone was cut out, not by human hands, and it struck the statue on its feet of iron and clay and broke them in pieces. Then the iron, the clay, the bronze, the silver, and the gold, were all broken in pieces and became like the chaff of the summer threshing floors; and the wind carried them away, so that not a trace of them could be found. But the stone that struck the statue became a great mountain and filled the whole earth.

Daniel 2:31-35

This book is dedicated to the dead who aspired to the unification of Africa and to the living who continue to pursue this goal.

ACKNOWLEDGMENTS

My first thanks go to Fred McBagonluri whose book *A Woman to Marry* inspired me out of my slumber to undertake this project. My indebtedness goes to Philip Townshend who painstakingly went through the manuscript from concept stage to the final work. Without his input this work would probably still be on the drawing board. I am grateful to my wife, Kande, my daughter Anaale and my son Simba whose valuable time I stole to write this book. I thank Mark McCabe, Raphael Adeyemi and Tuamunn Camynta-Baezie for proofreading the final manuscript.

CHAPTER I

September, 1990. 127 Juba Villas, Burma Camp, Accra.

"I've finished, dad," Mike called out.

Colonel Zinbalan came out of the house followed by his wife Takyiwaa and they both got into the car. Mike was already waiting in the back seat.

"Have you got everything?" Takyiwaa asked her son with mixed feelings. She was sad their only child was leaving home, but proud that he was going to the university.

"Yes, mum."

Mike couldn't wait for the 250-kilometre journey that would take him to Kumasi, Ghana's second city, to start his undergraduate programme in Chemistry. As they drove out of their driveway onto the main street that would lead them out of Burma Camp, Mike's mind wandered past the well-laid lawns, whitewashed fences and the well-cut hedges surrounding the officers' living area to the freedom he was going to enjoy at the university without the watchful eyes of his parents.

When they approached the main exit from the barracks Mike's attention was drawn to the soldiers at the checkpoint as his dad slowed down to acknowledge the salutes from the two soldiers staffing the exit. That's what I call respect, Mike thought. The salutes his dad got from other soldiers had always fascinated him and he had been thinking of becoming an officer after his graduation. I would like to travel like my dad, he would promise himself. He looked forward each time to his dad's return from missions abroad, not only for the presents but also for the wonderful stories his dad told him about those travels. The last time his dad had returned from a peace mission in Lebanon, he had brought him a digital camera and had told him Beirut was a beautiful city, although smaller than Accra.

Mike's thoughts were broken when his dad slammed on the brakes, bringing the car to an abrupt stop. Mike looked just in time as a driver missed hitting their car by inches from a side road.

"Damn this fool! Why can't people learn how to drive?" Colonel Zinbalan cursed.

"Just be careful," Takyiwaa cautioned. "I'm surprised there are not many more accidents with this driver anarchy," she added.

"I think the authorities should put more emphasis on driver training," Mike said.

Takyiwaa chuckled, turned her head to look at Mike and said, "In three years you will graduate and come to help our dear country dying for effective leadership."

"What would you like to do after your graduation?" Colonel Zinbalan asked.

"I will join the army."

Colonel Zinbalan's heart sank. He had observed his son iron his clothes and polish his shoes to military standards. He even noticed the similarity in the way Mike walked and had been concerned his son would want to join the army one day. It is probably my fault, he had thought, because he had never told his boy about the high risks in all the military operations and peace missions he had undertaken.

"Wait till you finish your degree," Colonel Zinbalan advised, hoping situations and friends at the university would change his son's mind. He was going to add something when he saw Mike dozing off through the rear mirror.

Mike woke up just as his dad turned off from the main road into the gravelled yard of the Travellers' Rest Stop at Nkawkaw three hours into their journey. "Thanks dad, I could do with a leak."

"I'm hungry, I don't know about you two," Colonel Zinbalan said, pulling the car into the parking lot.

Mike returned from the washroom to find his mother talking to a boy about his age. "There you are," his mother said, "Mike, come and meet Kofi Mensah. He is going to the same university as you."

"Which hall are you, Kofi?" Mike asked.

"Unity Hall."

"I'm in the same hall, Room 407."

"I'll see you on campus," Kofi Mensah said.

An hour later Colonel Zinbalan pulled into the parking lot in front of the Unity Hall of Residence. Mike looked at the two eight-floor towers opposite each other thinking, I'm going to like it here with no parents watching over me. He joined a couple of students at the Porter's Lodge for registration and when he collected his keys, he signalled to his parents.

"Where is the lift?" his mother asked.

"The lifts don't work. They haven't in the last ten years," the Porter told her.

"Which floor is your room?"

Mike looked at the writing attached to his keys and said, "8th Floor."

"I guess we will have to leave you here then," Takyiwaa said, embracing her son. When she let go, Mike could see the tears in her eyes but he pretended not to notice, holding back his own tears.

Colonel Zinbalan embraced his son, patted him on the back and said, "Call us if you need anything."

Mike waved until his parents got into their car before struggling up the flight of stairs with his suitcase. He got to the 8th Floor exhausted and when he got to Room 407 the door was already opened. "Hi, you must be Kutini. I'm Mike, your roommate."

"Come on in, Mike, make yourself comfortable. I'm just sorting out my clothes," Kutini said, picking a shirt from the bed behind him.

Mike lay on the other bed, closed his eyes and stretched himself.

"You must be tired. How far did you come?" Kutini asked.

"Accra. I haven't been on a long journey for some time."

"The inter-city coaches are not exactly comfortable."

"My parents came to drop me, but the roads aren't particularly good."

"You're a big boy; you should be able to travel on your own," Kutini teased.

***

Kutini came from a humble background. Early in the morning of the day before Kutini bade farewell to his parents in the large compound house built of mud and wood based on medieval architecture believed to have come from the ancient Sudanese Empires, his father, Andi Bomanso, had called him to his inner chamber.

"Sit down my son," Andi said, pointing to his left side of the mat spread on the floor. On his right were three items: a calabash containing water, a piece of broken earthenware containing ashes and a piece of chalk. "You're embarking on a very important journey so I'm going to ask our ancestors for their protection and blessings."

Kutini didn't believe in spirituality but said nothing as he watched his father draw a circle on the floor with the chalk.

The old man pinched some ashes between his fingers and sprinkling them within the circle saying: "The spirit of my fathers and grandfathers I call upon you. My great grandfather Dabaga, I call upon you. All the good spirits of our land, I call upon you. Today my son, Kutini, will be embarking on a long journey to go and study. I ask you to bless and protect him." He took some more ashes and while sprinkling them continued his incantation. "Just as these ashes were once fire, I invoke you to turn any trouble that might come his way into ashes."

Andi Bomanso shook the rest of the ashes from his fingers and picked up the calabash of water. "My ancestral spirits, here is some cool water, drink. Anything that might heat up Kutini's life – sickness, disease or evil – cool it down with this water. Just as you protected me while I was fighting in foreign lands, I commit Kutini's protection and well-being to you."

He drank some of the water and passed the calabash to Kutini. "Drink, my son," our ancestral spirits will protect and guide you to great things."

"Thanks father, for your blessings."

There was silence for a few seconds, then Kutini rose to go.

"Son," the old man called, "there is something I haven't told you."

Kutini sat down wondering what other dark secrets his father was going to reveal to him.

"Do you know why you were named Kutini?"

"I know it means conqueror of death." Kutini would have said he didn't want to know but his deep respect for his father restrained him. He also knew from his father that their house was called *Bomanso Dabuo* because his great-great-grandfather

Bomanso had established the household when he founded the village, which was why they were the kingmakers but couldn't themselves inherit the throne.

"Yes, but I suppose you don't know why that particular name was chosen."

"No."

"When you were born, for nearly two weeks, you wouldn't stop crying and wouldn't feed so, I consulted the gods. It was revealed that you were my grandfather who had been reborn to complete an unfinished business. The only remedy to your crying was to call you by my grandfather's name. You were on your mother's lap crying when I returned home that day. I picked you up and said: Grandpa Kutini, if you're really the one, show us a sign. To our amazement you giggled, then stopped crying and for the first time your mother fed you without trouble. Afterwards, you slept for almost twelve hours. Since then, as we watched you grow, we realised that there was something special about you. The spirits be with you."

Kutini sat, his forehead in his palm, his elbow resting on his knee. He didn't know what to believe or think. His mind just wandered to a similar occasion seven years earlier when he was leaving home to start secondary school. His father's last statement had been, "Remember, the people who have power are those with the pen, not those with the gun." The statement had sounded familiar. Where had he heard it before? 'The pen is mightier than the sword.' He couldn't remember who had said it but from that day on he hung on and analysed every news item in the printed media and by the time he finished his A Levels he had accumulated seven years of the *Daily Graphic* newspaper.

Kutini had an amazing memory and could recall specific news items and events with fine details; he would often back up his statements with relevant sources.

"Thank you father," Kutini said and rose. As he started to go out of the door, his eyes caught his father's military uniform hanging on the wall. He moved closer and examined them as though he was seeing them for the first time. The parade uniform of the Royal West African Frontier Force, a distinctive khaki drill with red fez, scarlet zouave style jacket edged in yellow and red cummerbunds, hung inside transparent plastic. The badge on the fez was a palm tree. Next to it, in similar protective plastic, was his artillery unit blue jacket uniform with red and blue braid and a round kilmarnock cap. The additional yellow braiding on the front of his blue jacket distinguished him as a warrant officer, the highest rank an African could attain.

Kutini turned to see his father standing behind him. He gave a military-style salute which his father acknowledged with a slight bow before leaving the room. Kutini followed him out, full of respect and admiration for him.

To most people in Sankana, Retired Warrant Officer Andi was known as *Dabble-U-O*; to the others he was simply *Sojaman,* a veteran of the Second World War who had fought in Burma for the British Government with the RWAFF.

In 1939, when Second World War broke out the RWAFF had been transferred from Colonial Office to War Office control under the leadership of General George Giffard, General Officer Commanding West Africa. It had been the basis for the formation of 81st and 82nd Divisions both of which saw service in Burma. It was in the 82nd Division that Andi Bomanso had served after he had been drafted into The Gold Coast Regiment three years into the war.

As Andi watched his son go out, he felt proud that Kutini was going to the university. One day he will be talking to the whole country just like *Osagyefo* did, he thought. He remembered how he had been taken from the village one early Harmattan morning by force and enlisted in the Gold Coast Regiment in 1942. A year later, he was in Burma fighting in the War. When he returned in 1945 he had continued to serve in the RWAFF until 1959, two years after the Gold Coast became the first black African nation to declare independence from Britain, when all of the Gold Coast Military Forces were withdrawn from the Royal West African Frontier Force. With the country's change of name to Ghana, the Gold Coast Regiment was renamed as the Ghana Regiment.

Andi Bomanso still remembered 6th March 1957, Ghana's Independence Day. It was the first time he had worn shoes outside of combat. He had stood in parade as the first indigenous head of state inspected the guard of honour before mounting the rostrum to deliver his famous speech, "… the Independence of Ghana is meaningless unless it is linked to the total liberation of the entire African continent…"

Warrant Officer Bomanso had looked in awe, oblivious to the speech, as the larger-than- life leader had finished his speech with: "Ghana is free forever." As the crowd cheered, the only words that had made sense to Andi in the entire speech were 'Ghana is free'. To him what mattered was that Osagyefo, as Dr. Kwame Nkrumah had become known, had defeated the mighty British Empire and Ghanaians would no longer be ruled by the white man and forced to fight other peoples' wars.

Andi was standing in the courtyard, his mind still in the past, when he saw his wife, Ponaa, coming towards him. He had married the princess from the neighbouring village of Nator three years after Ghana's independence and they had been blessed with two daughters and a son.

"Kutini is ready, have you given him money?" Ponaa asked her husband.

"I've given him his transportation fare."

"But that won't be enough; he'll need pocket money."

"I can't afford anymore. You know my pension pay is not much."

"And you spend it all on drinking."

Andi ignored his wife's comment. He had heard that accusation several times and didn't want to be drawn into another argument.

"He is your son; your only son," Ponaa continued.

"I'll send him some money when I receive my next pay," Andi promised.

"You'd better," Ponaa said and turned towards Kutini's room.

Kutini had finished packing when his mother entered. He had heard his mother's accusations of his father many times and didn't like them but he couldn't do anything. He was aware of the cash-flow problems in the family and had survived his secondary education through his own enterprise supported by the fee-free education accorded to Northern students.

"Here is some money I've been saving for you. It's not much but it will help," Ponaa said to her son. Her income from *pito* brewing was small but it contributed to the family subsistence.

"Thanks mother, it's more than enough," Kutini said without counting the money.

Ponaa wished she could do more for her son. "No matter what people tell you, remember that you have royal blood," she told him.

It was midday when Kutini finally bid farewell to his parents and walked through the maturing groundnut fields. Very soon his mother would harvest his three months' worth of labour in the fields; she would send him money from the proceeds, Kutini thought as he followed the footpath towards the village market. An hour later the once-a-day wooden truck that linked the village with Wa, the regional capital, stopped at the lorry park. Kutini sat on the wooden edge along one side of the truck among other male passengers. Inside the truck women traders sat on top of their wares chatting. As the dust trailed the moving lorry towards Wa, Kutini wondered when development would reach his part of the world.

In Wa, Kutini boarded the improvised passenger truck and sat uncomfortably among seven others in a sardine-like packed row. He arrived in Kumasi at the early hours of the morning after an excruciating thirteen-hour overnight journey along the bumpy 450-kilometre dirt road. He cleaned himself of dust, collected his baggage, then boarded a *trotro* to the university.

Four hours later, Mike walked into the room.

***

Mike had finished unpacking and was lying on the bed. He turned, adjusting himself and tucking the pillow under his head. At that moment, there was a knock on their door.

"Mike, aren't you coming for the orientation?" Kofi Mensah asked as soon as the door opened.

"When is it?" Mike asked with a sleepy voice.

"In an hour's time."

Mike got up from the bed and introduced Kutini to Kofi Mensah. "We met at the Traveller's Rest Stop at Nkawkaw," he said.

The three freshmen sat in the front row at the Great Hall as the Registrar welcomed them to the University. "As you all know this year the government is introducing the residential lodging fee scheme as the first stage of the university commercialisation programme. Details of the next stage will be made available in the second semester," the Registrar announced, "the University will of course put in measures to ..."

There was a clap and a foot tap, instantly picked up by the rest of the students in the packed hall, in a clap-clap, tap-tap, clap-clap rhythm. The students did not stop until the Registrar left the stage.

The next day at the Junior Common Room Committee meeting of Unity Hall of Residence Kutini rose to contribute to the debate on the students' lodging fees. "In my view, the government's commercialisation scheme imposed as part of an IMF package is unethical given the salary levels and the general poverty in the country. In 1972, the current Finance Minister led a group of students to attack the Prime Minister at the time for proposing a similar package. It would be suicidal to reintroduce this scheme without first addressing the country's economic situation. I would therefore like to table a motion against the scheme."

There was a loud applause as the students cheered Kutini's motion.

Kofi Mensah caught up with Kutini and Mike after the meeting and said, "I like the way you provide references to back up your arguments."

"It's good to know at least one person agrees with me."

"Several people share that view."

"Let's go for a drink," Kutini suggested.

During the rest of the semester the three friends were mostly found together and had become known as *The Three Musketeers.* Mike was the quietest of the three and would often listen as the two went into long political conversations. He was always amazed at the depth of Kutini's political knowledge and enjoyed listening to him discuss the merits of an African State with Kofi Mensah.

"One African State would be difficult, it would have to be a federation," Kofi would argue.

"What matters is a united Africa, not what type of unification," Kutini would respond.

***

Mike had just returned to his room from his last examination paper when his dad called.

"Should we come and pick you up tomorrow?"

"Hold on dad," Mike said and confirmed with Kutini they were going by coach. "No, I'll get the inter-city coach. I'll see you tomorrow," he said to his dad.

"How did your first semester go?" Colonel Zinbalan asked when Mike arrived.

"It was good. I enjoyed the lectures and I've been thinking of how I will apply them when I join the military."

"Did you make any friends?" Colonel Zinbalan asked, changing the topic.

"Oh, my room mate, Kutini Bomanso, is brilliant. He spoke at the Student Representative Council Forum at the Great Hall and he has since been the talk of the university."

"Politics is quite an interesting field."

"Kutini studies Computer Science. He is just an excellent speaker."

"Do you want to be like him?"

"No, dad, I want to be an officer like you."

Colonel Zinbalan swallowed hard, fighting his inner self. He didn't like to impose his wishes on his son. "Mike, military life is not as easy as it seems. If I had a choice I would be in a different profession."

Mike detected the worry in father's voice. "Dad, do you have problems at work?" he asked.

"Not really, it's just this soldier who has been assigned recently to my unit from Sandhurst. He is a law unto himself." Colonel Zinbalan had never discussed his work with anyone, but hoped somehow he would be able to dissuade Mike with his own personal experience.

"Who is this soldier?"

"I don't think you know him. He is called Amankwa Amofa.

CHAPTER 2

Amankwa Amofa had always wanted to be in the military since his youthful days. He was sportive and had been playing for his school's football team since the age of six. He had joined his secondary school's cadets at the age of fourteen and by the age of sixteen his height and build had earned him the rank of cadet commander. His physical structure and his determination combined with a genealogy of combativeness made him an ideal candidate for the military.

Amofa joined the Military Academy after his A Levels and worked tirelessly to graduate as the best all-round Officer Cadet, which earned him a place to go to senior officers' training at Sandhurst, UK – a well sought after opportunity in the academy. It sorted the men from the boys, as they put it.

While at Sandhurst Amofa had attended the Chelsea Flower show where he first encountered the concept *feng shui*. The award-winning garden had drawn Amofa's attention to the designer and they talked at length about gardening. Amofa had bought some books on the subject and returned to Ghana a year later with loads of aspirations and expectations.

When Amofa was offered the piece of land on which his house now stood he started dreaming of how he would transform that barren land into a *feng shui* garden. The house, which would become his retirement home, was situated at a strategic part of the rich residential suburb of Accra called McCarthy Hill, named after Sir Charles McCarthy, one of the Governors of the then Gold Coast.

The house sat on a hill, the main entrance about fifty metres away from the access road. From the left, round the back, and to the right was a valley. There was water during the rainy season but it dried up with the dry season, leaving a small creek of water at the back of the house.

This valley together with the road formed a boundary around the ten-acre property on which the house sat. In a way it was an island and he intended to turn it into a garden oasis.

When the house itself was completed, he started to design the garden. He wanted *feng shui* principles to be evident in the exterior landscaping, to reflect the open modern interior their house designer had created.

Amofa had read that for the natural forces of energy to be present in every dwelling unit to attract peace, harmony and tranquillity, he would have to incorporate the five elements of water, metal, fire, wood and earth both in the interior and exterior designs. The stream flowing round the house provided the first of the five elements – water. With *feng shui* principles shunning strong, straight lines, the presence of the natural stream and planted edges provided the required flowing curves with its sense of movement.

Amofa's love for gardening had started as an interest and then it became an obsession until he found another use for his garden.

He had been working on the watercourse one day when a soldier he had sent on an 'assignment' came to report to him. Amofa had asked the soldier to 'take care' of an officer and to make it look like an accident.

The country was under military rule and Amofa took advantage of his position to settle personal scores. He would usually say if the ruling body was a family, then he was part of it and no one could touch him.

"Is it done?" Amofa asked.

"I tried to . . ." the soldier stammered.

"All I want to know is whether or not it's been done."

"Sir, his car skidded off the road before I could make full impact."

"Did he see you?"

"I don't know, sir," the soldier answered.

Amofa was furious and dreaded the consequences of the officer finding out the truth.

"What are you going to do about it?" Amofa asked.

"What would you like me to do, sir?"

"To shut up, forever," Amofa said as he drew a pistol from his pocket. The sound from the single shot was no more than the sound from working the earth.

Amofa returned the pistol to the holster and started to dig deeper into the ground along the watercourse where he was working. It became the unmarked grave of the missing soldier, one of many, who would remain missing for eternity. When Amofa had finished digging, he checked the pockets of the soldier and removed all identifications, held the corpse by the feet, and dragged him into the pit.

As he dropped the first scoop of earth onto the body, he said, "May your poor soul rot in hell." When he was done, he compacted the soil over the body and took a break.

Inside the house, which was yet to be inhabited, he sat on a kitchen stool, lighted a cigarette and started to smoke. It was the first one in many days. He had tried unsuccessfully in the past to give up smoking, because he would always keep a pack ready, just in case, and he always found a case.

A couple of minutes later he got up from the stool holding the soldier's identity papers and walked over to the kitchen sink. He held the papers over the burning end of the cigarette and watched as they burst into flames, became ashes and fell into the sink. He then turned on the tap and smiled as the last of the ashes went down the sink drain.

After killing the soldier, Amofa decided he would take care of Brigadier Mills himself. A week later, Brigadier Mills was working late when Amofa went to his office. "I've been asked to take you to Gondar Barracks, sir," Amofa said, referring to the headquarters of the ruling military junta.

Brigadier Mills stared blankly past Amofa, dreading the consequences of going to Gondar Barracks. He knew few officers who went there made it back. Since the military junta took over the ruling of the country there had been no respect for the rule of law, and discipline had broken down in the military. For a brief moment Mills thought of resisting, but realised the consequence of that action would be dire, so he obliged and went with Amofa into the waiting military vehicle.

After about ten minutes of driving, Brigadier Mills noticed they were not going in the direction of Gondar Barracks. "I thought we were going to Gondar," he stated.

"Damn well, we are not. This is for blocking my promotion." Amofa's statement and the sound of the unsuspected bullet were simultaneous. Seconds later, with his right hand, Amofa pushed the dead body out of view and continued to drive towards McCarthy Hill.

Thirty minutes later Amofa pulled into his drive and dragged the body out of the car under the cover of the night sky. Further along the watercourse in his garden, he dumped the body of Brigadier Mills into the hole he had dug previously. As he covered the body with earth, Amofa was thinking about how he would cover up his secrets forever when an idea came to him: he would make sure there was flow along the watercourse all year round. To achieve this, he provided an artificial water source using special valves to allow a gentle trickle of water to flow from within the house's main plumbing via a duct into the creek as though it were natural spring water. This was easy to achieve due to the steep slope of the land into the creek. The overflow from the creek then forced water into the course of the stream.

The source of the water itself was a thousand-litre plastic tank, raised on a platform of concrete behind the bathroom window of the house. Just before the water entered the stream a submersible pump was used to feed the stream through an additional outlet from a boulder. This way, Amofa was sure the stream would always have water flow and perpetually bury his victims.

Amofa had installed this additional feature to the garden after he had moved into the house with his family. Amofa described in detail the installation and its functions to his daughter Maa Abena, who had shown keen interest in what her father was doing.

Amofa was fond of her, because she reminded him of his deceased mother, whose name he had given to his daughter.

"The design here," Amofa said to Maa Abena, pointing to where he had incorporated ornamental grasses and herbaceous perennials, "provides restrained hints of colour and texture to the garden."

However, the *overdams* formed upright pillars, and when the wind blew across, they seemed to be saying to the rest of the world, "we are proudly covering the secrets of our master."

Amofa stopped, knelt down and touched the *overdams*. "Be good," he said, thinking of two other civilians he had buried there.

"Daddy, why are you speaking to the plants?" Maa Abena asked.

"It gives them nourishment," Amofa answered as he rose, looking beyond the garden. Ironically, the *overdams* also created divisions within the garden, which when viewed from the point where the land started its steep slope downward, provided fleeting glimpses of the water feature beyond.

Amofa mounted cobbles on strong metal rods to create imitation seed-heads giving the garden an unusual feature – a feature that also helped him to cover up his heinous crimes.

To add a sense of movement and lead the eye to a focal point within the garden, Amofa had used double and triple depths of logs to soften the feature and to form a fluid backdrop to the planting. He added this sense of focus to take the attention of prodding eyes away from his buried secrets, thinking of how easy it was to disguise a burial and make it look so natural.

Amofa's first promotion came when his garden was maturing, its full beauty becoming evident. And why not, he thought. He had become a master of all he surveyed and he had to change with the times. His promotion to Captain also came at the time the ruling military junta that Amofa was a member of was returning the country to constitutional democracy after their 'house cleaning exercise', which had seen summary trials and executions by firing squad. He became the Adjutant at the 4th Battalion of Infantry, Gonda Barracks, Burma Camp in Accra, under Colonel Zinbalan.

CHAPTER 3

Colonel Zinbalan took his job seriously and was quick to discipline soldiers who failed to meet his high standards of performance and despised Amofa's arrogance. Soon after the hand over from military to civilian rule, he started receiving information regarding Amofa's knowledge of some of the missing people. Zinbalan opened a file, labelled it X, and started compiling evidence and information on Amofa. Each day he would leave his office, carrying file X in his briefcase.

Colonel Zinbalan had compiled a significant amount of information on Amofa, but one question kept bothering him: if all these are true, then where did he leave the bodies? He had been pondering this question for several weeks when he heard Amofa one evening boasting to his colleagues about his house and his garden with all these wonderful designs. A garden, Colonel Zinbalan had thought – could it be the place? He inserted a note in his X-File that read: *Garden of the Dead*? He closed the file and went to the washroom.

Amofa walked into Colonel Zinbalan's office soon afterwards. There was no one there. He looked at the time on the wall clock behind his boss' desk thinking, I will be late in going home, when his eyes caught the X-File. Amofa listened for movements, then opened the file: *Captain Amankwa Amofa is alleged to have knowledge of the disappearance of Brigadier Mills* . . . He read the first line, then he heard the familiar footsteps, closed the file and withdrew behind the desk.

As soon as Colonel Zinbalan walked in Amofa saluted. "Permission to fall out, sir?" he asked.

"Before you leave, make sure all the doors are locked."

"Yes sir."

***

Amofa had been thinking about the X-File. Now he was no longer Captain Amofa, he was simply X. Suddenly he was on a mission: to find and destroy the X-File. He had tried all the locked drawers in Colonel Zinbalan's office with forged keys without success, then he observed the file stayed with Zinbalan in his briefcase.

At home one evening, Amofa was thinking about how he would get the file from Colonel Zinbalan's car when he heard a knock on his door.

"Lieutenant, to what do I owe this honour?" Amofa asked as he let Lt. S. S. Bambi into his house. Lt. Bambi had been the past Head of State under the previous military government of which Amofa had been a member.

"Anyone with you?" Bambi asked as he sat down.

"No, it's just me. Something important?"

"You know, the ruling government is selling the country to the West."

"What are they up to?" Amofa asked, sitting up.

"They are in consultation with the IMF. My sources tell me they will privatise all the state-owned companies."

"We can't let that happen."

"We have to stop them before we become slaves in our own country"

"This X-File nonsense has to stop," Amofa said almost to himself. He could already see his chance of rising above the law again.

"What X-File?"

"Oh, it's some stupid allegations of my knowledge about certain disappearances."

"This government is using excuses to hide their incompetence. The corruption is now worse. We have to do something."

"Who else is with us?"

"Two other guys: Sergeant Homeka and Captain Sanda."

"We should get together."

As the four soldiers planned their operations, Amofa was also planning his own personal post-coup agenda. He had no doubt about the success of the coup, knowing from experience how the security apparatus of the country operated. He was surprised how the civilian government took security for granted.

On the eve of the coup, the gang of four met in Amofa's house. Lieutenant Bambi looked at his list, pulled hard on the roll of cannabis he was smoking, passed it to Amofa and asked, "Captain Sanda, are all your men ready?"

"We're all set."

"Amofa and I will take Broadcasting House and make the announcement when you've secured the Castle," Bambi said, thinking about Osu Castle, a fortress first built by the Danes in 1482 as a trading post called the Christianborg Castle. It was now the seat of the Ghana Government and taking it was the key to the success of their coup.

"I'll send you the signal when it's secured," Sanda replied.

"Sergeant Homeka, what's your situation?" Bambi asked.

"My men will be at their designated positions at the key military installation around Burma Camp at the appointed time."

"Excellent, it sounds like things are working as planned."

The four men passed round their rolls of cannabis and talked about how they would bring power to the ordinary Ghanaian after their revolution. In their minds they were the liberators whose actions would be an expression of the anger of the masses.

On the night of the coup, Lieutenant Bambi and Captain Amofa with their men were in position around the precincts of the Ghana Broadcasting Corporation when the signal from Captain Sanda came in.

"Target on sight and in firing line," Amofa spoke into the handset, lying flat on his stomach, his finger ready on the trigger with his eyes fixed on the night vision telescopic view of his gun.

The night was pitch black and cold from the dry windy harmattan blowing from across the Sahara around this time of the year. The only lights around were those coming from the guard post to the entrance of the Ghana Broadcasting premises.

The solitary shadowy figure of the guard at the entrance was only a silhouette to Amofa. He shifted his body weight from his left hand to his right for a temporary relief. That was when the order came.

"All ready." The voice was unmistakable; it was the message Amofa had been waiting for. He took aim and pulled the trigger. A few hundred metres away, a sharp, almost inaudible noise came out from the guard as he crumbled to the ground.

With the skill of a Sandhurst trained and the speed of an Achiase Jungle Warfare graduate, Amofa reached the main entrance, pulled the man into the guard post and took over. Seconds later, a military jeep carrying his colleagues stopped at the gate. The soldiers, carrying AK-47s, moved cautiously into the main building of the broadcasting station.

Amofa smiled as Lieutenant Bambi walked past. Even in the dark, he was unmistakable in his military camouflage; the light skin of his face gave him away as he signalled Amofa to follow.

Amofa obliged, giving the leader cover as they made their way into the main television broadcast room. Amofa almost stepped on a dead body left behind by a colleague.

When they reached the building some of the soldiers took positions and the rest continued outside the newsroom. At the signal, Amofa burst into the room, his gun swung from left to right to cover the three news reporters in the room.

"Nobody moves," Amofa commanded. There was no need; the unarmed civilian news broadcasters were already terrified.

Amofa gave a signal and the leader came into the room and took over while he tied up the newsmen and brought them to the controls.

It was five in the morning. The leader spoke into his handset and listened for the response. All his units were in position, except those going to the Castle.

"How long will it take?" the leader asked cursing under his breath.

"Thirty minutes," the reply came over his handset. He turned the handset off and waited. At precisely 0530 hours his handset came to life. "The Castle is all covered." He immediately understood what they meant as the Castle had become synonymous with the official residence of the President of Ghana.

Inside his bedroom, the President of Ghana had finished his usual morning prayer and had routinely turned on his radio. For the next ten minutes, as the President shaved, the song *Yen ara ya asase ni* continued to play uninterrupted on the nation's broadcasting station. It was unusual for that time of the morning, so he reached for his phone as he walked into his bedroom.

"Freeze," Captain Sanda commanded, as three more soldiers took positions in the President's bedroom. Sanda then removed his handset and said: "We have the President."

"Excellent," the coup leader replied and turned to one of the newsmen tied to his chair. "I want you to put me on air in five minutes."

"Country men and women ..." Lt. S. S. Bambi started.

***

Amofa removed his world receiver pocket radio and tuned it to the station. He couldn't hear the words the leader was saying on his radio, so he checked to make sure he was tuned to the right station, then he realised the trick being played by the newsman.

Amofa neither hesitated nor wasted words; the sound of the bullet ripping through the heart of the newsreader did all the speaking.

"You," Amofa said, pointing to the other newsreader, "Get us on the air, now."

The newsreader looked at the lifeless body of his colleague swimming in a pool of his own blood, wiped his sweat from his own forehead and proceeded to put the military leader on the air.

"Fellow countrymen and woman," the leader started his rehearsed speech the second time, "the ruling government has been overthrown by a group of patriotic junior military officers. This is a revolution borne out of the anger of the people. The worse ever government in this country has been deposed. Corruption was widespread and they were selling the country to the west by going for the IMF and its stringent conditions. We can no longer afford to be slaves in our own country. The constitution is suspended forthwith, parliament is dissolved, and the Forces Revolutionary Council will replace the government. You will be hearing more from me during the course of the day, good morning."

As soon as he finished, he started to sing and was joined by Amofa and two other soldiers:

Arise Ghana youth for your country
The nation demands your devotion
Let us all unite to uphold her
And make her great and strong

We are all involved
We are all involved
We are all involved
In building our motherland.

That speech and the song that followed ushered in the dawn of another *dawn broadcaster,* a phrase that had come to be synonymous with coup makers in Ghana.

New Year;

New King;

New Rules.

Ghanaians woke up in the New Year to a new force. The self-imposed 'revolutionary' government overthrew the constitution, dissolved parliament and took the law into their own hands to settle personal scores.

CHAPTER 4

On that chilly January evening, a week into the violent military take over that overthrew the constitutional government of Ghana, the home of Colonel Zinbalan had visitors.

The harmattan winds were blowing and the evening temperatures were low by tropical standards where anything below ten degrees Celsius was considered cold. 127 Juba Villas was a popular place for senior officers to meet and play board and card games on weekends. Even though the Officers' Mess had a well-stocked bar with a fantastic atmosphere, the attraction of 127 Juba Villas was unique.

Madam Takyiwaa was not only bubbly and full of life, she also offered something the other officers couldn't find elsewhere in the barracks. *Ogogoro,* the local gin, served with *Aponkye nkrakra,* was a delicacy only Madam knew how to serve well.

Takyiwaa had maintained her maiden name after many years of marriage, as is the case amongst most middle-aged married women in Ghana. In the absence of the title Mrs, she had come to be known to the associates of her husband and neighbours as Madam. Her *Ogogoro* was reputed to be the best gin in the barracks and people praised her *Aponkye nkrakra* saying, "The combination of goat meat, and hot chilli and ginger sauce ensure free bowels."

Madam had just served her last customer for the evening.

"This will keep me warm for the night; my wife is on a business trip," Afro Moses said as he took his last gulp of the hot stuff before finishing off his last piece of meat. "I'll come for the recipe when my wife returns."

As far as Takyiwaa remembered, Afro Moses had said that countless times.

"Goodnight and dream about your wife," Takyiwaa shouted as Afro Moses headed for his car, still nibbling on the bone from the meat.

"Night, night," Afro Moses mumbled back.

When Takyiwaa entered the living room, Colonel Zinbalan was alone watching the late news. "Conuba, has Mike gone to bed?" she asked.

Takyiwaa was the only one who still called Colonel Zinbalan by his first name since his mother died five years before. Most people didn't even know that name. The title Colonel was enough.

"I think he is watching a . . ."

There was a sudden bang on the door, so hard the lower hinge came off, leaving the door dangling at an oblique angle. Takyiwaa screamed as Colonel Zinbalan rushed to the door coming face to face with Captain Amofa.

"Are you out of your mind?" Colonel Zinbalan shouted.

"Damn right, I am," Amofa replied, half-finishing his sentence and hitting Zinbalan across his right ribs with the butt of his gun, breaking two in an instant.

Mike screamed, running towards his mother who was also screaming for help.

"On the trot, *big man,*" Amofa shouted.

Before Zinbalan could protest, Amofa hit his head with the butt of his gun shattering his brains. The first shot went through the lungs of Takyiwaa and the bullet buried itself in the wall behind. Mike was transfixed, could neither scream nor move and Amofa saw the look in the boy's eyes. It was one that spelled death.

"The iniquities of the fathers shall be visited on the sons," Amofa mused, taking aim.

In her agony, Takyiwaa saw the next shot coming. It went over Mike's head as she pulled him and they fell together.

With a single step Amofa was out of the house, his right shoulder hitting the dancing door and yanking it from the pathetic hinge, half-crashing to the floor with it. He regained his balance and jumped into the passenger side of the military jeep. The man in the driver's seat tossed Colonel Zinbalan's briefcase containing the X-File to Amofa. He then released the hand brake, let the clutch up, the accelerator down and sped the vehicle off with a screeching sound into the chilly January night.

Juba Villa residents came rushing out, the officers holding their guns, but it was too late. The post-mortem report the next day stated Colonel Zinbalan had died from multiple injuries to the ribs and the head and Takyiwaa from a fatal bullet wound to the lungs.

***

Kutini picked up the *Daily Graphic* from the Porters' Lodge of Unity Hall on his way out. As he walked towards the University library, he was wondering why Mike hadn't come back from his break. It was the third day after the Christmas break and he had expected Mike the previous day.

The Return of the House Cleaning Exercise.

The lead headline caught Kutini's attention and he read:

Last night three high court judges and a retired army officer were abducted from their homes and murdered in cold blood. The victims have been identified as . . .

At Burma Camp, home to the Defence Ministry, Colonel Zinbalan and his wife were executed in what has been described as the most brutal yet. Their son, who escaped death, is said to be in state of shock and is currently on admis-

sion at the 37 Military Hospital . . .but justice is as alien as the planet Pluto, and the culture of silence is the only free survival kit available.

The falcon can no longer bear the falconer, the centre cannot hold anymore; mere anarchy is indeed loose upon mother Ghana.

Kutini put the paper down, unable to think straight, tears running down his cheeks as he packed his books and left the library. He dialled Mike's number and listened as the phone rang continuously at the other end. There was no answer.

Later that evening Kutini tried the number again. "Can I speak to Mike please?" Kutini said when he didn't recognise the voice that answered the phone.

"He is too devastated to talk right now. Who's calling?"

"Kutini; I'm his room mate at the university. Is he still at the hospital?"

"I'm his uncle, Tweneboa. He is staying with me at the moment."

There was a brief silence over the phone as Kutini struggled to find the right words. He so much wanted to console his friend and ask if he could help him in any way, but thought, what can I possibly do to help him?

"I'll let him know you called," Uncle Tweneboa said.

"Please let me know when you schedule the funeral," Kutini said awkwardly.

Mike lived with his uncle Tweneboa in the small town of Akrokeri for the next two weeks following the funeral, keeping to himself. He would sometimes wake up in the middle of the night screaming "Daddy, daddy they are coming back," but there was no one he could share his problems with. "I'll kill the man who killed my parents," were the only words he had said to his uncle in a week.

"The law will take care of them," Uncle Tweneboa had replied, without conviction. It was the only time he had heard his nephew talk about revenge and he never thought about it again.

CHAPTER 5

Mike Zinbalan returned to the university after his brief stay with his uncle. On the evening of the day of his arrival Kofi Mensah came to visit him and for the two hours he spent, Mike refused to talk, preferring to stick to his books.

Before Kofi left, he called Kutini aside and said, "I think Mike will need a lot of support and you and I are the only friends he's got."

The Three Musketeers had just got their drinks at the students' bar when Kutini heard 'Secretary' and turned round to face his old school mate Chris Tagoe.

"Do you remember me?" Chris asked.

"How can I forget you, Chris?" Kutini replied. He had learned to be independent from age twelve retailing audio tapes and later CDs at his boarding school to supplement the meagre pocket money his parents could afford. At first he had felt jealous of rich kids, but he soon found out he had something the others didn't – confidence and self-reliance. Kutini had become the boy who knew all the latest songs and became the friend of many including teachers. His friends would not only come to him to buy CDs, but also for advice on their own personal matters, earning him the nickname Social Secretary.

Chris was one of the boys who used to tease Kutini for being a petty trader, but it had been his comment that had put Kutini on the path to popularity among the students: "You're a genius; you could make lots of money teaching students in your spare time," Chris had said after Kutini helped him to solve a maths problem.

Kutini took the comment literally and started organising maths classes with success. His popularity increased when he joined the school's debating society and helped in organising a debate on the topic: *The current UN Security Council veto system is anachronistic to modern times.* "You'll be a good lawyer," someone had remarked after the debate but Kutini had his own interests.

It had come as no surprise to Kutini's colleagues that he had passed his Ordinary Level examinations with distinction and his Advance Levels one year into the two-year programme.

"Please join us," Kutini said to Chris.

Kutini introduced Chris to his two friends and ordered the next round of drinks. He had just finished explaining how he came by the nickname *Secretary* when they heard a group of students had attacked the University Administration for conniving with the government to impose commercialisation on the students.

"Let's go and stop them," Kutini said.

"You must be out of your mind, the students will lynch you," Chris Tagoe said.

"No they won't," Kutini replied and started walking towards the administration block. Chris hesitated, but followed when Kofi and Mike followed Kutini out of the bar without question.

Upon arrival Kutini was shocked at what the student mob had done. They had disconnected the University's telephone lines and a group of students was holding the Vice Chancellor hostage.

Kutini calmly walked to the leader of the demonstration and collected the loud speaker. "*Choo boi,*" he chanted the indigenous war cry.

"*Yei,*" the students responded.

"*Choo boi.*"

"*Yei.*"

"Bravo, my fellow students," Kutini started, "err, leave the Vice Chancellor alone, he is a toothless bulldog," he said pointing to the group of students holding him. They looked a bit confused at first.

"Come on, let him go." Reluctantly, they let go.

"Good. Now, where were we? The elders say, 'there are several ways of killing the cat,' we can resolve this situation using our brains or resort to barbaric and unethical methods. What's it going to be?"

"Traitor," someone shouted from the crowd.

"Shut up, you moron," another person replied, then silence.

"Mr. Vice Chancellor, would you like to say a word to the students?" Kutini invited.

The Vice Chancellor hesitated, straightened his clothes, then came forward, took the microphone and in a shaky voice addressed the students. "You've shown that reason can prevail no matter the situation. I can therefore assure you that I'll strongly represent your concerns to the government, but first, what's your alternative?"

No one spoke and just as the silence was beginning to tense up Kutini shouted: "Give us interest free loans," and the students erupted in loud cheers of approval.

"Thank you and have a good day."

The students started to disperse.

Mike and Kofi were talking when Kutini joined them. "How did you do that?" Kofi asked?

"People will always choose the good from the evil when they are challenged with the two extremes."

"What do you mean?" Kofi was puzzled.

"The students chose to use their brains instead of being labelled barbaric, didn't they?"

Kofi opened his mouth to say something, then stopped as he heard someone shout, *the three wise men.* "Did you hear that?" he asked.

"What was it?"

"Never mind," Kofi replied and shook his head as they walked towards Unity Hall.

Inside their room, Mike asked Kutini, "How did you come up with such a crazy idea? There is no way the government would go for that."

"It was the first thing that came to my mind," Kutini replied.

Subsequent meetings with the government had led to the establishment of the student loan scheme for tertiary education.

A week after the demonstration, Kofi came to visit Mike and Kutini. "I want to stand for the President of the National Union of Ghana Students for the next academic year and I need your support. What do you think?"

"It's a great idea, but we need a strategy if you are to win the elections," Kutini suggested.

"I'm not sure what I can do to help," Mike said.

"Just stick with me during the campaign. The *musketeers* and *wise men* reputation will do the trick," Kofi replied, "and perhaps Kutini could ask Chris to help," he added.

"We will need a majority hall vote to win," Kutini said.

"We already have Africa and Unity Halls, don't we?"

Of the six halls of residence in the university, Africa and Unity Halls had traditionally taken a common stand on student issues emanating from a common history. When Unity Hall was built it was linked to the only female residence, Africa Hall, to signify African Unity.

"That's a safe assumption," Kutini replied, "who are the other potential candidates?"

When Kofi mentioned the names of the two other candidates, Kutini said, "One is from Katanga Hall and the other from Queens Hall, which leaves two neutral halls. That's where we will concentrate our efforts."

"Great plan." Kofi was excited.

On the night following Kofi Mensah's election victory, Mike woke up to find himself surrounded by a number of his floor mates, including Kofi.

Mike had had a terrible nightmare: the people coming for him had turned into animals and their guns had turned into horns. He had screamed in his dream, only the scream wasn't a dream – it was real.

Kutini had been so frightened he wanted to move out, but stayed upon the advice of Kofi Mensah.

Mike's nightmares grew to a point where he was always afraid to sleep at night. He would study throughout the night just to avoid sleeping and slept for short periods during the day. A blessing or a curse; the nightmares had turned Mike into a bookworm.

As his university days were drawing to a close, Mike had started thinking of what he would do after graduation. Graduate unemployment was rife and made worse by the government's freeze on employment. He would have to join the Europe bandwagon, he thought.

***

June, 1994. Mike sat among his course mates during his graduation at the Great Hall. His only guest, Uncle Tweneboa sat at the back. Mike was thinking: This is the day my degree will be conferred on me, then what? I wish my parents were here.

"First class honours, BSc Chemistry, Michael Zinbalan," the Registrar announced.

"Sharp-brain," Chris shouted above the noise of the clapping. Mike's parents must be proud, he thought; he had never been told about Mike's parents.

The Vice Chancellor stood up as Mike approached, removed his cap and with a slight bow shook hands with Mike. "Congratulations young man, I'm proud of you," he said.

"Why did the VC remove his cap?" Chris asked his colleague sitting next to him.

"He does that only to honour first class students."

Chris was wondering why Mike was still standing on the stage when he heard the VC's voice:

"On behalf of the University Senate I would like to present to Michael Zinbalan, one of *The Three Musketeers*, the United States Aid Scholarship to study for his Masters at Rutgers University in New Jersey, US."

Mike smiled as he received his award from the VC, wondering how he knew about *The Three Musketeers*.

Uncle Tweneboa couldn't hide his excitement for Mike and on their way home, after the graduation party, he advised his nephew of the good of travelling, but spoke at length about the difficulties it entailed, the time it takes to find one's feet and the patience it required. "To succeed, you need to think about yourself first. It's only then you can help others. Don't let the welfare of the extended family be your priority, our priority is you."

Mike was amazed at the depth of his uncle's knowledge. He had underestimated the old man. After his course he would work and show his uncle his appreciation for all he had done for him with a Lincoln Continental. It would be a surprise and his uncle would be the first Ghanaian to drive the latest Lincoln. He had grown to love the man he had come to think of as his father and would do anything to make him happy.

As he daydreamed about all the wonderful things awaiting him in the land of silver and gold, the land of milk and honey, a sudden thought occurred to him: Is America really what they say it is? He discarded the thought with: My parents would still be alive under the American system of democracy.

On the day of his departure, his uncle was at the airport to see him off together with Kutini, Kofi and Chris.

"I'm joining the military next month," Chris told his friends just before Mike's departure.

"Be careful my friend," Mike said, unable to hold back his tears.

As KLM Flight 724 lifted off the ground from Kotoka International Airport in Accra, Mike said to himself, "Thank God, this is the last time I'm seeing Ghana." He then said aloud, half to himself and half to anyone who cared to listen, "I wish someone would change the name of this airport from Kotoka to some dignified name. I hate military misadventurers."

A row ahead, someone turned to look at Mike and gave him the thumbs up. Mike acknowledged with a nod and a smile.

CHAPTER 6

Mike had spent the first semester at Rutgers University keeping to himself, afraid that if people got to know about his nightmares they would avoid him. He often spent his lunch time at the cafeteria.

He sat at his usual corner with his back to the wall, preferring this location because he could see whoever was entering or leaving the cafeteria. Mike had fallen in love with *The Godfather* the first time he read the best seller from Mario Puzo. "A real mafia must never expose his back," he would say.

Mike watched a woman come through the door and walk to his right. He hadn't seen this tall, slim, olive-skinned woman in the university before. He watched her walk to the bar, her hair running down her shoulders.

She got her drink, turned round and started to walk to an empty table when she noticed Mike and changed her mind.

"Hi, are you from Africa?" she asked as she approached Mike.

"Why do you ask?" Mike answered, half-angry.

"Ah, you *are* from Ghana."

"How do you know?" Mike's anger was giving way to amusement.

"I know from your accent," Effie answered, still standing with her drink.

"Please sit down."

Effie sat down, put her drink on the table and started to light a Marlboro. "Do you mind if I smoke?" she asked in the process.

"If you have to."

"I don't have to," she said, turned off the lighter and replaced the cigarette in its pack.

"I'm Mike."

"Effie," she replied, "I've seen you here a few times, always by yourself. Haven't you got any friends?"

"Not really," Mike answered, unsure if he wanted to make any friends. "What are you studying, Effie?"

"I am doing research in Linguistics."

"Is that how you knew I was Ghanaian?"

"Yes, I am doing a case study of English speaking West African countries. What are you studying?"

"I'm postgraduate chemistry student," Mike replied.

The two hours they had stayed in the cafeteria and talked had seemed like a few minutes to Mike. "I'll give you a call over the weekend," he said, when they parted company, but the following day they ran into each other again at the cafeteria.

"I'm giving a presentation on *The Influence of Culture in Spoken English in West Africa*, would you like to come?" Effie asked when they sat down to drink their coffee.

"When is it?"

"Wednesday, lunch time in the McPherson's Auditorium in the Ford Building."

"I'll see if I'm free that day," Mike said, showing some reluctance, as if unsure of something.

"Why are you always so evasive, you're either coming or you're not, what's it gonna be?"

Mike smiled, liking Effie for being direct and straightforward.

"I'll be there," he replied.

"You better," she said. Mike laughed and she laughed too enjoying his sense of humour.

"What coffee are you drinking? Is it espresso?" Effie seemed to notice the small size of Mike's coffee for the first time.

"It's Turkish coffee; I like to try different things."

"Well then, I'll make you Greek coffee sometime. It's the best," she said with pride that portrayed some aversion towards anything Turkish.

"I look forward to it."

"I'll see you on Wednesday at the presentation," Effie reminded him.

Mike was sitting in the front row in the auditorium when Effie walked onto the stage following her professor.

After a brief introduction, Effie took the podium and started her presentation with a map showing old empires of that part of the world until 1070 AD. She then went on to show the movements of people following the fall of the great empires to their present-day location, and how different languages and cultures had crossed during the process.

Mike sat, hanging on to every word Effie spoke, impressed not only with her knowledge of the linguistic structure of most West African languages, but also with how she delved into the intricacies of the cultures. Her elaboration on how the different cultures in the sub region had influenced both the language and the overall values of their society fascinated Mike.

"To conclude," Effie summarised, "the intricate mix of diverse linguistic cultures of the sub region is, today, manifest in the unique African American way of speaking. Thank you all for listening."

A loud round of applause erupted from the audience.

Mike was happy he had attended the presentation. "It was brilliant. I learned a lot from it," he said, when they met afterwards.

"Thanks. I'm glad you found it useful."

"Let's go and get some food at the cafeteria," Mike suggested.

"Let's go to my place, I'll cook you a real Greek meal."

When they got to Effie's apartment, Mike joined her in the kitchen. "What would you like me to do?" he asked.

"You cut the onions, I don't want to cry," Effie said. "The thing I hate most about cooking is cutting onions."

"Do you like cooking?"

"I love cooking," Effie said, with the enthusiasm of an eight-year-old who has just been presented with a new puppy. "Cooking is an art," she continued, "you have to get everything in the right proportions and in the right mix; the temperature has to be right to cook it over the right time period."

"Thanks for the lecture; I didn't know you were a cooking professor," Mike said, teasingly.

"Don't start," she said.

***

"Excellent food," Mike complemented her when they finished the meal.

"Thank you," Effie acknowledged. "*Greek* coffee?" she asked.

"Sure, how long?"

Mike was at it again, she thought. "Two hours," Effie replied and walked into the kitchen.

The coffee didn't seem to be any different from the Turkish coffee, but Effie's came with a hint of cinnamon giving it a unique flavour and Mike loved it. "Thanks for the treat," Mike said.

"My pleasure; any time."

They sat on the couch together watching the news. Effie lay on Mike's lap and could feel his hardness on her back. She got up, looked straight into Mike's eyes and said, "There is a naughty boy down here." Gently, she stroked his hardness and didn't resist when Mike held her. She kissed him, already beginning to feel wet inside. She held him closely, her tongue feeling the taste of Mike's lips, afraid to let go, as if he would disappear if she did. Gosh, she thought, I haven't felt this way for a long time.

Mike attempted to undress Effie. With a gesture of her hand she stopped him, then slowly and deliberately she undressed him, dropping each piece of clothing onto the floor as if time stood at her service. She teased Mike's nipples with her tongue, then stopped to unbutton her shirt.

Mike's body shook with spasm. His nipples had never been touched and he had always thought only the female nipples were sensual. He quickly helped Effie to undress, lifted her from the couch and asked, "Where is the bedroom?" Mike was still conventional when it came to making love – love should be made on a bed.

"Over there," Effie said, pointing straight ahead without any resistance.

Mike put her on the bed, climbed over her and started to explore her body until he could feel the tension of his full erection. When he couldn't resist anymore he tried to enter her.

With a gentle stroke Effie stopped him and started kissing his genitals from the G-spot, working her way up his testicles to the tip of the penis before removing a condom from her bedside drawer. She slipped the condom on Mike and lowered herself down over his erection in a slow, calculating manner.

Effie was in control, moving up and down on him and when she thought he was about to come she would slow down, bend forward and give his nipple a slightly painful, but sensual bite.

Mike felt his body shake as he reached each orgasm and each time he tried to push, but Effie would stop him. He was experiencing orgasm he thought he could only achieve through ejaculation. Mike's body started to shake with another orgasm as they both started to push in sync. First, he felt the hard pointed nipples of Effie on his chest, then the softness of her breast before feeling the full weight of her body. He smelled her breath, just before their lips met, then their tongues engaged and then his penis stretched inside Effie with each ejaculation. He felt as though a pipe had burst open, his own semen dripping from inside his condom down onto his pubic hair as he lost his hardness. There was a long moan of joy – joy he hadn't known existed.

When he woke up, Effie was in a nightgown walking towards the bed with breakfast. "You're incredible," Mike said, thinking, this goddess of a Greek girl is not only beautiful, but also a real goddess of sex.

"I know," Effie replied. That night Mike didn't have a nightmare.

At first Mike's relationship with Effie was casual and he would spend his weekends at her apartment. His nightmares had stopped and he was beginning to take their relationship more seriously. Three months into their relationship, Mike woke up one night in Effie's apartment screaming.

"Are you alright?" Effie asked in a sleepy voice.

"Just had a bad dream," Mike replied, and that was when he decided to see a psychiatrist. He realised he couldn't go on like that for much longer without breaking down.

"Here, have a cigarette. I think it would do your nerves some good."

Mike accepted the cigarette without question.

CHAPTER 7

In his second year after passing all his comprehensive exams, Mike took an opportunity to work as a part-time research chemist for Technologies International Group. During the three months he worked with the company, he became increasingly frustrated with the rudimentary laboratory procedures. He came home at the end of the third month contemplating whether he was in the right profession. He was sitting on his couch with a Marlboro when his phone rang.

"Mike, this is Kutini."

"What a pleasant surprise." Mike hadn't spoken to Kutini after their initial conversation when he first arrived in the US. He hadn't thought about Ghana since then and had also forgotten about the promise he made to buy his uncle a Lincoln, though he called him occasionally. Life in America was not as easy as he had thought.

"I wanted to let you know that Kofi Mensah has been made the Foreign Minister in the new government."

"That's excellent news. I'll call to congratulate him."

"How are you doing yourself?" Kutini asked.

"I'm not sure. I don't enjoy what I'm doing at the moment," Mike replied, explaining the source of his frustration.

"May be you could reprogram their analysis procedures," Kutini suggested without a thought to Mike's own academic background.

"Maybe I could," Mike said, half to himself.

Mike started looking at books on computer programming. He started teaching himself and then attended private lectures to supplement it. Without knowing it Kutini had introduced him to the world of programming and he had started writing simple routines to help him with his office work.

Ben Goldberg, the head of research at Technologies International, had first noticed Mike's potential when introduced the use of the tropical plant, *funtumia ditenalia* in the formulation of their eco-friendly adhesives for the automotive industry, earning them the industry's innovative technology of the year award.

***

Goldberg had reluctantly agreed to use Mike's new programs in their laboratory, but the results soon spoke for themselves and so when Mike proposed to pursue a Master's programme in Information Engineering at Virginia Tech, Blacksburg, Ben gave his support. He also made provision for Mike to work at their software development office there.

At the end of his first year, Mike was cited as the Highest and Distinguished Class Achiever, received the Myrtle and Earl Walker Scholarship from the Society of Manufacturing Engineers and became a visiting Scholar at the Schools of Aeronautics and Astronautics at the Air Force Institute of Technology at the Wright-Patterson Air Force Base, Ohio.

Mike was thinking how his two years in Virginia had passed quickly as he walked into the graduation hall with Effie – two master's degrees in four years. His thoughts were broken when Ben Goldberg, who he had invited, waved at him and moved to the guest area.

His first job had been Development Engineer for Technologies International where he had masterminded the development of Full Authority Digital Engine Controls and Multifunction Display Systems for the aviation industry.

Mike had a new career and his interest in the aerospace industry had gone beyond an obsession; it was madness. Avionics were now becoming more sophisticated than their predecessors, which were basic pilot-static and gyroscopic flight instruments with engine monitoring gauges. The 'glass cockpit' concept was now the order of the day.

Mike's rapid progression in his chosen profession had been based on performance and achievements. He had been surfing the net in his office one morning and had been so absorbed in what he was looking at that he did not hear footsteps stop behind him.

His boss had been standing behind him for almost five minutes looking at Mike using company time to surf the net. At first, he thought Mike was just having a quick check on something related to the project he was working on, but no, he was absorbed in his own world in some obscure part of cyberspace. He couldn't contain himself anymore, so he coughed, but Mike was oblivious to anything going on around him.

"Mike," his boss called.

Mike almost jumped out of his chair.

"You're supposed to be finishing work on the project. The deadline is a week tomorrow and here you are, wasting company time net surfing," Ben Goldberg said, not attempting to hide his anger and disgust.

Mike replied casually, "I left the report with your secretary this morning, have you not read it yet?"

Ben relaxed a bit but continued, "You obviously have nothing to do then."

"I have something important to show you," Mike said, still not aware of the anger in his boss' voice, "when are you free?"

"I hope to God this is really important. Come when you're ready," Ben said and walked away.

Mike sat opposite Ben in his office and presented him with a sketch of an architectural configuration of what he called a new revolution in the airline industry. In front of Ben was one of the most ambitious adventures he had seen in his twenty years in the industry. He thought, what the hell is this lunatic up to?

He had read Mike's report after their brief encounter and had been impressed. Mike had delivered the project a week ahead of schedule and the results were more than he had anticipated. He was already dreaming of how his end-of-year bonus would buy him a round-the-world trip on a luxury cruise.

"How long will this take?" Ben asked.

"Give me a couple of weeks."

"You have one week."

In exactly a week, Mike walked into Ben's office to schedule a meeting.

"Let's talk after lunch," Ben had said.

Mike had booked a room with a projector set up for the meeting. He was ready when Ben walked into the meeting room.

"Show me what you've got," Ben said.

Mike started his PowerPoint presentation by showing the familiar needles of the old-style Course Deviation Indicators of aircraft cockpits.

"This," he said, "requires a degree of mental agility to interpret. Why drive a stick when you can have an automatic?" he asked, moving on to the next slide.

"This is how General Aviation Cockpits would look like with our new system. It will have the Primary Flight Display in front of the pilot and a Multifunction Display System situated in the centre of the panel."

Ben, who was slouching in his chair, sat upright and listened attentively as Mike went through his slides.

"The Primary Flight Display will show the pilot comprehensive flight information while the Multifunction Display shows aircraft systems, engine readings, fuel status, radar, terrain, traffic, weather and navigation information."

Mike moved to the next slide and continued:

"The beauty of this system is its ability to incorporate an integrated moving map that displays airport layouts, approach charts, airspace, topography, obstacles and nearby traffic. No more near-misses."

Mike looked at his boss to see any disapproval signs. If Ben Goldberg had any reservations, he didn't show it.

"Fundamental to the system is Global Positioning Systems," Mike said, pointing to a satellite in space on his slide, "and one can feed an infinite amount of data. There is no shortage of information that could be integrated with General Aviation Cockpit systems ... and as you can see the system requires no special skills to interpret the information presented," Mike concluded his presentation.

"Brilliant. It's impressive, but I have one main problem. The global positioning system was developed for the United States Department of Defense. How do we get access for integration into General Aviation Cockpits?"

"That's where you come in Mr. Goldberg. If you can persuade the Federal Aviation Administration to get the Department of Defense on board, then we would be on to something big."

"Leave it to me and let's keep this confidential," Ben said before ending the meeting.

***

Ben had worked hard to get the two organisations on board and had completed the GPS design with supporting software.

The finished product now allowed GPS to be used to fly under Instrument Flight Rules and as an operational in-flight navigational aid.

Mike's epic success with the General Aviation Cockpit systems drew the attention of the defence industry. He had several offers, but he turned them down because, as he put it, "I like what I do and I'm happy where I am."

He had the freedom and the respect and he got promoted with a salary rise before he even thought he was due for one.

Ben's attitude towards him had changed from one of a boss to that of a colleague. His company owned the patent for the new system Mike had developed, but he had signed a contract with the company that entitled him to a percentage on each sale of the product.

Mike received one offer after another through the post with promises of better pay and promotion. One offer after the other went into his rubbish bin.

One Sunday morning, Mike was tidying up when he came across an unopened letter. It had being lying under a pile of newspapers for about a week. He opened it and thought it was one of the usual – an offer from The Boeing Company – but this letter was different from the others. A particular line in the letter caught Mike's attention, *even if you don't want to consider the offer, we will still appreciate it if you could let us know about your decision.*

Mike showed the letter to Ben Goldberg the next day and Ben suggested Mike take up the offer on the basis that Boeing accepted Mike on an attachment basis.

Ben knew Mike's potential and didn't want his company to lose out on such a cutting-edge state-of-the-art development. He wanted a piece of the action and he would achieve that through Mike. He envisaged himself giving a presentation to the Defense gurus from the Pentagon. Mike could see the excitement in Ben's eyes and he liked the idea. He hadn't thought about that possibility before. It was the beginning of a string of developments for the Federal Defense.

Mike loved America. "Why shouldn't America be great?" he would often ask his friends. America was a country where talents were sought after for what they were worth, not by colour, race, creed, sex or religion, but on what one could offer.

***

Mike's attachment with Boeing was in developing and testing the X-45A unmanned air vehicle. On May 22, 2002, he watched with excitement at NASA's Dryden Flight Research Center at Edwards Air Force Base in California as the X-45A made its maiden flight lasting a total of fourteen minutes, during which a maximum speed of 195 knots and altitude of 2,286m was reached.

Bill Lebstock, head of the Defense Advanced Research Projects Agency, watched as the outcome of their joint programme was played before their eyes. As a technology demonstrator the X-45A had relevance not only to the US Air Force's own UCAV programme, but also to the US Navy's UCAV-N project. The maiden flight of the X-45A represented the first flight of an unmanned vehicle designed specifically for a combat role.

Peter Gardiner, the head of NASA's Langley Research Center in Virginia, read the report by Bill Lebstock:

. . . A second X-45A is due to fly later in 2002, allowing the two UCAVs to operate together, as they would in combat. By fiscal year 2006 it is planned to be able to operate the UCAV in conjunction with manned aircraft in an exercise.

Mike Zinbalan of Technologies International is leading the Boeing Team to develop the control systems of a second scaled-up version of the X-45A, the X45B, as its submission for the US Air Force's UCAV requirement. The X-

45B is due to fly during 2005 or 2006 and is being built to a similar configuration to that envisaged as an operational USAF platform. Three X-45Bs are to be produced for the test programme. The USAF also wants 14 Block 10 versions of the UCAV for evaluation from 2008. The General Electric F404-102D has been selected to power X-45B, with the power plant company contracted to supply three engines for the test programme. . . .

Peter Gardiner's eyes paused and went back to the second paragraph of the report. His mind wandered absently on the name Mike Zinbalan. "I need that guy right here," he said aloud, picked up his phone and dialled.

"Rudolf Reinhardt," responded the voice at the other end of the line.

"Hi Rudolf, it's Peter here, what've you been up to?"

Rudolf and Peter had known each other as neighbours at Piscataway, New Jersey. They would usually hang out during their university days when terms were out, but they had pursued different careers.

Rudolf was now working for the FBI and responsible for investigations and compilation of dossiers at the request of the appropriate agencies.

"To what do I owe this honour?" Rudolf asked, trying not to sound formal.

"We have an interest in a guy and would like a background check on him. Name is Mike Zinbalan and works for Technologies International at their New Jersey office."

After a pause, Rudolf noted the information down.

"No problem. Are you visiting your parents this weekend?" Rudolf asked.

"Yes, are you?"

"I'll be in Piscataway, if you would like to pop in for a drink."

"I sure will, I'll give you a ring," Peter said.

The dossier on Michael Zinbalan was brief:

Mike was born in 1972 at Burma Camp in Accra, Ghana where he did his primary secondary and tertiary education before coming to the United States on a USAID Scholarship to do a Master's degree in Chemistry.

Mike later studied Information Engineering, before developing his General Aviation Cockpit Systems. He also led the team that developed the control systems for UAVs. He currently works full time as a Development Engineer at Technologies International.

Impressive. Very impressive.

His application for American citizenship is still pending. He is still single with no criminal convictions, no religious or social affiliation and no ties to any terrorist group. His father had been a military officer in the Ghana Army, but both parents had been murdered following a military take over.

Clean. Very clean.

On Peter's desk stood three labelled trays: IN TRAY, OUT TRAY, and ACTION TRAY. Peter closed the dossier and marked on the folder "PAR" to remind him that priority action was required on the file. He placed the dossier in the ACTION TRAY, got up from his chair, and walked to the window of his office. He could see the White House across the Potomac River. He loved the view from here.

Peter removed a pack of cigarettes from his breast pocket, opened it, and gave the middle part a gentle tap; three cigarettes thrust forward. He pulled the foremost cigarette with his lips, replaced the pack in his pocket and lit the cigarette. He then moved to the front of his desk, transferred the cigarette from his right hand to his left and reached for the telephone.

Each time Peter had to speak to someone he didn't know, he would light a cigarette and stand up. The confidence this action gave him, he believed, was carried across to the person he was speaking to.

"Good morning, Technologies International, how can I help you?" the voice at the other end responded.

A week after Peter had made contact with Technologies International, Mike was sitting in a room with him. After briefing Mike about the nature of the job and the high level of security involved, he asked him if he would be interested in the offer.

"It'll be a challenge, but I'll do my best to meet it," Mike replied.

"Very well," Peter said. "Your induction will involve various levels of security training and we would undertake background search about you."

"What will be my responsibilities?" Mike asked.

Peter looked down on the file in front of him then looked at Mike over his glasses without raising his head. "We will come to that," Peter replied putting Mike's question on hold. "Do you have any objection to our doing a background search?" he asked.

Mike wondered why he would be sitting there that minute if they hadn't already done a search about him. "No, of course not," he replied.

In Peter's twenty-two years experience, he knew one could always find out more about a person directly than what a background search could ever throw up. "If at any time we think you're a security risk, we will advise you." Peter's final words were more of a warning and Mike understood.

CHAPTER 8

Soon after Mike went to the US, Kutini left for the UK to pursue a Masters degree in Computer Science at the University of Newcastle upon Tyne, where he met Franklin Williams, another Ghanaian student, during the International Students' orientation. They met afterwards for a drink at the Student Union Bar and their conversation revolved initially on silly jokes about women, sex and drinks.

"Why don't you drink alcohol?" Frank asked.

"Women say people who drink alcohol can't satisfy them in bed."

"Ah, so you are the ladies' man then."

"Yeah, once they've tasted it they can't have enough of it. And I also treat them with respect."

"How do you attract them in the first place?" Frank was curious.

"That's the easy bit. Get them to talk to you using an obvious genuine compliment."

Kutini had been known among his colleagues to be the ladies man. Even though he claimed to treat women with respect, his colleagues thought he just used them and changed them at will. Most of them admired his ability; others despised him or were simply jealous.

"It's easy to get them to talk, then what?" Frank wanted to know more. He had had some relationships, but he was generally unsuccessful with women. As he listened to Kutini speak there was only one thing on his mind. He had secretly admired Phyllis, a woman he had met at the Afro Caribbean Society meeting, but hadn't been able to tell her how he felt for fear of losing her friendship.

"What do women admire most in men?" Kutini attempted to draw Frank into thinking.

"Intelligence?" Frank suggested, even though in his mind he was thinking women like good-looking guys.

"No!" Kutini exclaimed. "They love men who can cook."

"So?" It was an anticlimax to Frank. It didn't make sense. "What has that got to do with attracting women?"

"Simple. Direct your conversation towards food, and let her know how good a cook you are." Kutini finished his discourse on attracting women.

"I don't know how to cook," Frank said exasperated, "most guys don't.

"Just learn to cook one of your favourite meals well. All you then have to do is to invite them for a home cooked meal and leave the rest to them. Remember to provide an expensive wine with knowledge about its history and brewing process."

"Women enjoy sex most when they are tipsy," Kutini said, happy to share his knowledge with this complete stranger. There was no secret involved in this.

"Wow!" Frank exclaimed with excitement. "How many women have you dated?"

"Not as many as people would like to believe, I am selective when it comes to women."

Frank was already visualising Phyllis and himself in his room having a meal together – her eyes sparkling and glowing from the candlelight.

He heard her say, "You are so wonderful, Frank, you make me feel special," and he responded, "You are special to me."

"Would you like another drink?" Kutini asked, waking Frank from his daydream. "Yes, I will get it. What would you like?"

"Red Bull."

"Do the women love guys with wings as well?" Frank joked as he walked away to get the drinks. As he waited at the bar, his eyes wandered around the room, resting momentarily on the sign *Martin Luther King Jr. Room* with an arrow pointing straight ahead. He had seen it several times, but for the first time his mind went to his famous speech "I have a dream ..."

"Why is it named after Martin Luther King Jr.?" Frank asked Kutini as he placed the drinks on the table.

"He was given an honorary doctorate degree by the University and the students named this room after him," Kutini explained. "Why do you ask?"

"It's such a shame that some people still think his dream will forever remain exactly what he said it was – a dream. I just hope a leader like him could one day rise in Africa and unify it."

"You can do it. You're just as capable as anyone else."

"No, I am not," Frank interjected. "I'll help in any way I can to achieve that goal, but I am not the one to lead."

"Let me lead you then," Kutini said humorously, "If it's worth achieving someone's got to lead the way, somehow."

***

One evening Kutini was just about to get to bed when his doorbell rang. Reluctantly he answered; it was Frank.

"Frank, you know it's late."

"I know, I've just come to show you something really important," Frank insisted.

"It certainly must be. Come in."

"We are not going to be poor students ever again."

"Why, have you won the lottery?" Kutini asked.

"No, it's better than the lottery. Come let me show you," Frank said as he sat by Kutini's writing desk.

"I found out how to get access into Barclays Bank's computer system. I just transferred fifty thousand pounds into my account."

"You're kidding me."

"No kidding."

"But that's fraudulent."

"Hey, I didn't come here to learn ethical and moral lessons. You're either in or out. What's it gonna be?"

"How did you find out?" Kutini asked.

Frank explained how he came across a hacking code by accident when he was doing the class assignment for automatic teller machines. His first point of reference in writing the program source code was the internet where thousands of codes were freely available. He had copied a source code, made a few modifications and had run the program. There was a flash on his computer screen, went blank for a few seconds, then sprang back to life again, this time opening up a web page. At first, he was puzzled, but then he realised he was in the Barclays Bank computer systems.

What Frank had accidentally stumbled upon was a hacker's code to the Barclays computer system and he had quit the program. He came back later to transfer money into his own bank account. The world of computer hacking was now open to Frank.

Over the rest of Frank's student days computer hacking had become his hobby. He could easily get the passwords of organisations and peek into their computer systems. On the advice of Kutini, Frank had stopped hacking into banks and stealing money, but had become addicted to hacking for the fun of it. For him, it had become a game; an addiction. He played hacking games with the likes of Kevin Mitnick as if it was some kind of a chess game and his identity soon became known to the computer underworld as *The One*.

Kevin Mitnick's name had become a legend associated with hacking. He was believed among the American Law Enforcement community to have the ability to launch intercontinental nuclear missiles by whistling into a telephone and was considered such a dangerous hacker the FBI spent a year hunting him down. When they caught up with him on a rainy September night – after a nerve-jangling cat-and-mouse game between Mitnick and a rival hacker who turned out to be working with the police – little did they know that the previous day he had lost to a more formidable rival hacker: *The One.*

Each time Frank went into the Department of Defense computer systems, he couldn't help being confused. The weaknesses of their systems were public knowledge, yet nothing was being done to increase security. He would wander round the system reading new information on the continual conversion of guided missile systems from computer-based laser to satellite-based laser guided systems. The potential for a disaster should be obvious to the Defense Information Systems Agency. He wondered why terrorists went to the extent they did when they could simply target America using their own missiles.

Frank had become increasingly intrigued about North Korea's nuclear research programme and the impunity with which they defied America and was curious to know what they really had. He entered into the Department of Defense computers by looping through Rome's Air Force command and control computer network. He created a highly complex web of interactions so he would not access the computers directly, which would have been easily traceable.

He gained control of Rome's support systems and used their Lab computers to break into the North Korean Nuclear Research Institute. Once inside, Frank was disappointed to find that all the information was written in Korean. "What was I thinking?" he asked himself. He was about to leave the site when a thought occurred to him: the Yankees will be able to interpret it. Frank downloaded what he thought would be critical information from the North Korean system and put it on the US Department of Defense computers. He left the Department's site with the signature, *The One.* It took three days for the Air Force to become aware the system had been compromised.

Frank knew that in the computer underworld, if you were a good hacker, everyone knew your name. If you were a great hacker, no one knew who you were. He chose to be a great hacker and had since stopped using his underworld signature. He would just peek in and get out of a system without a signature. As far as the computer underworld was concerned, The One had ceased to exist. Once he went into the federal government's computers and found a worm called Code Red. It was a bug designed to disable the network on the first of each month. Frank had designed a counter-virus, A Few Good Men, to devour Code Red. He left no signature.

The following day, Frank had told Kutini about his latest exploits in the computer underworld. Kutini, wanting to change the subject had asked, "Is Phyllis aware of all these?"

"No, not a chance," Frank had replied. "By the way, Phyllis and I are getting married after our graduation."

"That's wonderful news. I think it is the right thing to do."

Soon after their graduation, Frank and Phyllis got married with Kutini as their best man. Kutini sat next to Frank at the wedding reception at the Ballroom of the Royal Station Hotel in Newcastle upon Tyne. They were chatting when Kutini spotted a woman in a silky lilac dress walking towards their table with steps that reminded him of Naomi Campbell. Their eyes locked onto each other for a brief moment and she smiled, walked round to Phyllis and whispered something into her ear.

"Who is this woman?" Kutini asked Frank, his gaze still fixed on the woman as she walked away from their table.

"I think she is one of Phyllis' guests, she is called Laz."

The music was playing with only a few people including the bride and groom on the dance floor. Laz was chatting to another woman when Kutini approached her. "Would you like to dance, Laz?" he asked, his arm stretched.

Without answering Laz took Kutini's hand and followed him to the dance floor.

"How do you know my name, Err . . .?"

"Oh, my name is Kutini, a friend of Frank and his wife. Are you at this University?"

"No, I'm starting my MBA at Oxford University," Laz replied. "Did you graduate with Frank?" she asked.

"Yes, but I've been granted a PhD fellowship for the next three years."

"Well done," Laz said, "what's your research topic?"

"I haven't decided the topic yet, but it's going to be about computer network security."

"Wow, you must be very proud."

"It was nice meeting you," Kutini said after the dance, "I hope to see you again soon."

"I'm having my birthday party in two weeks, if you would like to come?"

"Sure, I would love to?"

Kutini and Laz began dating, but it wasn't until Laz had finished her Masters programme that she moved to join Kutini in Newcastle. On the weekend of Laz's arrival Kutini took her to see a stage play of Anthony Burgess' *A Clockwork Orange.*

"What do you think of the play," Kutini asked afterwards.

"I loved it, thanks. It's the kind of story that gets you thinking."

"It's got a lot of social and political implications, hasn't it?" Kutini asked.

"Sure. The main character, Alex, said something like 'neither the church nor the state has taught us how to use our energy and so we must use it to destroy ...,' this is exactly the yob culture we see in this country today."

"I was thinking of that line myself in the context of poverty and the civil wars across Africa."

"Hmm, I think that's got more to do with greed. Don't you think?"

"You're quite right, it's much broader than that," Kutini replied. "Something to eat?" he asked.

"Good idea."

***

Laz had found a job with a small company – a job she didn't really enjoy. She told Kutini she would find a better job in London once he finished his programme. She looked forward to the day they would live together as husband and wife, but as the days went by she was getting worried that Kutini had never discussed marriage.

The couple had been living together for a year when they took a holiday on the east coast of Ireland. They had spent a romantic summer weekend together in the small fishing village of Dunmore East. They woke up on a bright Saturday morning and after having their breakfast Kutini brought out a map of the area showing the coastline and asked Laz, "Where would you like to go?"

"What about a walk along the cliffs?"

They had been walking for about three kilometres when they came to a spot where the grass looked as though it had been specially planted.

"This is beautiful," Laz said, lying down, unable to resist the invitation of the lush vegetation. "… and the ocean is …"

"Shhhh, I've got something to tell you," Kutini said.

Laz sat up, looked straight into Kutini's eyes thinking, this is it; he is going to ask me to marry him. Laz had been waiting for this moment, sometimes getting frustrated and doubting Kutini's word that he loved her.

"Yeees."

"I know you don't like your job in Newcastle. Have you started looking in London?"

Laz lay back on the grass, closed her eyes to hide her disappointment wondering if she was wasting her time with Kutini. She felt love for him, but she also wanted to get married. "No," she said, "why do you ask?"

"I just thought it might be a good idea to start looking for a property as well."

"I don't see why not," Laz answered indifferently.

"Laz."

"What?" she asked, still lying on the grass with her eyes closed.

"Laz, will you … will you marry me?"

She opened her eyes to see Kutini on his knees. She lay there for a moment unable to decide if she had heard him right.

"Please," Kutini pleaded unsure whether he had chosen the right moment. For all the time they have been living together he had been looking for the right moment to ask Laz for marriage, but now he felt his best plan would not be enough.

"Marry me, please."

Laz sat up and looked into Kutini pleading eyes. With a sudden gust of strength she grabbed him by the head, pulled him closer and kissed him. She held on to him, their bodies merging into each other, motionless, afraid to let go and anyone passing by at the time would think their merged bodies were in suspended animation like a statue, captured in time for eternity.

"I thought you were never going to ask," she said.

Kutini removed a ring from his pocket, placed it on her finger saying, "this is the best day of my life."

"Mine too," she said and pulled Kutini forward. They both landed on the grass rolling over each other. The late morning sun smiled gently on the couple as they lay on nature's carpet, lost in their own world, unaware of the waves constantly pounding the face of the cliffs fifty metres below.

They had being lying quietly for a while, their breathing beginning to return to normal from exhaustion when Kutini asked, "How would you like to get married?"

Laz lay, as though she was waiting for an inspiration to answer. "I don't know. Getting married is more important to me than how I get married."

"What about getting married in a small church in St. Lucia, just you and me?"

Laz jumped up with excitement. "How long have you been planning this?" she asked.

"I take that as a 'yes'," Kutini said.

CHAPTER 9

19 July 2004. Inside the Roman Catholic Church in Castries on the Caribbean Island of St. Lucia, Laz and Kutini walked down the aisle, the empty rows of chairs staring at them from either side of the room. Ahead, the Minister was waiting for them behind the altar flanked by two newly ordained priests.

The couple stood in front of the altar, Kutini feeling nervous, struggling to remember the rehearsals they had had and wondering how Laz felt when the Minister started the ceremony.

"Kutini Bomanso, this woman whom you hold by the hand is to be your wife. She has given you one of the most sacred things under heaven: a woman's life and a woman's love. ... Do you vow here, as you have promised, that you will be true and loyal, patient in sickness, comforting in sorrow, and forsaking all others ... so long as you both shall live?"

"I do."

"Laziema, this man whom you hold by the right hand is to be your husband. On your life, your love and devotion he will lean for strength and inspiration. ... Do you vow here, as you have promised, that you will be loyal in adversity ... so long as you both shall live?"

"I do."

"You may now share your vows with each other."

As the couple spent their two weeks' honeymoon mostly in their hotel room on the Island, Laz, had one thing on her mind: to get pregnant. "How many children do you want?" she asked.

"You name it and I'll give it to you," Kutini replied.

They both laughed.

***

The couple returned to the UK after their honeymoon. Kutini collected the presents that had been left with their neighbour and they were going through them when Phyllis called. "Are you alright?" he asked.

"It's Frank," Phyllis said, sobbing, "He has been arrested and charged with internet fraud."

I knew it, Kutini thought, "Is there anything you would like me to do?" he asked.

"No I just wanted to inform you. He has asked me to contact his lawyer, Carl Ingram."

"Let me know if you need any help."

Two days later, when Kutini still hadn't heard from Phyllis, he called. Frank picked up the phone.

"When were you released?" Kutini asked.

"Today, my lawyer got me out on technical grounds. There are no existing laws on gaining access into an organisation's computer systems, especially when no crime has been committed."

"Who is this Carl ...?"

"Carl Ingram is a young bright lawyer I met here in Birmingham. He also studied in Newcastle, at the University of Northumbria.

"Be careful," Kutini said, hoping Frank would stop hacking because it violated privacy even if no crime was committed. What material benefit did Frank get from hacking? Kutini's thoughts were drifting to the possibility that Frank might be gaining somehow from his activities. It couldn't just be addiction.

How ironic, Kutini thought, that I should be studying computer network security when my own friend is exploiting the security loopholes.

He was six months away from completing his research programme and had started applying for jobs in London. Now he was thinking about the possibility of teaming up with Frank to set up a computer company. *Computer Network Security,* he smiled at the thought of the name, knowing Frank's knowledge in hacking would contribute to providing bespoke network security solutions to clients. First he would have to complete his thesis.

Kutini had been working late into the night in order to meet his deadline. He was still lying in bed on this bright Saturday morning when Laz opened the bedroom curtains to let in the sunlight. Kutini woke up suddenly, blinked a few times and asked, "What time is it?"

"It's ten o'clock, come on, get up."

"Thanks for waking me up, I need to go and finish some work."

"You're not going anywhere," Laz said, "it's a weekend, the weather is good and you need a break. Let's go to Tynemouth."

The only reason why Laz liked Newcastle was its proximity to the coast and Tynemouth was one of her favourite places.

"Wow, that's a good idea," Kutini replied, stretching as he got up from bed.

At Tynemouth, the couple had come out of the caves into the sandy part of the coast. They were sitting in the sand watching the hundreds of people who had come out for the good weather.

Kutini heard the chortle of a child behind them and turned round. "Oh, she is so cute," he said to the parents as they walked past with the baby.

"It's a boy," the mother corrected.

"He is so beautiful," Laz said and waved as the couple moved away. She turned to Kutini. "I have something to tell you."

"Is everything OK?" Kutini asked with concern.

"I'm pregnant."

"This is wonderful news," Kutini said, hugging and kissing. "How many weeks is it?" he asked out of excitement. It had been six weeks since they returned from their wedding in St. Lucia, but it seemed only a few days ago to him.

Laz laughed, stroking Kutini's nose. "It shall all be revealed – when I've been to see the doctor."

"I can't wait to hold my first child," Kutini said.

"Patience is a virtue."

"Well, I've got to get my research work out of the way before you pop the baby."

"You do that. I'll need all the help I can get."

The news of Laz's pregnancy had been a source of extra energy for Kutini. He was determined to complete his PhD programme and get a job before the baby arrived. As the days went by Kutini had two reasons to look forward to each next day: his work was progressing in the right direction and the sight of Laz's growing stomach brought its own excitement to him. Kutini would put his hand over it to feel the movement of the baby and say, "Daddy loves you."

As Kutini approached his submission date he had also started attending job interviews. He had submitted his final thesis and was waiting for his exam when he got a job offer with Digital Solutions based in London. A week after the exam the couple moved to London and Kutini started his new job.

As soon as they had settled into their home in London, the couple started planning for the baby. As her due date approached Kutini became more and more anxious, providing all the support he could give to Laz.

Laz was still in bed when Kutini left for the office two days after her due date. He had kissed her oversized belly before leaving. "All is ready for you little one," Kutini said for the ninth time as he stroked Laz's stomach. "Call me if you need any help," he added as he left for the office.

Just before midday, Kutini received a call from St. Thomas Hospital in London. "Mr. Bomanso, your wife is in labour."

"Which ward?" Kutini wrote down the details as he listened to the directions. When he arrived at the ward, Laz was still having minor contractions. He kissed her and asked if she was alright.

"Just some pains."

"Are you still up for the video recording?"

"Sure, if the hospital will allow it."

After checking with the nurse in charge, Kutini set up the stand for the camcorder and got it ready for the final hour.

As soon as the baby was delivered, Kutini was ready to collect it. "It's a boy. Welcome home, Amiga," he said and almost at the same time the baby cried. Kutini held on to his son until the umbilical cord had been cut.

A nurse collected the boy and, after cleaning him, gave him to Laz, who was looking tired and frail. "You're so cute, Amiga; you look like your dad."

Kutini was glad he had been there for his son's birth and nothing could have made him happier.

***

Kofi Mensah was among the guests during Amiga's Christening. "Congratulations," he said.

"I'm glad you could come. How far have you gone with the Liberian crisis?"

"I'm glad you asked, Kutini. The Government wants your involvement in the peace standoff."

"What standoff?" Kutini asked. "All you guys have to do is get the rebel Charles Taylor out of the scene. He is the main stumbling block to peace in the region."

"Charles Taylor is very slippery. Remember, he escaped from a US prison and fought for about a decade before seizing power in Liberia."

"Here is what I think we should do..." Kutini started. The plan was quite elaborate: Charles Taylor, who was still wanted by America for breaking jail, was due to arrive at the Ghana peace talks aboard the luxurious yacht, the *Akosombo Queen,* on the Volta Lake. The security personnel would be on hand to arrest him and hand him over to America.

***

Charles Taylor's arrival at the venue for the peace negotiations was an hour overdue. Kutini was inside the *Akosombo Queen* chatting with some of Liberia's opposition rebels when Kofi Mensah came in, apologised for the delay in the start of the meeting and announced Charles Taylor's plane had landed. "The meeting will start any time soon," he added.

Outside on the tarmac, disguised security personnel waited for Charles Taylor to come out of the plane. The plane, which had stopped at the end of the runway of the small airstrip, turned round and taxied towards the waiting vehicles. As soon as it reached them, the plane increased speed, taxied towards the other end of runway and took off.

The security personnel watched in utter confusion as the plane disappeared into the clouds carrying their prime target.

"Tell me it's not true," Kutini said when Kofi Mensah told him what had happened. "Someone must have tipped him off," he added in exasperation.

"After all these months of planning," Kofi said with clenched fist. "What do we do next?" he asked.

"All is not lost yet," Kutini replied, "let's talk to the other groups, find out their proposals and get a consensus."

"There will be no consensus without Charles Taylor," Kofi Mensah said in frustration.

"I wouldn't say that," Kutini counted.

Aboard the yacht Kofi Mensah apologised for the unexplained actions of Mr. Taylor, proposed they carry on the meeting without him and introduced Kutini Bomanso.

"The main agenda for today's meeting was to discuss the appointment of a transition government. In the light of what has happened, what do you propose we do?" Kutini asked the other opposition parties.

The *Akosombo Queen* rocked gently as the anchor was raised and moved into the deeper waters of the Volta Lake, reputed to be the largest man-made lake in the world. The leader of the main rebel group, Prince Henry, caught his balance as he removed papers from his briefcase. "We cannot sit here to negotiate when the man stalling the peace process is not sitting at this table."

"This meeting was called by ECOWAS due to the deteriorating political situation not only in Liberia, but also in the surrounding countries. The regional body has the mandate to enforce any decisions we make here today, with or without Charles Taylor," Kofi Mensah noted.

"Good point," Kutini said, "any objection?" Kutini made some notes when no one objected. "Any other suggestions?" he asked.

"In the light of what Mr. Mensah just said, I propose we go ahead and make nominations for the formation of the transition government," Prince Henry said.

After the confirmation of the leader and key members of the transition government, Kofi Mensah announced the Nigerian Government had made provisions for the enforcement of the agreement. "Nigeria is leading ECOWAS military forces into Liberia to enforce today's decisions." All members present applauded the announcement.

***

Under the pressure of the Nigerian-led regional force, Charles Taylor accepted a political asylum.

Kutini sat among African leaders who had gathered in the Liberian capital of Monrovia to see to the peaceful departure of Charles Taylor to make way for a transition government. He watched as the Presidential jet lifted off with Charles Taylor and his family bound for the Nigerian federal capital of Abuja.

While the exit of the rebel leader signified the return of peace to Liberia, another phase of the precious-mineral related war was taking a different turn in the Democratic Republic of Congo that would involve Kutini in a life and death diplomatic mission that would change the course of history.

CHAPTER 10

"Mr. President, thank you for making time to meet me."

Tony Conrat sat down opposite President Louis Kilunda of the Democratic Republic of Congo. It was the first time he had been in the President's official residence in Kinshasa, a different setting from the jungle clearing where Conrat had made a deal with Louis' father for the control of the country's minerals.

Conrat's company, Bankroll Resources International, had financed Louis' father in the overthrow of Mobutu, but the deal did not materialise until after his death. Now, Conrat was here to claim what he thought belonged to his company.

"It's my pleasure to meet you. How may we help you?" Kilunda asked, knowing why Conrat had pursued him to Kinshasa.

"I'm here to ask for your approval and cooperation in implementing the deal my company had with your government," Conrat said.

"Mr. Conrat, I'm afraid the deal you had with my father did not involve the people and government of the Democratic Republic of Congo."

Kilunda was well aware Conrat's company had financed his father's military campaign, but he had plans of his own, plans for the people of Congo and they didn't involve selling the wealth of his country for a pittance.

"The deal was done for the benefit of your people and my company is committed to the welfare of the people of Congo," Conrat persisted, employing all his textbook knowledge about negotiating skills.

In the past, Conrat had never had to negotiate. He bought his way into whatever he wanted. He believed everyone could be bought and his aggressive dealings had catapulted him from the job of mining engineer to his present position as head of the company's operations in the Congo.

Conrat did not want to be drawn into negotiation. With Louis' father, the deal had been quick and straightforward: he needed arms and Conrat's company needed access to the nation's resources. Simple. He had not been prepared for Kilunda's cunningness and caution.

"I will discuss your proposal with the government and we will get back to you," Louis Kilunda said finally.

Conrat abandoned his diplomatic politeness. "Do remember to point out to the members of your government," he said, putting his last cards on the table, "that Bankroll Resources International financed your rise to power."

"My government is fully aware of your invaluable contribution to the war because of my late father," said Kilunda with refined restraint, "and that will be considered in any decisions we arrive at." He stood up to signify the end of the meeting.

A presidential aide showed Conrat to the door, where a military guard took over and escorted him out of the building.

As Conrat left the compound he couldn't fail to notice the heavy security surrounding the presidential compound.

As soon as Conrat was out of the room, the aide handed over a document to President Kilunda who went through it. As a military officer, he had distinguished himself by his ability to read fast and grasp large volumes of material and to take decisive actions. He was a natural leader and it had been a matter of choice rather than inheritance that brought him to power when his father died.

The fifty-page document contained a proposal for mineral exploration and mining, and a contract for granting mining concessions to Bankroll Resources International. Kilunda studied the financial details of the contract and handed the document back to his aide.

Louis Kilunda knew the dealings of Tony Conrat too well. His business was minerals and his passion was money, which transcended all his morality. Conrat had financed several rebel groups during their fight to take Kinshasa. Louis' father had happened to be the one to topple Mobutu's government. Conrat was still financing some rebels who controlled other parts of the country, so Kilunda decided he wasn't going to do business with him.

Conrat waited two months without hearing from the President. In the meantime, he had information that letters had been sent out to several mining companies to bid for mining concessions. Bankroll Resources International was not among them.

Conrat called Kinshasa and was put through to the office of the President, but not to the President himself. It was obvious orders were in place to stall him. "Can I make an appointment with the President?" he requested.

"The President is very busy. His diary is full for the next two months."

Furious, Conrat shouted down the line, "Your President is a crook and this country is going to pay for his stupidity. You Congolese think the minerals are yours, they are …"

The line went dead as the person he was talking to hung up.

"…they are ours," he spat through clenched teeth. "Son of a bitch," he swore, as he slammed the receiver down.

***

The diamond trade left a murderous trail leading out of a logistics network stretching from local rebel leaders' landing strips in the African bush, through presidential palaces, via the weapons markets of the West to the offices of diamond traders. Following the submission of a study of the inhumane business of blood diamonds, the United Nations Security Council had imposed a ban on diamonds from certain countries. This prompted the head of De Bertz Company, Nora Goldstein, to pull out of Angola, but it was a miscalculation. A previously unknown Russian diamond trader, Ivan Yuganov, moved in to secure an exclusive diamond contract with the Angolan government and within a few months had elevated himself to a formidable competitor for De Bertz.

The head of De Bertz had to come out with a different strategy. If Antwerp were the diamond capital of the world, it was Nora's creation and she was, therefore, the President of the Nation of diamonds.

Nora had come to the office on this Saturday morning as usual. She had been so busy building her diamond empire that marriage had passed her by and so she did not have any family to worry about. She was sitting at her desk in her Antwerp office looking out of her window enjoying the whiteness of the previous night's snow. It was the first December snow which increased her hopes for a white Christmas.

As Nora watched the snow her mind wandered from a Christmas with her parents to how eternal diamonds were: Diamonds are indeed forever. After all, about four million years ago, or so the experts say, the earth trembled causing giant primeval trees to come crashing down and in the humus of decaying foliage grew new trees, which in turn fell and rotted – first to peat, then to coal. Several kilometres below the earth's surface, the carbon melted under the massive pressure and was compressed into diamond. Volcanic eruptions propelled the cherished stones towards the earth's surface as if extending a gift to humankind: a present to lovers whose wishes are their loves could be as eternal as the stones that shine brilliantly upon their fingers and through their décolleté.

Nora, the goddess of diamonds, would continue to extend her love symbol to lovers and would stop at nothing to get it even if this symbol of love and of purity was stained.

She had formed a complex network with neutral diamond producing countries to certify her blood diamonds as though they originated from those countries. Her power and influence in the global trade transcended the business world into politics, with key figures in European and African governments in her payroll. She used this to good effect, but the loss of the Angolan government had left a gaping hole in her company's profits and reputation as the world's largest diamond trader.

She called Viktor Mamphele, the South African Consul in London and told him, "We need a regime change in Angola as soon as possible." Nora was not the one to get into arguments with. She had absolute power most governments could only dream of and she used it to her company's advantage.

"I will contact Tony Conrat; he is our man on the ground."

***

At the small airstrip in Makunu, Tony Conrat met with General Angelo Binda, a commander of the Goma-based faction of the armed Rassemblement Congolais pour la Démocratie (RCD) in Makunu and his assistant Jean Tshilongo.

"My company is ready to continue to assist your movement to liberate Congo," Conrat said to Binda.

"We appreciate your support," Binda replied. "What have you got for us?"

"Some beautiful babies," Conrat said. He opened a door on the side of the aircraft to reveal an assortment of assault rifles.

Binda picked up an AK-47 and with the speed of a combat soldier, turned and pointed it at Conrat followed by the sound *ta ta ta ta ta ta.*

Conrat fell to the ground.

Binda stopped the sound from his mouth and helped Conrat to his feet. "That's how fast I'll destroy the enemy."

"Don't ever do that again," the bewildered Conrat said, struggling for the right words.

Binda saw the anger in Conrat's eyes and said, "Come on, I'm not going to kill you. How will we get these babies otherwise?"

"I want to get the hell out of here."

"Follow me. I'll show you something that will calm your nerves," Binda said.

Conrat took a deep breath and followed as Binda led the way down a series of stairs into a room. Down in the basement, Binda removed a briefcase from one of the cabinets and opened it.

Conrat's eyes brightened and his mouth fell open. Inside the briefcase were several diamonds. Conrat picked up a stone and said, "Come to papa. Papa loves you."

"I have got something else to show you," Binda said, opening a box to show Tony a consignment of the mineral columbite-tantalite (coltan) used as an integral part of miniature circuit boards in cellular phones and laptops, and known to the local population as tantalum.

"This is the new big thing," Conrat remarked, overcoming his initial shock and glad to be the main power broker in this new and exciting trade. "I don't trade in drugs. I'm a legitimate businessman in precious minerals," he would often tell his friends in the West, oblivious to the fact his trade had killed more people than drugs.

Tony Conrat inspected the tantalum and nodded his head in acceptance. "Let's get this stuff into the plane," he said, picking up the briefcase.

"I'll get the boys to do it," Binda said as he led the way out of the hut.

As they came into the forecourt Jean Tshilongo was waiting with a number of soldiers. "Happy sir?" he asked Tony Conrat.

"You bet," Conrat replied.

"Alright guys let's move it," Tshilongo instructed.

The soldiers disappeared into the hut to load the tantalum into Conrat's plane and then offloaded the guns and ammunition delivered in exchange.

When the barter side of the trade was complete Binda passed his foreign account details and that of Tshilongo to Conrat to pay their share of the cash proceeds into.

Conrat collected the piece of paper with the accounts information, folded it and put it inside his diary. "Can Tshilongo be trusted?" he asked. There was something about Jean he didn't like but he couldn't figure out what it was.

"Tshilongo is very loyal," Binda replied, "When should we expect the next delivery?"

"In a fortnight," Conrat said, thinking, I can always buy their trust.

***

As soon as Conrat left, Binda invited Tshilongo into his hut and told him about an attack by the Mai Mai in the village of Badungu.

"The leader there was killed in the attack and I would like you to go to Badungu to take charge of the unit."

Tshilongo arrived at the camp amid cheers and shouts from other soldiers and was let through series of mud houses into a room serving as the armoury.

The soldier in charge pushed a writing desk aside, then pulled an old rug on the floor aside to reveal a wooden door. He pulled it open, climbed down a ladder and beckoned Tshilongo to follow. The armoury stored in the basement started Tshilongo thinking about all the glory a major victory would bring to him.

The soldier briefed Tshilongo as he escorted him to inspect the rest of the camp. The two men sat down afterwards and went through a war plan. Tshilongo called a parade later that afternoon and informed the soldiers of a military campaign to start at dawn.

The cocks' cock-a-doodle-doo from the village announced the arrival of dawn. A heavy downpour and accompanying thunderstorm drenched the soldiers as they prepared for the march into the village. As though by design, the dark clouds gave them the perfect cover and the thunder drowned out the sound of their movement.

Jean Tshilongo and his armed men entered the village of Badungu like hungry wolves in search of prey under the cover of the late night darkness and started raiding houses.

Inside a large compound in the middle of Badungu local Mai Mai militiaman woke up, blinked to adjust to the darkness and sniffed the air. He smelled smoke. Quietly, he woke the rest of the militia up. Through whispers the word was passed round as they grabbed their weapons and went out into the rain and laid an ambush. The rhythmic sound of gunfire was now distinguishable from the thunder.

Tshilongo and his men were moving towards a house when they heard a single gunshot from behind and froze. The whole place went quiet for a few minutes.

The Mai Mai militia, who were waiting for the gunshot signal, came out of their positions. They crawled on their bellies towards Tshilongo's men, surrounding them from behind. A movement in front alerted Tshilongo's men to the presence of armed men and they opened fire.

"Cease fire," Tshilongo shouted out when he realised they were outnumbered.

Tshilongo could hear the shrill jubilant voices of child-soldiers firing indiscriminately in their direction. He whispered to the soldier next to him, "Prepare your hand grenades." The message went round and as soon as they were all ready, Tshilongo shouted, "Now."

Tshilongo watched as the rain of grenades fell into the positions of the Mai Mai tearing through flesh and metal, filling the air with the dismembered bodies of the child-soldiers. As the noise of the explosions died down he could hear the cry of a wounded child-soldier calling out to his mother.

"Bastards," Tshilongo swore, as they made their way through debris of body tissue mixed with metal, bones and blood. Tshilongo stopped by the child-soldier still crying out for his mother, knelt beside him and asked, "Do you want some breast milk?"

"My mother begged me not to join the army, but they forced me. Please don't kill me."

Tshilongo looked at the boy trying to drag himself into a pleading position with both legs blown off and asked, "How old are you?"

"Twelve, sir, please don't …"

"Go fuck your mama. I'm sure she would thank me for this favour," Tshilongo said, blowing the boy's brains out, then got up to catch up with the rest of his soldiers.

"Where is the Mai Mai leader's house?" Tshilongo asked one of his men.

"It's at the end of this footpath, the last house on the outskirts. We can't miss it."

Pierre had fallen asleep that night playing with the camcorder he had received from his elder brother in France as a birthday present. He was still clinging to it when his father, the Mai Mai local militia leader, woke him up. "Take your mother and get out of the house through the back door."

"Is everything OK?" the eleven-year old Pierre asked. Just then he heard bullets rip through their front door and quickly followed his heavily pregnant mother out of the house. He paused as he heard a cry of pain from his father and wished he had a gun, then he realised he was still holding his camcorder.

"Search the house," Pierre heard the command and started running. He lay in the bush with his mother, holding their breath and watched as the armed men came out of their house carrying heavy sacks, which he suspected would be his father's tantalum.

Almost without thinking, he raised his camcorder and started to film the scene. A few metres away one of the soldiers turned round and threw a grenade into the house; the explosion set it on fire.

Pierre almost screamed; he held his hand to his mouth to stifle the sound. Then, he heard a movement next to him and turned round to see his mother break cover. He almost followed her, but, as though by instinct, he looked in the direction of the armed men to see Tshilongo take aim. He froze, his camcorder still focused on them.

Tshilongo and his men were moving towards another house when he heard a movement behind him and turned to see a woman running in the opposite direction. He took aim and pulled the trigger.

The woman stumbled from the impact of the bullet from behind and fell face forward, landing on her oversized stomach. Tshilongo watched until there was no more movement from her before turning round to go. At that moment, he heard a baby cry.

At first, he thought it had come from the burning house. He started towards it but a second cry drew his attention towards the fallen woman. As Tshilongo reached the woman he saw to his fury that she had given birth in the process and it was the newborn baby crying.

He looked at the baby, hesitated, and shot it. "This should put you out of your misery," he said and walked towards his colleagues, issuing fresh commands as he went.

***

Pierre lay in the bushes afraid the sound of his pounding heart might draw the attention of the killers. His heart jumped with each sound of gunshot or grenade explosion he heard. Above him the clouds began to clear and the first light of day was returning to the village. At the same time he was hearing less and less gunshot.

Pierre didn't come out of his hiding place until late morning when he could no longer hear movements. He lifted his head first, looking all around him for signs of armed men. When he didn't see any, he got up and ran towards the spot where his mother lay, dropped on the ground beside her and wept. He did not hear the two people approach until a voice spoke behind him. He leapt up with fright and started to run.

"It's OK. Please come back. I'm Karen Walker, a Red Cross doctor. We are here to help you."

Pierre stopped running, but hesitated to return.

"It's alright, please come." The two were not armed but Pierre approached them cautiously.

"I'm Phil Jones. Is this yours?" he asked, showing Pierre the camcorder.

"Yes." His voice was almost inaudible.

"Let's go."

"No," Pierre protested, "I can't leave my mother."

"It's not safe here. There are still armed men roaming about."

Pierre reluctantly followed as Karen led the way towards a parked Land Rover. Phil waited behind to film the dead woman and her baby before joining them for the short drive to their camp where Karen gave Pierre food and a blanket.

"Where is my father?" Pierre asked without touching the food.

"We don't know. We are still assembling all those alive and will be able to tell you shortly," Phil replied.

"Why did they kill my pregnant mother?" Pierre was crying.

Dr. Karen Walker came over to Pierre to console him and persuaded him to eat some food, then asked, "Is it alright if we see your film?"

"Yes."

Karen wept openly as she saw the horror of the killings.

"It's OK," Phil consoled her, "may be we should show this to the media," he suggested.

The next day CNN aired edited pictures from Pierre's amateur video together with an interview of Karen and Phil.

"The images you are about to see were taken by a brave

amateur we know only as Pierre," the reporter said, "they are very disturbing images and some people might want to look away now." The dark blue background of dawn gave the horrific pictures a more gruesome tinge.

We will now take you to Badungu where our CNN correspondent, Sam Tuki, spoke to Pierre and his rescuers."

"Dr. Walker, what can you tell us about the raid?" Sam asked.

"It was a killing field out there. They raided every house in Badungu and burnt most of the houses there. We believe some of the inhabitants managed to escape, but most of them were killed."

"The local militia, what happened to them?"

"Sam, in Badungu here the Mai Mai militia were mainly forced child-soldiers, some as young as nine years. We found about a hundred of them killed at one spot."

"About this boy, Pierre, how did you find him?"

"Phil and I had been moving from house to house trying to help the wounded after the raid when we came across Pierre lying next to his dead mother."

"What about his father?"

"At the moment we don't know. Pierre said he was in the house when they left. We believe he died in the fire that engulfed their house."

Sam turned to Pierre and asked, "Have you got any relatives somewhere?"

"My brother is in Paris," he replied crying. "I want to go to my father", he added.

"What are your plans for Pierre, Dr. Walker?"

"We would like to appeal to anyone who would like to adopt him to contact any of the Red Cross offices in South Africa."

"Do you have any message for the international community?"

"Yes, Sam, if we don't get the international peace keepers here soon, I'm afraid it will be Rwanda all over again."

"Pierre was lucky to escape with his life in this region where the decade-old war has claimed millions of lives including the child-soldiers you saw in our report. Sam Tuki reporting for CNN, Democratic Republic of Congo."

CHAPTER 11

In August 2005 on the local news station, the President of South Africa, Joseph Thebe, listened to the news item with anger. He picked up the phone and called his Foreign Minister. "Have you seen the news about the new phase of the Congo war?"

"Yes, I was going to call you to discuss it."

"I would like us to convene a meeting of African leaders this weekend. Would you like to organise it?"

In the South African city of Cape Town, African leaders heeded the worldwide call and convened an emergency meeting to find a solution to the long-standing hostilities.

The waterfront in Cape Town had been turned into a security fortress as armoured yachts carried leaders arriving from Cape Town airport. Their destination: Robben Island.

Robben Island had been chosen for this meeting for two reasons. First, it was the spiritual home of freedom fighting, for it was from a prison cell on this island Nelson Mandela had fought apartheid in South Africa for twenty-seven years. Second, it was the best place in which to ensure maximum security within a short time.

The day before the meeting, security personnel with sniffer dogs had swept the entire island. Police patrol boats circled the island to see off any unauthorised boats. Helicopters hovered overhead.

The meeting was scheduled to start at 1100 hours and by 1030 hours all the leaders had arrived.

"Thank you all for responding to this urgent call," Thebe said, plunging straight into business. "There is only one item on the agenda for this meeting: finding a lasting solution to the decades of civil war in the Democratic Republic of Congo."

After a long and hard debate that went on into the early hours of the morning, the leaders emerged with a working plan. A delegation of foreign ministers would go to Kinshasa the following day to persuade the government to declare a ceasefire. Within a week, a group of peace negotiators would follow to try to get the warring factions to allow multinational forces into the country to help with security.

"We need five countries to volunteer to provide peace negotiators," Thebe said.

The Foreign Minister of Ghana, Kofi Mensah whispered to his President, Ebo Mettle. "We will provide a negotiator," Ebo Mettle offered.

Nigeria, Egypt, and Kenya followed, then the room fell silent.

"We need one more country." Thebe looked uncomfortably around the room. The South Africa Foreign Minister scribbled something on a piece of paper and passed it to Thebe. "Err, South Africa will provide a negotiator," he announced.

The meeting closed with a clear commitment to bring peace to the Congo and to establish a standing committee made up of foreign ministers to monitor and coordinate the process.

On their flight back to Ghana, President Ebo Mettle asked Kofi Mensah, his Foreign Minister, "Who will be the best person for this job?"

"I know just the person – Kutini Bomanso."

"Mr. Bomanso turned down the position as your deputy and didn't respond to our call to serve on the Information and

Communications Technology Committee. What makes you think he will accept this job?"

"He will see it is a moral obligation - instead of being drawn into politics. He is a very capable negotiator."

"How are you going to get him to do it? We have other capable people."

"Leave that to me, Mr. President. I'll arrange to meet him in London as a matter of urgency."

***

The next day, Kofi Mensah was on his way to London. He hadn't called Kutini in advance. He preferred to meet him face to face. Whether he would find Kutini in London was a gamble he was prepared to take.

During their university days, Kutini had negotiated a favourable deal for the students during a stand-off between them and the authorities. He had become an instant superhero on campus, earning as many friends as jealous enemies. The Minister had been one of those who had been secretly jealous of Kutini's achievement, but when he had realised Kutini was a natural leader he had tapped into his friend's talent for his own political ambitions.

The past government had used Kutini's skill in brokering peace in Sierra Leone and he had been instrumental in the Liberian peace negotiations, so he was confident he wouldn't turn him down, if only for old times' sake.

He rang Kutini as soon as he checked into the Embassy's guesthouse at Hampstead Heath in London. The phone was answered after the first ring.

Kutini picked up his phone to hear the voice of his old school mate, the Ghanaian Foreign Minister. "Is it your job you're offering me this time?"

"Don't be daft, Kutini, I'm in town and would like us to meet tomorrow evening, say eight o'clock?

"I'll see you at eight tomorrow."

At exactly eight the next day Kutini pressed Kofi's doorbell and was answered promptly.

"Good to see you," Kofi said, sounding rather formal.

Ever since Kofi became the Ghanaian Foreign Minister, Kutini had observed his friend change from a buoyant easy-going, fun-loving person to a personality that made mockery of a stereotypical English upper class and reminded Kutini of the British soap opera, *Keeping up Appearances*. Even though Kutini didn't know it, that was probably what put him off from getting involved in politics.

"What does your government want from me?" Kutini asked, defensively.

With calculated diplomacy, Kofi asked, "Would you like a drink?"

Kutini was surprised at the change of subject. "Sure, something hot."

Kofi got the kettle boiling. "It's not what my government wants. It's what Africa wants."

"Kofi, you know I don't want to get into politics. I'm happy with what I am doing."

"This is not about politics, Kutini. We need your help in negotiating peace in the Democratic Republic of Congo."

Kutini was silent. He remembered how he had felt when the news of the killings was broadcast on BBC I. His wife had wept and he had turned the TV off to console her. But now he was thinking about his wife and son.

"What happened to our hot drink?" Kutini asked, trying to buy time to decide.

"Sorry, I forgot. I'll go and get it."

"You know my son is only five months old and I can't leave him and my wife on their own," Kutini said after Kofi had returned with his drink.

The statement brought some relief to Kofi as he thought; at least he didn't turn me down outright like he had done in the past.

"You're our best negotiator and I've given my word not only to the President, but also to the African leaders that you would help. Please don't disappoint me."

"I've got to discuss this with my wife and I'm not promising anything."

"We can arrange for a house help for her," Kofi offered.

"That wouldn't be necessary," Kutini said, "Is this why you came to the UK?"

Kofi looked away from Kutini's piercing stare feeling uneasy. "As a matter of fact, yes," he replied, the grin on his face doing little to hide his desperation.

"Well, I'll let you know my decision tomorrow. I must be going."

"I'll be waiting for your call."

When Kutini got home, he told his wife, Laziema, about his meeting with Kofi.

"I hope you're not thinking of honouring the invitation?" Laz asked.

"I told Kofi I was going to discuss it with you first."

"Then tell Kofi the answer is no."

Only Kutini's steps on the wooden floor broke the silence in their living room as he walked away, one part of him wanting to say, "How insensitive."

"I thought we had decided we were not going to get involved in politics," Laz said after him.

Kutini stopped and came back to Laz. "This is not about politics. It's about helping to save innocent lives and from the way you felt when we saw those pictures in the news, I thought this would be an opportunity to help."

"What about me? What about Amiga? Don't we matter? Don't we need help?" She couldn't hold back her tears, her voice going up with each question waking up Amiga. She picked him up when he started crying and said, "Your dad doesn't love us anymore."

"Kutini sat down next to Laz, held her and started drying her tears. "Laz, you know I will always love you and I'll do anything for you. When Kofi calls tomorrow I'll tell him I can't make it."

Amiga had stopped crying and Laz, who was resting her head on Kutini's shoulders, sat up and said, "No I can't do that."

"It's OK, I'm staying."

"I could be selfish and say don't go, but for the sake of the lives you would save, I couldn't possibly stop you."

Those words touched Kutini. "I hope it will be worthwhile," he replied.

"It will be, you've never failed on such missions," she said.

When a call came in the next morning Kutini knew it would be Kofi before he answered the phone.

"Have you got news for me?" Kofi asked.

"When would you like me to come?"

"We have a reservation for you on British Airways. We are hoping to meet all the commission members in five days in Accra, so confirm your reservation to suit you."

***

Kutini sat in the first class of a British Airways flight on his way to Ghana. He was expecting a VIP welcome. At the back of his mind he knew a peace mission to the decade-old war in the Democratic Republic of Congo was not going to be an easy task. He was all too familiar with the situation there as he was with similar situations in other parts of Africa.

Kutini's mind wandered to his mission and the innocent women and children who had died because of these senseless wars. The shrill crying voice of a baby two rows ahead of him broke his thoughts, then he thought about the woman and her baby killed in the Congo. He held his head in his hands and cried. Children are the most endangered species in Africa, he thought.

They were about four hours into the six-hour flight when he fell asleep, only to wake up to the announcement of the final descent to the Ghanaian capital of Accra. He was met on the tarmac by Kofi and taken to the Ministerial Lounge at the Kotoka International Airport before being driven directly to Akuse, home to the Peduase Presidential Lodge on the shore of Lake Volta. A meeting of all the commission members would take place the next day.

The next morning, Kutini Bomanso was the last to arrive at the meeting room, but still ahead of the scheduled time for the meeting. Sitting in the luxurious surroundings of the Presidential lodge, he was away from the immediate call of both telephone and email and looking out over the rolling countryside making conversation with the group of four strangers he'd just introduced himself to. However, he didn't feel relaxed.

From the moment he arrived, he was being scrutinized – the clothes he wore, his hairstyle, and even his age were all being used to determine whether he was going to be in the running. As a successful senior manager and a member of the board of directors of a company he part-owned, Kutini had realised that to be successful knowledge wasn't enough. He had to look and play the part.

Clearly the rest had chosen either to rely on the uniform of the old formal suit or blazer with some odd colour combinations, and the frail looking man who was later introduced as Rahim Mubarik had even donned a knitted pullover, forgetting the hot climatic conditions in the tropics. It didn't make any difference as they were driven in air-conditioned cars to air-conditioned rooms.

Kutini was dressed in smart casual clothes, looking urbanised in a light blue shirt over khaki-coloured viscose trousers and navy blue jacket. He had chosen them with care. In the competitive environment where Kutini worked, appearance was everything and first impressions had always been his catch phrase.

Kutini was particularly conscious of Rahim's scrutiny and was delighted to be wearing his new glasses. They gave him that look of confidence, made him feel totally comfortable and which he was told, also gave him 'an air of authority!' His thoughts were interrupted when he saw his friend Kofi and two others enter.

"Thanks, gentlemen, for honouring our invitation. I'm Kofi Mensah, Ghana's Foreign Minister," he started when they were seated. "We also have with us here Ayoshegun Bamidele, Nigerian Foreign Minister who will provide us with the background to the conflict and James Nziza from Kenya, who will lead the commission." He passed round copies of a document on the commission's role in the Congo. "Let's start by introducing ourselves."

"Yaro Tunde, Nigerian, based in Boston, USA."

"Kutini Bomanso, Ghanaian, based in London, UK."

"Rahim Mubarik, Egyptian, Alexandria, Egypt."

"Alfred Xuma, South African, based in Toronto, Canada."

Bamidele then gave a brief background to the conflict, what role they were expected to play and the goal they had to achieve before asking James Nziza to give a detailed insight into the conflict.

For the first time Kutini Bomanso became aware of the complexity of the conflict. He listened as James Nziza enumerated the various factions in the war. First, there were the Hutu members of the former Rwanda Armed Forces believed to be responsible for the genocide of Tutsis in Rwanda, who were now fighting the government of Rwanda. Then the Mai Mai, a loose association of traditional Congolese guerrillas who fought the influx of Rwanda refugees. Another group, the Alliance of Democratic Forces, made up of Uganda expatriates and supported by the Government of Sudan, was fighting the Government of Uganda.

Several groups of Hutus from Burundi fighting the Tutsi-dominated government of Burundi also had a playground in the Congo. To make matters worse, there were subdivisions within some of the groups.

"The war in the Democratic Republic of the Congo has become the widest interstate war in modern African history, involving nine African countries and affecting the fifty-five million Congolese population." Nziza paused and looked around the room. He could almost hear the breathing of the members through the silence.

"The war claimed almost two million deaths between August 1998 and May 2000 alone, with over fifty-thousand child-soldiers killed within any one year. We have been entrusted with negotiating peace. This is our responsibility and also our challenge."

After the briefing, the group interacted to get to know each other. Alfred Xuma passed a copy of an article to James. "I am sure you will find this an interesting read on the conflict."

James looked at the cover of the article entitled, *The Geopolitical Stakes of the International Mining Companies in the Democratic Republic of Congo,* authored by Pierre Baracyetse.

Alfred was a peace activist and had found the facts in the article as compelling as they were damning. He knew too well what was at stake in this war and the article confirmed it.

Kutini walked up to the two and said, "That was an insightful briefing, Mr. Nziza."

"Call me James," he said, shaking his hand.

"It's nice to meet you, James, I am Kutini."

"It's nice to be part of the team," James responded. "Have a look at this article; it tells part of the Congolese story."

Kutini was glancing at the paper when a burst of laughter came from the other end of the room where Rahim Mubarik and Yaro Tunde were talking.

"It seems we have a good team here," James said.

"We need good team work for Africa to succeed," Alfred added.

"It will take a great deal of effort to stop these international corporate pirates and scoundrels," Kutini noted.

"That's a good point," Alfred said. "Our own governments have added to the cause of corruption, violence, murders and political upheavals."

"This team will have to prove we can meet the challenge," James concluded.

More laughter came from the other two, who had been joined by Bamidele. Kutini moved over to make his acquaintance.

"We have quite a handful of challenges to meet," Kutini said, after a brief introduction.

"It will take more than just living under city bright lights to meet such challenges," Rahim remarked. "Excuse me," he added, then left.

"I will catch up with you guys," Bamidele said and also left.

If Kutini took offence at Rahim's statement, he did not react. He was thinking about Yaro and Bamidele. There was something about Nigerians that struck Kutini. They were bold. They were smart and confident and, although sometimes overbearing, Kutini admired these characteristics.

Kutini and Yaro shared the information they had about the Democratic Republic of Congo. "I am really not at ease about this mission. The situation in the Congo is still chaotic," Yaro said.

"That's precisely why we are on this mission."

"I think the UN should just split the Congo among the warring factions."

"It's an interesting point Yaro; let's talk about this after dinner."

At dinner, Kutini Bomanso sat next to Yaro Tunde. After warming to each other with conversation on football and how an African nation had come close to winning the world cup they started to talk about themselves and their school days.

After dinner, the two men went to the lounge, ordered drinks, settled in to a corner and continued their conversation about the silly things they had done in school.

"I remember one night during a school sports festival we had a disco dance in the school's assembly hall. During the dance I saw the Regional Minister go out with one of the student girls, so I sneaked behind them. Before long they were making love behind the back of his car. I shouted at them." Kutini paused.

"What happened then?" Yaro asked, laughing loudly.

"The Minister went into his car and drove away leaving the girl running back to the assembly hall."

"I once told my teacher she had a big mouth for picking on me every time. It was translated literally by the headmaster and I got punished for being 'the most handsome boy' in the school," Yaro told his experience.

They both laughed and Kutini noticed they had attracted the attention of a group of people sitting at the other end of the lounge. "This lodge was built under the rule of Kwame Nkrumah as the Presidential Retreat," he told Yaro, changing the topic of the conversation

"I know," Yaro replied, "Kwame Nkrumah was one of the greatest leaders Africa ever had. He could have united the people."

"We can still implement Nkrumah's visions," Kutini suggested.

"But how?" Yaro asked, thinking about Africa's degeneration into despair. He couldn't think how Africa could unite with all these wars and the numerous language barriers.

"The unification of Africa will not happen by accident, but will be born out of a deliberate, systematic and conscious effort by a group of young Africans who are not willing to compromise."

"And just where are we going to find such group of young Africans?" Yaro asked with scepticism.

"Right here, right now, you and I could form the nucleus of such a group," Kutini said.

Yaro didn't say anything for a few seconds; he seemed to have fallen into deep thought. "You are right, my friend," he said, coming out of his deep meditation. "The youth are angry and militant, the old are desperate and in despair. All they need is a little more information and a dash of inspired leadership."

"Exactly; this is the inspiration we could offer them." Kutini was getting excited about their converging thoughts.

Yaro's mind went to the clandestine Free Africa Movement (FAM) his late father had told him about, which had the ultimate objective of creating a federation – the Federal African Republics. His father had failed to persuade him to join the military and he had shown little interest in his Movement. As he thought about his father's ideas and unfulfilled aspiration, he hoped his soul would forgive him for his refusal and have eternal rest in perfect peace.

Yaro looked at his watch. It was just after midnight. "Let's catch some sleep and continue on our way tomorrow," he said.

"Sure, we need to stay alert if we're going into the lion's den," Kutini replied.

CHAPTER 12

South African Airways Chartered Flight 571 took off from Kotoka International Airport headed for the Congolese capital of Kinshasa.

"Welcome aboard," the huge pilot who could pass more for a wrestling champion than a professional pilot said as the plane attained maximum altitude. "This is your captain, Samuel Biya... Make yourselves comfortable and enjoy the flight." He had been in the Air Force and had risen to the rank of a Flight Lieutenant before resigning to train as a commercial pilot. It was because of his background that he was responsible for flying South African Airways Chartered flights and most of his passengers had been high-profile government officials and diplomats. He engaged the autopilot, looked at his co-pilot and smiled. For the next few hours they had less work to do.

Aboard the flight all five members of the peace commission sat around a desk in a conference-like fashion that reminded Kutini of a scene in the film Air Force One. When the plane reached cruising speed and the pilot had turned off the seatbelt sign, James Nziza, the leader, pulled his briefcase from underneath his chair, removed a file and put it on the desk. "I hope you are all comfortable?" he asked.

"I hate flying; I fly only when I have to," Rahim replied.

"Gentlemen," James started, "according to our plan, we will meet the government and depending on the outcome we will then meet the Interahamwe, the Mai Mai, the RCD... Is there anything I have left out?"

"I suggest that we alter our schedule. If we visit each group in turn the process will be long and other factions might be apprehensive," Kutini said.

"I thought we had already agreed to the plan," Rahim countered, feeling his dislike for Kutini increase each time he heard him speak.

"What do you suggest?" James asked.

"I don't think this is the time for suggestions; let's get on with the agreed programme," Rahim insisted.

"Would you like to hear me out?" Kutini pleaded, his impatience with Rahim turning into burning frustration inside him.

"No, Mr. Bomanso."

"Why not?"

"Because you're cheeky, rude and sarcastic, and that's just an introduction," Rahim finally let out.

Kutini opened his mouth to say something, but stopped and just inhaled the surrounding air with a deep breath using both his nose and his mouth.

"That is taking a step too far, Mr. Mubarik," James said, bringing order back into the deliberations. "Remember, we are a team and every view counts."

"What were you going to suggest Kutini?" Yaro asked with eagerness.

"I wanted to suggest that we invite all the warring factions to a central location..."

"I think it's a brilliant suggestion," Yaro said and they all agreed except Rahim, who just kept quiet and after some time dozed off.

The Airbus 300 was flying over northern Gabon when Rahim woke up with a fright and pushed a fallen piece of luggage from his knees. Without warning the plane seemed to fall from the sky and he saw the food service trays, carts and luggage tossed about in the cabin. Instinctively, he went into the emergency landing position with his head bent forward.

Then, the pilot's voice came over the microphone, "We are experiencing some turbulence. Please remain seated with your seatbelts fastened."

Is this the sign of bad things to come? Rahim was thinking aloud. He sat uneasy as the plane flew unsteadily through the pockets of warm air for about an hour. He was just wondering when the turbulence was going to stop when he felt the relative smoothness, then the pilot's voice: "We are starting our descent into Kinshasa."

Mashaallah, Rahim said quietly.

***

Underneath the shade of the young palm tree in the deserted village of Manuku, Jean Tshilongo sat playing cards with one of his armed men. He had ignored the faint and distant noise earlier, but it was becoming louder, clearer and closer.

He looked up, his gaze going past the rebel-ravaged houses in front of him towards the cloudless skies above him. He got up leaving his cards face down, adjusted his binoculars round his neck to lie behind him and shifted his American-made M16 sub machine gun from his right shoulder to his left. The M16 was a rare weapon among the RCD fighters. It was booty from one of his raids and he carried it with pride.

With his equipment ready, Tshilongo moved out of the shade into the open and looked through his binoculars. He was facing the plane and couldn't see any of the writings, but assumed it couldn't be a civilian plane. Since the fighting began, no civilian plane had flown over Congo.

Tshilongo reasoned that this might be a cargo plane carrying arms and could be the answer to his prayers. They needed more arms and ammunition and he had asked for supplies from the head office, but he had no idea when it would arrive or if it would arrive.

He called to the soldier. "I think the plane is carrying arms."

"Possibly," the soldier replied, joining Tshilongo

"Get your launcher ready."

"Yesssa." The soldier got the launcher into position, loaded the rocket and aimed at the flight path. "Ready sa."

"Get it down."

The soldier looked through the telescopic viewer turning round and moving the launcher to follow the flight path. "It's in sight."

"Fire."

Tshilongo watched as the rocket raced up with full power in pursuit of its target; it went past the plane, missing it by a wide margin. He turned to see the soldier gazing up, his mouth open. "Give me that and get the other launcher," Tshilongo said, taking over. He loaded and took aim. Why can't we get hold of some precision missiles? He adjusted the launcher, pointing some distance away from the plane. By his estimation the plane would be at that point by the time the rocket reached there; he hoped.

Oblivious to the now visible inscription on the plane, Tshilongo fired. The rocket lifted itself up with the faithfulness of a loyal servant towards its target. He started to reload when he heard another sound behind him – the sound from the other launcher; the two rockets raced each other in pursuit of one target. As he took aim the second time, he saw his first rocket hit its target. He fired his second one but it went off target as the plane hung precariously in the sky for a few seconds then tumbled forward heading towards the ground, nose first. Putting his two index fingers into his mouth, he whistled. In the distance, five of his soldiers responded to the bird-like sound signal.

"Let's go after it," Tshilongo said to his colleague, as he walked back to the tree. He picked up his bag and gun; then turned the soldier's cards in the process. They were two sevens and a jack of clubs. "You lost," Tshilongo said, as they hurried out of the ghost-village.

Inside the cockpit, Samuel Biya had seen the ferocity of the approaching monster, and in a desperate attempt he had banked the plane but his heroic measure hadn't been enough. The impact had jerked the plane, spinning it out of control and waking all the passengers in an instant. The pilot, realising that he had lost one of the engines, quickly sent out an SOS message. "We've been hit," he told the terrified passengers.

Biya wiped the sweat from his brow with the back of his left hand as he punched buttons with his right hand in a desperate struggle to regain control. He looked as if he'd seen his own ghost as he saw the dials on the altimeters falling very fast. Outside, he could see the open fields of farmlands. He struggled desperately with the controls as the ground rushed up in haste to meet them.

Inside the plane, the horrified passengers bent forward, holding their heads down in accordance with the pre-flight safety instructions.

"Oh Jesus," James prayed.

"Allahu Akbar," Rahim said.

Kutini bowed his head, wanting to pray, but nothing came to his mind. He couldn't remember the last time he prayed. "Our father, who art in heaven ..." he started, as he remembered the prayer from school.

The plane hit the ground, bounced and glided over the fields for a split second before crashing again. It continued with force ploughing the ground underneath for about three hundred metres before coming to a stop.

Samuel Biya had reduced the speed drastically and had turned the engines off to avoid explosion on impact. When the plane came to a stop, he waited for few seconds before turning on the electrical circuit to release the emergency doors.

***

The five team members and the co-pilot had been running away from the crash site through what appeared to be cornfields. Suddenly they stopped.

"Nobody moves."

They all froze in front of armed men who seemed to have appeared out of nowhere with their guns ready to shoot.

"Hands on your heads and turn round," a fresh order came. "On the trot; back to the plane."

A sudden panic had given way to calm bewilderment as the captives jogged back to the crash site and struggled into the plane on the orders of their captors. No one said anything as two soldiers took positions as if on guard and a third, looking more relaxed and in control, paced through the aircraft, covering all the passengers with his eyes at all times. One of the two guards went into the cockpit and brought the pilot, who was trying to get radio contact, to sit among the rest.

"Gentlemen," Tshilongo started in a voice that carried authority, "you are now in General Binda's custody. From now on, you will all do as you are told and no one gets hurt." The last statement brought the reality of the situation home.

On the orders of Tshilongo, the other soldiers started to search the plane for arms.

"Who is General Binda and who are you?" Kutini asked, without the slightest thought as to what their host might do to them.

Tshilongo answered in a calm and calculated manner. "You were in violation of our airspace and we operate under the instructions of General Binda, the supreme commander of the RCD. As for me, I am a humble servant of His Excellency," he said, sounding more like someone used to having his own way.

"We are here under the instructions of African Heads of Government to negotiate peace. I demand that you let my men go," James Nziza said, rising to the challenge of the situation.

There was a loud blinding slap that caught James from behind. In a flash, he saw the brilliance of the stars. It took a few seconds for the pain to register and, momentarily, he couldn't hear or see what was going on around him.

The slap had come from one of the armed men standing guard. A warning look from Tshilongo was all it took to bring the guard back to his position.

"I suggest that you cooperate for your own safety, as my men can occasionally get out of control. You're lucky to have survived the crash," Tshilongo continued as though nothing had happened. Silence befell the rest of the group.

"What do you want from us?" Kutini asked.

"That's not for me to decide; we are only carrying out instructions and will do what the General says. As a routine, we want to make sure that you're not carrying any arms."

Tshilongo motioned to his soldiers and they frisked the group one after the other. When they had finished, Tshilongo spoke into his hand-held radio. "All clear," he said to the unseen face somewhere in an unknown part of the world. He then called the other three soldiers on the ground to come up into the plane and search it.

The soldiers searched through the passengers' personal luggage. "What have we here?" a soldier asked removing a pistol from the pilot's baggage.

Tshilongo turned round, took the pistol and rolled it round in his hand with professional proficiency, bringing it to face Alfred Xuma, who instinctively raised his hands. With another quick movement Tshilongo brought the pistol into his trousers' side pocket. "Good find; keep searching."

Xuma, who had openly defied South Africa's apartheid regime and survived, suddenly found himself trembling in front of these rebels. Just as he was beginning to enjoy his hard-earned fame in South African politics, death was staring him in the face. As he watched the terrified faces of his colleagues, he thought: If I get out of this alive I'll campaign to bring an end to all civil wars in the continent.

James Nziza stood there, terrified and unable to think straight, only: What can I do? I'm the leader and the others would expect me to do something. Somehow he wished he wasn't the leader; then he saw Kutini looking at him and mustered courage. "We may be able to help you, if you tell us..."

"Just shut up," Tshilongo shouted as he moved into the cockpit where a soldier stood with a gun to the head of the pilot.

"Open the door to the baggage compartment," Tshilongo ordered.

Samuel Biya pressed a button on the control panel, but nothing happened. "It's damaged. I can't open it," he said.

"Can't you open it through the cabin? Just go and open it."

The pilot led the way with two soldiers behind him with guns ready. When he opened the door, one soldier jumped inside and turned on his flashlight. After a couple of minutes, he emerged.

"Any goodies?" his colleague asked.

"Negative."

"Damn," Tshilongo said. "What are you carrying?" he asked the pilot, holding the pistol to his forehead and releasing the trigger catch.

Nziza answered. "I told you, we are peace negotiators not arms dealers."

"What?" Tshilongo said, spinning round to face Nziza with the pistol. No-one spoke. He then leaned out of the plane and gave orders to the soldiers waiting on the ground to come into the plane. "Blindfold everyone except the pilot. These two should be taken to Watara Camp," he said pointing to two of the captives, "those two will remain in this camp and we will take the other two to Mobutu Camp. The pilot will be interrogated and join those in this camp," he finished his orders.

Kutini and Yaro were led away by Tshilongo and another soldier along a footpath through the deserted village and beyond. Two soldiers marched another group in a different direction.

***

After failing to get any useful information from the pilot, the soldier doing the interrogation was ready to take the pilot out into the camp. After all, they could still come back to search the plane, he thought.

"Let's move," the soldier commanded.

"I'm afraid I can't. I have to contact the airline," Samuel Biya said and stood his ground, his huge body casting a shadow over the soldier.

"You will do no such thing," the soldier said, pointed his gun and shouted, "Move."

The pilot started to move slowly. He heard the footsteps close behind him and with a swift move he swung round and grabbed the barrel of the gun, catching the soldier off balance.

It was a mistake. The soldier had his finger on the trigger and the sudden movement let the gun go off with devastating consequences. Rounds of ammunition ricocheted inside the plane. Some of the bullets missed both men and buried themselves in quick succession into the gadgets in the cockpit. As the two men locked hands into a frenzied struggle for life on the floor of the plane, the effect of the bullets was becoming evident. Smoke was coming from the direction of the cockpit.

The soldier, who was first on his feet, grabbed his gun and hit the pilot with the butt from behind. The pilot fell heavily with the full weight of his body, then blacked out. The soldier noticed the smoke and went into the cockpit without the slightest idea what he was going to do. Inside the cockpit, he could just see a loose wire burning. Without thinking of what he was doing he hit the loose wire with the butt of his gun. He had unknowingly triggered the shut door button and the plane doors started lifting up.

The soldier rushed back into the cabin and saw the pilot regaining consciousness. He was groaning when the soldier kicked him on his side. "Get up," the soldier shouted.

"What's going on?" the pilot asked, his voice a hoarse whispering sound audible only to himself.

The smoke in the cockpit was turning into flames. "Go and open the damn door," the soldier screamed when he noticed the plane door was shut.

Slowly and painfully, the pilot lifted himself from the floor with excruciating pain in his back. This is pain made from hell, he thought, as he made his way towards the cockpit door, but before he could reach it the flames swept into the main cabin, sealing off the passage to the cockpit.

The soldier rushed to the back where he started hitting the emergency exit with his gun in frenzy. He looked in the direction of the cockpit and saw the flames spreading slowly towards him. In a silhouette, he could see the huge figure of the pilot turning round in the fire as if possessed and dancing to ritual music. He turned to the door, shot at it, and waited. Nothing happened and the smoke almost choked him. He removed a grenade from his backpack and slowly moved forward to place the explosive close to the door. He then moved back and waited for the detonation. It was a fatal miscalculation.

The sound of the explosion was like the eruption of a virgin volcano. A loose seat hit the head of the soldier, splattering his brains. A second explosion followed, then multiple explosions as the fire spread through the plane and finally sent a huge fireball into the sky.

Inside the dark prisons of their blindfolds the hostages heard the explosion.

Tshilongo and the other soldier brought their two hostages to a momentary stop and looked back to see the fireball. After a few seconds they continued to march the hostages stumbling slowly and painstakingly along the stump-laden footpath.

They travelled in silence and that scared Kutini. Not even the soldiers spoke and the only sound he could hear was that of the wind and the wild life. The distant voices of children broke the silence and Kutini assumed they were passing through a town or village.

After what seemed like an eternity, they stopped and the soldiers led Kutini and Yaro into what seemed like a house with their blindfolds still in place.

Tshilongo said to his colleague in French, "you take care of them."

Kutini panicked, picking up the French words. He hadn't used his French for a long time and thought that he had forgotten it, but what he heard scared him, making him wish he had forgotten it. What are they going to do to us? he wondered.

When Kutini's blindfold was finally taken off, he could hardly see for the first few seconds. He blinked several times and slowly his eyes adjusted to the daylight.

"Where are the others?" Kutini asked the soldier who had taken off his blindfold.

"Don't worry about them; they will be well taken care of."

Kutini was very scared as he read his own meaning into the soldier's response, but had neither the will nor the strength to act.

As their eyes got used to the environment, Kutini found that they were in a large stately room with high ceilings adorned with chandeliers. The L-shaped room was large enough to host twenty guests, with its huge mahogany dining table running across the length of the room and matching leather-trimmed mahogany chairs.

At the leg-end of the L, Kutini could see the start of a glass cabinet that would have once held a variety of exotic drinks for the important owner of the house. Kutini tried to look around for windows. He didn't see any. The room curtains hung from ceiling to floor.

Kutini sat, wondering why the soldiers had brought them to this place. He thought that the rebels couldn't have shot down their plane only to bring them to meet their leaders to negotiate peace. Or had they realised too late that they were peace negotiators?

Tshilongo didn't help Kutini's confusion when he brought them each a plate of yams and a sauce made with lamb. The food came with a bottled coke each.

Coke? That was a good sign, Kutini thought, even though he didn't like coke and would have preferred water or fruit juice.

The two ate in silence and when they had finished Tshilongo came to show them to their beds. Only then did Kutini look at his watch and realised that it was half past eight.

CHAPTER 13

The golden sunrays that invited themselves into the room where the two captives lay announced the arrival of the next day. Kutini woke up and as he walked out of the door, the soldier met him.

"Anything I can do for you?" the soldier asked in a sleepy voice. "I need to attend to the call of nature," Kutini requested. Tshilongo showed him a bathroom, which also contained a toilet.

The only thing that gave away its lack of use was the dust and cobwebs at the corners of the room, every thing else from the toilet bowl to the cistern and the bath looked immaculate. He saw his reflection in the mirror and realised that he needed to shave, but had nothing to use. He remembered that they had left their luggage in the plane.

As Kutini came out of the bathroom onto what was like a balcony, the full impact of their situation was apparent. The building they were being held in was in the middle of the bush; there was no other house as far as his eyes could see. The structure was made of wood on a concrete foundation. Its beauty was marred only by apparent lack of use. He saw the improvised tank made from an empty oil drum with burned wood underneath. The connecting plumbing work suggested that it was used to supply hot water into the house. It was hardly required.

Kutini went into the dining room and found Yaro already there looking through the partly-drawn curtains into the vegetation outside.

"What sort of place is this and why are we here?"

It was a rhetorical question, but Yaro answered with a question. "Can you see the fence surrounding the house?"

Kutini joined Yaro at the window and saw that the shrub hedge was interwoven with thorns from different plants.

They didn't have to wonder for long as Tshilongo walked in without notice and introduced himself for the first time. "I am Tshilongo. I am responsible for you both until it's your turn to meet General Binda."

He made his speech as if he had been rehearsing for a special occasion. "Until then, I advise you not to even think about escaping. If you do, the lions will have a wonderful meal. Your death will be more heinous and gruesome than through the bullet," Tshilongo warned. "So you see, my work is very simple. I don't even have to keep an eye on you."

"Where are we?" Yaro ventured.

"This place used to belong to Mobutu. It is in the middle of what used to be his private game park with lots of specially imported wild animals." Tshilongo saw the bewildered looks in the faces of the two captives and felt pleased, glad that he had given them a fright. It was the truth. The only way he personally kept the animals at bay was using his gun and he didn't want them to start having ideas.

That explains the splendour of the house, Kutini thought.

"The thorn fence," Tshilongo explained, "keeps the lions away from the house."

As if to confirm what Tshilongo was telling them, the two watched as an impala strutted gracefully along. Suddenly, a group of lions that were lying in ambush rushed towards the impala. Kutini looked on, hoping that the impala would survive the ambush.

The impala sensed the approach of the lions and took off. The lions went after it. "Good luck, my friend," Kutini said after the impala. Unconsciously, he was thinking about how they were going to escape from their captors. He thought about his wife and son and decided that he wasn't going to die in the bush.

***

On their third day of captivity, Tshilongo went out for almost four hours and came back with game. Together with the other soldier they lit the barbecue in the yard and prepared the meat with skill as the two hostages watched. Tshilongo invited them to join him.

The four sat down and ate in silence. Tshilongo was hardly eating the meat; he was busy with his bottle of whisky. As though he had just thought about it, he held the drink towards the hostages but they both declined.

Tshilongo took a chunk of meat and went into the house, emerging after about twenty minutes holding a bottle of champagne. As he walked towards them, he was obviously drunk.

"Today must be a special day for you?" Kutini asked in impeccable French.

Tshilongo seemed suddenly sober. "You speak French?"

The animosity he had shown over the last two days gave way to a friendly engagement.

"Yes," Kutini acknowledged, still very much aware of their plight. "You look very happy," he continued, hoping to keep the conversation going. He had tried previously to engage Tshilongo in conversation without success. He was certainly in luck today.

"I am celebrating my son's graduation at the Sorbonne University in France," Tshilongo said with a broad grin. "Would you like to join me?" he invited, handing Kutini the bottle of Champagne, which he accepted out of courtesy.

"It must have cost you a fortune. How did you pay for his education in France?" Kutini asked, taking advantage of his newly found language-relationship.

"That's no problem at all. I have lots of diamonds and I put my money in a bank account in Paris where the money is transferred directly to my children's school."

"You have more than one child in France attending school?" Kutini was dumbfounded. Tshilongo was drunk, but clearly being very honest.

Kutini knew about foreign corporate bodies looting Congo's wealth using foreign soldiers. However, it was only when he looked at the happy, drunk face of Tshilongo that he realised the complexity of the conflict.

An end to the war will be disastrous for the likes of Tshilongo, Kutini thought, looking directly into his bloodshot eyes. How could he support even one child in a university in France on a soldier's salary? Kutini asked himself. "Excuse me, I need the loo," he said and went into the house.

Kutini was on his way back to rejoin the others when he heard series of gun shots and froze. Outside, an impala had jumped over the fence into the compound trying to escape from two hungry lions, one of which had charged through the gate and headed directly towards Tshilongo. His colleague had jumped in a fright, grabbed his gun and had started shooting at the advancing lion, but with a giant leap the lion had charged at the soldier, knocking his gun flying in the process and digging its claws into his heart.

Yaro rushed into the house and had just shut the door when the soldier's gun landed behind the closed door.

"Are you alright?" Kutini asked.

"Yes," Yaro replied, still in a state of shock.

"Stay here," Kutini said, then drew the curtain to see Tshilongo shooting unsteadily at the fighting lion astride his dying colleague. Just then he saw the second lion start towards Tshilongo. Without thinking about his own safety Kutini opened the door and reached for the gun lying outside.

"What the hell do you think you're doing?" Yaro shouted from behind.

Tshilongo saw Kutini with the gun. "Don't even think about..."

Kutini pulled the trigger, cutting Tshilongo short. The lion stumbled and let out a loud roar.

Tshilongo turned round to see the lion fall and heaved a sigh of relief. "Thank you, Mr. ...," he turned to face Kutini pointing the gun at him.

"Put the gun down," Kutini said.

"Take it easy, you just saved..."

"I said put the gun down."

Tshilongo dropped his gun. "Without me you're not going to get out of here alive," he said.

Yaro ventured out of the house and picked up Tshilongo's gun. "You will show us how," he said, backing into the house.

"Keep him covered, I'm going to find something to tie him up with," Kutini told Yaro and went inside the house looking for a rope. He was opening drawers in the kitchen when his attention was drawn to a folder on the dining table marked confidential, which aroused his curiosity.

Kutini opened the folder and flipped through the contents. He stopped at one with the title Regime Change. He started to read it:

Dear General Binda,

... The proposal for a regime change in Angola is a step in the right

direction. As soon as we achieve it, which should be a matter of days, our man, who you know and trust, will be in charge of the new government that will be responsible for implementing democratic elections. With our support he will get the peoples' mandate as their elected leader...

To ensure that the plan for regime change is fool-proof, our financiers are providing the best of the best in military hardware and the best mercenaries money can buy. ... Nigel Woods, whose accomplishments are legendary and well known to you, will lead the mercenaries...

Attached is a list of our financiers and their respective roles in the entire operations. Others would like to remain anonymous until the completion of the operation.

Signed

Mike Stoner.

Kutini's hands were shaking as he removed the letter with the accompanying attachments, folded them and put them in his pocket. He then continued his searched for the rope. He stopped in the living room, pulled the curtain open to let in more light, then stopped. These curtains would do.

After tying Tshilongo up, Yaro asked Kutini, "What do we do next?"

"I don't know. We have to think of something."

That night Kutini couldn't sleep. His mind was like a whirlpool and his thoughts went from one problem to the other. It was ironic that the control of mineral resources had become the driving force behind the war in the Congo, yet no international embargo on the export of such minerals as tantalum, diamond, copper, cobalt and gold from or to Congo, Uganda, Rwanda and Burundi had been imposed.

Kutini was angry at America for the complete lack of support in putting a stop to the conflict, thinking that the capitalists continued to participate in the illegal exploitation of the country's natural resources causing the deaths of so many, yet America looked on unconcerned.

He wondered how many people Saddam had killed with his elusive weapons of mass destruction that had prompted America to go and liberate the Iraqis. As far as he was concerned, America could stop the loss of innocent African lives, the death of African children and African women by imposing a freeze on the assets of such companies, but they were not interested in the welfare of the people. America had interests indeed, but no friends. Kutini had made up his mind. He would tell these trigger-happy criminals what he thought and would achieve his aim or at least die trying. There was no middle ground.

CHAPTER 14

Kutini woke up the following day still wondering how they would handle Tshilongo. "Do you think we can use him as a hostage to buy our way out?" he asked Yaro.

"It sounds good to me."

"Tell us how to get out of here," Kutini said to Tshilongo.

"You won't make it out of here on your own even if you know where to go. The RCD controls this whole area."

"You will lead us out then," Yaro said.

"Why would I do that?"

"Because if you don't we will feed you to the lions," Kutini replied.

"And if I do General Binda will feed me to the vultures."

Yaro and Kutini looked at each other. No one spoke. Then, they heard Tshilongo's radio calling:

"Buffaloes, HQ calling, do you read?" There was a pause and the message repeated every few seconds.

"Someone has to answer that radio," Tshilongo said.

Kutini brought the phone, held it to Tshilongo's ear and said, "You answer it."

"What do you want me to say?"

"Just tell them that we want a safe passage to the capital," Kutini said.

"Buffaloes, Buffaloes, HQ, HQ, do you read?"

"Buffaloes, reading HQ loud and clear," Tshilongo acknowledged.

"Why did you shoot down the plane carrying the peace negotiators?"

Tshilongo heard the thundering voice of General Binda and looked at Kutini and Yaro as though to get an inspiration; there was none. "We thought the plane was carrying arms to the government."

"Where are they?"

"Two of them are here at Mobutu Camp, Sir."

"I'm sending a Jeep. I want all of you here as soon as possible."

When the Jeep arrived, Kutini saw three armed soldiers jump out and move cautiously towards the house. A fourth soldier, who was also the driver, stood by the vehicle with his gun ready. Kutini skipped a heartbeat. Was it a trick to come and recapture them? Should they use Tshilongo as a hostage? As several questions rushed through his head, he realised that his resolve to confront these people was waning. He had to survive. He had a family to take care of and many other extended family members depended on him. He couldn't afford to fail his family and he couldn't afford to disappoint his dependants.

As the soldiers entered the compound Yaro reached for a gun.

"That won't be necessary," Kutini said, putting a restraining hand on Yaro. "One way or another we have to meet these rebel leaders. Let's do it now."

They got into the Jeep and drove off into the jungle. Above everything else Kutini was thinking of was how to get out of the situation alive.

***

Their journey ended in Makunu. They were driven to a large house at the outskirts of the town where the two were brought before General Binda. "Welcome, gentlemen."

"What do you want from us, General?" Kutini demanded, the sarcasm in his voice unmistakable.

"There is no need to be rude," Binda cautioned. "We are all here for the same reason – peace; isn't that right?" he said as if he had the situation under control. "All we want is democracy in this country."

"How can you achieve democracy by the use of force?" Kutini asked, throwing caution to the wind, ready to confront the rebels head on. "You want democracy your way?" Kutini continued his questions, unconvinced that Binda was fighting for democracy. "I understood democracy to mean the rights of people even to misgovern themselves without the use of force."

"That's where you're wrong. The army is part of the people, and we represent the anger of the people," Binda said, convinced that they had the right to resort to arms.

"The army! How do you sustain your army?" Kutini asked in dismay, taking advantage of Binda's willingness to talk.

"They pay us dollars for this precious thing without which you would have no mobile phones," the towering but lanky-looking leader of the group replied, showing Kutini a piece of tantalum.

"How much do you get from selling it?"

"I have no idea how much it costs. That is not my concern; Bankroll Resource International sells it."

Binda's response shocked Kutini and made him more curious to know how much this precious mineral was worth to the group to warrant the lives of the innocent.

Unknown to Binda, he had exposed some of the underlying causes that fuelled the war in the region. What he didn't tell Kutini was that his rebel group, the RCD, was the largest shareholder in Bankroll Resources International and was supported by the Rwandan government.

"Do you know that with tantalum alone the Congo could be one of the richest countries in the world?"

"We don't mine it; we only get paid for having the mineral on our soil," General Binda countered. "We are only using the money to fight for democracy for our people."

"You can get democracy by laying down your arms," Kutini told the General, conscious of the rifle he was holding whilst talking; his men were standing guard ready to take orders.

"No, we have to fight for it; that is the only way."

Kutini took a deep breath, looked directly into Binda's eyes and asked, "Do you want to go down in history as one of the greatest nation builders or obscured in history as one of the hunted rebels that committed genocide?"

General Binda suddenly shot into an unexpected rage. "You imbecile; who do you think you are? Who are you?" he thundered while drawing one of the two pistols strapped to his waist.

For a moment, Kutini thought he was going to shoot him and did not interrupt as Binda continued to shout obscenities.

There was a sudden bang on the table. Kutini started with fright before realising that Binda had put the rifle he was holding on the table, but with such force that it brought two of his soldiers running in.

"Out!" he shouted at them and they both disappeared behind the doors.

"We are peace negotiators sent here by the heads of African Governments," Kutini told the General.

"I know that," Binda replied in a sobering voice. "Congo and Rwanda, we're all one people, but how can we come together? There is division; there is war. Everyone wants to control the wealth and it's the women and children who suffer."

There was a confused look on Kutini's face and silence hung inside the room. It was emotional for Kutini to find so much compassion in a war-hardened general like Binda. Yaro seized on this new insight and spoke for the first time since they had come to meet Binda.

"We can help you if you let us. That's the reason we came to this country, but we need both your cooperation and your help," Yaro said.

"You have my word on both," Binda promised.

What good is the word of a rebel? Kutini thought and to test the commitment of Binda, he asked that they be reunited with the rest of the team.

"They are already on their way," Binda replied.

At 1700 hours the rest of the commission members and the co-pilot were brought to join Kutini and Yaro. They were filthy and unshaven, but looked healthy, except James Nziza, who was bleeding.

"Who did this?" Binda bellowed.

One of the soldiers started to explain. "I hit him with the gun because he wouldn't stop talking."

"You were under orders not to hurt anyone, you idiot." The sentence finished with the sound of the gun. No one saw Binda draw the gun.

The bullets caught the soldier on the left side of his chest. For a second, he stood there as if in suspended animation; a bewildered look on his face. His mouth was open, but no sound came out, then his feet gave in from lack of blood flow. The impact of the falling body on the concrete floor took away whatever life remained in the body which now lay in a pool of blood.

"That wasn't necessary," James said with sorrow. Binda ignored him and instead ordered two soldiers to remove the body.

"Where is the pilot," Nziza asked. The soldiers were looking at each other in turn until Tshilongo spoke, "The plane exploded; I believe he was caught up in the explosion with one of my men."

"Allahu Akbar," Rahim said.

"God is great," Kutini agreed, "but the pilot was the victim of a godless act of terror."

No one spoke for a brief moment, then Binda looked at James' bleeding eyebrow and asked for first aid to be administered, then asked, "What sort of cooperation and help do you want from me?"

"First, we want to establish contact with the government in Kinshasa, then contact all the other factions involved in the war." Kutini paused and looked round in anticipation of requests from his colleagues, but they were all silent. What he then wanted to say was give me a damn phone to call my wife, but instead said, "We need your help in arranging a meeting with the parties in the war."

"I can't help you with your meeting arrangements, but I will see what I can do about your first request," Binda replied.

CHAPTER 15

On the second night following the reported disappearance of the peace negotiators, an official from the Ghana High Commission in London visited Laz.

"Is my husband alright?" Laz asked.

"I'm sorry to inform you the entire team went missing yesterday and the government is doing all it can to find them."

"What happened?" Laz asked with tears running down her cheeks.

"We don't have any more information, but if there is anything we can do to help you, please ..."

Laz had lay in bed all night crying, scared to imagine the worse case scenario. She woke up the next morning with swollen eyes, picked up her son Amiga who was crying in his cot and said, "Pray your dad comes back alive." I should not have let him go, she thought.

...The entire team went missing ... Laz recalled the message from the official and wondered what they were hiding from her. She had rung various African embassies in London to establish the true situation.

When Laz eventually got a call from the High Commission about the safety of her husband, she didn't know whether to trust them. She had the phone with her all the time, cutting short any call not related to her husband in case he called.

When the call finally came she couldn't express her happiness. All she could say was, "Kutini, please come back immediately."

***

The disappearance of the peace mission had made international news and so when their release was announced it was greeted with jubilation among the people of Congo and the African leaders.

In the Congolese capital of Kinshasa the group finally met the rest of the leaders of the warring factions. Kutini listened with keen interest as the leaders of the RCD, the government of the Democratic Republic of Congo, the MLC, the Interahamwe and the Mai Mai were introduced. After the introductions Kutini looked towards James Nziza to start the meeting, but James who was still feeling unwell from his headache asked Kutini to address the leaders. The speech James had prepared had been lost in the plane so Kutini had to improvise.

"Gentlemen, with courage and honour we salute you. The saying goes that in unity lies strength. Our forefathers had a more powerful visualisation of the age-old adage. It's said that one of the powerful kings of our land on his death bed called all his fifty-five children to gather round. He brought out a broom from under his bed and as the children wondered what their father wanted them to do with a broom he ripped open the string holding the broom together and gave a twig of the broom to each son. He then asked each one of them to break the twig into two. With ease they each accomplished the wish of the dying King. He then removed another broom from under the bed and asked them to take turns in breaking the broom as a whole. When they had each tried and failed he said, 'Go my children and be like the broom and not the twig and you will never be defeated.' With those words the King passed away."

The silence in the room was eerie.

"Look around you. There is a greater move towards a unified Africa for us to live in peace and harmony. The presence of the Africa Union's first-ever peacekeeping mission in Burundi is a positive sign of a unified Africa. We can all choose to be part of it or be relegated to history as rebels who reign through terror and rape our land. Do we want our endowed natural wealth to be an endowed natural curse? Angola exports more oil to America than Kuwait, but where does Angola's wealth go? Do we want a situation like the shelling of the Rwegura hydro-electric power station in Burundi?"

Kutini paused to let the impact of his statement sink in and to assess how his audience was receiving the message before he continued.

"We are here today because our countries have been torn apart by wars. The question is: who are the beneficiaries of these wars? The real beneficiaries are those who wage and support wars in Africa – the greedy capitalist multinationals. The impact is to perpetuate poverty and insecurity, thus encouraging mass migration of the skilled and able. The effect is another form of slavery, which ensures the continuous supply of cheap and skilled labour for the capitalist world. As we discuss the way forward let's bear in mind we are one people and can only achieve progress by working together as one. Thank you."

Kutini could see a few heads nodding.

African intellectuals generally acknowledged among themselves that the interest of the capitalist multinationals was to systematically throw the entire continent into chaos by creating, financing and inciting conflicts and genocide. Their goal would be to control the vital natural resources of not only the African continent but also the world with their insatiable appetite.

The intellectuals have long admitted this situation would impair the ability of African countries to build an infrastructure and it would overburden governments with debt they cannot service, let alone repay. The result would be to create a system that would retard self-determination and self-dependence, while assisting in the corruption and temptation of the African leadership. The end product would be bondage and servitude, masquerading as foreign aid and loans – a recycling of the pillaged resources.

A representative from the Interahamwe group was the first to speak, reading from a prepared speech:

"There is ethnic discrimination against *us,* the Kinyarwanda-speaking citizens in the Kivus. Direct military involvement of external actors, multiplication of local warlords and active exploitation of natural resources now complicate our situation. It's akin to the era of the slave trade, where internal conflicts were created to perpetuate the heinous crime."

For the first time, Kutini noted the forgotten crucible of the Congolese conflict – the Kivus – was brought to the fore.

"With so many interests in the Congo I wonder how we can sustain a ceasefire. It's been tried on several occasions without success because some of the groups thrive on the continuation of this conflict," the RCD representative told the group.

The government representative had heard so much of this kind of stuff and for him enough was enough. He told the group: "We already know people who are visceral critics of the Congo peace process, but those who say it cannot be done must not stand in the way of those who are doing it. The fact we've assembled here today gives hope to our aspiration for peace in our country."

"We are men of action, not of words. May I suggest we agree to an immediate ceasefire while we discuss the process of political integration," the MLC man said with all the enthusiasm of a military man ready for action and not vain talk.

That night, while the rest of the commission members slept in the comfort of their hotel rooms, Kutini and Yaro spent the night working. They planned at length how to get the leaders to commit themselves to a peace plan and more importantly how they would come together as one democracy for the advancement of their own people.

When they had finalised their plans on what to do in the present conflict, Kutini put forward to Yaro his idea of uniting the entire African continent under one federation.

"You must be psychic!" Yaro exclaimed, "I have been having this thought since we embarked on this mission. The trouble is as long as a united Africa is not in America's interest any such plan will never see the light of day."

"You're right," Kutini agreed, "but willingness paves the way to success. Let's persevere and not give up."

In the few days Kutini had been with Yaro he had come to trust him. He told Yaro his plans.

Yaro was ecstatic. "I can't wait for us to start implementing them!"

"We have to sort out the Congo first."

"From the contributions in the last four days, I'm confident we will have a ceasefire in place tomorrow."

"I hope so," Kutini said.

On the fifth and final day of the deliberations, the parties agreed in principle to call for a ceasefire and put in place an interim government to take the country into a democratic government.

As the parties greeted the ceasefire deal with jubilation Kutini quietly felt the victory more than everyone else did. The mission wasn't over yet, but he felt the implementation of the ceasefire would lead to stability and the subsequent establishment of a representative government. They would go to Uganda, Zimbabwe and Rwanda. Where Sir Ketumile Masire, the former Botswanan President and Facilitator of the Inter-Congolese Dialogue, hadn't succeeded, Kutini Bomanso was bent on excelling.

At the airport in the Rwandan capital of Kigali, the last of their missions, military personnel were being deployed, armed with heavy machine guns and assault rifles. Sixteen armoured tanks were positioned at vantage points along the airport periphery. On the tarmac two fighter planes stood with their engines running, ready for action. No plane was allowed to take off, only incoming planes could land.

As soon as the Hercules carrier touched down two armoured vehicles flanked it with soldiers pointing their guns at the plane. The Hercules was escorted from the runway on to the tarmac away from the terminal building.

Five Rwandan soldiers stormed into the plane before the door was halfway opened. They escorted the twenty-three passengers and the pilot into a waiting bus under heavy military guard. As the bus left the airport with the captives towards an unknown destination the plane carrying the peace negotiators touched down. Government officials in a convoy of limousines were on the tarmac to meet them.

"What's going on?" Kutini asked, as he settled into one of the limos.

"We have just arrested a group of mercenaries on their way to overthrow the Angolan government. They arrived in that plane," the Rwandan Foreign Minister, Fred Musaka said, pointing to the Hercules on the tarmac.

Kutini could still see the military activities around the plane as they drove out of the airport. He felt his trouser pocket as his mind went to the document he had stashed there, but couldn't feel it, then he remembered he had changed clothes after their release. He made a mental note to check the trousers later in the evening. "Who's behind the mercenaries?" he asked.

"We are not certain yet but someone has been arrested in South Africa," Fred Musaka replied.

"Who's this person?

"Tony Conrat."

It wasn't a name Kutini could recollect from the list of names he had. He made another mental note to check when he got back to his hotel. For now he had urgent business to attend to.

Their meeting with the Rwandan government was the last on their schedule.

"What can we do to help your peace process?" the Rwandan president asked.

"We would like you to withdraw your troops from the Congo," James Nziza said.

"There are no Rwandan troops in the Congo," the President said.

"According to our reports," James said, "Rwandan militia operate in ..."

"I'm not bothered about what your report says, what I'm telling you is the government of Rwanda does not interfere in the internal affairs of another sovereign country."

"Mr. President, what we really want is your view as to how we can achieve progress in the Congo," Kutini said.

"Right," the President started, "if you want my opinion, I would say let's get the warring factions to agree to a cease fire, then send in the African Union peacekeeping mission and increase the forces of the United Nations observer mission (MONUC) to take charge of a transition process."

"That's a good point," James said. "Would your government contribute towards a peacekeeping mission?"

"Certainly, the people of Rwanda would like to see peace in Congo and the rest of the region."

"Perhaps I should have mentioned this earlier," James said, "but all the factions we have spoken to have agreed in principle to a ceasefire. We have a tentative date of 19th July for a meeting to set the agenda for the process to begin. Would this date suit you?"

"Fred will liaise with you to work out the details," the President said with a nod in the direction of the Foreign Minister.

As soon as they came out of the meeting Kutini looked at Yaro and they both smiled. This was just the beginning and they understood each other.

"You know the mercenaries have been arrested, don't you?" Yaro asked.

"Sure, I'll check my list at the hotel about the man arrested in South Africa."

Kutini got to his hotel room, found his trousers and removed the documents from the pocket. He scanned down the list of financiers, allowing his eyes to follow his index finger down the list. "There it is," he said as found the name, Tony Conrat. He heaved a huge sigh of relief and tucked the list back into his trousers. He picked up the phone and called home. On the first ring he heard his wife's voice at the other end of the line.

***

Laz was at Gatwick when the British Airways flight from Ghana landed on schedule. It will take a fair bit of time to get through immigration and collect his luggage, Laz thought, and mentally calculated this would take about half an hour.

For the first time in his travels, Kutini didn't have to wait in a line or be subjected to irrelevant questions. Thanks to his assignment with the commission he was travelling on a diplomatic passport.

As they came out to the waiting area a limo door opened and a well-dressed gentleman said, "This way Dr. Bomanso."

Kutini looked confused and turned round to his wife who gave him a nod of approval and entered the limo.

"Welcome, Kutini," he heard as he entered.

"What a pleasant surprise, Kofi," Kutini responded, as he recognised his friend the Ghanaian Foreign Minister.

The pop of the Champagne cork and the cheers were spontaneous. They drank and talked as the limo made its way out of Gatwick onto the M23 towards central London.

"Where are you taking me?" Kutini asked, sensing they had some more surprises in store for him.

"Just enjoy the ride," Kofi replied, aware of the suspense building inside Kutini.

The limo stopped outside of the Grosvenor Hotel and Kofi led the way. Kutini and Laz walked side by side behind him. At the reception they were directed to the Ascot Room.

As they entered the room all the guests stood up to welcome Kutini. "Wow!" He said looking round with surprise at the presence of friends and well wishers in the room. "What is this?" he asked in disbelief.

"It's a dinner in your honour," Kofi said.

After dinner Kutini was invited to tell his story. Reluctantly he recounted his experience, telling them an abridged version of their encounter and playing down his own role in the entire scheme of things. He chatted with people afterwards retelling his story again through curious questions.

Outside the Grosvenor Hotel Kofi Mensah held the door open for Laz and waved as the limo took off.

"Where is Amiga?" Kutini asked as they settled into the limo.

"He is with my friend Vicky."

When the limo brought Kutini and Laz home he went straight for the shower, then to bed for a dreamless night.

CHAPTER 16

Kutini woke up to the late spring Saturday morning in their London apartment. He could barely make out the noise of boats on the Thames River. He was glad he had bought this apartment with the view over the river. Rising twenty-nine storeys above the Thames and commanding a 360-degree view across London, Ontario Tower provided the reference for future residential developments in the city. The streamlined structure, a fusion of glass and steel offered Kutini an apartment of extraordinary sophistication, supported by a range of services and facilities redolent of a luxury hotel. He enjoyed living in that trendy part of London, but with Amiga starting to crawl, he needed more space and he had to start looking for a house.

He looked at his wife sleeping soundly in his arms. He imagined she felt secure sleeping in his protective arms.

Laz stirred in bed and opened her eyes. "It's so good to have you back."

"It is good to be back," he replied. "You have no idea how much I missed you, sweetheart." It felt so good to be holding his wife next to him and he felt too lazy to get out of bed. He guessed the time to be around 0900 hours. He hadn't had a good sleep for all the time in the Congo.

"So, tell me all that happened," Laz said as she brought a tray with their breakfast to the bed.

Kutini started to narrate the story to his wife. Occasionally he would stop talking and just close his eyes, hoping to shut out some of the gruesome details. Each time Laz noticed he had closed his eyes she would ask, "Are you not eating?" Kutini would then open his eyes, start to eat again and continue the story.

"... and so we managed to come out of the situation and to continue to achieve our goal," Kutini concluded.

"You are my darling hero," Laz said, and planted a kiss on his lips.

It was past midday when they finished having breakfast. Laz washed and got dressed. "I'm going shopping. Would you like me to get you anything?"

"Just get me the *Sunday Times.*"

Later that evening Kutini was reading the newspaper when an item caught his attention: The Angolan Foreign Minister, Edivaldo de Alvares, was in London and in collaboration with the South African High Commission was trying to gather evidence against the mercenaries who had been arrested in Rwanda.

The implications of the arrests stunned Kutini as he read the rest of the news report, feeling the message was directed to him as though they knew he had the information they were after. Slowly he turned round and went into his study. From a shelf above his desk he took his briefcase, opened it, removed the letters detailing the coup and read through the names on the list.

"Are you coming to bed? It's late," Laz said, walking into the room.

"I have to see the South African Consul," he said to his wife.

"What for?"

"Here," he said, giving the document to Laz, "it contains the list of the financiers of the mercenaries who were going to topple the Angolan government."

"I thought you had promised to stay out of politics."

"I'm just providing evidence to convict wrongdoers."

"I don't like this," Laz said and left the room. Kutini followed her to bed.

The next day Kutini called the South African High Commission to make an appointment to see the Consul and the Angolan Foreign Minister. When he mentioned the subject, he was transferred directly to the Consul, who agreed to see him the next day.

Kutini arrived promptly at the High Commission and was met personally by both the Consul and the Angolan Foreign Minister.

"I'm Viktor Mamphele, the Consul, and this is Edivaldo de Alvares, the Angolan Foreign Minister. Thanks for coming."

Kutini explained the circumstances under which he had obtained the documents. When he finished, he handed them over to Viktor.

As Viktor read the document he felt his hands start to shake and held the paper firmly to prevent the shaking. I should have met this man alone, he thought. When Kutini first called to say he had information about the mercenaries Viktor had assumed it was one of those hoax calls, as they had had several and he had agreed to meet Kutini on that basis. Now he felt he should have acted differently. How could they let such sensitive information get into the wrong hands? He had been promised the correspondence, which was hand-delivered, would never get into the wrong hands.

Thank God my name isn't on the list, he thought. He still dreaded what the consequences might be. If the list went out it would implicate some top officials in the British government and might eventually get to him. It was too late to do anything. He was sure even if he managed to destroy the documents given to Mr. de Alvares, Kutini might still be keeping copies somewhere. He passed the documents on to de Alvares.

"Very revealing," Edivaldo de Alvares said when he had finished reading. "Thank you very much."

Viktor Mamphele excused himself, went into the washroom and washed his face. He had been sweating inside the office, even though the temperature was below room average. He was thinking about what he would do to stop the information becoming public knowledge. When he returned to the office Kutini and Edivaldo were laughing apparently over a joke. "Is it alright to contact you if we need further information?" he asked.

"Certainly," Kutini replied and gave them his contact details.

"The people and government of Angola will remember you for your gallant act," de Alvares said as he saw Kutini to the door.

Kutini left the consulate satisfied with the hope his efforts would not be in vain, but would help to nail some of the promoters of war on the continent. What he hadn't realised was his action had put his life and that of his family in danger.

Viktor waited until Edivaldo had left his office before he made a call to Nora Goldstein, the head of De Bertz Company in Antwerp. Nora listened without interrupting, her anger rising, as Viktor narrated Kutini's find to her. "Do what you've got to do," she said in the end and put the phone down. Victor sat there still with the phone is his hand and a couple of words hanging in his mouth. He replaced the receiver and allowed his mind to wander for a few minutes, then made another call.

Later that evening Viktor walked into the Elm Tree Pub in North London and found an empty table. Another man joined him after five minutes.

"Sorry for the short notice, Carlos, but we have a situation," Viktor started.

"Don't be silly, there is nothing like short notice between us," Carlos replied, "it's not about my colleagues, is it?" he asked. Carlos was one of the mercenaries who had been contracted to go and overthrow the Angolan Government, but he had to pull out at the last minute because of a knee injury.

"It's worse than that. A man came into my office today with a letter detailing the entire operation and a list of all the major financiers behind the plan."

"That's no problem, I can take him out," Carlos offered. The retired Special Forces soldier from the British Army, whose real name was Graham Pelma, had earned the name 'Carlos' during the first invasion of Iraq in 1991 with his marksmanship, killing some of the Iraqi generals and eventually forcing the Iraqi government to order the soldiers to retreat.

"It's not that simple," Viktor cautioned, "he may still have information elsewhere; we just want to make sure he doesn't use it."

"What do we do then?"

"Keep him under surveillance and provide me with a weekly update of his movements," Viktor concluded.

***

That evening Kutini was surfing the internet for information and updates on the mercenaries when Laz walked into the study. "I almost forgot," she said, "your friend Yaro Tunde left you a message on the phone."

When he had finished surfing he picked up the phone and called.

Kutini arrived at The Albert, a bar near Windsor House and New Scotland Yard. Yaro Tunde was already at the bar.

He was staying at his mother's place in London for a couple of weeks before going to Boston.

"Nice to see you again," Kutini said, giving him a warm embrace. "How're you doing?"

"Wonderful," Yaro replied. "I've asked for a Bud. What will you drink?"

"I'll have coffee. I've a long day ahead."

The bartender placed a bottle of Budweiser on the counter and asked if they wanted anything else.

"Coffee, please," Kutini asked. He thought about the number of times he had told himself to cut down on coffee. He was addicted to the stuff, yet it could hardly keep him awake. The coffee came and they found an empty table close to the window and sat down. Kutini took off his jacket and hung it behind the chair.

In his white suit over a navy blue shirt with a matching tie and a hat Yaro looked like Al Pacino in *The Godfather.* He placed his hat on an empty chair next to him.

"Do you want anything to eat?" Yaro asked as they looked through the menu on the table.

"No, I've got my packed lunch in the office," Kutini replied. "You look great in your suit," he observed.

"I am playing the lead role in a film about my life story," Yaro said, without any expression.

"Really?" Kutini asked with amazement.

Yaro laughed. "You bought that, didn't you?"

"You got me on that one," Kutini acknowledged.

"I'm sorry I didn't tell you before, but today is my birthday," Yaro explained, "I'm meeting up with some old friends later on and I will go there from here."

"Happy birthday!" Kutini said and started to sing, "Happy birthday to you ..." A group of people who were drinking joined him.

After the song a guy asked, "How old are you, my man?"

"Twenty-one," Yaro replied.

"For how many years now?" the guy continued, unconvinced. He looked at Yaro thinking, this bloke must be in his mid thirties.

"Oh, let's see," Yaro looked up, pretending to be thinking, "I've lost count, man."

They laughed.

"You wanted to tell me about FAM," Kutini prompted.

"You know I'm half Ghanaian, half Nigerian?"

"No, you forgot to tell me."

"Well, it's my mother who is Nigerian, my father is Ghanaian," Yaro started. "It's a shame to say so but my father and his colleagues were instrumental in the overthrow of the government of the People's National Party, mainly for abandoning the socialist ideology and flirting with the IMF, and they started the Free Africa Movement (FAM) within the Ghana Armed Forces."

"Why was the FAM project left unfinished?" Kutini asked.

"According to my father the military regime was abandoning its socialist ideology and going back on its promises and so they spoke against it but became victims of the monster they had created and had to flee."

"Is that how your father came to this country?"

"Yes, he came here as a political refugee because his life was under threat."

"How was the movement going to go about forming a Federation?"

"The idea was to influence political and social change, which would have the effect of uniting Africa under a federal government that would free the continent from basic poverty and provide a home for Africans everywhere."

"Couldn't your father and his colleagues have used civil society instead of the military?"

"The movement was set up to systematically pursue the African Home Project by *any means necessary* and to the army clearly it was war or the threat of war; Ghana was to be the staging post."

Yaro's response reminded Kutini of an article he had read about the European Home Project, but his thought was interrupted when he noticed some movements outside of the restaurant. He heard a police emergency siren in the distance and saw a few police officers walking briskly in the direction of Victoria train station.

Kutini hated the police because they gave him the creeps. He always felt as though the next moment a police officer would put a hand on his shoulder and say, "You're under arrest, *sonny*."

Two guys walked into the pub and sat two tables away from them talking about the police activity outside. "How could they even think about it, with Scotland Yard just a walking distance away?" Kutini overheard one of the guys say.

He primed his ears to their conversation as they talked about an attempted daylight bank robbery at the HSBC Bank on Buckingham Palace Road close to Victoria Station. One of the armed robbers had fled; the other was holding a hostage in the bank.

Kutini sighed with relief; the police were not after him. There was no reason for them to be; he was a law-abiding citizen who wouldn't even exceed the speed limit.

Yaro was still talking, but Kutini was only half listening. He was thinking about the last statement Yaro had made and how Nkrumah could have developed Ghana with the resources available instead of wasting the money on a phantom called African unity, but he still believed this dream could become a reality.

"I believe if each country concentrated on its own development," Kutini said, "the time would come when they would be individually strong enough to join together without coercion."

"That's precisely what the problem is," Yaro agreed. "The FAM's *raison d'être* was simple; the breaking up of Africa by the Europeans at the Berlin Conference in 1884–86 was at the very bottom of Africa's problems. Africa is, therefore, in chains. To free her from the grip of basic poverty, the continent needs a big voice on the world stage. To get a big voice, Africa has to be united under one government."

"I am not a pessimist," Kutini put in, "but how would bringing together African countries with different ethnic, social and cultural backgrounds, and with diverse linguistic barriers be possible?" Kutini wanted to know more about FAM's approach and to confirm his own convictions about the concept of an African super state.

Yaro's father and his colleagues had obviously done their homework, Kutini thought, as he got more and more into the subject. He wanted to learn all he could about this clandestine movement that was supposed to work magic in Africa.

"The history of countries like America, Russia, China and Germany," Yaro continued, "shows size was the dominant factor in their development."

"I think we are now in a new era where this theory is obsolete," Kutini suggested.

Yaro had an answer. He had obviously devoted his life to that subject area. "To be a great power and to be in a position to develop economically a country should possess a maximum zone of resistance and manoeuvre to external interests and predators. This zone should contain within it necessary and adequate resources to develop without having to search for such materials from outside. Such a country must have the ability to close ranks with the rest of the world and mobilise its internal resources for development."

"That is communism!" Kutini exclaimed.

"Not necessarily," Yaro countered. "Even if we don't close ranks to mobilise we still need the size."

"By equating growth and development to size we can safely assume only America, Russia and China meet your criterion; what about countries like Japan, Britain, France and Italy who lacked the size? Surely they are great powers in their own rights?" Kutini queried eagerly as he was being led into a world to which hitherto only a few had been privy. He had earned the trust of Yaro for him to divulge such secret information to him.

"You don't understand, Kutini. The truth is these countries were imperialists who simply went out to colonise others in order to mobilise resources unavailable to them to fuel their industrial programmes." Yaro's impatience was beginning to show.

Kutini looked at his watch. "Germany had few colonies which they lost to the allied forces during the War, so surely your theory breaks down."

"Your lunch break must be over," Yaro said, picking up the cue.

"I'm afraid I must be going," Kutini said getting up from his chair. "How come you know so much?"

"My father was hoping I will join the military and carry on his plans, but I'm surely not the leading type. I'll send you some information."

As they came out of the pub Kutini noticed the increased police presence on the street. The bank hold-up must still be going on, he thought as he walked through the glass door into Windsor House.

Kutini could not concentrate on work that afternoon and as soon as he got home he called Yaro and asked: "How did your guest appearance at the film premiere go?"

Yaro laughed and replied, "You should have been there; the young ladies were all over me and I couldn't sign all the autographs."

"Next time don't leave me out."

"I like your sixth sense."

"My sixth sense?" Kutini asked confused, and wondered whether Yaro was actually going to star in a movie of his life story.

"Your sense of humour, man," Yaro laughed, "we all talk about the sense of humour but nobody realises it is the sixth sense."

"You never told me you were a philosopher," Kutini said, laughing. "Can you send me the other stuff through the post please?"

"I told you that you'll love what you hear; you can't wait to have more, can you?"

"No I can't."

"I'll send it as an email attachment," Yaro promised.

Kutini received the material from Yaro the following day and spent the next couple of nights reading. In the FAM document he read:

FAM would launch military takeovers in participating countries to create an impulse to war and galvanize Africa's military institutions to pursue unity under the flag of a civilian political leadership.... The Atlantic Charter that established the IMF and the World Bank seeks to perpetuate the dictates of the Berlin Conference of 1884-86 that officially divided Africa. As a result, under the leadership of Kwame Nkrumah, when Ghana together with Guinea and Mali formed a federation to control a sufficient supply of bauxite it could not be allowed signalling the beginning of the end of Nkrumah's rule.

Kutini sighed, put the article down and asked himself: "Is the track record of the IMF and the World Bank a reflection of the backdrop against which it was set up?" He paced back and forth through his living room thinking of the next step to take.

That evening, Kutini was going over more of the information Yaro had sent to him and decided he would like to meet him again. When he called, Yaro had a more interesting thing on his calendar.

"Let's have dinner at my place on the weekend," Yaro suggested.

***

Kutini arrived at Yaro's house in East London holding a bottle of wine wrapped in a soft white paper, pressed the doorbell and waited. A woman opened the door.

"You must be Kutini, please come in," the woman said, "I'm Julie. Yaro, your friend is here," she called out, as she led Kutini to the living room.

"I thought you were coming with your wife," Yaro said as he walked in.

"She had to stay home to take care of Amiga."

"How old is he?" Yaro asked, leading Kutini out into the garden.

"About nine months," Kutini replied.

They had been sitting in the garden for about fifteen minutes when Julie called. "Come on kids, let's have some food."

After dinner, Kutini and Yaro had moved from the dining area to the living room and Julie heard Kutini say to Yaro, "The information you sent to me was quite revealing."

"Sorry, but no political discussions in this house, right?" Julie cut in, pre-empting any discussion that would lead to a political subject. She was all too familiar with how they came to be political refugees in a foreign country.

"I've some books here you can take with you," Yaro said, "they are about the history of Africa's struggle for independence, which my father gave to me before he died."

"I didn't know your father had passed away. Sorry to hear that."

"It's a few years ago and that was when I moved to Boston to study for my Masters in Environmental Engineering, then got involved with Greenpeace."

"Thanks for the books and a lovely evening. I really enjoyed it," Kutini said as he prepared to leave.

"Thanks for coming; it was nice seeing you again," Yaro replied.

"Pop in any time," Julie said as Kutini bade them farewell for the evening.

CHAPTER 17

Kutini had never been a good history student, so he was surprised to find himself reading about the history of Africa in books and on the internet, first to corroborate what Yaro had told him, then to gain more understanding of what had happened and what was currently going on. He found out Africa's yearning for unification went back beyond the days of Marcus Garvey, beyond the days of independence.

Kutini was amazed at the wealth of knowledge out there. He was particularly intrigued at how other leaders had tried to advance their own ideas of African unity through militarisation and political ideologies that were short-lived and became obscured in state-sponsored military misadventures.

The conception of the militarisation of all African countries was contrived in the most grandiose of ways and the execution was going to be brutal, heinous and bloody. The process had been masterminded under the guise of a new universal ideology and was to be systematically implemented from one country to the other through military take-overs. Formidable leaders opposed to the concept had nipped it in the bud, with the backing of unseen powers. The dream was in tatters.

Kutini found the desire of African leaders for unification had been expressed through the rebirth of the Organisation of African Unity as the African Union. How were they going to go about it? What conditions were they supposed to meet to unite? What form would the unification take? What was their timetable? These and many others were questions Kutini could not find answers to.

The former South African President had called America a threat to world peace and lambasted the leadership as 'a dinosaur, towering like a moral colossus over the present century'.

Kutini was interested in the most inclusive and comprehensive revolution that would change the whole of human history. He could do it with just three technological whiz kids. Each recruit would be a highly disciplined individual with a high level of commitment, sincerity, and above all willingness to sacrifice. People give their best when they do what they believe in without the need for a reward of any kind, he thought.

In his pocket notebook, he turned a page and made the following entries:

4-POINT PLAN

1. *The test*
2. *Financial freedom*
3. *Military control*
4. *Unification*

Kutini liked to plan. He had always believed in the statement proper planning prevents poor performance, which he had internalised as proper planning promotes peak performance. He was an optimist and did not believe in the use of negatives – 'accentuate the positive' was his catch phrase. A revolution, he surmised, was a fundamental change in one or more of the three major domains of collective human existence: the political, economic and social systems. First, he would have to achieve a strong political African Unity that would stimulate economic growth through wealth creation and lay the foundation for a social system that would be uniquely African.

Kutini spent the next three months elaborating on his four-point plan. To ensure he didn't leave traces of incriminating evidence lying about he would shred each paper he wrote on and flush it down the toilet. As he refined his plans he would mentally go over each one memorising the details of each step.

Kutini's initial steps were crystallising in his mind as well as a few names he would contact; Yaro was first on his list.

***

"I'm glad I'm finally going to do something that will give eternal peace to my father's soul," Yaro said as they sat on the grass in the serenity of Kew Gardens in London. "What's the plan?" he asked.

Kutini had used the occasion of Yaro's visit to his mother to set up what he called the inaugural meeting. "Are you sure you can handle this?" Kutini asked, still unsure what he was about to say would not scare Yaro away.

"I believe my life was saved in the Congo for a reason and I intend to live for that reason, whatever it is."

"Good man," Kutini said. "As long as America is in a dominant position Africa will continue to be poor and divided."

"Kutini let's face it, America is going to dominate the world for a long time, so by your own admission Africa is doomed. I thought you had a plan."

"We need to attack America's source of dominance, which is their military might."

Yaro laughed, so loud he almost choked. When he was able to control himself he looked around to ensure he had not attracted undue attention, then asked, "You and me taking on the American military? Are you sure you don't need a psychiatrist?"

Kutini ignored Yaro's comments and continued, "America's military might is now almost entirely dependent on computer technology and that, I think, is their Achilles heel."

Yaro stared directly into Kutini's eyes with his full attention. He was now beginning to see the bigger picture. America under the control of a couple of Africans, he loved the thought.

"All we need to do is take control of America's defence system and they will do our bidding," Kutini added.

"You make it all sound like a comic book story. How would you gain control of the Pentagon?"

"Leave it to me Yaro. Don't forget I hold a PhD in Computer Science."

"I see, you plan to hack into the Pentagon computers."

"Call it whatever you want, but that's the idea."

"What would be my role in the grand scheme of things?"

"We need to know the locations of America's nuclear warheads and their nuclear submarine movements."

"That will be an easier job," Yaro said. He had been campaigning with Greenpeace for some time and some of their protests had taken them to military installations with suspected nuclear warheads. He remembered seeing literature on the movements of nuclear submarines.

"I wouldn't call it easy; we will need the exact coordinates or an address to work out the coordinates from."

"If you're going to hack into the Pentagon, then surely you should be able to have access to this sort of information," Yaro suggested.

"Good thinking, except it would be quicker in programming terms," Kutini replied. "Oh, another thing, we need to know all the military satellites orbiting in space."

"Who else is in this?"

"For now it's just you and me," Kutini replied, "I'll let you know when we need to bring in other people." Kutini had no intention of telling Yaro about other peoples' involvement. The less people involved in the scheme the less chance of jeopardising it.

It is time to give Mike a call, Kutini thought, as they strolled out of the quiet of Kew Gardens into the busy streets of London.

CHAPTER 18

At midnight, 1900 hours in New York, he called Mike Zinbalan.

"Hey, what's up?" Mike asked when he heard Kutini's voice at the other end of the line. "Are you in America?"

"No, I'm calling from the UK."

"I heard about your ordeal in the Congo and tried to get in touch, but you had changed your number again."

"I'm planning a holiday in America for next month with my family."

"Brilliant, then you can attend NASA's award evening with me."

"You've done it again, haven't you?" Kutini was curious.

"I'm not saying anything."

Kutini had always known Mike was a smart and intelligent guy and who had graduated with first-class honours, so Kutini instinctively knew he might have excelled somewhere. In fact he had excelled as the first Ghanaian ever to have commanded and controlled a spacecraft in orbit under the auspices of the US National Aeronautical and Space Administration.

Kutini was excited about meeting Mike. He knew Mike well enough to want to discuss his plans with him. He also knew Mike had the skill and the ability, but wasn't sure if he had the will power. Mike had always been the technical type doing impressive things that were difficult to understand.

Kutini next called Yaro Tunde in Boston to tell him about his planned visit to the United States.

"I'll have the information ready. Are you coming to Boston?"

"My family is with me. I was hoping we could meet in Washington DC."

"Not a problem. I'll meet you there. Let me know when you're here," Yaro said.

As Kutini counted the days to his holiday he would mentally go over his plans and try to resolve any potential difficulty. His mind had become a mental chessboard, making moves and counter moves. Would Mike be committed? If not, would he try to sabotage him or even report him?

When Kutini arrived in America with his family the first thing on his mind was to meet Mike. It so preoccupied him that his wife began noticing his absentmindedness and asked if there was something wrong. Kutini explained he was just excited about meeting his friend who was going to receive an award.

The two old school mates met at the Smithsonian Museum on the first weekend of Kutini's visit, the weekend of the awards ceremony. It was as though they were back in their university days.

"You haven't changed, Mike," Kutini observed. Mike was just as he had known him, with the same sense of humour and as witty as ever.

"You haven't changed either. Still the people's magnet?"

"Well, I guess it's just a natural part of me," Kutini answered.

It was a late afternoon programme so Mike and Kutini wandered around the Museum, their conversation briefly dwelling on the displays and gradually moving to personal details.

"What have you been up to since we last spoke?" Mike asked.

"Nothing really, I'm just working to keep body and soul together."

"I thought you wanted to go back home and establish yourself in business?"

"With all the stories of hardships coming back from friends and family, I decided against it."

"Africa abounds in talent, yet our continent is so impoverished and on the brink of self-destruction."

"Our leaders lack any sense of purpose or direction; all they are concerned about is self aggrandisement," Kutini acknowledged.

"All we need is the right leadership and self sacrifice."

"It's interesting you say that, I just came across the Africa Unification Front on the internet last week and signed up for membership."

Kutini had been on the net that evening reading the usual news from around Africa when he saw the link. He had clicked on it, gone into the site and been amazed at the amount of information and the activities of the members. The membership was made up of like-minded individuals from a background or with an interest in Africa. Their website hosted information, from requirements necessary for Africa to achieve unity to collective actions taken by members to achieve the stated objective through governments. Without hesitation, he had signed up.

"I've been a member for the last two years," Mike said.

"We are typical Ghanaians, aren't we?"

"Why is that?" Mike asked with a confused look in his eyes.

"It's said no Ghanaian conversation is complete without politics," Kutini explained.

"That's so true. I haven't thought about that one."

From the museum they went to have a meal together and continued their talk. Mike said he had never been to the UK and was planning a week in London in the summer.

"London is famous for sightseeing," Kutini noted. "Any ideas what you'll be doing?"

"Nothing in particular; I'll just take in the sights," Mike replied. "Any suggestions?"

"It depends on your interests," Kutini said, thinking of several places he could take him to. He knew London well and had become the unofficial tour guide for his friends from Ghana who came to London mostly on government business.

"I'm easy," Mike said.

"I will send you some information to have a look at."

Just as Kutini finished his sentence Mike's phone started to ring. "Excuse me," he said, answered the phone and went into what seemed to Kutini like a monologue with an invisible face that had a voice.

"Hello, Tuuro, how are you doing? … It's good to hear your voice ... I'm dining out with a friend from England … I'll call you when I get home … Talk to you later, bye."

"That was my cousin calling from Ghana," Mike told Kutini.

"I'm sure he wants to come to America."

"Certainly, only this time he wants a mobile phone."

"Most people think the streets of America are littered with money," Kutini said.

"I want to help him, but I would like him to come when he has finished his Advanced Level exams. Ghanaians here are sending their children home for education to protect them from peer-group pressure."

Kutini was silent for a few minutes and then said, as though the idea had just popped into his mind: "Teenagers in the West are at greater risk of getting into trouble than those in Africa." He was thinking about the high levels of independence and materialism in the West that were less common elsewhere.

"Certainly," Mike agreed, "here in America parents worry the negative values of self-denigration some children fall into will hamper the quest for social mobility."

"With the experience from home people learn to pick and choose from the different cultures."

"Like a buffet, eh?"

"And the parties," Kutini added and they both laughed.

"Seriously, here a lot of teenagers just focus on what party to go to," Mike said.

"It is time, I think," Kutini said, anxiously rubbing at the deep furrow in his brow, "to make home a better place to live."

Mike looked at his watch and said, "It's time we got going," and rose up.

At the awards venue Kutini sat on the front row of the large Auditorium at NASA with a camcorder rolling as Mike's name was mentioned to receive the US Sapphire Award for outstanding performance. He listened as the citation was read out.

"Congratulations," Kutini said after the ceremony, "how did you achieve this?" he asked.

"It wasn't anything spectacular. I was involved in the design and development of a future aircraft that would undertake some complex space missions to Mars. I also helped in the development and implementation of low-earth orbiting, deep space inter-planetary missions."

"Your role must have been pioneering."

"I only worked as part of a team, but my colleagues must have been impressed to nominate me."

"You must have made one big impression to deserve all the accolades."

"The one achievement I can call mine was the design of *HuLos*."

"What's HuLos?"

"Human Locator System – it's a nanotechnology-based microchip used to locate human beings anywhere on the planet using satellite communication and global positioning systems."

"Wow! Can you explain it in English please?"

"Come on, Kutini, you know what nanotechnology is. It's a miniaturised device that can be implanted under the human skull, skin, bone, or teeth and activated when required."

"Remember me when you make your millions."

"Actually, I'm in the process of securing a patent for the design," Mike said with pride.

When they parted, Kutini knew he had a working partner who felt the same way about Africa as he did. Like most Africans, Mike yearned to go back to a better Africa where he would be respected for who he was and not used as a tool. That yearning, Kutini thought, was what would push Africans to do what they had to do to make Africa a home to go to and not a pool of resources to be exploited and neglected.

Kutini's first assessment of Mike was very good, but he had to be cautious. Summer was not far away so he would wait until then to put the proposal to him when they met again in London.

The next day Kutini met Yaro at the Meridian Hill Park, about four kilometres north of the White House. They made their way towards the lower south side of the park; Kutini could not help, but admire the water cascade of linked basins as they walked along. As they continued down the slope until they got to the plaza at the foot of the hill with a rectangular reflecting pool and sat down.

"What have we got?" Kutini asked when they had settled by the pool.

"I've got some information about the defence satellites. I got it from the web. I don't know how useful it will be," Yaro said, handing a list to Kutini.

"Let's have a look." Kutini took the list and read: CRRES, LESAT 5, LES 9, GPSB II (PRN 24) . . . He read each satellite's relative orbital trajectories and the countries each one covered over a 24-hour period.

"This is excellent information. I'm surprised it's public," Kutini remarked.

"Don't you think it's probably part of America's propaganda strategy?"

"What do you mean?"

"They make their defence and military capabilities known. Sometimes I think some of them are exaggerated to scare and bully other countries."

"With America you can't rule anything out," Kutini acknowledged. "What else have we got?" he asked.

Yaro passed another list to Kutini containing the locations of America's nuclear facilities saying, "If you're going to get into the system I thought you could find this information yourself."

"It's easier when you know what you're looking for," Kutini replied. "What about the nuclear submarine locations?" he asked.

"That would be difficult information for me to get hold of. What we do in our Greenpeace campaigns is to follow a particular sub when we have suspicions about its activities, but they keep changing their positions."

"We might be able to track them with the satellites. I'll see what I can find," Kutini said.

"I'll leave the hi-tech stuff in your capable hands."

"Right, I've got to go and take the family out, otherwise I'll have a divorce letter waiting for me when we get back to the UK."

"Enjoy the rest of your stay."

CHAPTER 19

Kutini had just put his son, Amiga, into his cot on this late Saturday evening. He was still standing by the cot singing a lullaby when Mike called to say he had arrived and checked in to his hotel in central London.

On Sunday Kutini met Mike. "Hey, Mike, it's nice to see you again," Kutini said as he shook hands with him in the hotel lobby.

"You look well."

"Yeah, my wife's been taking good care of me," Kutini acknowledged. "Have you figured out where you want to go?"

"You tell me, you're the Londoner."

The two friends went to Buckingham Palace, waited to see the Changing of the Guards, then walked to St. James's Park where they wandered around for a few minutes before settling on the grass.

"I've some packed lunch for two," Kutini said. He spread a beach towel on the grass and unpacked the food from the rucksack he was carrying. "I've a proposition to make," he said

Mike wanted to say something, but hesitated when he saw the serious look in Kutini's face.

Kutini continued, "Africa needs to be united and I need your help."

"How do you propose to do that?" Mike asked, assuming Kutini was thinking about financing a continent-wide lobby group.

"The idea is not new and people have tried various options, including a military approach," Kutini said.

"So, what's your revolutionary new idea?"

"Well, err," Kutini struggled to find the right words, "I mean the political atmosphere is ripe in Africa. The main problem is the fear of Western interference." Kutini attempted his well rehearsed explanation that seemed to be eluding him at the crucial moment.

"What is this Western interference and how do you propose to overcome that obstacle?"

"Mike, my proposition is simple; we can eliminate that fear by taking control of America's nuclear weapons and jump-start the unification process."

"I don't understand," Mike said, sitting up and looking like someone waking up from a frightful dream.

"What I've in mind is to take control of America's defence computers and their military satellites." Kutini had dropped the bombshell.

"You must be crazy!" Mike exclaimed.

"Yes, I am. I'm crazy about the treatment meted out to Africans everywhere. I'm crazy about the exploitation of the continent. Most importantly, I'm crazy about seeing Africa brought together *by any means possible,*" Kutini said with all the passion he could muster.

"Why are you telling me this, Kutini?" Mike asked, angry, "I could report you and you would be incarcerated for the rest of your miserable life."

"You wouldn't do that; you're more passionate about Africa than I am and you would do anything to promote her development," Kutini challenged.

"You're out of your mind. You know I work for NASA and you're asking me to undertake a suicidal mission. I'm out of here."

Mike got up and starting walking away, turned round and said as an afterthought, "thanks for lunch."

After Mike had walked about a hundred metres, Kutini got up and followed him. He caught up with him and they walked side by side for a few steps. "Look, Mike, forget about everything I told you and let's go to Parliament House."

"Just leave me alone, will you?" Mike demanded.

"OK, I'm sorry," Kutini said, slowing his pace and falling behind Mike, then watched as he walked away.

"You never succeed if you don't try," Kutini said aloud as he made his way out of the park, wondering what he would spend the day doing tomorrow. He had taken a week off work to be with Mike. Kutini knew even if Mike did not go with him he would not report their conversation to anyone. His main worry was to find another person.

Mike went straight back to his hotel and as he lay on his bed that afternoon his thoughts wandered. He found himself thinking about his cousin, Gladys.

***

It was midnight in Washington DC and he had only just managed to drop off to sleep when his phone rang. At first, he had heard the ring in a dream and woke up to the reality of it. He had ignored the ringing and it had stopped, but started again almost immediately.

Who could be ringing at this time of the night? Grudgingly he picked up the phone. "Hello?"

"This is Gladys," she said, sobbing.

He was suddenly wide-awake. "Are you alright?" he asked, worried.

"The police broke into our apartment and took my husband away," Gladys said, now crying uncontrollably.

Mike could barely make out what she was saying. "What happened? How can I help?" He asked eagerly to find the underlying cause of the problem and offer help if he could.

He had been aware of the immigration problems in Israel, where a large number of migrant workers had left Israel of their own accord. An Israeli immigration official had acknowledged the papers of foreign workers had been checked, 'on the street, in their homes', and a number of complaints about violent behaviour by the police had been reported … "but if people don't open their doors – and we enter every home – there's no choice but to make the arrest in a violent manner."

"If our contacts with illegal migrants are unpleasant, we apologise," the immigration official stated, adding that brutal encounters shouldn't happen, but they had in the past and they would in the future as their mission was so complex and so unpleasant by its very nature, that sometimes this was inevitable.

As the targets of 'unpleasantness' various groups in the migrant-worker community had suggested ways to deal with their problem more humanely, proposing the government paid the return plane fare of workers who entered the country with legal work permits but subsequently left their employers.

"The drive to oust illegal foreign labourers is gathering pace," Gladys continued, while Mike listened in silence as she narrated the entire incident.

The police had come knocking at their door at the dead of night. When they hesitated to open, an axe was brought in to hack away at the wall and wooden doorpost, destroying them so the steel-reinforced security door could be lifted off its hinges. About seven police officers – some of them not in uniform – and others, probably immigration officials, went in and ransacked their rooms, possibly searching for their passports.

Their two daughters had been crying in terror, so the police had removed them to the hall. When she protested the police officers had thrown her against a wall and had slapped her.

"My husband was manacled hand and foot, beaten and kicked in the groin and carried down the stairs, head first," Gladys related with deep anger.

She told him how five of the six apartments in their building in the Neveh Sha'anan quarter of south Tel Aviv had been spray-painted with *fuck the niggers* at the entrance. These were the apartments raided that night. The sixth apartment, occupied by an Israeli family and with a sticker bearing a Jewish star on the door, was *passed over,* she added.

"Where is your husband?" Mike asked, finding the entire mental spectacle he had of the situation too ugly to contemplate.

"They have probably taken him to Ma'asiyahu Prison in Ramallah," she sobbed.

"I can understand a country's policy to protect its own workers," he said angrily, "but why do they have to humiliate you in this way? You're not criminals."

"We're here without the requisite documents – no doubt, but that's no reason to treat us like animals," Gladys fumed, choosing her words carefully to avoid using the word 'illegal'.

"We think of Israelis as God's people – we learned that from the Bible – and we treat them with love and respect in Africa, but here, their behaviour is poisoning our minds against them."

"I will send you money to get out of the country. I will call you tomorrow," he said.

He had known too well what was going on with illegal immigrants in Israel. Israeli television had broadcast live some of the raids on buses and homes of foreign workers as part of a government campaign to send tens of thousands of foreign workers packing. The television images portrayed a complete lack of compassion and had pained and shocked him. He was thinking of calling Gladys to persuade her one more time to leave Israel.

Gladys was his first cousin and he had paid for her plane fare to Israel. He had always been there whenever she needed him. He was not going to let her down now. He was always edgy about her continuous presence in Israel amidst the daily suicide bombings and had urged her on different occasions to leave, but her husband was adamant. He was glad Gladys would be leaving Israel; he would at least have peace of mind without worrying about her safety on a daily basis.

He could not sleep for the rest of the night. He would have to do something about this sort of thing. One day …

***

Kutini had just finished his dinner when the phone rang. He answered it. The last person he expected to hear from was Mike.

"Hi, Kutini, this is Mike. I called to tell you I'm sorry about the way I reacted this afternoon at the park."

"That's OK. I should have been more sensitive. Are you still up for tomorrow?" he asked.

"If it's alright with you," Mike replied, unsure of what Kutini's reaction would be.

"Certainly," Kutini replied, "I'll see you tomorrow then, as planned." He had lost a partner, or so he thought, but at least he still had Mike as a friend.

The next day Kutini met Mike at his hotel and they went to the Houses Parliament. Throughout most of the day they avoided the topic and it wasn't until they sat down at a café Mike asked, "What role did you have for me in your grand scheme?"

"You haven't changed your mind, have you?"

"I thought about it and I still think you're are crazy, but then it's the crazy people who rule the world," Mike replied.

"The plan is to start simple," Kutini said, removing a piece of paper from his pocket, "I wanted to show you this yesterday." He laid the piece of paper in front of Mike, who studied it for a few minutes.

"You're really crazy; this is impossible," Mike concluded, when he had finished reading it.

"You don't have to get involved, but if you do you can suggest alternatives."

"I don't mean it would be difficult, I mean we could be found out," Mike explained.

"Well, part of our job would be to design a foolproof system."

Mike wasn't convinced the approach was right so they spent two hours debating the issues and alternatives.

Finally, Kutini said, "Consider everything we've talked about, have a think and let me know tomorrow."

When Mike told Kutini the next day after dinner he would go along with the plan Kutini was excited. "I am so glad you've agreed to join hands with me. Future generations will thank you for your foresight and sacrifice."

They worked out the details of the plan before Mike went back to the United States and started working on it right away. Mike's first task had been simple: write a program that could allow a mobile phone to be used to control the flight of an aircraft. That was not a problem. It needed some thinking about, but as he always said, "If you can think it, I can do it."

When Kutini made his proposal, the first thing that came to Mike's mind was Peter Gardener's last statement during his interview at the Langley Research Center in Virginia: *If at any time we think you're a security risk we will advise you.* That was almost a year ago, but the words came back as if they were being said at that moment.

Mike had thought long and hard before committing himself to Kutini's plan. He had reasoned that if their actions would eventually lead to the development of Africa or even advance the progress towards her development, he would make that sacrifice.

Mike Zinbalan had programmed the phone to link to flight cockpit information via GPS. His knowledge of the use of remote control systems stemmed from his background as an aeronautical engineer and from his sheer love of experimentation with technological gadgets. His work had been simple and straightforward: any equipment with infrared facility can be used to link to any other system with infrared.

Mike had learned this when he found out his TV's remote control could work his hi-fi as well. He had dismantled the remote control, removed the chip and had placed it in a slot in the open motherboard that lay next to his computer. He had typed a few strokes on the keyboard and up on the screen came the entire program code for the remote control. He had scrolled down, turned it off and had reassembled it and put it back near the TV. He had not thought any more about it afterwards.

Mike spent two weeks writing a code for a mobile phone he had paid forty dollars for. It had been a gamble the phone was new as the guy claimed, and the gamble had paid off. It was one of the new handsets and the guy had probably stolen it or needed quick cash. It did not matter to Mike.

When he was ready to test the code, he came across his first major challenge. The phone was blocked. He had two options: to look for another phone or to write a code to unlock it. No, he had a better idea; he would search the net for an unblock code. Why reinvent the wheel, he thought. There were people out there who would post all sorts of codes on the internet just for the sake of it. Mike's search for an unblock code yielded a lot more than he had expected.

There were free program codes for performing different activities ranging from the mundane to the illegal and the bizarre. He had only ever searched for sites related to his own field, provided by professionals. This time, he had entered the computer underworld. The sheer volume of potentially dangerous codes, more dangerous than computer viruses, made the web look like a vast growth of brambles, weeds, or even poisonous clumps of hogweed that had spread through the web like some wild epidemic. It was a jungle, an untamed cyber hell, where even the most avid computer user stumbled.

As he stared at the thousands of lines of code he wondered why there were not already large numbers of computer crimes being reported. The computer was the most deadly weapon ever invented, but also the cheapest and legal commodity to lay hands on.

When Mike studied some of the code he realised how easy it would be for terrorists to use. Right under his fingertips, in the luxury of his apartment, was a weapon of mass destruction. Of course, not with me, he thought, but in the wrong hands, it would be. He had always thought of terrorists as cowards, but now he was also convinced they were amateurs.

It was now four weeks since Mike had started out on his project, working late into the night after his normal daily work to accomplish his task. He was enjoying the challenge and did not realise how late he worked each night. He tested his program with a dummy plane that simulated the real flight controls of a commercial plane using actual satellites.

After Mike's third successful test, he was thinking: I could make millions selling this to the aviation industry. Then there would be no need for pilots, and planes would be controlled from base. What if it got into the hands of terrorists? What if Kutini's real motive for this project is for terrorist activities?

The more Mike celebrated his success with each test, the more he found himself in a moral dilemma. He had just completed another successful test and was sitting down in his basement replaying what had taken place during his encounters with Kutini and could not think of anything pointing to suspicion. Kutini is just the one to dream up crazy ideas, he concluded.

Mike decided there was no reason to back off the plan at this stage and was about to call Kutini when his phone rang.

CHAPTER 20

Kofi Mensah was ringing to inform him about the first sitting of the National Reconciliation Committee his government had set up after the South Africa example of The Truth and Reconciliation Committee, which promised to heal the wounds of the past. "Amankwa Amofa would be testifying two weeks from today and I thought you might want to follow it."

"Thanks," Mike said painfully and replaced the handset. Instead of investigating crimes committed against humanity, the best this government could do was reconciling. How can I ever reconcile with the likes of Amofa? he asked himself.

That weekend with a feeling of pain Mike said to Effie, "I'm off to Ghana next week, for a couple of weeks."

Effie felt both excitement and sadness: excited because she assumed Mike was going to see his parents, sad because she was going to miss him – their feelings were mutual, but for different reasons. Effie had come to look forward to her evenings with Mike. The days seemed longer than she had known them to be. They had both come to consider each other as a life partner and had started talking about living together.

"I'm happy for you," Effie said, wrapping her hands around Mike's neck. "When was the last time you saw your parents?"

Mike felt a sudden pain in his chest like a million needles piercing his heart, all at the same time. Effie's question had brought back memories of pain and anguish. He remembered the incident now as it happened several years ago. The memory was indelibly etched into his mind. The pain was sudden and lasted for a split second, but he let out a shrill sound of pain, buried his head in his hands and started to sob.

"Are you alright?" Effie asked with concern, surprised to see the emotional side of Mike for the first time.

"I'm alright," he said without conviction.

"Are you sure?" Effie persisted.

The whole episode that led to the death of his parents came back to him. He was replaying the same movie from his mental recorder. He had never spoken about it until now. "I have no parents," he started and when he had finished telling Effie of the calamity that had befallen him, he was not sure if he expected her sympathy or otherwise.

For the first time, he felt as though a huge weight had been lifted from him, but he was not sure whether it was because he had spoken about it or because he had finally taken a decision on what to do about his parents' death. Either way, it did not matter; this moment had become the defining moment of his life.

When he got back to his apartment he called his travel agent.

***

Mike Zinbalan sat in the front row to hear what General Amofa had to say about his parents' heinous death at the NRC hearing. Mike did not recognise anybody in the room and no one took any notice of him. He was motionless and felt spasms of cold chill as three different people narrated their ordeals.

The pains were piercingly sharp. The wounds were deep, lying in hibernation beneath the shiny scars and pore-less skin, waiting for the slightest prick like the hearing to open them up again. The tears ran freely with emotion, soaking the handkerchiefs that were occasionally used to wipe them and the narrations were chilling to the bone. The progress of the Committee was meant to heal, but it was slow and to Mike it simply brought back memories of pain and anguish; memories he would rather forget.

Some of the victims of the darkest days in the history of modern Ghana had not lived long enough to tell their stories. They had died both defenceless and violently, gasping in agony as life was forced out of them. When the avenue was open for those still alive to tell their stories, they were so grotesque both narrators and listeners were awestruck. The horrifyingly macabre and ghoulish experience of some of the victims made public hearing so inappropriate they had to be told in camera.

The adrenalin level of a seventy-seven-year old property owner shot up suddenly as he told his story of how angry soldiers accused him of illegally acquiring wealth and, like gangsters, pulled down his building, gang-raped his wife in broad daylight, forcing him and his children to watch. "When I tried to protest, the soldiers dug out a hole on the ground and asked me to make love to mother earth. When I resisted I was beaten and left for dead," the man emphasised.

Suddenly reliving the pain, the impotence, the deep emotional scars of the inhumane sight of being forced to witness the rape of his own wife and the humiliation he had suffered over twenty years ago was too much for his frail body to bear. He paused to gasp for air, but his lungs refused to accept it and he choked on his own carbon monoxide. He collapsed to the floor and before the medical emergency team could get to him he was dead.

The incident led to the adjournment of the hearing to the following day.

Mike Zinbalan lay in bed that night unable to go to sleep. Each time he tried to close his eyes the nightmare revisited him.

He lay awake, replaying all that he had heard that day. Tomorrow, he thought, I will hear what Amofa has to say.

He was suddenly aware of Amofa standing at the foot of his bed and said, "You don't have to wait till tomorrow; I can tell you what you want to hear now. I've been waiting for this moment, now you can join your parents in hell." He removed a gun, pointed it at Mike, and pulled the trigger.

He struggled to free himself, while *they* struggled to pin him to his bed. Mike Zinbalan slowly relaxed, opened his eyes, felt his wet body and saw four hotel staff holding his limbs to the wet bed. A fifth poured cold water over him.

"Are you alright?" the person holding the water asked.

"What's the matter?" Mike asked.

"You were screaming and wouldn't open the door, so we had to let ourselves in. Are you all right?"

"I'll be fine."

When they left, Mike looked at his watch. It was five in the morning. He took a shower, dried himself and sat on the dry twin bed in the room. He would not sleep again for fear of another nightmare. It had been his worse one for many years.

At seven o'clock, Mike had his breakfast and made his way to the hearing, and again found himself a seat on the front row.

Avoca, a tortured victim of the brutal regime, was the first to take the stand at ten in the morning. Tears were running freely from Mike's eyes as Avoca narrated his ordeal:

"I watched as three mask-wearing soldiers cut flesh from the back of my friend Tanko, whose screams were muffled by a gag and sellotape over his mouth. Then, they forced my mouth open, shoved it down my throat and forced me to eat it. I was then given my own urine to water it down. I was blindfolded and stripped of my clothes. Two men held my legs apart and as I was wondering what it was about, I felt fire burn my penis, then I felt the tip being slashed, then I felt something like a needle being pushed in; that was when I passed out, unable to bear the pain.

When I regained consciousness, we were taken into a waiting vehicle and sent to another unknown destination. Someone came and asked me to co-operate with him. He said guns had been found in my house and I was to admit knowledge of those guns. I was also given a list of names of people who, I was told to confess, were plotting to overthrow the government.

Tanko and I were given detailed guidelines as to what to tell the bosses and made to rehearse our storylines. When I made mistakes they jumped on me again and started caning my mutilated penis. The pain was simply unimaginable. I broke down and started begging them to stop so I would do whatever they wanted me to do.

Avoca's seventy-five year-old mother, who was sitting in the audience and hearing her son's story for the first time, fell to the floor with shock and passed out. For the second time, the hearing was temporarily adjourned as the medical team moved in to resuscitate the old woman who was later taken out into a waiting ambulance.

When the hearing resumed, Avoca continued his narration:

"Tanko and I were separated and I was kept inside a room just big enough for me to stand straight with a container for me to pee, but no lights. During all this time, my urine was the only water I had. For about a week I was made to rehearse the story; when I was finally perfect by their standards I was taken to the BNI headquarters, where my blindfold was removed for the first time, to meet a panel of investigators. There, I was asked to tell my story. When I asked what story, someone, who I later found to be General Amankwa Amofa, said I shouldn't waste his time and that I knew the story I was to tell them if I didn't want to go back to where I had come from. I had no choice but to accept statements I was told to confess to."

Mike Zinbalan wiped his tears and waited. His death wish for General Amofa had just become an obsession as he watched the man responsible for his parents' death take the stand dressed in a navy-blue suit.

Cool and collected, General Amofa spoke, referring intermittently to his notes and on two occasions the audience applauded when he gave answers to some questions. On two brief occasions, Mike's eyes met Amofa's without any recognition at all by the ex-soldier. To Amofa, Mike was just another curious member of the audience.

The Counsel of the Commission, who was leading the retired general to give evidence asked, "Do you deny your involvement in the heinous crimes levelled against you by several people who have testified to the Commission?"

"Do I have to insult you?" General Amofa replied. "What you have been told are mere speculations and your question is presumptuous. What's your evidence?"

Some members of the audience were taken aback and stretched their necks to take a better look at him. Several people had gathered in the room to hear the confessions of the retired general, hoping he would show remorse and ask for absolution, instead he was arrogant and justified the actions of the military government at the time on the basis their actions were revolutionary and in any revolution there are bound to be casualties.

"Do you deny the testimony of Madam Kisiwaa," the Counsel for the Commission said pointing to a woman who had previously testified against him, "about how she lost her entire family at your hands and escaped with her own life only because she had been held up in traffic on that fateful day?"

"I think your woman is a pathological and demented liar," Amofa replied.

The pain on Madam Kisiwa's face was beyond description and as Amofa continued a loud noise was heard from the direction of the woman who had just spoken. All eyes turned in her direction. She fell from her chair, hitting the floor hard with her full weight, and passed out. She was later pronounced dead on arrival at the hospital. It was the second time in as many days such an incident had happened since the beginning of the hearing.

"The arrogance of it," Mike Zinbalan's voice was barely audible as he left the hearing. "I've had enough of this rubbish. I can't take any more of this man's bullshit."

Mike had come to the hearing with the hope of getting a confession and possibly an apology from the retired General who had turned his life into a living hell. He was burning with rage as he walked onto the main street and hailed a taxi.

As Mike Zinbalan looked out of the taxi window, he could see the wretchedness of the country he used to think of as home and thought about the hopelessness of the political and economic environment.

"Amofa will be paid back."

"Excuse me, are you talking to me?" the taxi driver asked.

"Let me get off here."

"Sure."

Mike got off, paid the driver and started walking; he had no particular destination in mind. He had resolved to avenge the perpetrators of the inhuman crime committed against him. He didn't know how, but from now on vengeance was going to be his life, or his death.

***

Mike's return to Ghana had become an emotional one for his uncle. Two days after Mike came back from the Committee's hearing in the capital he was sitting all by himself, gazing into the distant stars of the night sky, when Uncle Tweneboa joined him. He asked Mike about America and listened to him talk about his experiences and impressions of the country that seemed to his uncle the new Heaven he had heard so much about in church. As Mike talked, Uncle Tweneboa was glad he had, at least for a while taken his nephew's mind away from his parents' deaths.

"What sort of work do you do?" Uncle Tweneboa asked. "I hear most Ghanaians abroad engage in cleaning, security work, care work and, you know, menial sort of jobs."

"It's just like every country: there are those doing those sorts of jobs and there are those in highly skilled jobs. Mine is a hi-tech job using computers to develop new technologies."

"Can this kind of technology be established here in Ghana?" Uncle Tweneboa asked.

"Of course, but it's capital intensive," Mike replied.

He had not thought about it before and he honestly did not know the amount of capital required for this kind of venture.

"With the new government lots of Ghanaians are coming back to invest, including some of those in political exile," Tweneboa noted.

Mike was silent while his mind analysed his uncle's last statement.

"People coming back from exile," he said mainly to himself and asked his uncle, "why are leaders always associated with extra-judicial killings causing people to go into exile?" It was more of a rhetorical question.

"Leaders always kill," Tweneboa started to explain. "They are the same wherever you find them. Do you know why crocodiles can only be hunted under the authority of the King and rulers of our people?"

"No."

Tweneboa explained how, at the height of the Ashanti Kingdom, the rulers would use crocodile bile to eliminate any opposition to the monarchy, whether from within or without.

"Crocodile bile! Why that?" Mike asked, surprised.

"It's highly poisonous – more poisonous than the venom of a viper or even a cobra," Tweneboa explained.

He told Mike how the rulers would ensure the killing of a crocodile for its skin and meat was supervised, and the bile taken to the palace. This would be used mainly in a drink or sometimes in food to eliminate any opposition within, or to, the monarchy.

At this point Mike was half listening. He was already contemplating how he could get hold of crocodile bile. His chemist's mind sprung back to life. Mike decided he would find some crocodile bile and investigate the chemistry behind its poison.

His first contact with crocodile bile came earlier than he had anticipated. He walked into the local craft shop to buy presents for Effie and his boss. He wasn't sure what to buy yet, so he was just window-shopping when something attracted his attention.

"Excuse me," Mike said drawing the attention of the shop assistant, "what skin is this?" he asked pointing to a long scaly reptile-like skin hanging from the roof of the shop.

"It's a crocodile skin," replied the shop assistant, "it's a beautiful skin. I can give you a bargain," the shop assistant added with enthusiasm, hoping to make a sale.

"I'm interested in crocodile skin, but I would prefer a fresh skin."

"Why do you need a fresh skin?"

"I want it to undertake some research in America," Mike replied.

"It would be difficult."

"I'm sure you have the contacts," Mike said and placed a hundred-dollar bill in the seller's palm. "I'll come and get it next week and I need the bile as well."

"I'll try for you, sir," the seller replied with a slight bow after seeing the value of the money he was holding.

Mike returned a week later to find his treasure waiting for him. He took the bile, still fresh from the freezing container, and handed the seller another twenty dollars.

"God bless," the seller said.

Mike started to leave the shop when the seller said, "Sir, you have forgotten the skin."

"Ah yes, where is it?"

When Mike was shown the skin he had a good look at it, pretending to be interested, and asked if the seller could get it treated for him to pick up in the next couple of days. He then gave a few instructions as to how he would like it treated and left. It was the last time the seller saw him.

***

Mike had returned to the United States with a new sense of purpose. He had found a new obsession that would consume him and had perfected MZ-X3 as a potent and dangerous poison. Then he planned his next trip to Ghana.

His nightmares had taken over his life and he was going to Ghana to end it all, but first he had to meet Kutini. He called to inform Kutini he had finalised the program.

"Can we meet at the weekend?" Kutini asked.

"Yes, I don't have anything planned."

"I'll let you know my flight details when I book."

Mike picked Kutini up at Baltimore Washington International Airport and drove him directly to the Lincoln Memorial in Washington DC. The two wandered quietly around the memorial for a while, then took a short stroll to the banks of the Potomac River. It was late evening. Kutini could see the lights at the dome of Capitol Hill come on and said to Mike, "When I was in school I used to think Capitol was spelt incorrectly and should be Capital."

"Come to think of it," Mike started after a short pause, "it's the *capital hill* of the world. Decisions made here affect millions of poor, innocent people who will never even know about the existence of Capitol Hill."

"Unfortunately, that's the world's economic and political order."

They reached a bench and sat down. "Well, how are we going to reverse the order?" Kutini asked.

"I think we've got the plan right here."

"Have you any further thoughts about its implementation?" Kutini asked.

"Yes," Mike answered, elaborating his suggestions.

They went over the fine details of the plan verbally until they were both satisfied.

"Thanks for all the good work."

There was a brief moment of silence, then Kutini said, as though to himself, "I'm wondering how soon we can get the phone to Ghana."

"I'm going to Ghana at the coming weekend," Mike said.

"For how long?"

"Oh, just for a couple of weeks. I hear General Amofa is going to be cross-examined at the National Reconciliation Committee hearing. It would be an opportunity to hear what more he has to say about my parents' killings."

"I'm sure the law will catch up with him sooner or later."

"It better be sooner, or someone else might catch up with him before the law does," Mike replied.

"You're not suggesting revenge, are you?" Kutini asked unsure how to interpret Mike's last statement.

"Kutini, between you and me, life has been a living hell. Not a day passes without me having nightmares about my parent's deaths."

"Don't be silly, the law will take care of him."

"Thanks, but I will leave my options open," Mike answered.

"Be good when you go to Ghana."

"I'll try," Mike replied, thinking: If only he knew. Sometimes he felt he was insane and dreaded actually becoming mad. General Amofa will pay for taking innocent blood, he thought.

CHAPTER 21

Chris Tagoe had quit the military in Ghana after a series of frustrations from senior officers prevented him achieving his deserved rank. He had moved to America and joined the US Army starting from the bottom. His previous military background, however, gave him an advantage over the new recruits he was training with and he soon emerged as the best officer.

He had come to Ghana to get married to his fiancée, Mariam. The traditional marriage rites proposed by Chris' family had been turned down by the parents of his would-be bride on the basis they did not know Chris in person. Underlying the refusal, however, was Chris' humble background.

Chris' father had started life as a fisherman without any basic education and had been struggling to maintain his family until he came in contact with Indigenous Business Empowerment, an international non-governmental organisation, which introduced him to micro finance. His frugality and determination, supported by his wife, had turned him into the owner of several fishing trawlers but despite the business success of Chris' family they were still considered fishermen.

Mariam's father was a professor of law at the University of Ghana and her mother was a practising lawyer and a Member of Parliament. To Mariam's father the fact Chris was in the army made the marriage even more untenable.

Chris had come with the hope his presence would convince Mariam's parents of his love for their daughter, give them the chance to look at his individual achievement and accept him as their son-in-law. There would be, Chris hoped, a traditional marriage rite between the two families followed by an official wedding. He was on his way to Mariam's house and had stopped for lunch at Chopsticks, a Chinese restaurant at Osu in Accra.

Mike Zinbalan walked into an internet café along the Osu High Street, logged on to his bank's website and made transfer payments through his internet banking facility to Kutini's account. He then decided to go to Chopsticks Restaurant before visiting his father's old 'friend' – General Amankwa Amofa.

Chris saw Mike walk in. He wasn't sure at first if it was Mike Zinbalan, the same old friend who had left for the US soon after their graduation.

Mike on the other hand simply shouted out, "Chris, is that you?" They embraced each other and sat down together for a meal.

The waitress, a beautiful young woman, came to the table and placed two menus in front of them. Mike looked at her as she walked away towards another table. He dreamt in his pants. If only I could live another day, but I am not James Bond, he thought. Chris' eyes were following the woman with a sparkle, his mouth open. He turned round to see Mike's eyes fixed in the same direction.

"Whatcha looking at, nigger?" Chris asked, displaying his acquired African American accent. Mike smiled.

"You haven't lost your sense of humour, brother?" Chris asked and patted him on the back.

They studied the wine list and Mike said, "Let's share a bottle of Champagne."

"That sounds like a celebration," Chris remarked.

"We haven't seen each other for donkey's years. Why not, come on, let's celebrate this reunion."

The two were talking when the waitress came with the champagne and opened it with a style that made the pop sound so different. He could not help but express his admiration; it was more than just admiring the way she opened the champagne.

"Beautiful. How long have you worked here?" Chris found a chat up line.

"Oh, just on and off."

"What do you do when you're off?" Mike queried.

"I study at the university," she answered and moved on to take orders from another table.

I hope we meet again in the after world to share fantasies together, Mike said to himself, and blew a kiss after her.

The food came and the two old pals gladly shared what they had each ordered while they recounted memories of the good old days. Mike seemed exceptionally happy, with undertones of sadness that were difficult to detect. They finished the meal and a waiter this time came to collect the plates.

The waitress came back a moment later to ask if they wanted dessert. They both looked down at their stomachs and said, "No," in unison as if they were rehearsing a part in a movie.

"Can I have your phone number, Betty," Chris added reading from her name badge.

"I am not allowed to," she replied.

"Then, I will give you mine," Chris said, wrote his number and gave it to Betty.

"What the hell was that? I thought you said you were getting married," Mike asked when Betty had left.

"Chill out, it's still a few days away. Come on, we've got to live life to the full," Chris joked.

"Be careful," Mike advised.

"What are your plans for the day?" Mike asked Chris while they were waiting for the bill.

"I'm going to see my fiancée at Legon," Chris answered.

"Are you driving?"

"No," Chris responded, adding that the type of driving in Ghana was crazy and he preferred going by taxi. He wondered why there were not many more accidents than there already were, even though Ghana had one of the highest accident rates in Africa.

"Look, Chris, I'll give you a lift. We will go to see a friend of my late father, then I'll drop you off at yours. We can catch up on the way."

"Sure, I'm in no particular hurry," Chris replied.

"Could you also do me a favour and give this phone to Sapel Namaal please? It's meant for my cousin Tuuro at the village," Mike said as he scribbled the name and an address on a piece of paper and handed it to Chris. "I've a very tight schedule before I return to the US."

The traffic from Osu to McCarthy Hill was a nightmare. They sat in the car talking about their individual pursuits in the United States.

Mike told him about his achievements in America, omitting the finer details of his work. Chris was impressed, "You're a lucky man, Mike, I wish . . ."

"Wishes are not horses," Mike interjected. "When preparedness meets opportunity, the uninitiated calls it luck. What luck? Hard work and determination are the rules of the game. My boss is a Jew, and you know what? They work hard and they support each other. You hear that? They support each other. What do we Blacks do? Stab each other in the back. The Jews always want to support and help us because of our common history – slavery. The Jews were slaves for hundreds of years under the Pharaoh's weren't they? We Blacks haven't yet broken out of the bonds of slavery."

Chris looked out of the car window absent-mindedly as Mike continued with his monologue.

"All they need to see in us to help is trust, one virtue we have in abundance. It has its own disadvantages though. Blind trust can be disas—"

There was a sudden stop; Mike slammed hard on the brakes. There was the screeching sound of the brakes and tyres together. The car swerved precariously to the right. Not finding its balance, it swerved back to the middle of the road willingly obeying Mike's commanding hand movement on the wheel.

"In the name of the Holy Ghost, are you a one-man suicide squad?" Chris yelled. "I told you driving in this country is a death trap."

A taxi driver had swerved in front of them in an attempt to reach a passenger before another taxi did.

"Cowards die many times before their death …" Mike started to quote from Shakespeare's Julius Caesar, ignoring Chris' caution.

"If you want to die be sure you leave some piece of you for your family to pay their last respects."

"All die be die," Mike replied in typical Ghanaian parlance. "By the way," he added, "if I die accidentally, be sure not to touch my body."

"Did you drink anything in addition to the champagne?"

"Come on, we're here. General Amofa will be surprised to see me," Mike said as he pulled the car onto the side road.

Mike knocked on the door of General Amankwa Amofa while Chris stood a couple of inches behind him like a lioness guarding its prized catch for the benefit of the kittens.

"Can I help you?" a woman asked behind the half-open door.

"We've come to see the General," Mike replied. "Is he in?"

The low, but stern tone of Mike's voice and the brevity of his response did little to disguise the alarm signal sent to the woman. They were both well dressed and well groomed and nothing in the looks or appearance of either of them betrayed any intentions.

"One moment," Esther said and closed the door. She felt uneasy. Her sharp instincts developed through the revolution days as the wife of a military general told her something was amiss.

Mike and Chris waited.

A few seconds later, the door opened and a tall, slightly stooping middle-aged man stood in the doorway. There was a moment's hesitation as he held the door open, almost imperceptible. Shreds of recognition flashed through his mind. But he couldn't remember where he knew one of the young men.

"I'm General Amofa; I understand you would like to talk to me."

Amofa had retired early from the army soon after the military turned civilian government finished its second and last term of office and handed over power.

Even in retirement he was still addressed as General. In the neighbourhood where he lived with his family, General had come to be his name and he had accepted it.

"My name is Zinbalan, Mike Zinbalan and this is my friend Chris Tagoe."

Just as he mentioned the name everything came back to General Amofa in a flash. The look in Mike's eyes – the same look. After eleven years, just when he thought life was beginning to take on a new meaning, a new positive meaning, the past was back to haunt him. He wasn't going to allow this. He asked the children to go down to the creek to play. Esther also took the cue and disappeared out of sight.

"Mr. Zinbalan, to what do I owe the honour of your visit?" Amofa asked in a sarcastic voice. He now remembered seeing Mike Zinbalan's face during his testimony at the National Reconciliation Committee hearing.

"You know me?" Mike asked surprised.

"Are you not the son of the late Colonel Zinbalan? He was my *Ogbo* at the barracks."

Chris sensed the two wanted to talk in private. He casually looked out of the big windows whose blinds were pulled open and instantly fell in love with the well-mown lawns, the beautiful flowers, and the three summer huts in view.

Chris turned to Amankwa and said, "General that's a beautiful garden you've got there."

"Thanks," Amankwa replied, "that's where I'm investing my retirement time."

And the revolutionary loot as well, Mike thought.

"Can I have a look?" Chris requested.

"Sure."

Chris opened the sliding door leading from the living room and walked into the garden. He could not help but admire the beauty of this property, the pattern of the landscape and plants. The house itself sat at the leeward side of the hill with the creek hidden to the back of the house. The lawns were cut with military precision, a vocation Amofa had come to love and cherish in his retirement.

Chris found General Amofa's children playing at the creek and joined them. Maa Abena was twelve and Nana Kwadwo had just turned seven. The reason the creek never dried was the wooded vegetation surrounding this part of the land provided cover from the sun, which prevented evaporation. The shade also made this part of the property the favourite place for the children to play. They were usually with the house-help, Serwaa, to keep them from hurting themselves.

"This is a beautiful garden," Chris said, not to anyone in particular, gasping for breath and settling on the grass beside the children.

"My dad calls it *feng shui*." Maa Abena responded to Chris' statement.

She explained to him that her dad was very passionate about the garden and how he would spend long hours getting it together. "He has a book," Maa Abena had explained, "which he studies before starting his gardening work."

Chris had little knowledge of *feng shui*, but now he knew what he would do when he finished building his house. It seemed to Chris that from whatever book Amofa had copied his design he had added his own innovation to create this masterpiece of a garden. He was sure the designer of the original garden would marvel at this wonderful piece of work.

Maa Abena was full of pride when she explained how the water system worked. She had spent the whole week with her father and the workmen to achieve what seemed to be her father's wish. She had asked questions, some of which were ignored, but she did not seem to realise, as she had her own answers.

While Chris was with the children at the creek admiring the opulence of the property Mike and Amofa continued their dialogue.

Mike had come with a mission and did not want to waste time. "I know you worked with my father and he was a kind, hardworking man. Tell me why you kill him and if you had a grudge against him, what about my mother?"

Mike presented his request in a well-rehearsed speech. Inside him he felt differently. He wished Amofa dead that moment, but he needed to know why he had done it. He was not sure why he needed this information; he was simply following his instincts.

"I didn't kill your father."

"Who did?"

"How would I know? Those turbulent days of the revolution resulted in so many deaths and we can't possibly find the killers of all the unfortunate victims," Amofa said, choosing his words carefully. "Besides, even if the killers are known, under what law will they be prosecuted? The former regime is covered by the constitution's immunity clause."

Mike was getting impatient. Unfortunate victims indeed, he thought. Did he not know about the indemnity clause? He had come to take his revenge, knowing the law was not on his side. He wanted to end it all and the time was now.

"Can I use your wash room?" Mike requested whilst the adrenaline was rushing to his head. He was desperately trying to keep his calm, but this arrogance of an ex-soldier was not helping matters. He had asked to use the washroom without the usual courtesy of the magic word *please*.

"Through this door; first door on your left. The lights are movement sensitive," Amofa directed.

Mike entered the washroom and took his time to pee. When he finished, he flushed the toilet, conscious there was a camera watching him.

As they had entered the living room at Amofa's invitation, Mike had noticed a small television was on with static pictures moving a few seconds at a time to show different parts of static objects. He had caught a glimpse of a WC on the TV screen, but that did not concern him and he was not going to change his plans.

He moved to the sink, washed his hands, and reached into his breast pocket. He extracted what looked like a flat aluminium foil containing capsules of medication. He extracted one capsule, put it in his mouth and with his hand cupped, brought some water to his mouth and swallowed. Just then, he started singing:

This world is not my home
I'm just passing through
The treasures are laid up
Somewhere beyond the blue
The angels beckon me
From heaven's open door
And I can't feel at home in this world anymore
. . . .

He sang, still conscious of the camera, but aware it had no film to record and no sound facility. The capsule he had just swallowed under normal conditions should have delivered to him instant death, but not the way Mike had prepared it – death would come in an instant, but not for a short while yet.

Mike walked into the living room just as Amofa turned away from the television screen to face him. Mike knew he was being watched. Amofa had seen him swallow some 'medicine', but there was nothing abnormal about that and he was sure the two visitors did not carry any weapon.

General Amofa had elaborately installed a metal detector at his front door, which he had built himself to ensure no one knew about its presence. In this technology age, why employ people to guard you when technology can do much more? Besides, people's loyalty can be bought and he had come to trust no one but himself. When a metal object was detected on a person passing through the doors it triggered his wristwatch to bleep like an obedient alarm undertaking its dutiful responsibility to the delight of its proud owner. Not that he ever stopped anyone triggering the metal alarm; he only used it as an early warning system to get ready for any eventuality.

Even though the arrival of Mike and his friend had not sent any physical alarm bells, the psychological alarm still warned him to be ready. He carried a small hand-crafted Soviet-made pistol, a prized machine he had stolen from a Hizbollah fighter during his duties in Lebanon. He loved the pistol more for its artistic value than as a weapon.

"General Amofa," Mike resumed from where they had left off, "I am not concerned about the law. I just want to know who killed my father. Maybe then I will have a personal reconciliation and carry on with my life."

"I am sorry I can't help you and if you asked my advice, I would say let sleeping dogs lie."

For a second, no one spoke. In a deadly voice that suddenly broke the silence and sent chills down the spine of Amofa, Mike asked, "Why did you kill my father?"

For the first time in his life Amofa was scared and started to shiver, but stopped himself. He knew his instinct to carry a gun was right. Once a soldier, always a soldier, he thought.

"How dare you come to my house and accuse me of your father's death?" Amofa bellowed. "Go to the law if you want to accuse me. Your dad was a brute and deserved to die. Get out of my house, now," he screamed.

"I'm not leaving this house until you've had your last opportunity to make another kill before going to hell." Mike delivered his death sentence in a tone that typified sympathy more than a death treat.

For an instant, the message did not register. "What?" Amofa asked. Just then, Mike got up with the speed of a cheetah and made a movement as if he wanted to draw a gun for a shot. The sound of the gunshot was loud and the echo could be heard down the creek in the valley and in the surrounding houses.

Amofa's wife was not far away. She heard the sound of the bullet. One bullet. The echo in the house was like a thousand drums being beaten at the same time.

She had sensed danger as soon as those two visitors walked into the house and wanted to know their mission without her physical presence. She had stayed in the garage, within earshot from the living room, where she was listening to the conversation and had just started to enter the living room when the shot was delivered.

"Holy Jesus," she screamed. The bullet went through Mike's right shoulder. He fell into the chair and rolled down onto the floor in a heap and was dead instantly.

Retired General Amankwa Amofa was a decorated marksman from his military service. He had shot Mike with the intent to disarm and had hit him on his right shoulder. He had his retirement days to look forward to and did not want to consider jail as a possibility. After all, he thought, he had served his country well and was living life as a normal law abiding citizen.

Just as Mike fell to the floor Amofa reached to check if he was carrying a weapon. The bend that lowered him to the search took him down to the ground. The fall was heavy and loud. He exhaled exactly three short breaths, each lasting a fraction of a second and Amofa was dead.

Esther rushed to hold her husband, asking, "Are you . . .?"

Those were her last words. Mike's poison was working as planned.

CHAPTER 22

The sound of the bullet that hit Mike ricocheted through the woods; the birds fluttered and filled the evening air with miniature shadows and shrill sounds of fear bringing Chris and the children to a stop. They instinctively headed for the house.

Maa Abena ran ahead of the other three as they raced each other to reach the house. She obviously knew the short cut and followed it. Chris was running behind Serwaa and Kwadwo. Maa Abena was already inside the house when Chris saw the back entrance and raced in ahead of the duo.

He heard the cry "help" from Maa Abena just as he entered the room, but before help could come, death had claimed its fourth victim. Chris saw the pile of bodies on the floor and felt like throwing up.

His first impulse was to stop the others from entering the house. He met Serwaa and Kwadwo at the entrance and said in a stern and military-like voice, "your dad says you should wait for him on the lawn." They obeyed without question.

Chris re-entered the house looking for a phone. Finding none, he reached into his pocket and extracted a wrapped parcel, ripped it open and dialled the emergency number 999.

The operator at the end of the line asked, "Police, ambulance or …"

"Both of them," he cut in, "to Amofa's residence, McCarthy Hill."

He turned to the bodies lying on top of each other at the foot of the sofa and reminded himself not to touch anything until the police came. As Chris pondered what to do next he noticed that apart from the small drop of blood, an inch or so away from Mike's shoulder, there was no blood visible anywhere else. The four deaths could not all have been gunshots, he thought. He then recounted hearing only one gunshot. He tried to run the sequence of events through his mind. Mike said he was visiting his father's friend, so why would the man kill him? It did not make sense; nothing made sense. Chris was confused. He looked at his watch; he was getting impatient. Even though he had made the call only five minutes ago, it seemed a long time ago to him and neither the police nor the ambulance was in sight.

He walked across from the back of the house towards Kwadwo and Serwaa. They were still sitting on the lawn, not convinced all was well, but afraid to come into the house.

"Your daddy will come out soon," Chris said to them, knowing they would soon find out, and wondered if the police would implicate him in the crime.

Chris' thoughts were suddenly jerked back to reality when he heard the sirens close to the house. The police were the first to arrive – two of them. Chris met them and explained what had happened as he led them into the house.

"Whatever you do, don't touch any of those bodies." Chris warned, but the police ignored his warning and as they approached the bodies Corporal Inusah focused his camera and took a couple of snap shots from two different positions. At that moment, Detective Sergeant Yankey knelt down to examine the pile of bodies lying on the floor.

"I said don't touch …" Chris did not finish his sentence. "An idiot of a policeman," he swore in exasperation.

The lifeless body of Sergeant Yankey lay next to Maa Abena as if trying to pull her away from death.

"Just shut up," Corporal Inusah shouted as he rushed back to the police car, removed the mouthpiece of the communication equipment and pressed the on-button on the panel board. He then turned a knob to select a channel. This was the first time he was going to use this special channel that linked directly to the head of the specialist SkyHawks Team.

"SkyHawks, state request and location," came the voice from the team.

"SkyHawks requested immediately at Amofa's residence, McCarthy Hill."

"We are on our way," the voice replied.

Inusah replaced the handset and got out of the car knowing the SkyHawks team would be there shortly. He saw Chris and said, "Keep an eye on the children." He then went to seal off the crime scene by putting the cordon tapes across the main entrance of the completely fenced house.

The ambulance arrived, followed closely by a big dark van. It stopped by the side of the ambulance and one American and a Ghanaian jumped out of the van almost in unison. A third person, a Ghanaian, Alari Kanbe, opened the driver's door and stepped out leaving his door open. He walked towards the American.

Kanbe was the head of the SkyHawks Team, an elite team set up as a collaborative effort between the Federal Bureau of Investigations and the Bureau of National Investigations following the serial murders of women in Ghana. Despite his expertise in poisonous gases and vast experience in the field, his role was more figurative than functional.

The other Ghanaian, Faiza Iddris, was a trained poison gas and surveillance expert who worked with the SkyHawks team. The American was Rudolf Reinhardt.

Rudolf spoke briefly to Inusah and then to Chris. Together they went into the room where the five dead bodies lay. Kanbe followed closely behind. It was obvious that whatever substance they were dealing with was a poison, but certainly not gas.

Rudolf and Inusah came back from the crime scene and spoke to Faiza by the van. Inside the van was a cabinet with protective clothes and equipment. It also had on a separate shelf with a pack of half a dozen body bags, which were specially made with protective inside lining to prevent any contamination through handling. The rest of the van was like a moving lab holding various surgical instruments, chemical substances and a bed in the centre.

After Rudolf had briefed the team they all donned their protective clothes, which covered them from head to toe, and took five body bags. As they came out of the van Kanbe went over to the ambulance staff, opened his visor and spoke to them, briefing them on the delicate nature of the victims and how they required specialist handling. Faiza went into the house following Rudolf with Kanbe trailing behind, while Chris was asked to wait.

Inside the room they opened the first body bag, lifted the police officer from the pile of bodies, carefully placed him on the bag and zipped it up. Then using a broad tape made from a special adhesive sealed off the zip, ensuring the contents had absolutely no contact with the outside world.

Faiza Iddris brought a trolley from the van; the body was lifted onto it and she pulled it to the ambulance. The ambulance staff had been asked to stay clear because even in the sealed state they could not take chances. They placed the body in the ambulance and continued with the process, taking their time, until all five bodies had been put in.

News of the deaths had spread quickly and reporters were already at the crime scene, transmitting live information to their respective media, but with limited access to the proceedings inside the house.

When all five bodies had been put in the van the vehicles moved out of the property in a convoy: first the police together with Kwadwo and Serwaa, who were being taken away into protective custody. They were followed by the ambulance and then the SkyHawks van. The police sirens cleared the way for the convoy, which was now more of a funeral procession heading for the morgue at Korle-Bu Teaching Hospital.

Three other cars were following the emergency vehicles in a less convoy-like fashion. Among them was a Nissan saloon car in which sat a woman, Theresa Amole.

At the morgue, the bodies were carefully removed and placed in individual refrigerators with the label 'highly contagious, do not open' written in red. The writing itself stood out, predator-like, as if it was the contagious element itself ready to pounce on its prey.

At the entrance to the hospital the police were screening vehicles entering, allowing only hospital staff and emergency vehicles in. The press and all the relatives that followed the emergency vehicles were denied access. The press waited, while wailing and crying of family, relatives and friends continued.

"Oh, my dear Yankey, what have you done to me?" Theresa Amole was crying, "My dear Yankey, who will look after me?"

"Do you know Yankey?" a woman's voice asked from behind her.

Without thinking, and still very emotional, she replied, "Oh Yankey, my boyfriend, who will take care..." trying to hold on to the person asking in a sympathetic embrace. The slap that brought her to reality was enough to tell her it came from no ordinary hand.

Corporal Okumi was the wife of Yankey and they lived in the police barracks together. She had always suspected her husband had a mistress but she had had no evidence. The ensuing chaos got almost everyone involved either trying to stop the fight or fuelling the fight they were trying to calm. The electronic media had a field day transmitting live events on their breaking news programmes.

While the rivals clashed, the SkyHawks team slipped out of the hospital. Detective Corporal Inusah came to the gate and said to the crowd, "We would like only one relative, preferably the next of kin of each of the deceased, to come to the head office of the Criminal Investigations Department."

The crowd started to disperse. Inusah then drove off, but they were not going to the CID head office, instead they headed for the SkyHawks' office. Inside the police van was Chris Tagoe who was going to be interrogated by the specialist team handling the case.

The next morning, the local newspapers carried similar front-page headlines: *Wife or Mistress: who dominates in the love-lost relationship with the dead?*

The matching photos to the headlines showed two groups clashing, each led by a woman.

CHAPTER 23

People living and working around the two-metre high fence wall housing the Bureau of National Investigations Headquarters were awed and intimidated by the sheer size and myth surrounding the buildings and activities within the inner periphery of the wall. The inhabitants of the buildings had not themselves done anything to allay the fears or even attempted to demystify the place. If anything their silence, alleged activities and their powers had added to the myth.

Several buildings were contained within the headquarters, one of which belonged to the SkyHawks team. Reinhardt's office was directly opposite that of Kanbe. Faiza Iddris used a third office. A fourth and larger room housed the big round table with eight chairs used for meetings. The fifth room in the building was where the office machines and documents were kept and through it a door opened into another room, hardly used, but the most important in the entire building. It housed chemicals and equipment for testing and analysing substances, blood and body tissue. It was more than a forensic laboratory and could be used to perform complicated autopsies where conventional hospital equipment could not be used.

Towards the back end of the building were a kitchen and a washroom opposite each other. A passage led from the front of the building to the back and opened on to a garden and a space connected to the other buildings in the vast compound.

Inusah was invited into Kanbe's office and joined later by Reinhardt to hold a briefing on how the investigations of the McCarthy Hill deaths would proceed. It was the first time Inusah had been in the BNI building in his seven years as a police officer. His eyes scanned the spacious but modestly furnished office of Alari Kanbe, resting momentarily on the air-conditioner where the humming sound was coming from. The place looked ordinary and did not justify the myths he had come to associate with it, he thought, wondering what the BNI boss' office would look like. Inusah's thoughts were interrupted when Kanbe started to speak, explaining the sequence of procedures they would have to follow.

"We will keep you informed about developments and will contact you when we need your help." With that, Kanbe dismissed Detective Corporal Inusah.

While Inusah was being briefed Faiza Iddris searched Chris, took all his personal belongings and locked them away in their safe. Faiza then gave Chris a notepad and a pen to write a witness statement about the events that led to the deaths at the McCarthy Hill residence.

The events were still fresh in Chris' mind as he started to write. "I met Mike Zinbalan for the first time in many years at Chopsticks Restaurant at Osu in Accra…"

After over an hour and several interruptions from Faiza, Chris finally signalled he had finished writing his statement. Faiza took it away and led him to the conference room where the other SkyHawks members were already seated.

Alari Kanbe sat at the round table at the back end of the meeting room. To his right sat Rudolf Reinhardt. Faiza Iddris showed Chris to a chair and took her seat.

A video camera was ready, pointing away from them. In front of each of them were a notepad and a pen. Sitting across from them, facing the video camera was Chris Tagoe.

Chris was made aware he was the first suspect in the McCarthy Hill deaths and he was required to assist the SkyHawks with the investigations. He was also made aware of his rights to remain silent and to an attorney. Chris chose to talk without an attorney. After all, I am innocent, he thought.

Reinhardt looked intensively at Chris, observing his nervousness as Kanbe read the details of the crime, befitting the devil himself.

"Can I use the washroom?" Chris asked when Kanbe had finished.

"Sure," Kanbe replied, led Chris to the washroom, and stood by the door waiting.

After listening to the charges, Chris wondered if he didn't need an attorney after all. He needed time to think. If I ask for an attorney they might presume I'm guilty, he thought as he washed his hands.

When Chris came out, Kanbe was looking out of a window in the corridor and following his gaze Chris saw a Mitsubishi four-wheel drive pull up in front of the building opposite. Two uniformed police officers ran towards the car, one standing to attention whilst the other opened the back door of the car. A small man, ordinarily dressed, stepped out of the car and the two policemen saluted. The man acknowledged the salute with a slight nod and was escorted to the front door, held open for him.

"Who is this man who just got out of the car?" Chris asked Kanbe.

"Paul Nadan is the BNI director," Kanbe replied. "Shall we?" he added, pointing to the meeting room door.

Chris had heard of this legendary name. The fear his name evoked in Ghana overshadowed that of the president. Even as a military officer with the Ghana Armed Forces, Chris knew the name of Paul Nadan sent a cold chill down the spines of people, and so he was expecting to see a huge, well-built, athletic figure, not the diminutive frail figure he saw disappearing into the building.

Back in the meeting room, Kanbe asked, "All ready?" His colleagues acknowledged their readiness with silence. He pressed a knob on the video gadget next to him and said, "Right, let's begin.

Mr. Tagoe, we would like you to tell us the details of the McCarthy Hill incident, stating everything you can remember. We would like you to start by providing your full name, your permanent and current addresses and contact details, the names and addresses of your parents or guardians as appropriate and current work place and address of your current employer. Start when you're ready."

"My name is Chris Tagoe …" he started. "Mike and I ran into each other yesterday at…" Chris continued and spoke for forty-five minutes, stopping occasionally to remember something he had omitted.

No one spoke throughout his narration. Each member of the SkyHawks team was concentrating on the statement Chris was providing and taking down notes or writing down questions they would like to ask afterwards. There was a long pause after Chris had finished.

"Carry on, Mr. Tagoe," Kanbe said not knowing Chris had come to the end of his narration.

"That's all there is," Chris replied, looking exhausted and sweating in the air-conditioned office.

"Mr. Tagoe, did you know Mike was carrying poison on him when you agreed to go with him to General Amofa's house?" Rudolf asked.

"No, I did not," Chris said defensively.

"How did you know not to touch him when he was dead?" Rudolf continued his line of inquiry.

"During our drive to the house we encountered a near-accident situation. I recalled him saying I shouldn't touch his body when he was dead. At the time it didn't register because I thought it to be one of those flips he alone understood. The statement came back to me when I witnessed the death of the kid." Chris finished a bit angry because he had stated all that in his account.

"Would you have touched them if you hadn't witnessed the kid dying?" Kanbe asked.

"No, as an army officer I know not to tamper with crime scene evidence," Chris replied.

Kanbe looked to his left and to his right, anticipating more questions. There weren't any. He still asked, "Any more questions for Mr. Tagoe?"

Each person declined.

"Could you provide us with your personal details again please?" Kanbe requested.

They wrote down his full name, Christopher Austin Tagoe, and his details. His account did not reveal any suspicious motive. They had no immediate evidence to charge him with murder but they couldn't let him go yet; he would be held as a prime suspect until they had more information. They would have to talk to other witnesses.

"You do understand you are the prime suspect and we have to establish the truth of your story. I am afraid we can't let you go yet," Kanbe told Chris.

"But I have a wedding to arrange, you can't keep me here," Chris protested.

"I'm sorry," Kanbe said and nodded to Faiza. Together they took Chris and led him away, his hands cuffed.

In the meeting room the three-member SkyHawks team compared notes and reviewed the videotape. When they had finished, Faiza took the video tape into the documents room, opened the door to the high security cabinet built into the wall and placed the marked videotape inside. She locked the door and returned the key to Kanbe. The whole compound was a high security area and everyone who worked there was vetted, but since occupying that building they had installed extra security including this tamperproof cabinet for highly sensitive information.

***

Chris' wife-to-be had been waiting outside the building because she was not allowed inside and her eyes were sore from crying. Was Chris involved in the murders? Was he being tortured by the BNI who were notorious for their crude methods? Were they going to cancel the wedding? She looked at her watch; it was past seven o'clock in the evening and there was nothing she could achieve by her continuous presence outside the BNI compound, so she left.

When she got home, her parents were waiting for her to have dinner but she refused to eat and went straight to her room. Her parents ate their meal in silence and when they had finished, her father went up to her room and asked what had happened. She told him Chris was still being held by the BNI.

"Listen to me," her father started, "as far as I am concerned this marriage is not going to happen. I cannot let you marry a murderer."

"He is not a murderer," she screamed at her dad.

With a controlled voice that did little to hide his anger her father said, "He is a prime suspect and that stigma will always be there. The marriage is off."

***

The next day at the BNI office the SkyHawks team spoke to Amofa's surviving son and the nanny who confirmed Chris' alibi he was with them when they heard the gunshot. After they had spoken to the children, Chris was brought in and told he was free to go. "We would appreciate it if you could make yourself available if your help was required any time during the investigations," Kanbe added.

Chris promised to do so and provided them with a brief schedule of his movements for the following three weeks before he returned to the US.

Faiza Iddris returned Chris' personal belongings to him and escorted him to the heavy security-manned metal gates to the BNI compound. Two armed police guards saluted as Faiza approached. She nodded to a third policeman who opened the pedestrian gate and held it for Chris to leave. "Thank you for your time, Mr. Tagoe," Faiza said, as Chris stepped out of the compound.

As Chris left the SkyHawks office, the first thing on his mind was to see his fiancée. He walked the four hundred metres around the BNI building to the side of the main road opposite the Canadian Embassy and flagged a taxi. The driver stopped about a hundred metres away and waved at Chris to hurry.

When Chris got into the taxi, he asked, "Why didn't you stop over there?" pointing to where he had been standing for the last half hour.

"You get arrested if you stop there," the taxi driver replied.

"Oh, I see. So why did you stop?"

"I took the risk. I saw you standing there waving taxis a little while ago and I knew you were a stranger here."

In his confused state of mind Chris hadn't noticed the signal the other taxi drivers were giving to alert him it was a no stopping zone. To make matters worse, there were no signs saying taxis should not stop. In his time in America he had forgotten that in Ghana the rules were different.

"Where would you like to go to, sir?" the driver asked.

"Roman Ridge."

"Twenty-five thousands cedis, sir," the driver quoted the fare in the local currency.

Chris did not say anything. He was wondering why nothing ever seemed to change in Ghana. In America the fare would be determined by a meter but here he was being charged by how much the driver thought he was worth, not by the standard fare.

When they got to his destination Chris removed a ten-dollar bill and gave it to the taxi driver, knowing he would have paid over twenty dollars in America for similar distance.

"I can't change this, sir."

"Keep it," Chris said.

"Thank you sir, may God bless you," the taxi driver said, looking at the crisp ten-dollar bill in his hand. He was already calculating how much he would get in the local currency. He had made his day's income from this customer. "Should I wait for you?" he asked as Chris walked through the metal gate into his fiancée's compound.

"Yes," Chris replied as an afterthought. It would be a good idea to take his fiancée out for a meal and explain the entire mix up to her. "I will be right back," Chris added.

He pressed the bell and waited. He was about to press it again when the door opened bringing him face to face with his fiancée's father. "Hello, I've come to…"

"Mr. Tagoe, I've called off the marriage and I don't want to see you in this house again. Do I make myself clear?"

"But, Sir I…"

Chris heard the sound of the slamming door as it shut in his face. He went into a momentary trance. Am I dreaming? This isn't happening to him. This can't be real.

Chris stood in front of the door dumbfounded. His world had fallen apart; his feet simply gave way to the weight above. He crumpled onto the floor and cried. He thought about all the preparations he had made for the wedding: the horse-drawn carriage he had imported, the people he had invited and the honeymoon he had planned. Now through no fault of his own, fate had turned its ugly face at him. He got up afterwards and walked out to the waiting taxi.

"Where next, sir?" the driver asked when Chris got in and closed the door.

"Just drive."

After about twenty minutes of unsuccessfully trying to make conversation with Chris, the taxi driver asked, "Are you alright, sir?"

"I'm alright," Chris replied. "Can you take me to Abeka Lapaz please?"

"Wherever you want, sir."

For the next thirty minutes no one spoke. Chris sat in the taxi wondering whether the events of the last two days had been just a terrible nightmare. He was still struggling to come to terms with the circumstances surrounding the deaths. Maybe there is a curse on the house, he concluded, unable to find any logical explanations. Chris was surprised to find himself thinking that way as he didn't believe in superstition.

"We are at Abeka Lapaz, where should I go?" the driver asked.

"Go straight and take the second turn on your right," Chris replied, thinking that in America all he would have done would be to hand a cab driver an address. In Ghana, if one didn't know where to go the driver would stop and ask several people on the way, taking twice the time and end up asking for more than what they have already overcharged.

"Which way should I go?" the driver asked, as he turned into the side road.

"Stop at the third house on your left."

Chris found Sapel Namaal at home when he arrived. "I'm sorry I couldn't make it yesterday as promised," Chris said and went on to explain the circumstances. He then gave him a mobile phone and a letter. "Mike asked me to give this to you. I had to use the mobile phone to make a 999 call when the incident happened."

CHAPTER 24

At the SkyHawks office, the team was discussing the next stage of their investigations when Chris had left.

"We have to do the autopsies to find out the mysterious death agent," Rudolf said.

"I'm not still convinced of Chris' alibi," Kanbe said. "What if it was all planned and Mike Zinbalan was also an unfortunate victim?" he asked.

"There is only one way to find out," Faiza said.

"Yes?" Rudolf asked.

"Let's put him under surveillance."

"Good point, young woman. That's a job for you," Kanbe said, "anything else?"

For a few seconds no one said anything. "Unless there is anything else to discuss I suggest we take a break and prepare for the post mortem after lunch," Kanbe concluded.

Kanbe was the senior pathologist in charge of the autopsies and had trained as a medical doctor from the University of Science and Technology, Kumasi. The existence of the School of Pharmacy alongside the School of Medical Sciences provided an excellent basis for good rapport between the medical and pharmacy students. The relationship was carried into the professional field. As a medical doctor at the Military Hospital, Kanbe had employed this relationship to his advantage. He would always confirm his prescriptions with his pharmacist colleague before issuing to patients. The result had been a high cure rate and his popularity as the best doctor in the hospital.

Fame, however, came with it own price – or reward. He was granted a scholarship to pursue a specialist programme, coming back as a pathologist. His reputation kept increasing until he was drafted into the security service and subsequently became the head of the elite SkyHawks team with his American counterpart.

Before the autopsies began the two pathologists held a meeting to discuss the procedure they would follow due to the complexity of the task ahead. This was the first time they had seen people dying from touching a dead person who had died from poisoning.

They discussed the time scale for the five bodies and the careful handling of the bodies and body parts to ensure their own safety. They planned the layout of the surgical instruments and assigned to themselves responsibilities for the various sections of the body according to their individual speciality and experience.

The autopsy on Mike's body was the first to be performed. The two pathologists wore gloves and protective clothes designed for high risk handling of poison-related deaths.

The post mortem examination was delicate and difficult. Kanbe had the difficult role of searching the pockets of the victims to confirm their identities and Rudolf had the delicate role of taking skin tissue samples from the bodies.

Inside Mike's breast pocket was a dozen-capsule pack. One capsule was missing. The label on the packet read 'Vitamin C'. Rudolf checked the body for mortal wounds or any physical damage and noted Mike Zinbalan had a gunshot wound to his right shoulder. It would be the only external wound among all five bodies.

The two men examined the rest of the external part of the body. They noticed a thin film of water – sweat, most likely

– covered the pores of the body in a spotted pattern. A biopsy was inevitable. A tissue sample was taken and kept in a preservative solution for this purpose later. For now they would have to continue with the autopsy.

Rudolf opened up the body. He was a pathologist without a background in Medical Science, having qualified in Biochemistry, and held an MPhil in Physiology. Using a scalpel with scales marked on its blades he made a Y-shaped incision from shoulders to mid-chest and down to the pubic region, pausing at the left shoulder to remove the single bullet buried deep inside. There was almost no bleeding. The incisions were carried down to the rib cage and breastbone and the cavity which contains the organs of the abdomen. The scalp and the soft tissues in front of the chest were held back and together while they looked around for any abnormalities.

Kanbe, using a special vibrating saw, opened the skull vault making two saw cuts, one in front and one in the back. He still remembered the legal problems he had had with his first autopsy where the dead person's family would not accept the body back because of the visible cuts. He had since discovered this was an important safety feature to ensure the cuts do not show through the scalp when it was sewn back together. This way, he assured the family the pillow on which the dead person's head rests would conceal it.

Rudolf was responsible for the chest area. He had performed autopsies on behalf of the Federal government alongside a team of pathologists. It had not been by choice, as his boss had recommended him for a pathology course and he had obliged. He cut the cartilages joining the ribs to the breastbone in order to get to the chest cavity using a scalpel. He did not expect any fractures and was not surprise there weren't any because there was no cardiopulmonary resuscitation.

Rudolf brought out the oesophagus, stomach, pancreas, duodenum and spleen from the abdominal cavity. He opened these, checked them and saved a portion of the gastric contents to check for poison. He then removed the liver, weighed it at one thousand six hundred grams and noted it was a hundred grams more than normal. He examined the inner structure and found it to be fatty. It was too light, too orange, and a bit too big. Perhaps he had been drinking heavily for a while, but that wasn't his concern.

They were nearing the completion of the autopsy and Kanbe was preparing the big needle and thread to sew up the body. They returned all the internal organs, except the portions they had saved, to the body cavity, conscious of the appropriate laws and the wishes of the family. The breastbone and ribs were replaced in the body. The skull and trunk incisions were sewn shut in a baseball-stitch fashion. The body was washed and put away.

Kanbe performed the histology on the blood, urine, bile and the fluid they had extracted from the eye for the suspected poison or any other substances in the body. He produced microscopic slides and examined the sections, keeping the glass slides and a few bits of tissue.

When they finished they carefully cleansed the surgical instruments in chemical solutions, removed their protective clothes and went into their respective offices to write their sections of the report.

Tomorrow the next body would be done.

***

Rudolf decided on the third day of the autopsies he was going to give up meat. By a strange coincidence he found out his colleague, Kanbe, was also a vegetarian for the same reason, but hadn't given up meat until he started his specialisation as a pathologist. He had seen enough of cutting up dead bodies in three consecutive days. It was too much for him. The night before, he had woken up sweating and shaking. He was back in America and had visited a Bobby Van's Steakhouse in downtown Washington. He had walked down 15th St., NW, entered the restaurant and had ordered the porterhouse steak accompanied with a la carte orders of potatoes and various garnishes.

A waitress wearing strange clothes came to serve him. He reached for the cutlery and lifted an axe and a large garden rake. He looked down to his food and dug the rake into the steak and started cutting, but instead of an axe he was cutting with scissors. He took a bite from the steak. It was raw and when he looked at his food he found out he was cutting through a human body. He woke up with a scream. Thank God it was just a bad dream, he thought with relief as he lay in bed.

Rudolf loved steaks and he had been to Bobby Van's on several occasions. "It's a man thing," he would say to his colleagues. As a beef connoisseur the reputation of Peter Luger's in Brooklyn as the quintessential American steakhouse didn't escape his notice and so on a vacation to New York he had decided to verify this reputation.

A landmark since 1887, Luger's had remained little changed, maintaining its reputation with a single main course. Rudolf finished his meal at Luger's and decided on his verdict – Bobby Van's was better. They were more adventurous with their recipe. The steaks were tastier, with style and variety.

Suddenly, the thought of his exploits at Peter Luger's made him want to puke. He got up and went to the bathroom, but except for a short string of saliva nothing would come out of his stomach. He checked the time and it was half past three. He went back to bed, but could not sleep and then he decided not to eat meat ever again.

In this age of technology, why do we still use this crude method to perform autopsy? Rudolf thought. His colleague Bill Anderson at the National Space Biomedical Research Institute in Houston had told him about new developments in medical technology… How a near-infrared spectroscopic technique could be used to test blood without having to extract it with a needle, or test skin tissue without having to cut into it. Rudolf thought a technique that would do autopsies without having to cut the dead bodies open would be a breakthrough.

***

As Rudolf lay tossing on his bed the sunrays crept through every single space into his room, gradually increasing in brightness. He was in Ghana where the sun never forgot to rise in all its majesty every morning. He checked the time again. It was quarter to six when he dragged himself out of bed and prepared to go to work. He got there early.

In the next two days the team finished the autopsies and finalised their reports.

Kanbe read the entire report, then walked across to Rudolf Reinhardt's office.

"Oh, I see you're still reading the report. I'll come back later," Kanbe said.

"No, take a seat; I'm almost through with it."

"Strange eh?"

"Yeah, how could they have died just through skin contact?"

"It's not through food or drink; there is no evidence of any."

"Sergeant Yankey wouldn't be part of their party."

"What do you think?" Kanbe asked finally.

Rudolf had been doing some serious thinking long before he read the report. He had concluded it was poison all right, but not in gas form. Chris and the rest would be dead otherwise. It wasn't food or drink. Sergeant Yankey would be alive otherwise.

What poison would kill on skin contact? The question glided through his brain like a phantom through the night sky. He was clueless. Was Chris responsible? He had had the opportunity but what was the motive? Why would he involve Amofa's family? It was a puzzle – a puzzle he knew he had to solve. The solution, he knew, lay in the capsule, but the test showed they were normal Vitamin C capsules. Something still told him the answer lay in there, but he could not substantiate it.

"I don't know what to think," Reinhardt said to Kanbe matter-of-factly, then looked at his watch. "We have a meeting with Paul Nadan in half an hour."

Alari Kanbe and Rudolf Reinhardt sat next to Paul Nadan in the plush office of Ghana's most feared security chief. Local myths abound about Paul. He was believed by many to have the magical powers to become invisible and that also made him invincible against his enemies, of whom he had many.

The most potent of all the myths about Paul Nadan was he could read people's minds. This myth was given credence by the fact that each time he was personally involved in interrogating someone the truth always came out. Perhaps the psychology of the myth had its own mythical powers over his victims.

Paul had a folder in front of him which contained exactly five pages. Each page held a report of the autopsy on each of the five victims. He had read the reports earlier. He opened the folder and said, "Let's start with Sergeant Yankey."

Paul took this particular case personally. Besides the fact that the incident was unprecedented, Sergeant Yankey had been his friend. They had grown up together at the Burma Camp Military barracks because their fathers were military officers. They had attended the Armed Forces Primary School as kids and gone on to Achimota Secondary School together.

Yankey joined the police service after secondary school while Paul went to university, but they maintained their friendship and so Paul had been upset when he heard the news of Yankey's death. He had gone to give his condolences in person to the bereaved family.

The report concluded Sergeant Yankey had died from excessive amounts of a venom-like poison. The only other thing was Yankey's liver was found to be fatty and the report concluded he might have been a heavy drinker. Didn't Paul know that? He had often teasingly told his friend to drink in moderation but Yankey had been drunk when he was called to the crime site. This probably contributed to his lack of discretion at the crime site and ultimately caused his death.

Paul turned to Mike's report. Apart from the difference in weight and sizes of the organs, the only significant difference was Mike's report contained an additional section – Missile wound. The rest of the reports were similar and the conclusion of the cause of death in all five was the same – high doses of poison.

"What is the next stage of the investigation, gentlemen?" Paul had two things in his mind: what sort of poison had been used and why the crime had been committed.

Kanbe was the first to respond. "We are still interviewing neighbours and relatives," he answered, relishing his position as the leader of the SkyHawks team. He needed to prove to his boss he was in control of the situation.

Paul had suggested Kanbe specialise in pathology and had helped him to arrange for the necessary government funding. Paul had later recommended him to head the SkyHawks team.

In both his personal and professional life Paul had built around himself a group of loyal friends. He had a way of finding out where one's talent was and telling it back to the person like a fortune-teller, which gave him a great advantage.

Paul would encourage and persuade people to develop themselves, building trust and loyalty in the process. He would provide the support if it were within his means and the people he helped became his eyes and ears. They would volunteer information to Paul even if this endangered their own lives because they either owed him a favour or they were confident he would not betray their trust.

"What I mean is how you are going to progress with identifying the poison?" Paul clarified, this time looking in the direction of Rudolf. Paul was the type who liked to get to the bottom of things – and quickly.

"We intend to take the samples to the United States for further laboratory tests." Rudolf answered without previous thought on the matter. He hadn't had time to think seriously about it but felt obliged to answer as he interpreted the look on Paul's face as an invitation to provide an answer.

They discussed this new development and agreed for advanced tests to be conducted in the US. It was also agreed Rudolf would personally take the samples and lead the investigations in the US. He was more experienced to take up that responsibility.

CHAPTER 25

Rudolf was a man in his early forties. He had graduated from an Ivy League University, Yale, with a first class in Biochemistry. He was a specialist in chemical and biological warfare and had been the main advisor to the United Nations Weapons Inspection Team in Baghdad after the first Gulf War. Rudolf was known among his contemporaries as a methodical person who paid much attention to detail.

As a student Rudolf had stunned the FBI gurus during a meeting in their Virginia office. He had attended a conference where Craig Brooks, who was then leading a team to investigate some mysterious deaths among veterans of the Vietnam War, had presented a paper on *Vietnam War Syndrome – myths and realities.* Rudolf had approached Craig Brooks after the conference and had mentioned his theory about Vietnam War veterans' condition.

"Can we meet some time to discuss this?" Brooks had said and had given Rudolf his business card.

Rudolf had read about the veterans' condition in newspapers so he knew how they had developed symptoms similar to blood poisoning but would not respond to any blood-poison-related treatment. He was also aware of the veterans' account of how they got lost in the Vietnamese jungle and were sometimes stung by bees and bitten by other insects. He also knew about a certain blood-poisoning plant found in the jungles of Vietnam and inferred that if the liquid from this plant was somehow carried by the bees, which then stung their victims, they could get blood poisoning from this plant.

Brooks had given the go-ahead for Rudolf to take blood samples from veterans who had those symptoms and had matched the poison in their blood to the poison contained in that plant.

The next exercise was to find out how many of them had been stung by bees or other insects during their time in Vietnam. Rudolf found that though some of them could not remember, many of the sufferers remembered being stung by bees on one or several occasions. Rudolf then postulated that since bees would not normally take nectar from these plants the poison would have to have been externally introduced into a nectar-bearing plant used by the bees. He concluded with the theory that the soldiers were poisoned using bees or some other insects as the agents of transmission.

If his theory were correct, Rudolf reasoned, the Vietnamese would have an antidote to the blood poison. His reasoning stemmed from the fact that there weren't any known conditions like that among the Vietnamese veterans although the bees wouldn't differentiate between friends and foes. Besides, the infected bees wouldn't have lived their entire life cycle after sucking the poisoned nectar.

Rudolf's theory was a breakthrough for Craig Brooks. Together they had teamed up with a pharmaceutical company to develop a cure for the veterans. Rudolf's place at the FBI was assured and he had joined them soon after his graduation.

***

Rudolf Reinhardt had come back to the US to lead the investigation into the use of the deadly poison in Ghana from his office in Washington DC. The investigations were meant to establish the cause of death of the five people, but that was just the immediate reason. The long-term importance of this investigation was to identify a possible connection to biological and chemical attacks.

At the FBI research laboratory five samples, labelled sequentially from GH00I/02 to GH005/02 were tissue samples taken from the dead bodies. The sixth sample labelled GH00IA/02 contained the blood of Mike Zinbalan – the only blood found at the crime scene.

There was an additional exhibit labelled simply 'Suspected Substance'. Beneath the label was the word *Dangerous* written in red. This was the rest of a pack of 'medication' found on the body of Mike. After meticulous test procedures the suspect substance was found to be exactly what it said on the pack – Vitamin C.

The tissue samples were also tested and the results were similar to the findings from Ghana.

Rudolf was hoping to get some sort of a breakthrough and was quite disappointed that the results did not reveal anything he hadn't already known. The mysterious deaths in Ghana were taking their toll on him and he began to spend less and less time with his family, but the tests did nothing to provide answers to the kind of poison used.

According to Chris and Inusah, the police officer, Yankey had died upon touching the corpse. The only gun wound among the victims was on Mike's shoulder. This meant that all the others had died from touching Mike who was likely to be the carrier of the poison. This was further confirmed by the autopsy report that the gunshot wound was not fatal.

Normally Mike would not have died from such a wound. If these people had died from touching Mike then he must have swallowed the poison immediately after the gunshot, probably fearing that he was going to die. Why would he have carried the poison to the house in the first place? What had prompted the shooting? As Rudolf pondered these questions there was only one thing certain: Mike had the highest concentration of the substance in his body. It is logical to conclude that Mike had the poison in his body before or after he was shot, Rudolf was thinking. That was his theory for carrying on with his investigation. Hopefully he could have answers to some of these questions from searching Mike's apartment.

The search had been quite revealing. Mike was meticulous. The apartment was clean and tidy, and every thing seemed to be in its right place. Had he always been like that or had he just tidied it up prior to his departure for Ghana? Rudolf wondered. There was no sign of any suspicious substance and there were no medications anywhere in the apartment. Rudolf went through his recent phone bill and, apart from calls to utility companies and the occasional call to his company, there was one number that featured frequently. Rudolf dialled this number.

***

Mike's return from Ghana was a week overdue. He had not called since he went and all Effie's attempts to reach him had been futile. She was getting desperate when she got a phone call from the FBI asking if she knew Mike Zinbalan. Her heart skipped a beat when she answered, "Mike is my boyfriend; is he alright?"

"He is dead," said Rudolf.

"Call me later," she said and hung up.

Effie was shattered. She was too upset to talk. Her whole world had collapsed. Everything around her had suddenly turned dark and shadowy. Involuntarily, she let out a loud scream.

She had fallen in love with Mike and had started thinking about them as husband and wife one day. She knew she had a profound influence on Mike and thought that sooner rather than later he would propose to her. Just before Mike went to Ghana she had seen a wedding dress in a shop window and had spent time imagining herself in that dress walking down the aisle to take her place at his side.

She had, often on her own, said aloud to herself "Mrs. Effie Zinbalan," loving the way the names sounded together. She had dreamt about a five-tier wedding cake and imagined the honeymoon on the Island of Crete.

Rudolf sat in his office wondering if he should have approached Effie with the news in a less dramatic way. Perhaps he had underestimated the extent of their relationship. He decided that he would call her the next day to give her the chance to recover from the shock.

Just before Rudolf finished work for the day he decided to call Effie to console her. When she answered the phone Rudolf said, "This is Rudolf from the FBI. I called to tell you how sorry I am about Mike."

"Thank you," Effie replied.

For a second or so no one spoke, then Effie asked, "Was it an accident?"

"I was hoping I could come to talk to you about it tomorrow," Rudolf replied.

There was another momentary pause as though Effie was thinking about it when Rudolf added as an afterthought, "you could come into my office if that's OK."

"I will come to your office," Effie replied, "what time?"

"What time would be convenient for you?"

"Nine," she suggested.

"I'll see you at nine tomorrow then," Rudolf confirmed and explained how she could find him, hoping that his meeting with Effie would provide clues to the poison.

Effie walked into Rudolf's office at the appointed time. Rudolf was expecting her, but still pleasantly surprised at her punctuality.

"Thanks for coming at such short notice, Miss Demetriou," Rudolf said politely whilst gesturing to her to sit down.

"I had to come because I need to know the full story," Effie replied, still upset.

"Mike died from poison along with four others, including a policeman," Rudolf introduced the subject on a formal basis.

"Who poisoned them?" Effie was impatient.

"Our lab tests show that the poison originated from Mike Zinbalan."

"What? Mike wouldn't kill himself, no, not Mike." Effie was visibly shaken and couldn't believe that Mike had taken his own life.

Rudolf stopped the questions to allow Effie to regain her composure.

"What do you want me to do?" she asked, sobbing.

"We are hoping that you can assist us."

"I mean what will I do without him?" Effie said half screaming, forcing Rudolf to bow his head in silence. "I'll assist you in anyway that I can," she replied finally, thinking it was the least she could do.

"Tell me about Mike," Rudolf requested.

Effie gave an account of her relationship with Mike. She said Mike had been a lonely and private person and didn't have any regular partner until she took the initiative in their relationship. They had grown to love each other, or so she believed. She had found out one day how Mike's parents had died and sympathised with him, and from that time the bond between them had become even closer.

Rudolf was half listening and half thinking. Was General Amofa responsible for the death of Mike's father? Was he taking revenge?

"Did Mike talk about avenging his dad?" Rudolf asked, keen to establish a link. A theory was already developing in his mind.

"No, he never talked about his parents again," Effie answered with certainty.

"Did he mention who his father's killer was?" Rudolf continued with his questions convinced that he was nearer the truth behind the deaths.

Effie was thinking, "He might have done, but I can't remember any name."

"What about any living relative?"

"Yes, I do remember him mentioning his uncle Twi, Two... ne... boa." Effie struggled to remember the pronunciation.

When Effie left, Rudolf went back to his desk, picked up his phone and pressed the number 1 on his phone pad. As the phone rang thousands of miles away at the SkyHawks office in Ghana, Rudolf was grateful for speed dial technology.

"I've got a name for you," Rudolf said when Kanbe answered the phone.

"What have we got?"

"I'm going to have to spell this one."

"Go on," Kanbe prompted.

"Tango, Whisky, India or Oscar, I'm not sure, November, Echo, Bravo, Oscar, Alpha."

"Tweneboa," Kanbe said, recognising the name, "the third letter must be Echo"

"Good luck," Rudolf said.

CHAPTER 26

Mike's relatives were the only ones who hadn't come forward so far. During Chris' interrogations he could only vaguely remember the town Akrokeri where Mike used to live, but did not know who he had lived with and what the town's name was and Sapel Namaal had been difficult to contact. Effie's mention of his uncle's name had added a vital piece to the jigsaw.

Kanbe and Faiza set off for the five-hour journey to Akokeri, which took them through Kumasi, Ghana's second city.

The road from Kumasi to Akrokeri also served as the main road linking the city with Obuasi, Ghana's premier Gold City, but in spite of Obuasi's reputation as home to the world-renowned Ashanti Goldfields Limited the road serving these two cities was narrow and treacherous. Large patches of the macadam had come off, making it an apology of a road.

Kanbe and Faiza experienced two near-accident situations.

"The road alignments have been designed for accidents," Faiza remarked.

"It's a death trap!" Kanbe exclaimed.

"Shouldn't the mines company contribute to improving this road?"

"I think you should be in charge of solving our road problems, not chasing ghosts," Kanbe remarked.

For the rest of the journey, the two intelligence agents sat silently whilst Kanbe concentrated on his driving. At Akrokeri junction, they turned left passing the Akrokeri Training College and entered the small town. It was not difficult locating the residence of Opanyin Tweneboa. People were gathered around the house in mourning clothes and Kanbe assumed they were mourning Mike's death.

The two visitors were directed to Tweneboa's door. Kanbe knocked and a woman in her twenties emerged, wearing mourning clothes. "Can I help you?" she asked.

"We are from the BNI and would like to talk to Opanyin Tweneboa," Kanbe announced, showing his identity.

"You are a day too late," she replied.

"Why, has he travelled?" Kanbe persisted.

"Well, you could say that, he went on a journey of no return."

"You mean he..." Kanbe struggled to find an appropriate word.

"Yes, he passed away yesterday," she said with tears running down her cheeks.

"I'm sorry."

"Can I help you? I'm his niece."

"We wanted to inform him about the death of his nephew, Mike Zinbalan."

"He knew," she replied indifferently and gave them an account of how Tweneboa had died on the Kumasi-Obuasi road along with three others in a road accident. He had heard of the death of his nephew days after his death and was travelling to Accra to claim the body when he met his own death. Their car crashed into a broken down timber truck on the carriageway around a bend.

Kanbe and Faiza were sad and disappointed. Tweneboa was Mike's closest relative and they had hoped he would provide them with information about him. Most of the family members knew of Mike, but no one knew anything about him.

"Did Mike have any other relatives?" Kanbe wanted to glean any information he could get from Tweneboa's niece.

"Uncle Tweneboa occasionally mentioned his cousin who lives in the north."

"Do you know which town?"

"I don't know," she answered, feeling uncomfortable to display her ignorance.

On their way back, Kanbe and Faiza noticed the timber truck that had claimed the life of Tweneboa. Kanbe was not a religious man, and was surprised to hear himself say a silent prayer for Tweneboa. Faiza was surprised however, for a different reason: the truck was still there waiting to claim its next victim, with no visible efforts by the authorities to remove it. It was a shameless waste of human life that could have been prevented with simple common sense, but Faiza did not share her opinion in case Kanbe thought she should be given the post of the Roads Minister.

Faiza hardly listened to international news, otherwise she would have realised that the occurrence of accidents on Ghanaian roads was akin to gun crimes in New York, only the number of casualties involved in each accident was more than each incident of a gun crime.

When Kanbe and Faiza got back to their SkyHawks office, there was a pile of information to go through. Kanbe was sitting at his desk in the midst of sifting through the piles in the hope that he would come out with something about the mysterious poison when his phone rang. Normally, he would have ignored the phone call, but it was the case hotline ringing. He picked it up hoping that this one would be important since a lot of information had come in, most of which had been followed to a dead end. Some of the information wasn't worth the time it took to make the call.

"Can I speak to a member of the SkyHawks team please?" the caller said.

"You're through to SkyHawks, how can I help you?" Kanbe replied.

"My name is Abubakar Al Hassan," he pronounced his full name emphasising the Arabic phonetics. "I have information about Mike Zinbalan."

"What sort of information do you have?"

"I think I know what killed him."

There was a brief hesitation. "Are you sure?" Kanbe asked, not convinced that the person knew what he was talking about.

"He used crocodile bile, which I think he got through me. He said that he was going to use it for research," Abubakar explained, with definite conviction.

Kanbe was transfixed in his chair and for a moment, the receiver hung loosely in his hand. This was the most informative call he had received yet, but could it be a hoax? He hoped not. "Where are you calling from," he asked.

"Tamale."

"I'll arrange for you to come to Accra on tomorrow's Air Force flight, is that alright?"

"That won't be a problem."

Kanbe wrote down some details about Hassan and gave him a reference code for the flight.

The next day the Air Force plane took off on its routine flight from Tamale Airport. The flight, dubbed Airlink, had been initiated for both the military and civilians to bridge the huge transportation gap between the north and the south of the country. This time it was carrying a very important person as far as Kanbe was concerned.

It was the first time Abubakar had been on a flight and his initial nervousness on take-off had soon given way to excitement when they were finally air borne. A few minutes into the flight he had relaxed, pleased with himself and started to enjoy his flight. So this is how it feels when tourists come from abroad to buy my artifacts, he thought. He looked out of the windows and saw the clear blue skies and the little houses and roads of Tamale from the sky. It was beautiful. He went into a deep, dreamless sleep and did not wake up until the plane touched down in Accra.

When the plane landed, Abubakar Al Hassan was met on the tarmac and escorted to the waiting BNI operations vehicle.

"I'm Alari Kanbe, I hope you had a smooth flight?"

"I did, thank you."

At the SkyHawks' office, Alari Kanbe turned on the dictation machine and sat quietly without interruption for the twenty-one minutes it took Abubakar to narrate his encounter with Mike Zinbalan.

Abubakar's information was the most significant revelation since the beginning of the investigation. Abubakar had recognised the photo in the newspaper as the person who had walked into his shop and requested a fresh crocodile skin. It was Mike Zinbalan all right, Abubakar had thought.

He had gone to see his suppliers with Mike who had persuaded them that he needed the crocodile bile to undertake research in America. The clan head, whose permission was required to deliver the bile to him, had granted his request. Mike had been given the crocodile skin and the bile the next day. He had paid them well, taking the bile with him and gave the skin to Abubakar to treat it for him to collect later on. He never returned.

Kanbe listened attentively whilst Abubakar gave his brief account of how Mike had acquired the venom. Kanbe asked a few questions, thanked Abubakar and arranged for his overnight stay and his flight back to Tamale the next day. He then went into his office and typed an email to Rudolf.

***

Rudolf read the e-mail with interest. This was an extra bit of the jigsaw in place, but there were still more questions. He was pleased that at least the motive, or a theory as to what it might be, had been established. Now they knew what poison had been used.

What remained to be answered, which was really what interested him, was why the poison did not kill Mike instantly. How was the poison transmitted through skin contact? He hoped Ben Goldberg might provide him with the answers that he desperately wanted.

Ben had received the news of Mike's death with a huge sense of loss. Mike's input into the company had brought many breakthroughs in their line of business worldwide.

He still could not believe that Mike was the suicidal type or one who nurtured any bitterness in him, biding his time to take revenge. He was always punctual, well dressed and approached his work with enthusiasm and drive. He also had initiative and was always ready to provide innovative solutions to the many problems they came across.

Ben's theory was that people who nurtured bitterness hardly performed at their best either at work or in academia. He told Rudolf that he was willing to provide any assistance that could help in finding out the cause of death of his once star employee.

"Can we come to talk to you tomorrow?" Rudolf asked.

"Sure, I would be happy to talk to you," Ben replied.

As soon as Rudolf walked into Ben's office he knew why Mike's apartment was in such an immaculate condition.

"I'm Ben," he introduced himself as he shook hands with Rudolf and his assistant.

"Rudolf"

"Amy Green"

"Nice to meet you."

The spacious office was well laid out and decorated. The mahogany furniture was modern, but with antique undertones. Two flowerpots exhibited with pride their tropical palms surrounded by ferns at the two corners of the office as one entered. Two three-seater sofas and a two-seater surrounded a glass centre table mounted on an elephant, shaped from ebony. On the huge desk were a laptop, an organizer, two telephones and a penholder.

An older replica portrait of Ben hung on the wall to the left on entrance to the office. The portrait was the first thing to catch one's eye.

By pure instinct, Rudolf knew that behind the portrait would be a door to Ben's secret safe where he would keep records of new products for the market.

The portrait was not meant to conceal because it would be the first place for any person to look for such a safe. Rudolf wondered what information the safe could be holding.

"That's my father Jacob," Ben pointed out as soon as he realised that the portrait had caught his guests' attention.

"You look like your dad, Mr. Goldberg," Rudolf observed whilst admiring the quality of work of this life-size portrait.

"He passed his looks on to me," Ben said with pride and thought to himself: He also inculcated in me the sense of real independence – financial independence.

"Please sit down," Ben said eventually to Rudolf and his two colleagues pointing to the sofas. "Can I offer you anything?"

They both declined.

"Ben," Rudolf started, "can you tell my why Mike would kill himself?"

"No, but Mike was a private person and looked stressed sometimes. Don't we all?"

"Did he ever talk to you about something bothering him?"

"He never complained directly to me and the only problem of his I ever got involved in was to do with his academic life," Ben recounted.

Rudolf and Amy were quietly listening as Ben gave them the background he knew and what he thought about Mike Zinbalan. Rudolf had suggested that they should not take any notes, just listen and watch carefully, but were free to ask any questions that they thought might help the investigations.

"According to my records Mike held a patent with your company and in the event of his death the company became the sole patent holder. Is that right?" Rudolf asked.

"That's right," Ben answered, wondering what that had to do with Mike's death.

"Is there anything you might have said that would prompt Mike to avenge his parents?"

"Is that what happened? He died avenging his parents? God have mercy."

"We don't know. That's what we are still trying to establish."

"We've never discussed his parents before. During his graduation I expected to see them, but I didn't and I never asked him why," Ben replied.

Rudolf turned to Amy and asked them if she had any questions.

"Do you mind if we take a look around the lab where Mike worked?" Amy asked.

"Not at all; you're also welcome to talk to staff members, they could be helpful," Ben replied and led them to the lab where he introduced Rudolf and Amy to his lab staff and showed them where Mike used to work.

They looked round for any suspicious object or substance and casually asked questions about some of the substances they saw in the lab. Amy noticed a set of lockers and asked what they were for. One of the research staff said they were lockers for staff members. "Which of these belonged to Mike?" she asked.

"That one," a staff pointed. "It's never been used since he left to join NASA."

Amy tried it, but it was locked. "Where is the key?" she asked.

"Mike had one, but there should be a spare somewhere," another employee answered and went searching for it.

When the key was brought to Amy, she opened Mike's locker and looked inside. It was empty and clean as Amy expected.

As Rudolf and his team left Ben's premises they spotted Ben standing in front of his office. "Thanks for your time, Ben," Rudolf said.

"You're welcome."

Back at Rudolf's office, the two agents sat down.

"Right, what have we got?" Rudolf asked when they were both settled.

Amy brought out the notes she had written from memory on their way back from Mike's work place and went over the interview. "There isn't anything useful we can get from there," she said.

"Let's get all the information relating to this case together," Rudolf suggested.

Amy got up to bring all the files and they went through all the evidence available from the various interviews and from the lab reports.

"Can you spend some time to put a report together please," Rudolf said, pushing a file towards Amy.

Amy spent the rest of the day transcribing the interviews. The next day they went through volumes of autopsy and lab reports. As the report gradually took shape a picture started to emerge – from Effie's accounts, Mike's parents had been brutally murdered under a military dictatorship. It had been established that Mike was a private person who did not discuss his innermost feelings with anyone and was therefore lonely, even in his relationships. He had bought the highly poisonous crocodile bile on his recent visit to Ghana and from the autopsy report he had died from poison, not from the gunshot. There was only one conclusion to be drawn – suicide vengeance.

CHAPTER 27

Rudolf read the report with interest. It fitted perfectly into his line of logic and conclusion, but there was still one puzzle – how was the poison administered? What had transformed the seemingly normal reptile venom into a highly contagious poison that penetrated through the human skin on contact? It was still a puzzle, but for now Rudolf was happy to issue the report and close the investigation. He would investigate the poison in his own time, so he went through the report and made corrections and suggestions for Amy to include in the final report.

Rudolf was reading through the final version, when his phone rang. "Rudolf Reinhardt," he answered.

"Rudolf, this is Peter Gardener. I have some information for you. Can you come to my office tomorrow?"

"First thing in the morning."

"I'll see you tomorrow then."

Rudolf replaced the handset wondering what information Peter had for him that he couldn't mention over the phone; I'll find out tomorrow. He finished reading the report, but decided that he would not issue it until he had spoken to Peter.

The meeting the following day was brief. Peter Gardener had found a private folder on Mike's computer and thought it might give the investigation team some clues to his death. Rudolf ran through the list of chemicals that Mike had stored. He could have used any one of the forty-two substances on the list or a combination of them. There would have to be a test on this.

"Can I take the computer with me?" Rudolf asked.

"Could you not just copy the information?"

"We would have to check the hard drive for any encryptions. Would that be a problem?"

"No, that should be OK."

Rudolf thanked Peter, took the computer base and left for his car.

Rudolf was on his way to the office when a thought started forming in his head. He slowed down the car to help him think and eventually brought it to a stop, turned it round, and drove off in the opposite direction, heading towards Mike's apartment. It was still a crime scene with the police cordon in place.

Rudolf went straight to the letterbox and opened it with the set of keys he still had to Mike's apartment. As he expected, there were stacks of letters in there, which he removed; then he got into his car and drove off to his office.

Amy Green was going through the report when Rudolf came into the office carrying the computer he had brought from Mike's work place. "Amy, I've got Mike's computer. I'll see if we can get any information about the poison. Could you go through these letters to see if we can find anything useful please?"

Amy picked up the letters, went to her desk and started reading them. As she read each one she was unconsciously placing them into categories:

Junk. Junk. Bills. Junk. Bi…"

She stopped and read the letter she was holding in detail. It was a bill all right, but not the usual utilities. Doctor DeWitt had sent a bill for $550 for professional services rendered.

Amy held the letter for a while, wondering why Mike would be paying medical bills when he would have been on insurance. Then, she looked at the designation of Doctor DeWitt. It read:

Consultant Psychiatrist. She left the rest of the letters and went into Rudolf's office.

"A letter from a psychiatrist," Amy said, handing it over.

Rudolf read the letter. "Let's go pay Doctor DeWitt a visit," he said.

When they got to the practice the secretary told them Doctor DeWitt was with a patient.

"Please tell him the FBI is here to talk to him," Rudolf said, showing his badge.

The secretary disappeared into the building and when she came back, she said, "Follow me," and led the way through the corridor into DeWitt's office.

"Doctor DeWitt, we have come to talk to you about Mike Zinbalan," Rudolf said.

"What about him?"

"We want to know what state of mental condition he was in when he last came to see you."

"That's part of patient confidentiality. I cannot tell you that."

"Mike Zinbalan is dead."

"I'm sorry to hear that, but that doesn't change the confidentiality."

"We think he committed suicide and your cooperation could help us to establish that."

"Right, sorry, have a seat."

Doctor DeWitt gave Mike's files to the agents and added that Mike was on treatment for a rare mental condition.

"And what would that be?"

"It's a condition which affects the part of brain that controls how decisions are made. In Mike's case, once he set his mind to a particular thing, it was difficult to change it."

"In other words, even if it was known that he was going to revenge his parents by his chosen method he couldn't have been stopped?" Rudolf asked.

"Exactly."

"What causes this type of condition?

"It could be hereditary or due to severe trauma caused by shock, which stops blood and oxygen supply to that part of the brain."

Back in the office Rudolf added a few lines to his report with a conclusion that Mike had taken suicidal revenge on General Amankwa Amofa. He closed the file and picked up a folder in his in-tray that Amy had left for him, opened it and started reading the summary of the contents of Mike's computer. He stopped at a page that contained the list of chemical substances. He read it and opened another folder called MZ-X3. Inside, he found pages containing elaborate chemical formulae together with detailed notes. The biochemist in Rudolf was excited as he looked at the complex chemical structures on the screen. He could not help but admire the attention to detail displayed through each step in the poison's development.

As Rudolf rose from his chair, there was only one thought on his mind: the equipment used in processing the poison must be found. He drove to Mike's apartment. It was the third time that he was searching it. He started from the living room, checking every item in detail as though he had all the time in the world. He opened Mike's cupboard at the end of the living room. There was nothing apart from clothes and shoes. He saw a pair of neatly polished shoes, but it was the glitter of polish that drew his attention. A hair lying on top of one shoe was unusually conspicuous. Rudolf bent down, picked it up and put it into a plastic container. He sealed it off and continued to the bedroom.

Rudolf had just left the kitchen area when a thought came to his mind: why was there no coffee in the kitchen cabinets? He went back into the kitchen and lifted the coffee maker. He did not recognise the brand name.

Rudolf returned to his office with the two items he had brought from Mike's house and passed them to the forensic department with a warning to be careful with the 'coffee maker'.

The next morning Rudolf got to work to find a file lying on his desk. He picked it up and looked at it, turning it round like a precious present from Santa Claus on a Christmas morning. Slowly he opened it and read the contents of the first report, then the second, before sitting down.

Mike had used the 'coffee maker' to synthesize the crocodile bile, thus allowing it to be absorbed into the blood stream within one circulation of the blood through the body. Since it took the blood thirty seconds from one heartbeat to circulate the entire system that would be how long it would take to unleash its deadly effect on a victim.

Tetrachlorium. Rudolf recognised the name of this substance. "Why would such a genius want to kill himself?" Rudolf asked himself in amazement. Mike had combined the *tetrachlorium* as a medium in his preparation to allow the poison to be transmitted through skin contact.

The second report showed that the hair found on Mike's shoe was from a hamster. "He used a hamster to test his concoction," Rudolf said quietly.

Rudolf went back to Mike's computer and started reading the chemical formulae again. The poison had been prepared in such a way that it would lie dormant in the body until an artery was fractured. The sudden rush of blood triggered the poison to attain maximum potency and the final blow came before the victim was aware of what was coming.

"MZ-X3," Rudolf said aloud and smiled, "Mike Zinbalan X3. What is X3?"

Rudolf took the file containing test results of sample GH001A/02 and compared the chemical composition of the poison found in Mike's blood to the composition found in his 'coffee maker'. They were an exact match.

He sat back, his expression a mixture of shock, amazement, admiration and indignation that such a brain could have been wasted in such a horrid, senseless manner.

Rudolf shifted to his own computer, made a copy of the case report and prefixed the file name with the word *classified*. He added a paragraph in the conclusion:

The chemical constitution of MZ-X3, the poison used in the McCarthy Hill deaths in Ghana, is so advanced that they have the potential to be used in biological warfare and should therefore be kept out of the public domain until we fully understand how it works.

When Rudolf had finished with the classified version he encrypted it and moved it onto a security-protected part of the electronic data system accessible only by the head of the FBI. He then issued the unclassified version to the SkyHawks office in Accra.

Rudolf rose from his chair, walked to the window and looked out. His stare went past the streets and buildings below, beyond the activities, around and into nothingness. Suddenly his face brightened up, relaxing his tensed muscles. Heaving a huge sigh of relief, he walked back to his desk and called his travel agent. I deserve a holiday, he thought as the phone rang.

CHAPTER 28

American Airlines Flight 675 took off at the Baltimore Washington International at exactly 0845 hours on schedule, bound for Miami.

Rudolf Reinhardt put down the Washington Post he was reading and looked out of the window, taking in the view. He liked the view from the air and never missed the opportunity to ask for a window seat when he booked a flight. He was looking forward to a week on the beach without any interference from work or family when the intercom interrupted his thoughts. The captain's voice came on the air. "Keep your seat belts on until the seat belt lights are switched off."

The plane continued on its ascent, gaining altitude and speed until it reached cruising speed when the seat belts light went off with the sound of a bell.

In the cockpit Captain Mooreland sat next to his co-pilot. For the next twenty minutes after take off Mooreland maintained manual control of the plane before he switched to autopilot. The flight was scheduled to arrive at Miami at 1125 hours.

Since 9/11, unknown to the rest of the world, all commercial planes had been fitted with direct access to the cockpit through a passage just below the cockpit. An automatic mechanism had also been added to the controls to shut all windows in the cabin to stop hijackers from seeing any approaching rescue fighters.

An opening had been created a foot from the front tyres, accessible only to rescue personnel that led to an enclosure big enough to accommodate two people. Inside the enclosure there were two small holes: a peephole and a gun hole. The peephole had two pins fitted to hold a specially designed camera. This facility gave the rescuers a direct view of the cockpit area without being seen.

***

0340 hours, local time. Tuuro Bondana sat in front of the TV in the dimly lit living room of their house in Takpo, a small village in the Upper West Region of Ghana. Next to the couch he sat on was a coffee table, on which there were two items: a cup of coffee and a mobile phone, which doubled as the remote control for the TV. He had clear instructions: switch the television to channel 51 at 0345 hours.

Tuuro had set his alarm to wake him up at 0330 hours. He was dreaming. He was in an airplane and people were running all over the plane shouting. The roof of the airplane was ripped open. He was flying the airplane. It was running on the road and overtaking all the vehicles. He stopped. A crowd came to cheer him.

Tuuro woke up sweating. He had never been in an airplane before, not even been to an airport. His only knowledge of planes was through verbal description and from television channels and films. "What sort of weird dream was that?" he asked himself. He looked at his watch; it was 0300 hours. He wouldn't go to sleep again.

He went into the kitchen and made a cup of coffee.

"I don't need stimulants to keep me awake," he would always tell his friends, but would not stop drinking coffee to prove his point either. He preferred the ground coffee he made himself, calling Nescafe 'toxic waste'.

0345 hours local time. Tuuro picked up the cup of coffee and took a long deep sip. He replaced the almost empty cup on the coffee table and picked up the mobile phone. He depressed the digit 5 followed by I in a deliberate manner as if afraid he would press some other digits by accident – one that he couldn't recover from.

The television burst to life. On the screen was an airport. He could see a number of planes. A plane was just touching down on a runway. He could vaguely read the outline of the words written on the tail. He could make out the letters LUF...

It did not matter. Airlines and their names meant nothing to him. To him, a plane was the means by which he would one day go abroad. Maybe his dream meant that it was time now, he thought. Why did his cousin want him to watch this programme at such an unholy time of night? His respect for his cousin and the fact that his dream of going abroad was dependent on him gave him a blind and unquestioning loyalty. Maybe his cousin wanted him to know how planes take off and land.

There was a plane with the distinct inscription 'American Airlines' just taking off. Tuuro was excited to see the way the plane was taking off. The nose lifted off first carrying the front tyres with it. The back tyres stayed on the tarmac for a few second and then lifted off the ground. As he watched the plane gain altitude he saw something come out from the underside of the plane.

At first he thought it was someone's feet. Someone was falling off the plane. Then he noticed that the tyres of the plane had moved in and the 'hanging feet' closed after the tyres. "Marvellous," he shouted. "I'm going to be a pilot one day," he promised himself with a feeling of excitement.

He looked at his watch. He had been instructed to switch it off at exactly 0430 hours. The programme was getting boring.

All he could see now was an outline of a plane flying and the grey skies with a cloud underneath. Two more minutes and he would go back to bed. Or, maybe his cousin would call him to tell him to prepare to go abroad.

Sapel Namaal had sent the parcel to Tuuro at the village without telling him that his cousin Mike had come to Ghana and had died. Sapel had found Chris' account of Mike's death too implausible to believe and wanted to find out himself before telling Tuuro.

It was 0430 hours; Tuuro picked up the phone, pressed the 'C' button and the TV went off. He went to bed. Unknown to him, 7,000 kilometres across the Atlantic and 11,000 metres above sea level, Flight 675 was under his control.

***

Flight 675 continued on its flight path, oblivious to the fact that it was under a more powerful and formidable 'auto-pilot'. Tuuro's phone had locked into the Cockpit control system via one of the numerous satellites orbiting the earth, which the aircraft control system was currently linked to, overriding both the autopilot and any subsequent manual control systems.

Captain Mooreland and his co-pilot Douglas Bratt were having their meal while talking about the new cabin-crew girl. Sara Fisher was an attractive young woman who had just graduated from the flight training school as an airhostess and was on her maiden flight. She had instantly attracted Douglas' attention with her sleek, slender body.

The two pilots stopped their conversation abruptly as Sara came into the cockpit with coffee for them. Douglas' eyes were following her movement as she placed the coffee down with her knees slightly forward, lowering herself in the process without bending her back.

She had an exquisite figure, and Douglas could not help but notice. When she had finished, she walked with the grace of a catwalk model into the first class cabin.

"She should be in the modelling business," Douglas remarked after she had left.

"Keep your eyes off her or else your numerous lovers will carve you into pieces," Mooreland cautioned as he thought about the number of women Douglas had dated in the last year.

"I'd love to see her on my private catwalk," Douglas said, ignoring Mooreland's caution.

"I'm too old for this model business," Mooreland observed, as he also walked into the cabin thinking how automation had made a pilot's work so easy. He would not have to touch the controls again until they were getting ready to land. In the aftermath of 9/11 leaving the cockpit door open was a security risk but he hated the idea of getting stuck in that narrow space for the entire flight duration.

On his return he saw on the LCD panel *aircraft u-turn manoeuvre at 10:15*. It was 10:13.

"*Boy*, you think this baby is some kind of Gameboy?" Mooreland asked his co-pilot while his eyes remained fixed on the display. The question was more of a statement, but his use of the word 'boy' signalled danger.

"What's the problem, Captain?"

Mooreland ignored him and continued staring at the information on the LCD.

Douglas followed the Captain's gaze and read the information. "I haven't touched anything, I swear," Douglas said, alarmed.

1015 hours. A new message on the LCD read: *u-turn manoeuvre in progress.*

Captain Mooreland sat at the controls, disengaged the autopilot and tried to regain manual control. The message on the screen changed to *action not recognized, aircraft returning to base.* Mooreland tried to maintain calm and rang the control tower to enquire about any emergency interference. There was none. Then he panicked.

"Mayday, Mayday, Mayday. BWI Radar. Alpha, Alpha. Boeing 747 Flight 675.

Aircraft moving in wrong direction, manual control impossible. Military escort requested. Overhead Atlanta, Georgia at eleven thousand metres, heading zero five zero. Full instrument rated, 353 POB."

"Alpha, Alpha. BWI Radar. Roger your Mayday," the distress call was confirmed at BWI Airport.

Mooreland pressed the button for the intercom and said, "This is Captain Mooreland; we have just been advised of severe weather conditions at Miami Airport. Planes are being diverted to the nearest airport. For your convenience we are returning to BWI."

Inside the cabin Rudolf's intelligence mind told him something wasn't quite right. He took a quick glance around him, got up from his seat and walked to the WC. He was standing behind the engaged door looking round to see if he could spot anything suspicious when Douglas walked up to him and asked, "Is everything alright?" Douglas had been asked by Mooreland to take a walk in the cabin and observe if there were any signs of terrorist activity.

"Sure," Rudolf answered, convinced by the way the question was asked that there was something amiss.

Douglas continued casually but cautiously down the aisles looking for people using computers, mobile phones, or some digital equipment that might interfere with the flying instrumentation. Most people were sleeping and the few still awake were reading newspapers, a book or just staring blankly into the cloudless sky above through the windows. Only one WC was occupied and Douglas knew it was the man he had passed who was inside. Everything else seemed fine, so he started on his way back to the cockpit.

As soon as Rudolf came out of the WC Douglas went inside and that alarmed Rudolf. He must be looking for something, he thought, but went to his seat and sat down.

Douglas walked into the cockpit just as Mooreland's headset came to life. "What's the situation?" the voice from the control tower asked.

"The plane is on its way back, and I can't control it."

"What's going on?"

"I don't know," Mooreland answered in exasperation.

***

Seymour Johnson Air Force Base. Two F-15E Strike Eagles took off carrying two passengers: Andy Whittaker and Ron Condola. Their role was to storm the aircraft and take control of the situation.

In addition to the two crewmembers the F-15E could carry a third and a weapon systems officer in the rear cockpit. The dual-role fighters had the capability to fight their way to a target over long ranges, destroy enemy ground positions and fight their way back out.

The 4th Fighter Wing at Seymour Johnson Air Force Base was the first operational F-15E Strike Eagle wing in the Air Force. It used an APG-70 radar system, which allowed aircrews to detect ground targets from longer ranges, picking up details like bridges and airfields on the radar display from more than

80 miles away, while detecting close-range targets as small as vehicles.

The aircraft's low-altitude navigation and targeting infrared for night (LANTIRN) system consists of two pods attached to the exterior of the aircraft. The navigation pod contained terrain-following radar, which allowed the pilot to fly at a low altitude following cues displayed overhead. The second pod, the targeting pod, contained a laser designator and a tracking system that marked an enemy for destruction from as far away as ten miles.

Once tracking had been started targeting information was automatically transmitted to infrared air-to-surface missiles or laser-guided bombs. The LANTIRN system gave the F-15E unequalled weapons delivery accuracy.

If the aircraft had been hijacked the hijackers might force the pilots to send false information. Ground control needed to know what was going on.

The camera had an infrared facility linked to controls in the F-15E which then relayed the pictures to the control centre at the Seymour Johnson Air Force Base.

Andy Whittaker and Ron Condola were among the first to train for this type of operation. In fact, they had both been involved from the conceptual stages, making suggestions as to the sort of equipment required. Ron's suggestion had resulted directly in the incorporation of the camera to the gun hole.

Andy was feeling the tension when Ron's voice came over the headset, "Ready to kick some ass, pal?" he asked with excitement as they drew close to the target.

"You bet I am," Andy replied without much conviction, wishing he was at home with his fiancée making arrangements for their planned marriage. The training period was over, now was the time for the real thing.

The two fighter jets were within radar range of Flight 675. They had travelled in one formation from their base. Five minutes to rendezvous and the rescuers could see the American Airline directly in front. The fighters banked in opposite directions as they approached and sandwiched the commercial plane.

Rudolf's worse fears were confirmed when he spotted the fighter planes. He got up from his seat and approached a cabin crew with the name badge Sara Fisher. Discreetly he showed his badge to her and asked, "Miss Fisher is there anything I can do to help?"

"The captain says everything is under control," Sara replied.

"I don't think so. We are being escorted by fighter planes; surely they must need some help. Can I talk to the captain?"

"We have been instructed not to interrupt."

"Is there anyone inside the cockpit beside the pilots?" Rudolf asked.

"No."

"Call me if you need any help," Rudolf said and started uneasily back to his seat.

The passengers had spotted the fighter planes on both sides of their plane and got alarmed – some had started screaming.

"What in heaven's name is the problem?" one passenger shouted to no one in particular.

The plane was on its normal flight path except flying in the opposite direction and the passengers were demanding answers.

Inside the cockpit, Captain Mooreland was battling frantically to regain control of the aircraft when Ron's voice broke his concentration.

"Is everything OK?" Ron asked.

"Everything is *not* OK; the damn controls are jammed," Captain Mooreland fumed with frustration.

Ron was beginning to have doubts about the hijack. He had a feeling that this was a technical glitch, but had to prepare himself for a hijack situation; no assumptions. He was ready when the F-15E bridge was released.

Midway beneath the fighter, a door slid backwards making way for a bridge to drop fifty metres down. A hundred metres away the other fighter released its bridge from the undercarriage allowing it to drop fifty metres.

The two bridges lifted slowly until they became perpendicular to the fighter planes, attracted to each other by a magnetic force. They joined underneath the American Airline with a click, prevented from wavering during the joining process by the magnetic pull.

The bridge, now complete, opened up to form a passage for the two combat rescuers to storm the plane. The three planes were now flying parallel to each other.

Andy checked his guns in their holsters, made sure he could get them out in a flash, and waited. He was a ranger and a bomb disposal expert but his focus now was to take out any terrorist before they had time to think. If it was a computer glitch he was sure Ron, the computer systems engineer, would handle the situation.

Andy saw the flash signal on what appeared to be a wristwatch, then lowered himself onto the bridge. At the other end he saw Ron also descending. The two armed rescuers, with straps holding them to the bridge, slid along, lying flat on their backs and propelled along the bridge's railing like a good old steam engine on its maiden journey.

The rescuers came to a stop underneath the massive commercial plane with their heads almost touching each other.

The mission was as dangerous as it was daring. They went to work right away, but it took them a good five minutes to get the underside cockpit rescue door opened, a job that had taken them five seconds under practice conditions. The wind power was so strong that at one point Andy thought the bridge was going to snap, but it was no ordinary bridge – it had been made with high-tension flexible material and tested under extreme conditions. With quick presses of the latches that held their straps in place to the rail the two were up. Ron went inside first, followed by Andy who closed the door behind them. The bridge separated, each half falling slowly into vertical position before lifting up and disappearing into the belly of the fighters.

Inside the enclosure Ron removed a camera from his back-pack. From inside the camera case he removed a cable and inserted it into the camera. He then removed a plastic cover above his head to reveal a small hole that opened directly into the cockpit. He waited two seconds, pushed the round end of the camera into the hole and turned it clockwise until he felt a click. The sound could hardly be heard.

With the camera in place and the cable dangling behind him, Ron removed his palm computer, plugged the other end of the cable into the computer and inserted the miniature wireless card.

When he was done he turned on the computer first, then the camera. He touched the camera icon on the computer. The screen went blank for a fraction of a second, then live again. He signalled to Andy who stretched his neck to see a display of the entire cockpit. At the same time the first pictures of the cockpit of Flight 675 were picked up at the military base.

Using the arrows on the computer key pad Ron moved the head of the camera round to look at all areas inside the cockpit. They could only see two people who appeared to be the pilot and his co-pilot.

"Are these two not the pilots?" Andy whispered his question.

"It could be anybody," Ron whispered back. "Ready?" he asked.

Andy nodded.

Ron pressed a button on his palm computer. The trap door opened and almost simultaneously Andy was inside the cockpit with his gun ready to fire. Ron was only seconds behind Andy also with his gun ready and assessing the situation in the cockpit.

After confirming the pilots' identities Andy asked, "Is everything all right?"

"I think it's a computer glitch," Mooreland replied, removing the headset from his head and attempting to explain the situation while the co-pilot kept his eyes on the display panel.

The two soldiers lowered their guns and put them in their holsters. Ron brought out a cable from his bag, connected one end to his palm computer and the other end to the plane's central processing unit. His diagnostic software would tell him any problem on the aircraft. He touched on the diagnosis icon and waited for a few seconds, but nothing happened. He tried a few things then realised that the computer had frozen. Nothing would make it work. He cursed under his breath and said to Andy, "Let's check the cabin. I'll go first, you cover me."

They moved into the cabin one after the other, noticing that apart from the scary looks on the passengers' faces everything else seemed normal. As they moved down the aisles, the passengers assumed the worse.

"Has the plane been hijacked?" a passenger asked as Ron walked past.

"No, it was a false alarm but for the sake of security we're escorting the plane back to BWI," Ron replied.

Andy, who was walking down the other aisle, stopped at Rudolf's seat and said quietly, "Miss Sara Fisher tells me you're an FBI agent?"

"Yes," Rudolf replied showing Andy his badge.

"Is there anything suspicious you would like to tell us?"

"I don't even know what is going on."

"The plane was thought to be hijacked, but so far we haven't seen any hijacker on board," Andy explained.

"I'm not sure I can help you, but I noticed two people using computers. Could they have interfered with the flight controls?"

"Possibly, do you know who they are?"

"The first one is two rows behind me on the aisle seat and the second is about four rows behind."

"Thanks," Andy said, moved away and called the base. "There is one FBI agent on board. His name is Rudolf Reinhardt."

Rudolf's name and description were checked at the FBI head office as he contemplated the soldier's explanation for their presence on board. To bring fighter jets to escort their plane meant there was clear and present danger, yet everything seemed normal except for the soldiers' presence. He wondered what might have happened inside the cockpit to raise an alarm warranting the need for military escort.

Rudolf's thoughts were cut short with the angry voices coming from the passengers as the two armed men walked down the aisles looking out for anyone using electronic gadgets.

Andy found the two laptop computers where Rudolf had told him. He asked the owners to surrender them, explaining that they would be returned to them on landing. Ron had also taken a third computer from a passenger.

When they had finished checking all the passengers, Ron went on the intercom: "Ladies and gentlemen, my name is Ron Condola, I'm here with my colleague Andy Whittaker, Special Forces from Seymour. The situation is now under control and we appeal for calm while we take you safely back to BWI."

Inside the cockpit Captain Mooreland had given up trying to gain control. He simply resigned himself to the unknown force, hoping that the plane would land safely. He could see the airport in the horizon and the plane had started its descent.

On the ground, every bit of information received was being scrutinised in detail, looking out for any message that might be encoded in everyday language as Andy Whitaker sent updated information of the situation on the plane to the control staff.

Voice analysers were being monitored to spot any distress in the messages being relayed. Although nothing unusual had been reported yet, the situation was still being treated as an emergency – all flights going out of the airport were cancelled and in-coming flights were diverted to nearby airports.

Security agents and emergency vehicles were gathering at BWI. Twenty emergency vehicles backed by armoured military vehicles lined the periphery of Terminal 3 where the plane was coming in to land.

Ron came into the cockpit as the plane started on its final descent into BWI. "Any new developments?" he asked.

"Same old story," Mooreland answered in a resigned tone of voice.

"Are we going to make it?"

"I sure hope so," Mooreland replied, turning on the microphone. "Cabin crew prepare for landing," he said as the plane descended towards a runway.

Three pair of eyes were all glued to the cockpit controls when the plane touched down. Ron's eyes were on the LCD as the screen flickered and the display changed to *Thanks for your cooperation, goodbye.*

The manual control sprang back to life and Captain Mooreland took over slowly bringing the plane to a stop in the middle of the runway.

A hundred metres from the ground the two F-15Es continued their flights as if heading for a collision course with the terminal buildings. They performed a ninety-degree manoeuvre, flew vertically upwards and disappeared into the clouds.

On the tarmac military vehicles surrounded the plane with their weapons aimed at it until all six emergency exits of the huge Boeing 747 opened to the relief of the terrified passengers.

"Mr. Reinhardt, you're required to proceed to the FBI operations room near the immigration area," Andy said and went for the microphone. "Please proceed calmly using the nearest exit," he announced.

Rudolf was one of the first passengers to leave. As he stepped onto the tarmac, he was amazed at the number of security agents and emergency staff helping passengers into the waiting buses to be taken to the passenger holding area under heavy security guard. He also noticed the presence of a SWAT vehicle and knew that forensic, computer and bomb disposal experts would be inside waiting to board the plane. Rudolf got on the bus, recalling details of the events inside the plane. He would have to tell the FBI investigation team what he had seen.

Ron and Andy were the last to leave the plane and as the two rescuers entered the terminal building they saw armed guards every hundred metres. Andy spotted one of his colleagues and waved as he walked past. As they approached the immigration desks Andy noticed the unusually long line. "Why the hold up?" he asked.

"I think it is security," Ron replied, pointing to a passenger being hand-searched after going through the security scan. Each passenger was then directed to the temporary office for questioning.

At the temporary office of the security agents, Rudolf introduced himself to the team of FBI who were conducting the investigations.

"Mr. Reinhardt, you have been directed to lead this investigation," an agent said, handing over a faxed document of instructions to Rudolf.

Rudolf read the instructions and then set out with his FBI team to conduct the interviews. The crew members were interviewed first. Rudolf listened to each member's version of the mental agony they'd been through, most of which he already knew.

"You were on the flight, you should know what happened," Sarah Fisher said angrily to Rudolf when it was her turn to tell her story.

"It'll be helpful if you could tell us anything that I might have missed, maybe something that happened in the cockpit;" Rudolf said.

The calm in Rudolf's voice meant to sober Sarah didn't achieve the desire effect. "The only thing that happened there was that those pilots didn't keep their eyes on the damned controls," she blurted.

"Thank you for your time, Miss Fisher," Rudolf said and watched her walk out of the room. What would the pilots know? he wondered.

As Captain Mooreland gave his accounts of the events on the plane, Rudolf grew more confused. Nothing made sense to him. Something wasn't quite right and the only emerging pattern was that the problem, whatever it was, came from the cockpit. Rudolf asked for the detention of the two pilots for further questioning.

After four hours of interviews and detailed scrutiny Rudolf and his team released all but six passengers. Two of those detained were on the police wanted list for botched bank robberies. The other four had no known criminal records but were held for the simple reason that three of them had been using computers during the flight.

The fourth detainee hadn't actually used a computer but was held for a possible link to a passenger who was using a computer. "The terrorists are out there, go get them and leave us alone," the detained passenger burst out in anger as he was led away.

***

The investigation into the 'hijacking' of American Airline Flight 675 had become a newspaper sensation but after a week of investigations and a complete check of the plane no evidence could be found of the alleged hijacking. The FBI couldn't find any link between the computer users and the strange behaviour of the aircraft. The two bank robbers were released without charge and handed over to the Montgomery County Police where the botched bank robbery had taken place.

Rudolf followed several leads but soon dropped each one of them and his only possible scenario was that the two pilots, or one of them, had sabotaged the flight. Whatever the reasons were, he was bent on establishing them.

Rudolf Reinhardt was getting impatient with the lack of progress in his investigations as he sat facing Captain Mooreland across the table in the interrogation room at the FBI office. "Can you go over what happened on the flight again please," Rudolf asked.

Captain Mooreland and his co-pilot had been detained under the terrorism act and as Mooreland sat there he was beginning to lose his patience and sanity. He could not believe the arrogance of this FBI guy. How could they even suspect him of attempting to hijack his own plane? The world has gone insane, he thought. He took a deep breath and for the fifth time narrated the events in the aircraft from take-off to the time they landed.

Rudolf scratched his head and moved the hair falling over his forehead backwards. How come this hair only falls when I'm thinking? he asked himself as he analysed the sequence of events in his head. The plane had taken off, attained the required altitude and speed. It had been turned on to autopilot and then suddenly out of nowhere the plane had begun to display unusual messages. The plane had turned itself round and landed safely where it had started. The pilots claim they had no hand in this. There was no malfunction in the autopilot and no one had claimed responsibility.

"Can you receive email or text messages on the cockpit display?" Rudolf asked, as though he had already solved the puzzle.

"Our systems are linked to the Global Positioning Systems so technically one could send messages through either medium."

Rudolf's face lit with excitement. That was it. Why hadn't he thought about GPS before? He looked at Captain Mooreland and they both nodded in agreement without a word being said. They understood each other. If Rudolf's theory was what Mooreland was thinking, the plane had been remote-controlled.

"But, why?" Mooreland asked.

"Tough question, but let's concentrate on the how. I will need to check the three computers." Rudolf had seven more days to hold the pilots.

Alone in his office Rudolf spent six hours checking information on all three computers which were still in the FBI custody. None of the computers had been connected to the internet during the course of the flight and no links to any of the aircraft's controls were found. Rudolf's eyes were still fixed to the screen of the last computer but he was not looking at anything in particular. He was gazing blankly on the screen, lost in thought. "Did we check all the mobile phones that people had in the aircraft?" Rudolf asked himself, as though he was responding to hypnotic suggestions. He took the list of the phone numbers and checked with the phone companies. The phone records of all the passengers were checked for the day of the incident but no such messages similar to those displayed on the plane cockpit had been sent through their respective networks.

Rudolf had come to a dead end. Not again! he thought, but somehow he still felt that the answer lay there somewhere. He could feel it had something to do with GPS, either using a computer or a phone. How? Still he thought Captain Mooreland was hiding something.

Rudolf Reinhardt walked out of his FBI office into the waiting crowd of news reporters who had been camping outside his office since the incident. Their cameras were flashing and questions from all directions muffled into one big noise.

"What was the cause of the hijack?" asked a reporter from Sky News.

"One of our theories is that the hijackers used a mobile phone or some similar gadget to remotely control American Airline Flight 675, but due to the diligence of our defence the situation was contained. We believe that the hijackers are linked to Al-Qaeda operating from deep inside Sudan," Rudolf replied.

"So, are we going to attack Sudan?" another reporter asked.

"That's for the President to decide."

CHAPTER 29

Sheila Quarshie had been following the news of the attempted hijacking of Flight 675 on a daily basis in the Ghanaian capital, Accra. She had read the latest that linked the hijacking to the use of a remote medium by the Al-Qaeda network in Sudan.

The inscription on the door to her office read *Network Security Officer*. In reality, she was a state intelligence operative on the payroll of the BNI. Her actual role was to keep a random check of all telephone conversations and text messages that came through the Areeba Network to ensure that state security was not compromised. She walked into the Areeba building and made her way into her office, put the morning newspaper she was holding on her desk and set to work. It was a job she revelled in.

As a security officer her pay was far in excess of what a top corporate head would earn in Ghana. Besides, her two children were studying abroad under government sponsorship. She was rich and enjoyed her wealth, justifying her life-style as the successful computer guru behind the success of Areeba. It had started late as a mobile phone network provider in Ghana but had grown to become the biggest and the most profitable, covering the entire country.

Sheila was an ambitious computer expert in a male-dominant profession and she was ready to make her mark. She had suggested the use of Areeba as a brand name to market Ghana Telecom's mobile telecommunications network. The 'funky' name, as the Ghanaian youth found it, had increased the company's market share.

With the new government, security had been taken to new levels with the help of other international security agencies. Ghana had learnt her lesson the hard way and had come to accept democracy as the way forward but could only thrive on a solid security foundation. Ghanaians had said no to military takeovers and it was up to the government to ensure that they did not happen.

With her influence, Sheila had suggested to her bosses that to be an effective intelligence gathering institution the coverage had to be nation-wide. The government had then supported the company to cover the whole country, which gave them an added advantage over their competitors. It yielded additional benefits too – most Ghanaians living abroad would connect their relatives, particularly those living in rural areas, to Areeba for easy contact.

Sheila was on her daily routine in front of one of several computers in her office scanning all messages and focusing on certain key words and phrases. On one of the computers text messages were scrolling up the screen. The program Sheila was using allowed her computer to beep when any suspect message was picked up and the information would then be written to a log file and printed out.

Thanks for your cooperation, goodbye, the text message flashed by; *u-turn manoeuvre at 10:15,* another message flashed by. She routinely looked at the text messages on the screen – they were just part of the long list of messages that she heard and read everyday; she carried on with her work.

Sheila had chosen Information Technology because it was the profession of the moment. She had dedicated herself to her study but now that she was reaping the benefits she wasn't sure if that was what she really wanted to do. She used to imagine herself writing huge computer programs that would do these wonderful things, but here she was scrolling through this screen day-in and day-out, occasionally laughing at people's stupid text messages. Her work had become routine but she still enjoyed the prestige that went with it.

Sheila picked up her newspaper on her way out for lunch. While eating her lunch she read through the headline stories. The Flight 675 hijack had ceased being a major headline story so she turned to the international news section to read about the latest development on the hijack. She saw the news item tucked into one column. It stated the pilot's version of events during that infamous faceless hijack. A transcription of some of the things the pilot read on the cockpit LCD was: *Thanks for your cooperation, goodbye.*

On her way back to the office after lunch Sheila felt something lurking in her mind, but she wasn't sure what it was and dismissed it. Sitting at her desk she checked her log files to see if any message had been picked up during lunchtime but there wasn't any. She turned her swivel chair to face the text message computer, then she remembered what was on her mind – the transcribed message of the pilot.

She took the newspaper, read the hijack story again and the message leapt into her face; she had seen it on her computer. The words in the text message hadn't met the criteria for it to be beeped or logged. She pressed a set of keys on her computer keyboard and the message sprang up. She matched the rest of the messages against the messages that were reported to have appeared on Flight 675. They were word-for-word the same. Her air-conditioned office did not help; Sheila was sweating. She took her car keys and her sunglasses and walked down the stairs that took her to the car park.

Sheila did not report to anyone at Areeba and did not have to tell anyone she was leaving. That was the privilege of being her own boss, she thought, as she walked towards her car. She drove directly to the BNI headquarters and at the entrance to the building the security personnel recognised her behind her designer sunglasses, opened the big metal gates and waved her through. She parked her car at a space marked Reserved – Network Security Advisor, walked into the secretary's office and asked to see the BNI boss. Paul Nadan was in a meeting with the heads of security, a routine meeting to assess the security of the country. Sheila scribbled a note and gave it to the secretary to pass it to Nadan.

There were some people in the outfit who had Paul's priority attention and Sheila Quarshie was one of them. As soon as Paul read the note he excused himself to the eight heads of security, came into the secretary's office and invited Sheila into a separate room.

When Sheila had told her boss what she had found out, Paul went back, apologised to the security chiefs that something urgent had come up and adjourned the meeting until further notice. With that he dismissed them and went into his office.

"Sheila, this is a top-priority case so we need to involve the head of SkyHawks and get to work on it right away. Can you wait?"

"Yes," Sheila obliged.

Kanbe had just finished talking to Rudolf Reinhardt in the United States about his ruined vacation when Paul called.

"Can you come to my office as soon as possible please?"

"I'll be right there," Kanbe said, picked up his brief case and walked across the grass lawn to the office of Ghana's intelligence boss.

"The reason I called this meeting at such a short notice is that Sheila has just discovered that the phone used to hijack American Airline Flight 675 could have come from Ghana."

"That can't be true! Rudolf was on that flight," Kanbe exclaimed.

"That's right, Mr. Kanbe. The phone was used right here in Ghana and the details are registered on our database."

"Is there any way we can identify the person?" Kanbe asked.

"I think we can trace the phone. That is, if it is still being used or switched on," Sheila replied.

"How long will it take to do that?"

"If the phone is turned on it should only take a couple of hours."

"If we do find this person can we make an arrest?" Kanbe asked.

"No we can't; no crime has been committed in this country. We can only investigate officially once we have had a request from the United States Government," Paul replied.

"What do we do now?" Sheila asked looking at Paul.

"I'll come back to you on that," Kanbe answered.

"Can I leave it to the two of you to work this out and keep me updated?" Paul asked and they both nodded in agreement.

As soon as Kanbe returned to his office he prepared a report and sent it through to Rudolf Reinhardt.

***

Rudolf read the report with growing anxiety and wondered how an incident that happened on an internal flight in America could have anything to do with Ghana. Since his assignment to the SkyHawks Team in Ghana he had witnessed several bizarre incidents.

Rudolf prepared a memo and sent it to Craig Brooks, Head of the FBI, whose rise to his current position was attributed to his ties to the President. Rudolf remembered when he first met Brooks at the conference. He was glad he had done so because following their joint work on the Vietnam Veterans, Brooks had made sure that Rudolf's job was guaranteed.

Rudolf looked at his watch; it was past his lunch hour and he was hungry but dreaded going out of the office building. The press had been gathered there since the Flight 675 incident and although Rudolf had been ignoring their questions he felt they deserved some information – only he hadn't any.

As Rudolf walked towards the main entrance there was only one phrase in his mind for the press: Nothing to report.

The first question Rudolf could make out from the jumbled sounds of a thousand voices was: "Who was responsible for the hijack?"

Rudolf ignored the microphones being thrust to his mouth and continued fighting his way out. Then someone asked a question that stopped Rudolf in his tracks. "Can American people trust the intelligence community to help protect the motherland?"

Suddenly, he felt that he owed it to the American people to let them know what was going on. Without a second thought, Rudolf spoke directly into the score of microphones in front of him. "We are working on the theory that the plane might have been hijacked by remote control. Thank you."

"I don't believe this," a reporter remarked.

"It's almost surreal," Rudolf agreed, and continued down the flight of stairs ignoring all the subsequent questions.

***

While Rudolf was on his way to lunch Craig Brooks had skipped his lunch break after reading the memo. He called the President and briefed him about the latest development on the Flight 675 hijack. The mystery surrounding the plane's hijack had caused the President to ask for regular briefings.

When the President finished speaking to the FBI chief he called the Head of Homeland Security and gave him a set of instructions. As soon as Bruce Atherton finished speaking to the President he made five quick successive phone calls.

At the Office of Homeland Security Bruce Atherton sat with the FBI chief, the CIA chief and three other computer experts from the Pentagon responsible for network, telecommunications and military satellite communications security. This was Atherton's first meeting regarding a direct threat to homeland security. He had to get it right. "Fellow council members, thank you for coming at such short notice. We are all aware of the events of the last two weeks with the hijack of Flight 675. What I would like to suggest is that the FBI and the CIA provide all the intelligence available to the Pentagon. We will also have intelligence coming in from our allies. In the meantime we have issued a directive banning the use of mobile phones, computers and electronic gadgets on all commercial flights."

The directive had devastating consequences on AirMobile, a company that had invested heavily in futuristic mobile phones in airplanes. News of the AirMobile's imminent collapse reached the Oval Office in the White House as the President of the United States was preparing to hold discussions with his Defense Secretary, the Joint Chief of Staff, the Security Advisor and the Secretary of State. He was furious about the impact this act of terror was having on the American economy. I cannot allow terrorism to destroy our civilised way of life, he thought as he walked into the Oval office where his 'war cabinet' was waiting for him.

"Fellas, I've asked Bruce Atherton to recruit the best people to take control of this new threat to our homeland security. At the same time we need to take military action against this Asian country."

"Ghana is in Africa," the Secretary of State, who was sitting next to the President, whispered.

"I require you to come up with a military strategy within the next two days," the President continued, ignoring the correction.

"The Government of Ghana is not directly involved in the situation and they are prepared to assist us; perhaps we should talk to them first," the Security Advisor suggested.

"Perhaps we need to find the person involved first," Brooks said.

"It better be quick. We can't wait for any more similar incidents. God knows where the planes would be directed to next," the President concluded.

After the meeting Brooks went back to his office and called Rudolf. "How close are we to finding the hijacker?" he asked.

Rudolf had just sent a request to his elite team in Ghana to provide details of the phone's usage and where to locate the phone and the user. "We expect to have some positive results soon," Rudolf told Craig.

"I need to know as soon as you have any information."

"I'll keep you informed."

***

Sheila Quarshie had been waiting for authorisation. She took the file marked *Flight 675* from her Action tray and opened it. Reading from it, she typed the phone number into a search space on her computer and clicked on 'search'. She focused on the screen, analysing the information she was reading. Apart from the control message sent to Flight 675 the only other use was the phone call made to the national emergency number 999 with a request for police and ambulance at Amofa's residence at McCarthy Hill.

As Sheila had expected the phone was not registered in anyone's name. Most criminals would give false information; in the case of Areeba no records of phone users were kept. People found their own phone, bought a SIM card and were connected. When the units ran out they bought more credit to top up and everyone was happy. Still, it was part of her new proposal to the Areeba Board of Directors that details of people who bought and used SIM cards should be kept on their database.

Sheila had been working for nearly three hours trying to locate the phone without success. It had not been used since the Flight 675 scare and it was effectively dead. She was beginning to get frustrated. The only possible option left was to find the location of the last place of use but she didn't have the technology to undertake that task. Besides, the user could have long moved away or even disposed of the phone or...

She bit her finger, her mind wandering; then it started to occur to her. Why hadn't she thought about it before? she asked herself.

Sheila remembered the gruesome deaths at McCarthy Hill. General Amofa had been an acquaintance and they had met a couple of times at the neighbourhood drinking spot. She had read the news about the mysterious deaths and wished she could know how it all happened. Now she was going to be part of the solution of those mysterious deaths because when she passed the information to SkyHawks she was almost certain that the arrest of the big fish was imminent.

Kanbe received the news that the phone that had been used in hijacking the American Airline was the same phone that had been used in making the emergency call. "If we find the person who last used the phone for the 999 call, we have our man," Sheila told Kanbe.

Kanbe sat down in disbelief as the events surrounding the deaths flashed through his mind. Chris had almost convinced him of his innocence during the interrogation with his sincere expressions and conviction of what he was saying, which was corroborated by Amofa's children.

Kanbe retrieved the case folder and read Chris' statement over again trying to spot any inconsistency, searching his memory at the same time, but he could not find any. His criminal records check had shown no previous convictions either in Ghana or in the United States and his military career had been spotless. However, this new development had put a new twist to the case and Kanbe started to wonder whether Chris had been acting. He brought the recording of his interrogation and watched it for about an hour, pausing occasionally and replaying some scenes.

He made a call to Rudolf.

"We have cause to believe that Chris Tagoe has something to do with the hijack," Kanbe told Rudolf, explaining the findings from Sheila Quarshie.

"We'll have his apartment searched immediately," Rudolf said, thinking that as a member of the US Armed Forces Chris would be investigated according to the rules of the military and if found guilty of any criminal act he would be charged under Military Law.

"Where is Chris now?" Rudolf asked.

"He is still in Ghana and under surveillance," Kanbe replied, glad that Chris was still under their watchful eyes.

Faiza Iddris had been assigned to Chris Tagoe as soon as he was released by the BNI. "We want to make sure that he doesn't abscond, so keep him in sight until we can bring charges against him," Alari Kanbe had told Faiza.

CHAPTER 30

Chris Tagoe woke up the day after his release thinking about the events of the last few days and hoping that they were just nightmares. As he lay in bed contemplating them with self-pity with no-one to turn to, an involuntary smile came over his face. The thought of Betty Brown flashed through his mind and in an instant he had forgotten about the pain and agony he had been through; he was thinking of how to make contact with Betty.

After all, he was innocent and if his fiancée refused him because of the mix-up life must go on. There are many fish in the sea, he thought. He had to take his chances with Betty.

He looked at his watch. It was ten in the morning and Chris dragged himself out of bed and went into the shower. After washing and shaving he went through his clothes deciding which to wear, finally settling on a white shirt over dark-blue trousers, and put on some Bulgari Black eau-de-toilette. He had to make an impression on Betty and could not afford to make mistakes.

It was lunch time when Chris got to Chopsticks restaurant where he hoped that Betty would be working that day. He took a quick glance, but he didn't see her.

"Table for one?" the waiter asked.

"Yes," Chris answered, resisting the temptation to ask for Betty right away.

After looking through the menu he ordered a vegetarian meal. The food arrived and as he started to eat it felt strange because he wished he was sharing the meal with someone he loved – Betty. He ate in silence, taking his time, as though he was afraid to finish the food. He wasn't really hungry; he had lost his appetite for food since the door to his lover's heart was slammed shut in his face and had come to the restaurant to look for Betty. He had hoped desperately that Betty would call him to console him, knowing that it was not going to happen. They hardly knew each other.

"Excuse me, is Betty working today?" Chris asked as a waitress came to clear his table.

"No," she replied, "but she is working tomorrow."

The next day Chris came back to the restaurant. He couldn't get Betty out of his mind. Maybe it was a blessing in disguise that he couldn't marry his fiancée.

"Hi, Betty, I've been waiting for your call," Chris said as she came to take his order.

"I have been busy at the uni," she replied.

"Have you got a minute?"

Betty looked round the restaurant. There were a couple more people in there. It was early afternoon and the restaurant didn't get busy until early evening.

"Sure," she responded.

"Are you free to go out tonight?"

Betty hesitated and then asked, "What have you got in mind?"

"I was hoping we could go to see a movie."

"I would love to."

"Does that mean a yes?" Chris asked with excitement.

"Yes," Betty replied shyly.

After the movie, they stopped at Afrikiko Gardens for drinks.

"Do you believe in love at first sight?" Chris asked Betty after they had ordered drinks.

"Yeah, I do believe you can fall in love with someone on a first meeting. Why do you ask?"

"I'm in love," Chris said.

"Ha, ha, really?" Betty asked unconvinced, but enjoying it all the same.

"What would you say if I asked you to marry me?"

"I would say I don't even know you."

"You never know anyone until you've lived under the same roof."

"True, but that's a level up in a relationship," Betty responded, enjoying the direction of the conversation.

The drinks came and Chris poured Betty's drink into her glass, then poured his own.

"Marry me," Chris asked.

Betty choked on her drink while laughing. "Couldn't you have waited for me to swallow my drink before dropping such a shocker?" she said. She stopped laughing when she detected a serious look in his eyes and her heart started to beat faster. She hoped he wouldn't hear it. "Marry you?" she asked, "we've only just met and I don't..."

"You just told me you believed in love at first sight," he said.

Betty fumbled with her drink and began to speak with a stammer that wasn't there before.

"Well, I did say I believed in it, but I didn't say it was a licence to marriage. Besides, I'm not even sure I'm attracted to you, let alone want to marry you."

"You're attracted to me and you know it," Chris said firmly, "your eyes betrayed you. Or you're not aware you have expressive eyes?"

In response Betty looked down, unsure of what to say.

"I don't think you would be here with me on a date if you didn't feel anything at all for me," Chris continued.

There was silence as Betty stretched to pick up her drink. Chris held her hand, brought it closer to him and said, "Look, we are adults and I believe in going straight to the point. I'm in love with you and as fate would have me believe I know that in your heart you know you're in love with me too. Let's not deny ourselves what we both know and feel is right. Marry me Betty."

Betty Brown felt Chris' grip tighten around her palm and she felt a wave of sensation shudder through her body. She had liked him when she first saw him at the restaurant, but to get married – she still wasn't sure. She would take her chances, she decided.

"Yes, I'll marry you. I know this is probably the craziest, most impulsive thing I've ever done, but I'll take my chances. Still I have to get to know you before ..."

"We have the rest of our lives to do that," Chris said with excitement. "Can I see you tomorrow?" he asked.

"OK," she replied.

They spent the next couple of days together. On the third day Betty asked Chris about his friend. Chris was silent so she asked, "Is he alright?"

"Have you not read the news?" Chris asked surprised.

She listened as Chris explained the circumstances surrounding Mike Zinbalan's death and how he had spent a day in the hands of the BNI.

When he finished, Betty held him close to her body. "I'm sure you'll be alright," she said.

"With you everything will be all right."

Betty's mind was racing. She had become comfortable with a feeling of security around Chris. She had no problem marrying him, but what would her parents think? She had finished her final examinations at the University but still had her dissertation to complete for her honours degree.

When Betty broke the news of Chris' proposal to her parents that evening she was expecting opposition and had prepared for that. She was pleasantly surprised at their reactions as the dreaded opposition from her father turned into music in her ears. Her father, Jake, had asked in an almost jubilant voice, "You've finally found the man of your dreams eh?"

Just as she was wondering if her father was being sarcastic and trying to play a wicked joke on her, her mother walked close to her, put her arms round her shoulders. "Do you love him?" she asked.

"Yes, Ma."

"Who is he? Betty's father asked.

Betty told her parents about Chris and his involvement with investigations surrounding the Amofa residence deaths. As Betty narrated the story her father was inwardly happy about the final elimination of General Amofa. Someone had had the balls to take care of him, he thought as he remembered the brutality of the General during his days.

"Just be careful," her mother had advised.

"I will," Betty had answered, thinking to herself: one can't be careful enough with men, just when you think you know them well enough they spring a surprise on you. Betty was determined to find out more about Chris during their weekend away at Lake Bosomtwe, about half an hour's drive from Ghana's second city, Kumasi.

On their second day at the Lake Hotel the couple were on the lake in a boat taking in the beauty of the scenery around them when Chris said, "I'm arranging our wedding in two weeks."

"We can't plan a wedding in two weeks!" Betty exclaimed, turning to face Chris. Her sudden movement made the boat, which was sitting idly on the water, wobble.

"Just get busy with your guest list, I will handle the rest."

Betty had brought Chris home the next day and introduced him to her parents on their return from the Lake. When he left Betty informed her parents that their wedding would be in two weeks.

"Why the haste, you still have your dissertation to finish," her father cautioned, but Betty had her own ideas. If they got married now she would join him in America as soon as she handed in her dissertation. She would not let this opportunity pass her by.

***

Saturday, 18 May, 1100 hours. The bridal party arrived in a well-decorated limousine. The ceremony was short and brief at the Marriage Registry in the Registrar General's Department. The family and friends of the bride and groom rose as the bridal party entered the marriage hall and took their seats. The officiating Attorney stood in front of the couple. "By the authority vested in me by the state I now pronounce you husband and wife."

Chris kissed his wife amid flashes of camera lights. As they came out of the marriage hall Chris led Betty away from where the limo and the photographers were waiting.

He had a surprise for her.

At the end of the walkway a carriage with two horses and two coachmen was waiting. Chris had shipped the Victorian horse-drawn carriage from England for his wedding. The four-seater carriage stood proudly enjoying the impact it was making on its admirers, showing off its classic black leather exterior and its gold-painted wooden wheels.

"Please," Chris said, and held the carriage door open for Betty.

She stood there, speechless and motionless. Her feet started to wobble as Chris helped her into the carriage and followed.

"Why did you do this to me?" Betty asked recovering from her shock.

"This was meant to be a surprise and the carriage is your wedding gift," Chris replied.

"You're heaven sent," she said and kissed him.

***

Faiza Iddris was up early on the day of Chris' wedding and had mixed with the filming crew, keeping her distance and making sure that she didn't stand out. The Victorian horse-drawn carriage carrying Chris and Betty, whom she was filming, fascinated her. It was the first time she had seen one outside of movies and television screens.

The horses moved along, uneasy at first, then stabilized after a few minutes. The hood of the carriage was brought down to reveal the immaculate velvet red inside, displaying her prized occupants with pride and glamour. The journey to the reception took the bridal convoy past the imposing National Theatre building and turned right at the traffic light towards Liberation Circle, followed by a convoy of family and friends.

Traffic had come to a standstill, not due to traffic jams, but to drivers stopping to catch a glimpse of this out-of-a-movie spectacle. The spectators had become one with the bridal convoy and together they lived a dream. Chris noticed a camerawoman who was not the official one filming the event. She held the camcorder close to them for a brief moment before the carriage started to roll again, putting a distance between them. Faiza Iddris got into her unmarked car and moved along with the wedding convoy. The carriage continued on its maiden journey drawn by the two majestic horses.

Chris looked at the dilapidated buildings around Flagstaff House with nostalgia as the carriage went past. The once-official residence of the first President of Ghana surrounded by army staff quarters now all stood in ruins.

As the carriage made a right turn opposite the Military Hospital into the Officers' Mess, where the reception was being held, Chris looked at Betty and smiled.

"Why?" Betty asked.

"You're beautiful," he replied just as the carriage came to a stop.

CHAPTER 31

When Faiza presented Chris' surveillance report to her boss following the wedding, she was in for a surprise. Kanbe went through the report, smiled at the last photo showing Chris helping Betty out of the carriage and closed the file. He then opened his drawer, removed an envelope and passed it over to Faiza. He watched as she opened it with a suspicious look.

"What is this?" she asked, her suspicion turning into surprise.

"You're going to South Africa tomorrow."

Faiza returned the plane tickets to the envelope and put them away in her hand bag. She had been on assignments abroad before but this would be her first time in South Africa. The trouble with her job was that she never got to enjoy her travels.

Alone in her office she went through her equipment, checking each item against her checklist. When she had finished, she packed them into her travel case and left for home. She finished packing her personal stuff, took a shower and went to bed, then felt something hard under her pillow. She put her hand underneath and felt the book she had been reading the previous night: *The Art of Being Invisible – The Agent's Survival Kit.* Faiza got up, walked to her wardrobe, selected a suit and some accessories, put them in her bag and went back to bed. It is going to be a long flight tomorrow, she thought as she went to sleep.

The next day at Kotoka International Airport in Accra, Faiza waited in the departure hall until Chris and Betty had checked in before approaching the check-in desk. The man behind the desk neither asked for Faiza's passport nor her luggage; he just winked at her, handed her a boarding pass and said, "It's a window seat behind the couple. I'll make sure no one sits next to you."

"I owe you one," Faiza said with a smile as she walked towards the departure gate. Faiza was the last passenger to board the plane and as she walked past the couple to take her seat she avoided eye contact. She sat behind Chris and Betty, fastened her seat belt and waited for the pre-departure safety instructions before setting her voice recorder. She then connected her headphones and put them over her ears making it look like she was listening to her own music. Twenty minutes after they were airborne the crew served their first meal and after Faiza had finished hers she reclined her seat, lay back and fell asleep.

Nine hours later the South African Airline plane touched down at Cape Town Airport. In the arrival hall Faiza watched the couple go to the Avis Car Rental desk. She waited until they had left before she approached the woman behind the desk.

As they pulled out of the parking lot and made their way out of the airport area Faiza was on their trail. She followed as they turned into the N2 Highway and travelled due east of Cape Town. After about twenty minutes Faiza wondered where they were going. At first she thought that the couple were spending their honeymoon in Cape Town and hoped that she would have the chance to see a bit of the city herself, but now she wasn't so sure, so she just followed. After a two and a half hours' drive the couple turned off the N2 into a property that seemed to be in the middle of nowhere. Faiza drove past them and about a kilometre away turned round and came back to find a sign to a bed and breakfast in Swellendam.

The ten-room bed and breakfast just off the N2 Highway linking Cape Town and Durban was situated on a forty-acre piece of land at the bottom of a valley with a splendid landscape. A hundred metres away from the guestrooms was a four-bedroom country house serving as the living quarters and an office for the owner. A stable stood another hundred metres away to the right of the living quarters and a quiet stream flowed behind the guestrooms. The natural setting of this place indeed provided the right atmosphere for a couple on a honeymoon, Betty thought as she lay next to Chris.

Unknown to the couple, Faiza had tapped into their phone when they were making a booking for the bed and breakfast in Swellendam and had made her own booking soon afterwards. She was looking out through the front window as Betty and Chris walked towards the building, hand in hand. She came out of her room as the couple disappeared into a room four doors away.

"Shit," Faiza cursed. She had hoped that they would be given a room next to hers. She would have to work out something fast to have any chance of keeping tabs on them. She mentally noted the room numbers either side of the couple's room before walking to the reception.

"Are you alright, my love?" the proprietor asked with a smile.

"Sure, a friend of mine is coming here tonight; do you have any more vacancies?

"Let me see," the proprietor replied, opening the guest book. Faiza looked beyond her to see if the keys to the rooms she wanted were hanging there.

"We have two vacant rooms."

"Is Room 10 vacant? It's closer to the stream, I'm sure my friend would like it."

"I'll reserve it for your friend."

"Can I book it now and take the keys? She will be arriving late."

"By all means," the proprietor replied, "what name and address should I use?"

Faiza gave false details, took the keys and was off to move her baggage into the room next to Chris and Betty. She then started to assemble her equipment. She removed a camdropper from its case, examined it and using the plastic suction components stuck it to the wall dividing her room from the couples' and then connected a wire from it to the small screen monitor positioned on the bedside cabinet. As soon as she turned it on, the pictures from the adjacent room came to life showing the couple's movements.

When Faiza was first introduced to the camdropper, she had been fascinated by the ability to use x-ray technology in surveillance, enabling the camdropper to take photos through walls. Although the technology wasn't advanced enough to penetrate all types of walls, it was good enough for most residential properties. The main challenge for Faiza was getting voice recording through walls. In spite of the wooden construction of the accommodation, she found the insulation prevented any voice recordings. After several attempts, she gave up trying to set up the voice recording equipment and settled down to watch the couple on her screen. She wondered why the ultrasonic technology used in oil and mineral explorations could not be adapted for surveillance – maybe Western intelligence personnel were already using them.

She watched the couple sitting at a table eating and realised she was hungry. She reached for her bag and removed her plastic food case containing bread, cheese, dried meat and butter. She ate her food and washed it down with coffee.

The couple were now lying on the bed and talking, but Faiza had no way of knowing what they were discussing. As she watched, her mind wandered away. She had fallen in love with Jones at university and had been looking forward to marriage after graduation, but Jones had left her for a Ghanaian-born American soon after their graduation and she hadn't had a boy friend since then.

It had been four years, but Faiza still couldn't bring herself to date another man for fear of suffering the same fate. Now she was thinking of giving Steve, who had been asking her out, a chance. She had drifted to sleep in her thoughts and had forgotten to put a tracking device on the couples' car.

Faiza woke up early the following morning and waited until the couple had finished their breakfast. She drove off before deciding what she would do. Chris and Betty had turned left at the exit from the bed and breakfast into Swellendam town centre so Faiza decided she would have breakfast before tracking them. From where she sat eating she could see any car coming from the town centre onto the main N2 Highway.

After breakfast Faiza had walked the short distance into the town centre going towards the Drostdy Museum Complex when she saw the couple come out. She then brought her binoculars up, pointed them in the direction of the Langeberg Mountain Range beyond taking in the picturesque view. Her sunglasses and her long braided hair made her look different from the woman who had been in the plane with short hair and no glasses. Thank God for wigs, she said to herself as she blended in with the many tourists in the town. That evening Faiza waited until the couple had gone to sleep, then came out of her room and stuck a magnetic tracking device under their car. That would keep them in touch, she thought as she opened the door into her room.

The next day Faiza was up with the rising sun. She blinked at the sudden bright light and looked at her watch. It was seven o'clock. She sat up, drank from her water bottle and hoped that the couple hadn't already left, but it wasn't until well after nine that they emerged from the breakfast room and walked back to their room. Faiza saw them put their luggage into their car and realised that they were going to check out. She removed her camdropper, assembled her equipment and packed her clothes. As soon as the couple were out of the property Faiza went to the reception and checked out. She turned her car onto the main road heading westward, a good three hundred metres behind the couple. After about two hours she came off a bend only to find out that they were not in front, so she increased her speed with the hope of catching up with them. For the next ten minutes, she drove without spotting them, then she checked her tracking device. At the next exit Faiza turned and followed the signs towards Stellenbosch. As she approached the town she saw the couple inside their car, parked on a dirt road off the other side of the main road. Faiza drove on looking for a place to turn round and wished she had wired their car to hear their conversations. She made a u-turn at the next roundabout and as she came closer to where Chris and Betty had turned off, she realised to her shock what they were looking at. A hill led out of Stellenbosch towards the main highway and as she climbed, spread in front of her like a painted piece of an antique watercolour painting was the sprawling Black township. The ramshackled houses, the lack of drainage and sanitary facilities, the substandard electrical wiring that were ever ready to devour the very masters they served in this post-apartheid South Africa era gave the gloomiest picture of what it had been like before. Faiza felt the warmth of her tears ran down her cheeks and let them run until she tasted the salty liquid on her lips. She wiped her tears, her heartbeat rose with her rising anger and frustration at the apparent lack of progress since the beginning of majority rule by the ANC.

In her angry mood Faiza failed to see the couple come out of the township towards the highway. When she realised they weren't there, Faiza started her car, checked her device and followed them. Thirty minutes later Faiza was three cars behind them in Cape Town. She had come to a stop behind the queued traffic at the steepest part of a road, facing uphill. The traffic started to move, so she had engaged first gear and was about to release the hand brake when she saw the car in front backing into hers. She pressed on the horn, but it was too late. The car crashed into hers forcing a backward ripple effect for about five cars in succession. She cursed as she got out of her car to confront a group of youthful holiday backpackers. She was confused.

"I've called the police," a driver from one of the affected cars told them.

"What do I do now?" Faiza asked with frustration.

"We just have to wait for the police."

Faiza waited with growing frustration for what seemed like a long time. When the police arrived, she found their accident reporting procedure to be painfully slow. It was late evening when she got through with the legal process and drove to the nearest Avis garage, but her frustration turned into desperation when she found out that she couldn't get a replacement until the next day.

The following day she picked up another car and worked frantically to transfer her surveillance equipment. As soon as she had finished reassembling the equipment she turned-on her tracking device and the monitor sprang to life. She checked the couple's location, started her car and drove off towards the city. Thank God for satellite navigation, she thought as she followed the direction towards Cape Town train station.

The distance to the car started to reduce faster than she was travelling. There must be something wrong, Faiza thought, then realised that the car was being driven towards her. She watched as the car drove past her in the opposite direction. She slowed down and prepared to stop and turn round when something struck her. There was only one person in that car, a male driver who Faiza didn't recognise. Her instincts told her to continue to the train station so she accelerated.

At the station she removed her two bags, one containing her equipment and the other her clothes, from her car and went to the passenger waiting area. On the information screen she saw the Rovos train was next to depart in thirty minutes.

"Where is this train going to?" Faiza asked a passenger on the platform.

"It's not a passenger train; it's for tourists going to Vic Falls."

"Thanks." Faiza was almost running towards the ticket office.

"You're lucky ma'am, a family cancelled their ticket yesterday," the woman at the ticket desk said, "but it's an expensive one because of the size," she added.

"I'll take it," Faiza said, pushing her credit card towards the ticket salesperson.

"Here you are. Enjoy your holiday."

"You're an angel. My friend Chris and his wife will be glad I made it," Faiza said, "do you know their carriage?"

"Err, let's see. What's his surname?"

"Tagoe."

"Ah, Chris and Betty, they are in Cabin 2 in the second carriage," the woman said, reading from her passenger information page on her computer.

"Many thanks."

Faiza walked along, looking around the platform. There were passengers getting into the train and some were standing waiting for the next commuter train. As Faiza came to the waiting area she saw Chris and Betty sitting in front of a café chatting. She turned round before they could see her and got into the second carriage. She found Cabin 2 and went in. She was impressed with the beauty of the interior décor but she had no time to think about luxury now. She went to work, fixing a radio transmitter beneath the double bed and placing the microphone underneath the sofa. She had just finished and was about to leave when she heard the door open. She froze, holding her breath behind the door. Racing in her mind were a dozen possible explanations of why she was there. She was about to meet them and say wrong cabin when she heard Betty speak.

"Let's check out the restaurant first," Faiza heard Betty say, then the door closed.

Faiza heaved a sigh of relief and waited a few seconds before stepping out of the cabin. How could she be so stupid? she asked herself. After all her main job was to ensure Chris did not disappear into thin air, but she thought any information she could gather would be useful.

The Rovos train left Cape Town Central Station at 1100 hours. Chris and Betty sat in their double room with en-suite facilities. In the next car, Faiza assembled her surveillance equipment and mounted the camdropper. The couple had just finished their evening meal and were snuggling up in their double bed when Faiza turned on her surveillance equipment. She sat, listening and watching as the couple made love. As she watched them, her mind drifted to how she would plan her own wedding and honeymoon. She thought about all the wonderful things Chris and Betty had led her to see and experience. As she thought about them she suddenly found herself asking the question: How could Chris and Betty afford this sort of expensive marriage? First, there was the horse-drawn carriage and now this expensive romantic journey. She looked at her surroundings and realised that but for her official assignment she could never afford this sort of thing. Could Chris be involved in something more than just the duties of a military officer in America? The more she pondered these questions the more she wanted to know about him.

The train trundled through the spectacular mountain ranges and scenic wine lands of the Cape on its 1,600-kilometre journey across the haunting wasteland of the Great Karoo to the gold-rich grassland of the High Veld. Five days after leaving Cape Town the Rovos train crossed the South African border into Zimbabwe heading for Victoria Falls.

"In ten minutes we will be guests of the world's most renowned spectacle. Ladies and Gentlemen, it will be my pleasure to present you Victoria Falls." The driver slowed the train down and from their deluxe suite Betty could see the spectacular view of the falls, reaching 200 metres into the river pool below. The wonders of mother earth, she thought, just when you think you've seen them all you come across yet another that leaves you searching for words to describe it. She started to sob and let a tear drop.

Chris watched as the tear, obediently yielding to the forces of gravity, continued its descent gracefully like a new love running into the open arms of a lover. It kissed the water below. It had been immortalised and would forever remain part of the pool of water. He turned and planted a kiss on Betty's lips. "There is a God out there," he said.

"Where are we going next?" she asked, resting her head on Chris' shoulder, her gaze still fixed in the direction of the Falls.

Their carriage was just passing the last of them. They withdrew their heads, closed the window and crawled back to bed, holding each other. Betty started to undress Chris as they rolled on the bed.

"To Paris," Chris replied as they pulled the covers over themselves.

***

As Faiza trailed the couple, she was increasingly frustrated that nothing they talked about concerned what she had been waiting to hear. She took consolation in what she was experiencing. Her fascination during their wedding gave way to intrigue on their honeymoon and she had started dreaming of her own future. She was drifting to sleep when she heard a distant voice ask: "What made you go to the General's house?"

Faiza woke up thinking it was someone in her cabin, but realised that it was Betty's voice coming through the microphone. Simultaneously, the voice was picked up at the operational office at the BNI in Ghana. Kanbe's excitement was visible as he thought this was going to be the smoking gun they had been waiting for.

"I've told you that I was accompanying my friend. What else would you like to know?"

"I didn't mean to upset you honey. I just want to convince myself that you're innocent. I don't want anything bad to happen to you and our future."

"I know I could have stopped it, but …" Chris started, but the train manager's voice cut in.

"In thirty minutes we will be arriving at Capital Park Station in Pretoria, our final destination. I hope you enjoyed our exclusive service."

"Damn," Faiza swore and walked over to the window.

"Just shut up," Kanbe shouted as though the train manager could hear him thousands of miles away.

Faiza was still gazing through the window when Chris looked out, and for a split second his eyes locked into hers. A flash of recognition went through Chris' mind, but he couldn't remember her. He withdrew his head struggling to remember the woman, unable to dismiss the familiar face he had seen. He vaguely remembered a resemblance to the woman who was filming at their wedding. He knelt by the bed and started looking underneath.

"What are you looking for?" Betty asked.

"Hidden cameras, microphones..."

"Why, are we in some kind of trouble?"

"No, but I think someone has been following us," Chris said as he pulled out an electronic gadget from under the bed. He then checked round for others and found the microphone under the chair. They sat in absolute disbelief.

"Why would anyone put you under surveillance?" Betty asked, breaking the silence.

"The Ghanaian security thinks that I'm a US spy," Chris lied.

Betty had her own opinion, but didn't say anything until they got into their hotel room. "Is it about the deaths in Ghana?" she asked.

"I think so."

"Why are they doing this?"

"I wish I knew."

When Faiza couldn't hear them anymore she knew that she had blown her cover, so she switched to Plan B. She went through her clothes, removed a particular set and put them on. She removed her braided wig, replaced it with one with straight grey hair and put on her prescription glasses. As she stepped out of the train Chris, seeing her, would have taken her for a wealthy, middle-aged woman on a vacation. With a broad grin Faiza approached the information desk to enquire about flights to Paris.

"There is a flight this afternoon from Joburg. The next direct flight is in two days."

"Thank you," Faiza said, her grin turning into a full-blown smile. She had come to love the way Black South Africans called Johannesburg 'Joburg' with such affection and love and a deep sense of belonging. Occasionally she came across those who called it 'Jozi', but she preferred 'Joburg'.

Chris and Betty boarded Air France Flight 025 at Johannesburg International Airport and when all the passengers had settled down, Chris took a casual look around where they were sitting and was relieved to find that the woman who had been following them was not on the plane. Directly across the aisle from where Betty and Chris sat, Faiza adjusted herself in her seat, fastened her seat belt and opened the newspaper. Her smart but somehow old-fashioned business suit, matching grey hair and her dated glasses would deceive even her own boss. *The Art of Being Invisible* – Faiza thought about her book; it was her favourite.

CHAPTER 32

Charles de Gaulle Airport, Paris. Chris and Betty landed in the city of love, the last leg of their honeymoon before going to America.

In all his travels what Chris hated most was immigration controls. It seemed to him that all immigration officers were hand-picked racists or had been trained to be such and they delighted in humiliating any foreigner. He obtained his Green Card after joining the US Army and he was looking forward to the day he would get his citizenship. He looked at the signs and read the English translations – the first sign with the shortest queue was for French and European Union citizens, the second sign with fewer people in the queue was for American citizens. The last one was for all other countries.

Betty and Chris joined the back of a long queue. Chris had the nagging feeling that they were going to have a hard time at immigration controls. As they approached the desk he saw a man's passport taken away. The man stood to the side looking anxious, probably entering France for the first time. An immigration officer beckoned to Chris and Betty. They moved past the waiting man to the immigration desk and handed their landing cards and their passports to the officer.

"D'où venez-vous?"

"Sorry, we don't speak French," Chris responded, already prejudiced and wondering why the officer thought everyone should speak French.

"Where are you coming from?" The immigration officer asked in perfect English with an almost imperceptible accent.

"South Africa." Chris was getting impatient.

"Business or pleasure?"

"We are on our honeymoon."

The officer stamped both passports handed it over to Chris and said, "Enjoy the love of Paris."

Chris was still standing there, not believing that it had been hassle-free. "Thank you," he said belatedly.

They followed the signs, which were written in both French and English. Chris mentally compared the two and concluded that with a bit of imagination one could figure out the meaning of the French words.

Betty listened as Chris tried to read the French signs aloud with rather English pronunciation.

"You thought you were cheating your French teacher," she said.

"*Mais, je peux lire le français,*" Chris continued humorously, making a mockery of the pronunciation.

Outside the terminal building the couple took a taxi to the Balmoral and checked into Room 57. It was not until five in the evening when they came out of the hotel and walked the short distance along the Champs Elyseés through the Champ-de-Mars gardens. They bought two tickets. First, they went to see the machinery of the 1899 elevator. The voyage underground took them into the world of Jules Verne, to discover the impressive hydraulic machines designed by Gustave Eiffel. The original machinery, which had been restored and computerised, was still in use. The wax characters of Gustave Eiffel himself, his daughter Claire and their famous guest, the American inventor Thomas Edison in his office, looked almost real.

The elevator took them up on a spectacular ascent providing glimpses of the extraordinary bold architecture of the monument, ending in a breathtaking panoramic view of Paris.

They looked over the city and took in the stunning view. "I've never been this happy in my life," Betty said looking at Chris.

He looked at her eyes, they were bright and her lips had become full and inviting. Against the spectacular illuminations of the tower, Chris could see the nipples of her breasts piercing through the cardigan she wore like some mischievous twins taking a peek into the night light from their bedroom windows. Betty looked more beautiful than Chris had ever imagined. Her slender figure, her full hips and the sparkle in her eyes were enough to make any man turn. Dressed in that cardigan gave her the elegance that would make Hollywood stars pale into insignificance. Chris started to dream about her in Hollywood, or maybe as a supermodel. No, not a supermodel, a Hollywood star is what he wanted.

He held her closer, feeling the firmness of her breasts against his chest. He gently squeezed her bottom.

Betty moved her head forward, kissed him and started to rub her hand against his genitals. She opened the zip of his trousers, moved closer and guided him inside her, shifting the front of the G-String sideways.

She sighed with ecstasy, oblivious to the tourists still walking past. She was living her fantasy. She had always dreamt of making love in the city of love, on the tallest structure, on the Eiffel Tower. As Chris succumbed to her fantasy, the world existed only for the two of them. Nothing else existed, at least not at that moment.

The 336-projector sodium lamps of the tower shot their beams upward from the inside of the monument's structure.

Betty, who had her back to the railings, didn't see the uniformed policemen, or the camera wielding couple – the press. The blinding flash and "*Excusez moi,*" were almost simultaneous.

The arrest for indecent exposure was swift.

A few metres away from the couple Faiza Iddris shook her head and turned towards the opposite direction. "I can't believe this," she said, "only a brother can do this."

***

"…the main news headlines…"

Rudolf Reinhardt stopped halfway up the stairs and came back to his living room. He took a sip of the coffee and sat in the sofa.

"Love in Paris brought to its most extreme yet: Sex on the Eiffel Tower," the headline stated.

Jacques Perez picked the phone. "Interpol Paris, how can I help you?"

"This is Rudolf Reinhardt with the FBI." Reinhardt's name was almost a household name among the global intelligence fraternity. It evoked respect, fear, as it evoked instant response. "The man arrested today for the indecent exposure is on the FBI wanted list, could you provide me with details of him, please?"

Jacques took some details from Rudolf and said, "Alright, I'll get back to you." When Jacques called back he told Rudolf that the couple were scheduled to arrive in Boston in two days' time. Rudolf took down the details with excitement and anticipation. His long search for Chris Tagoe was ending.

"Could you arrange for them to drop the charges so he can arrive here on schedule please?" Rudolf requested.

"I'll see what I can do," Jacques replied.

Rudolf Reinhardt picked up the phone and looked at the receiver as if unsure what it was. He replaced it and walked to the window of his apartment where he could see the neon lights of the city. It was just past one in the morning in Washington DC. He had been working late into the night since the mysterious deaths in Ghana and the remote hijacking of the American Airline plane.

It was a real help that his wife and two children were away visiting her ailing mother. Tonight in particular he had worked late than usual, and fate had smiled on him. Suddenly his face brightened. He knew what he wanted to do with that phone, but it was late so he decided he would wait till the next day. He still had two days, no need to rush.

Rudolf's call to Craig Brooks the following morning was picked up by an assistant, who told him that Craig was preparing for a meeting.

"This is urgent," Rudolf said firmly.

After a few seconds on hold, Craig picked up the phone.

"We need to arrest Chris Tagoe, but I want to do that when he arrives here in the United States, so I would like to ask the French to release him," Rudolf said.

"That's splendid. Why don't you go ahead and arrange that?"

***

At the police station where Chris was held, his cell door opened and a police officer shouted, "Chris Tagoe."

Chris blinked and moved forward. He was expecting to meet a lawyer. He had requested one, but the police officer just handed him his things and said, "You're free to go; your wife is waiting for you at the reception."

Chris couldn't believe what was going on. Why hadn't they been charged? Why had he given in to having sex in the first place? Women! – they were the cause of all mankind's woes, he thought. First it was Eve who had seen the two goats in the Garden mating and had asked to practise it with Adam, now it was Betty's fantasy. He stepped out of the police station feeling better that he had someone else to blame, then stopped.

The paparazzi were waiting for them. The flashes were almost blinding. "How did you feel having sex up there?" a woman asked stretching her microphone out to reach the couple. They ignored a barrage of questions and forced their way into the waiting taxi.

The paparazzi followed them to the Balmoral Hotel and laid siege at the entrance until the couple left two days later, staying inside the hotel until their departure.

At the reception desk the two telephone lines had become instant hotlines as couples called to reserve rooms in the three-star, family-run hotel. The arrival of the 'sex-couple' had turned the hotel into a magnetic field for lovers, holidaymakers and curious Parisians. The 57-room hotel was fully booked.

CHAPTER 33

0500 hours, Boston Airport. At the passport control Desk Number 10, a couple presented their passports to the immigration officer, who looked into the first passport. It bore the name Christopher Austin Tagoe. The officer checked his photo against the one pasted in front of his desk. Although Chris' hair had grown long and he was wearing a moustache that went down both sides of his mouth to meet his beard, the similarity was unmistakable. He then checked Betty's passport, returned both to the couple and waved them on. As the couple passed through immigration controls the officer spoke into her handset.

A few metres away Rudolf Reinhardt acknowledged the call and nodded to his assistant, Amy Green. The two FBI agents approached as the couple made their way towards the arrival hall. Betty was holding Chris' arm with one hand and the other clung to her handbag like a toddler holding tightly to a prized teddy bear. Chris recognised Rudolf and immediately sensed that there was trouble.

"Mr. Tagoe, welcome back. It's nice to meet you again."

"Nice to meet you err…"

"Rudolf Reinhardt, SkyHawks."

"Is there a problem?"

"We just require some additional information and thought that you might help us as you promised."

"What do you want to know?"

"We would like you to accompany us to the FBI office for questioning," Rudolf replied.

As they started to move Chris saw Amy exchange a few words with Rudolf, then turned to Chris' wife and said, "You can go home; I'm sure you enjoyed your fantasy together on the Eiffel Tower."

Rudolf and Amy listened as Chris narrated his story about the events leading to the death of Amofa's family and the police officer. As Chris told his story again he realised that the French had released him because he faced charges in the United States. "My involvement in the entire episode is the case of being in the wrong place at the wrong time," he concluded.

"Same story," Rudolf acknowledged. "What's your relationship with Mike?" he asked, looking into Chris' eyes.

"Mike and I have been friends from our university days in Ghana."

"Have you or Mike ever been charged with any criminal offence or inciting violence?"

The question from Rudolf took Chris by surprise. How much did these people know? He had to be careful. Rudolf was watching him as he stalled for a few seconds before answering.

"I don't have any criminal record and both the Ghana Army and the US Army did checks to that effect. I can't speak for Mike, but as far as I know he hasn't either."

Rudolf knew all about Chris' activities as a student leader but none of them constituted inciting violence. He turned to Amy Green and nodded.

Looking down on notes she had been writing, Amy asked, "Chris, how long have you been planning this crime?"

Before Chris started to speak his anger was visible. "Don't be so presumptuous. You have no proof that I am a criminal," he exploded.

"Then explain to me how you came to be in possession of the deadly mobile phone."

"Mike asked me to..."

"So you planned this together," Amy cut in.

Chris swallowed hard and started again. "Mike asked me to take it to Sapel who would send it to his cousin at the village."

"What were you doing at General Amofa's house on the day of the murder?"

Chris took a deep breath, looked at Amy and said, "Mike gave me a lift, but had to stop at a friend of his father's."

"What do you know about the phone?"

"I don't know anything about it. I was just asked to take it to Sapel. Is there anything wrong with the phone?" Chris started to feel alarmed.

Amy ignored his question and asked, "How did you know that the phone would work on the system in Ghana since the phone hadn't been registered?"

"I know that most phones are programmed to dial emergency numbers anywhere in the world. Besides, I was acting on impulse when I couldn't find any phone in the house."

Chris denied any knowledge of, or involvement in, either the poisoning or the alleged hijacking. It sounded believable, but the coincidences were just too overwhelming.

Rudolf was disappointed. He had hoped that Chris would be the last link to the phone, but his testimony left the trail open. He was determined that he would do whatever it took to find that person, so although he was due to return to Ghana after his vacation, he had agreed to stay to help with the failed hijack investigation.

After Chris' interrogation he was escorted to a prison cell and held for further questioning. Rudolf could not afford to lose him. Information from him would be vital in locating the phone and arresting the perpetrator of the attempted hijack. Rudolf sent the contact information and detailed description about Sapel Namaal to the SkyHawks Team in Accra.

***

Sapel Namaal had returned home from work and had just sat down to have his evening meal when the security forces moved in. Three unmarked police vehicles had been waiting outside his house at the Abeka Lapaz suburb of Accra for most of the afternoon. There was a loud bang on his door and when he opened it two armed policemen were standing there.

"Mr. Sapel Namaal?" a policeman asked.

"Yes, is there a problem?"

"We would like you to accompany us to the BNI office."

Sapel's heart skipped a beat, then started beating faster. "Am I under arrest for something?"

"We need to question you about the phone you received from Chris Tagoe."

"I was only asked to deliver it to Tuuro," Sapel protested.

"You can talk about that at the office," an officer said and escorted him to the police van.

Alari Kanbe was waiting when Sapel Namaal was brought to the SkyHawks office. He listened, without interruption, as Sapel explained how he came to be in possession of the mobile phone. After his narration, Kanbe made some notes, then asked, "What happened after you received it?"

"I sent it to Tuuro, together with the local currency equivalent of the one hundred and fifty dollars."

"Did you use the phone before sending it?"

"No."

"What's Tuuro's mobile phone number?"

"I don't know, Tuuro promised to let me have the phone number as soon as he got one, but later told me that because of the freeze on SIM cards he would have to wait until he could get a connection."

"Where is Tuuro?"

"He is in Takpo with his parents," Sapel replied and gave Tuuro's contact address.

"Thank you for your time," Kanbe said.

Alari Kanbe reviewed the new information he had received from Sapel and prepared a brief note. He then walked over to Paul Nadan's office to update him on the development and to get his permission to make an arrest.

CHAPTER 34

Daylight was waning and the shadows of the evening were stealing across the sky. The songs and the drums were sounding with renewed vigour. The citizenry of Takpo had come from far and near to celebrate the annual Wilaa Festival.

It was the largest gathering yet since the restoration of the traditional festival following Naa Widana's ascension to the throne. In the dimly-lit dirt forecourt of the King's palace, a small cluster of minstrels came to the end of a busy, bouncing song and the heaving mass of bodies burst into applause, whistles and ululations.

The man behind the xylophone drained the dregs of his *pito,* the local brew, before nodding to his fellows to take up their drums and with their *cheema* tied to their ankles burst into musical life again. The *cheema,* made up of pieces of metal strung together by a length of string, made a rhythmic sound in unison with each step of the dancers.

Inside the palace Naa Widana was receiving homage from all the dignitaries who had come. Outside it was cooling with the dry windy harmattan weather, the evening pulsating with life, song and spirit.

Music was the very essence of Dagaabas. From Wa to Nandom, from across the dialectical divide of north and south, the familiar strains of traditional Dagaaba music could be heard drifting from one end of the street to the other.

Inside many houses in the village, families and friends met to talk about life at their various places of abode. For some people their conversations had become unintelligible as the power of alcohol in pito took over. It had been the traditional drink for the Dagaabas dating back beyond the time when they settled at their present location.

Tradition had it that pito had the power to keep one cool from the dehydration effect of the high temperatures in this part of the country. Since it was brewed from only the grains of guinea corn without any additives or preservative the drink maintained its nutritional values.

During this time of the year the pito flowed freely and loosened peoples' tongues. It was time to identify the beautiful, up-and-coming young women of Takpo. Most marriages would start or end during this festival. The power of pito had both a social connotation, bringing people together, and an economic connotation, providing employment and income for the womenfolk during the off-farming season.

It had been the tradition to brew it over three days using the choicest of guinea corn, but a citizen had introduced a revolutionary method of brewing into the area. This relied on the household brewery concept, but allowed pito to be brewed in one day instead of three using the same procedure.

The darkness of the night had taken over and the powers of darkness were doing so too – the mystical night-time masqueraders, known locally as *simma,* were in control, with the dim glowing lights revealing little about them. They commanded a lot of respect with lots of myths about them.

Little was ever spoken about the night-time masqueraders. They were the all-powerful creatures from the underworld that could make or unmake things and were revered. As the masqueraders moved slowly and ghost-like towards the palace, the talking drums sounded in a rhythmic way, echoing the praises of Naa Widana, and the trumpets sounded his greatness. The talking drums, the first form of sending wireless message known to man, attracted the masqueraders drawing them in a slow, deliberate fashion towards the drums as though by some powerful forces seen only by them.

Of all the towns and villages around, Takpo had the highest reputation for traditional music, producing the best and the finest festivals in recent years. During the festive week Takpo held some of the best entertainment sessions overflowing with pito, which was to be found in almost every household during the week-long festive days.

Grazing lands surrounded the small village of Takpo, home to some talented, educated and industrious youth who had invested in cattle ranches. The village was thriving on farming and small-scale shea butter processing.

A footpath led from the palace past a house to the left through the rice valley to the Datuoyiri section of Takpo. As the footpath approach Datuoyiri *nim* trees lined both sides like huge sentinels, so tall that their branches interlocked, sheltering people from the sunshine. This section of Takpo was home to the rulers of the town.

Perched on the other side of the valley among a cluster of houses was the home of Tuuro. He was holding a party with his friends on the first floor of their family house. He put on one of his favourite songs, turned up the volume of the music and invited his friends to dance. He accepted a smoke from one of them, lighted it, inhaled and let the smoke out in a deliberate manner. Tuuro would not normally smoke but he was quite tipsy.

"Can we have some special coffee?" someone shouted.

The reputation of Tuuro's special coffee was known throughout the village. He took pride in calling himself *homeboy* because he processed his own delicacies.

On this occasion Tuuro had used cannabis as the herb instead of *nunum*. He had served the coffee and his friends had stopped dancing and were enjoying Tuuro's 'special brew'.

***

The music, drumming and dancing initially drowned the sound of the chopper's arrival. The searchlight swept through the crowd. At first, they cheered with expectancy thinking that this was the late arrival of a government official.

The chopper's searchlight continued along the footpath towards Datuoyiri. It hovered above the trees surrounding the house where Tuuro and his friends were partying.

The sound of the chopper and the bright beams of light flooding the house brought the partygoers to the windows and doors of the house. Tuuro, seeing the chopper so close, sensed danger for reasons he couldn't explain and started to run. The others saw him run and started dashing out of the house.

A tear gas canister fired from the chopper landed in front of the house and all hell broke loose creating pandemonium everywhere. The smoky gas meant to immobilise any moving target was filling the air. The soldiers had clear instructions to bring Tuuro in alive.

The chopper moved out of the line of the smoke in a simultaneous upward and sideways manoeuvre, hovering over the roof of the house. Inside the house, several people were dazed while Tuuro, still holding his unfinished cigarette, jumped out of a window and run into the nearby bush followed by some of his friends. The chopper banked sideways to the right as one of the soldiers spotted them and followed in the direction they were running. Tuuro heard the sound of gunshots, unconsciously dropped the rest of the cigarette he was holding and continued running through the bushes, thinking that their house faced bombardment from the chopper hovering above and sweeping the ground with the powerful searchlight.

The light from the cigarette Tuuro had dropped started to burn and burst into flames consuming the dry leaves of the savannah. The chopper lifted up, apparently to avoid the sudden gust of burning grass and the rising smoke. The ensuing fire engulfed the bushes around it. The dry harmattan wind had a much easier job to do as the dry bushes helped to spread the fire. The chopper turned around and lifted further up, its sound fading away leaving the fire to visit its fury on the village.

The sudden sounds of gunshots, the flames and the ensuing smoke brought the festival to an abrupt end. People started running for their lives, neither knowing where to hide nor what was going on – even those being pursued.

The powers of the masqueraders were no match for the fury that came with the people's fear. They were pushed over and some trampled on, their costumes too cumbersome for them to run in. The speechless and mournful-faced inhabitants of Takpo, running from the shadows of the raving fire, summed up their helplessness.

In the distance cattle could be heard mooing and sheep bleating as the fire engulfed them. It burned throughout the night and when morning came there was an abundance of ready-roasted beef, enough to feed the entire village for a year. The village itself stood intact as the dirt road constructed by manual labour around the village had a second use that day – it had served as a fire buffer zone. The fires had died down along the edges of the road for lack of a 'bridge' across to the other side, but the once-beautiful *nim* trees bore a simple and eloquent message that said much about the devastation caused by the fire.

The government delegation that visited Naa Widana at his palace in Takpo the next day was unprecedented in the history of the village. In spite of the prominence of people from Takpo the village itself had never attracted so much attention from the government. The official delegation made up of the head of SkyHawks, Alari Kanbe, the Foreign Minister, Kofi Mensah and the BNI chief, Paul Nadan, arrived with a brief message for Naa Widana: the Presidents of the Republic of Ghana and the United States would like Tuuro to help with the investigation into an attempted hijacking of an American airliner.

Naa Widana was furious. "If you knew you had the option of asking for my help in the first instance, why did you come to devastate the village with impunity? Why this particular time of the year? You dare to infuriate the gods of our land and incur the wrath of our ancestral spirits and then come here to ask for my help?" He turned to his linguist. "Show them to the door," he instructed.

Paul Nadan apologised for the oversight and promised that the government would compensate them for the damage and appease the gods and ancestral spirits of Takpo.

"You know the tradition of our land," Naa Widana said to Paul, "do you just walk into a chief's court without the usual courtesies?"

"Again, I apologise for ignoring tradition."

Naa Widana consulted with his linguist and said to the delegation, "I'll talk to Tuuro, please come back tomorrow."

Tuuro's response to Naa Widana's call was swift. Tradition was still well respected in this part of the world. Tuuro could defy anyone, even the government of Ghana, but he dared not defy the Chief who was not only the custodian of the land but also represented the gods and the spirits of their ancestors.

Naa Widana informed Tuuro that the government of the Republic of Ghana wanted him to help with an investigation regarding the use of his phone, which would require him to accompany the delegate to Accra.

"So they tried to kill me and my family because of a phone I have never used?" Tuuro asked in anger.

"I don't know what is special about the phone, but I implore you to cooperate with them," Naa Widana advised.

"If you ask me to."

The next day when the delegation arrived at Naa Widana's palace Tuuro was waiting anxiously. They asked if he had his mobile phone with him.

"Yes," Tuuro replied, wondering what his mobile phone had to do with the devastation following their failed attempt to apprehend him. He was the only one in the village who owned a mobile and his arrest did not come as a surprise to most people. His dad was happy to get rid of him because out of all his children it was Tuuro who brought him trouble and pain, but sad because he was the only son who was still around him. Tuuro was handcuffed and led into the waiting chopper. Inside, Tuuro's right foot was chained to his seat and the handcuff taken off.

"Why are you taking me to Accra?" Tuuro asked when they were airborne.

"You will find out when we get there, no more questions," was the short answer from Kofi Mensah.

Naa Widana had told him he was required to help with an investigation but he kept wondering what the investigation was all about and why they had sent a chopper after him that night of all nights if all they wanted was his help. The hour and thirty minutes' flight to Accra seemed like eternity to Tuuro. The rest of the passengers were talking and drinking and Tuuro strained unsuccessfully to hear, gave up and got lost in his own world of thoughts. Why had they taken his mobile phone from him, a phone he hardly used. He couldn't figure out the sudden interest in it and what his crime was.

When they arrived in Accra, Tuuro was picked up in a security van and taken to the SkyHawks office. He sat in a room with his hands cuffed and his foot chained to a hook in the wall behind him.

"You are charged with attempted hijack and hijacking through remote devices of American Airline Flight 675. You have the right to remain silent and the right to an attorney. Anything you say may be used as evidence against you in a court of law, but you will receive a lesser sentence if you cooperate with the investigations," Kanbe read out the charges.

Tuuro's account of his possession of the mobile phone was direct: he had received the phone from his cousin Mike but had never used it to make any call or send any text message.

"Tell us why you never used phone," Kanbe asked.

"I couldn't get a phone card to buy."

"You mean you've never used it for anything?" Kanbe persisted.

Tuuro sat, looking towards the end of the ceiling but seeing nothing up there. He was lost in thought, his mind occupied with mental images of when he had first received the phone. "I used it to watch a programme on TV once, that's all."

"Excuse me; you used the phone as a remote control?" Kanbe asked, shifting and straightening himself on his chair, alarmed.

"Yes."

"Which programme?"

"It was a programme about airports."

"Do you have any detail about that?" Kanbe asked, unable to assimilate what he believed to be one hell-of-a cock and bull story.

"It's in my wallet."

Tuuro's personal things had been taken from him when he was arrested and kept in a safe on their arrival at the SkyHawks office so Kanbe went and retrieved the wallet and brought it back to the interrogation room. He emptied out the contents and Tuuro pointed to a folded paper. Kanbe opened it, read the instructions written on the paper and passed it to Paul Nadan.

"I'm sure your FBI colleagues will be interested in this piece of evidence," Paul remarked after reading it.

***

Soon after Tuuro's arrest the United States Government made a formal extradition request for him to face charges in America under the Terrorism Act.

The President of the Republic of Ghana, Ebo Mettle, a lawyer by training and a politician by profession, sat with his best legal brains and his top security advisers at his Osu Castle office. Among them were the Foreign Minister, Kofi Mensah, the Attorney General, Gyimah Badu, and Paul Nadan. In front of each member present was a copy of the request letter from the United States.

"Gentlemen, what are the legal implications of this request?" President Mettle asked.

"We're not obliged to honour the request since we do not have any extradition treaty with the United States," Gyimah Badu answered.

"I think the situation goes beyond legal issues. If we look at it from the political angle the current global focus is on Africa. There have been pledges to cancel debts and increase aid. Surely this is Africa's decade and we cannot be seen to be in the way of America's war on terror," Paul Nadan said.

"Have you considered the price?" Kofi Mensah asked.

"What do you mean?"

"Poor countries would have to comply with stringent and unacceptable economic policy conditions. How can we be cutting spending on health and education, removing all agricultural subsidies, opening up markets to cheap imports to the detriment of local production and selling off local industries to foreigners in the name of privatisation and ever hope to make poverty history?"

"Surely, you don't expect debt forgiveness and increase in aid unconditionally," Gyimah Badu said in defence of Paul Nadan.

"Why not, these conditions often harm recipient economies and undermine democracy by denying elected governments and their parliaments or civil society a say in important decisions about the country's economic programmes. Wouldn't you agree, Mr. President?"

President Ebo Mettle listened as the discussion about the extradition request turned into an economic debate. He nodded his agreement and waited for the debate to continue.

"What about the doubling of aid?" Gyimah Badu persisted.

Kofi Mensah smiled, removed a document from his brief case and thrust it across the table to where Gyimah was sitting. "Have you not read this document?" he asked, "if all eligible thirty-eight highly indebted poor countries qualified today the deal on aid would only release an average of $1.5 billion a year. This still falls far short of the more than $10 billion a year needed immediately to have any significant impact on poverty reduction. With an estimate of one million children dying every year due to poverty, by the time aid gets to them over five million will die and that's about a quarter of Canada's total population," he concluded.

There was silence in the room for a few seconds before the President broke it. "Tuuro will stand trial in Ghana under our own laws, unless anyone has any objection."

There was none.

President Ebo Mettle had taken a gamble, because he knew the odds were in his favour. He was convinced that the American Government would not take no for an answer and would come to negotiate. The leadership of the Government of Ghana, had on assumption of office, entered into negotiation with a lesser-known lender in international finance – International Financial Consortium – for a loan of one billion US dollars to kick-start the country's ailing economy and bring its infrastructure to the level where it would attract the required investments from abroad.

The loan had been arranged and the first installment had been due for release to the government when the IMF injunction kicked in. When the date for the delivery of the loan came without the loan the Finance Minister simply told the people of Ghana that the government was no longer pursuing it. What they were not told, however, was that the United States had put pressure on the IMF's Chief Economist for Africa Region to stop Ghana from going to the international market to borrow money on non-concessional terms to finance her development.

***

At the White House, the President was informed about the refusal of the Ghana Government to release Tuuro to stand trial in America, so he convened a meeting with the Secretary of State, Gordon Ramsden, and the FBI chief, Craig Brooks.

"What is stopping the Ghana Government from releasing the terrorist?" the President asked.

"I think it's quite obvious. The International Finance Company loan that we stopped, using the IMF, is proving to be a stumbling block to any diplomatic dialogue," Gordon Ramsden said.

"We have intelligence to prove that the IFC resources come from wanted drug lords. Allowing that loan would have been sponsoring international money laundering; you know we can't allow that," the President countered, unsure of himself and looking towards Brooks.

"The security implications of not granting that loan would be the impoverishment of the people and a sure invitation to the return of the military whose allegiance we have no guarantee of."

"How much loan were they seeking?"

"One billion US dollars," Ramsden answered.

"See that it's arranged," said the President to Ramsden, "anything else?" he asked.

There was no response.

As soon as the meeting finished Gordon Ramsden made a phone call to President Ebo Mettle to inform him that the White House was supporting Ghana's application for a loan and were confident that the IMF would approve it.

The next day the IMF's Chief Economist for Africa held talks with the Finance Minister to discuss the details of the proposed loan. This was followed by a series of related events: the President of Ghana received two phone calls from two of the world's most powerful countries.

"Due to Ghana's acceptance of Heavily Indebted Poor Countries status the UK government is cancelling sixty percent of all your debts," the UK Foreign Secretary said.

The message from the US Secretary of State was more direct: the US was cancelling all of Ghana's debt owed to the US

Government in addition to supporting her application for a one-billion loan through the IMF.

It was also reported later in the local news that negotiations had begun between the government of Ghana and an Australian mining company for the latter to establish a one billion dollar bauxite refinery plant in the country and mine bauxite.

A week after the loan arrangement had commenced the US Ambassador to Ghana met with President Ebo Mettle and submitted a fresh request for Tuuro's extradition. The request was granted and after Gyimah Badu had prepared the legal documentation Tuuro was flown to the United States to face trial.

***

Kutini had been devastated when he heard of Mike's death. This is not happening, he had said to himself. Alone in his study, he had allowed his tears to run freely down his cheeks without the strength or the will to wipe them away. Mike had been a great friend and lately a partner in his grand plan to see a unified Africa in a nuclear-free world. He had been aware of Mike's nightmares and his suicidal tendencies but had thought the passage of time and his achievements had had a healing effect on him. He had felt so wrong, wondering what he could have done to stop Mike. Without him, the plan was as good as dead, he had contemplated. That was it, he had decided; he would go no further. He had been following the investigations into the deaths when suddenly the news about the plane hijack hit the headlines, defining a turning point in Kutini's resolve – Mike had done it after all.

Alone in the UK Kutini followed the hunt for the person involved in the plane hijack through the local news. As soon as he read about the arrest and extradition of Tuuro Bondana to face trial in America he called Frank. "Could you put me in contact with your lawyer friend please?"

"Carl only takes two clients at any one time and so I doubt he would take on any more," Frank replied. He knew better than to ask for reasons over the phone.

"Then make it your case. This is urgent."

After a short pause, Frank said, "OK, but only for this occasion."

"Only for this occasion," Kutini replied.

CHAPTER 35

Carl Ingram looked up from his laptop and straight at the wall clock ahead. It was quarter to midnight and time to go home, so he put the pieces of paper he was working on into a folder, shut down his laptop and got up. He picked up the computer and the folder, walked to the sidewall and lifted the huge watercolour of an English countryside to reveal a safe. He removed his wristwatch and pressed on a button to release a key from the side of the watch.

Carl inserted the key into the safe and turned it until there was a click. He then turned the combination knobs until there was a second click. He opened the safe, put the computer and folder inside and locked it. His client list was short and he had a policy of not taking work home.

Carl's law firm was located in the heart of a known hard-core criminal haven in Birmingham, UK, but as Carl walked the dimly-lit street towards his house he felt no fear as the footsteps drew nearer. More people knew him than he cared to know them; he was simply untouchable.

Just as the footsteps past him, he heard the word, "stop." He was suddenly facing a man with a hood over his head wielding a knife. "Give me your wallet," the man said. It was almost a whisper, but in the dark deserted street, it was audible enough for Carl to hear the demand.

"Easy," Carl said as he handed the man his wallet.

"Your mobile phone," the man demanded.

"I can't give you my mobile phone, I'm sorry," Carl answered calmly.

"What?" the man asked surprised.

"There is money in the wallet and you can have my cards, just take them and leave me alone."

The man opened the wallet, saw a stash of cash and started to back off. He took a few steps backwards, turned around and ran into the darkness.

Carl heaved a sigh of relief and continued towards his house. He always carried a hundred pounds in his wallet for situations like this. He called it a mugging survival strategy. His philosophy was that muggers' first sight of money would stop them from inflicting bodily harm. It worked for him. As for his cards one call would cancel them and they would be replaced within two days.

Carl had reached the front of his door, put the key in, and was about to turn it when he heard a voice behind him.

"Excuse me."

He turned round to face a huge man, about two metres tall, towering over him; his hand extended.

"Here is your wallet, Mr. Ingram, and I'm sorry about what happened."

Carl hadn't even heard the footsteps approach this time. "Thank you," he replied, took his wallet and opened his door. "What a day," he said as he entered and went straight to the fridge to removed a can of beer. As he slumped into the couch, his mobile phone rang. In his line of duty, he was on 24-hour call.

"Mr. Ingram, I have been referred to you by a good friend who is also a client of yours. Can we meet tomorrow at the Bull Ring Shopping Mall at half past one? I will be buying a digital camera at Jessops."

It was a demand and Carl knew better than to suggest otherwise. There were only two people who called him on that phone and whoever this person was could only obtain that number from one of his two clients.

Carl walked into the prestigious Bull Ring shopping mall in the heart of Birmingham and made his way towards Jessops. It was the second time he had been in there – when it was first opened and now.

Carl had just stepped into Jessops; it was not as large as the one he knew on Temple Row. As he walked towards the digital camera section he saw a man walking in that direction with a shop assistant who opened a cabinet and gave a camera to the man. "Do you think this will make a good present for an investigative lawyer?" the man asked the assistant.

"I'm not the expert in cameras. I'll get one of my colleagues for you," the assistant replied.

Carl recognised the man from the description he was given. Franklin Williams had rung earlier to inform him about sending his close friend Kutini to him.

"I've got a similar camera, they are good, Mr. Bomanso."

"Mr. Ingram?"

"Yes."

"Kutini. I'm glad you made it. Should we have a coffee?"

"That's a good idea."

***

"A friend of mine is going on trial in America for hijacking American Airline Flight 675; I would like you to represent him and one other person linked to it," Kutini said, when they had ordered and sat down.

Carl took a sip of his coffee, allowing the cup to rest at his lips for a moment, his mind analysing what Kutini had just told him. "The American legal system is different from here. It would be difficult for me to represent them there."

"My friend said you were the best and I'm sure you would find a way to do it."

Carl felt flattered by the compliment while knowing that it was true.

"I'll understand if you can't do it", Kutini said, breaking the silence.

"No," Carl said, "I can't disappoint your friend. Besides, it would be exciting to handle a case in America. What's your friend's name?"

"Tuuro Bondana. You'll find his details and those of Chris Tagoe in this file," Kutini said, handing Carl a manila folder.

Carl opened the file and the first thing he saw were two photos each with a name written underneath: Tuuro Bondana and Chris Tagoe. Chris' photo showed him in his US Military uniform wearing a smile, while Tuuro had an innocent boyish face. Carl's initial thoughts were that if there were going to be problems at all they would be with Tuuro. "I'll study the file and get back to you."

Back in his office, Carl spent the rest of the day studying the file. His initial concern was confirmed as he read from the file that Tuuro had actually controlled the mobile phone. With Chris, he knew without a doubt that, unless there was something else he didn't know, he would be able to get him acquitted.

When Kutini called the next day to find out if Carl would take the cases the answer was affirmative.

"Good. I'll make your hotel bookings and flight arrangements. Do you have any special requirements?"

"No."

"Can you travel tomorrow?"

"Let me see," Carl said as he scrolled through his electronic organiser, "I have some court cases this week. I can travel next week."

"OK, I'll send the accommodation and flight details to your office address," Kutini said.

As soon as Carl finished taking the call he phoned a law firm that handled his cases in Washington DC and informed them that he was coming over to work with them on a case.

***

A member of the hotel staff met Carl at Baltimore Washington International Airport. The following morning he walked into the plush office of Fletcher, Shawley & Co. Law Firm and was greeted by the senior partner, Nigel Fletcher. It was the first time Carl was meeting with the partners as his previous dealings with them had either been getting information from them or passing a case to them to handle in America.

Carl Ingram sat down with his two American partners to discuss the case and to prepare for the hearing the next day. Nigel went through the relevant sections of America's legal procedures with Carl highlighting the areas that he thought to be different from the British system.

Alan Shawley, who had been to the prisons to talk to the two persons involved, briefed Carl on his meetings occasionally referring to his notes. He had also done some research on the case and after the briefing he passed a file containing his findings to Carl.

"Thanks for the good work," Carl said after thumbing through the file.

The following day as Carl and his partners stepped out of their taxi and walked up the stairs towards the entrance of the Supreme Court Building in Washington DC he noticed something quite unusual. The court's relatively recent new home, designed in classical Corinthian architecture, sat in perfect harmony with the nearby congress buildings and across First Street from Capitol building, but this perfect harmony was distorted by the presence of armed police guarding the Supreme Court making it look more like a Taliban arms roundup.

Police dog handlers stood impassively near the metal gates to the rear of the court building while men in smart suits with neat hairstyles stood nearby trying to look as conspicuous as mafia hit men without their dark sunglasses, which would have looked a bit out of place on this damp Monday morning. It wasn't only the armed guard and the police dogs that were unusual about the Supreme Court, but the building was also being used as a High Court to try cases involving international terrorism.

Entry to the court building was via the full size metal detector frame and supplemented by a manual scanner wielded by civilian security staff. The courtroom was screened off and to gain entry there was a secondary scanning procedure carried out by armed police. Everyone, including the legal representatives of the defendants, was scanned and patted down in search of anything sinister.

Inside the courtroom though there were only two unarmed police officers discreetly placed and hidden away from the gaze of the jury behind the tinted glass of the public seating area. The public gallery of the courtroom contained close friends and family of those facing trial and alongside them sat plain-clothed police officers as the court was not open to the general public for the case on trial.

The defence legal counsel led by Carl Ingram sat in readiness as the presiding judge made his appearance. Directly behind the legal counsels at the rear of the court facing the judge's bench was a ten-foot high bullet-proof glass partition separating the prisoner's dock from the rest of the court.

"I would like to remind everyone present that the press is not allowed in this courtroom. Is there anyone from the press in here?" There was silence.

It was raining when the defendants arrived at the court building encased in a heavily fortified horsebox used to transport category 'A' prisoners. The first defendant, Tuuro, was brought out of the transport vehicle into the drizzle. As he felt the drops of rain on his face he had a strange feeling of triumph. This must be a good sign from the gods, he thought as his mind went to the *rain god* which his ancestors worshiped. While lost in his own world of supernatural security he was brought into the courtroom through a back door leading from the cell holding-area directly to the rear of the dock surrounded by six police officers. First he spoke to confirm his name and age, still looking overwhelmed and subdued by everything around him. Tuuro had lived most of his twenty years in his village and the furthest he had travelled was the twenty-four-kilometre journey to school during his college days. He sat looking nervous as the clerk read out the charges.

"Mr. Tuuro Bondana, you are charged with count one: conspiracy to hijack Flight 675 on June 24. Count two: Conspiracy to cause grievous acts of terrorism with Chris Tagoe and Mike Zinbalan. Count three: hijacking of Flight 675 on June 24. Count four: causing grievous acts of terrorism against the United States. How do you plead?" the bailiff asked.

"Not guilty."

Chris Tagoe was the next defendant to be brought in. Usually in such a case where there are multiple defendants all would appear together before a judge; not in this case. The judge had earlier been given instructions from the Attorney General on how best to deal with the defendants who were both considered 'high risk'. They were to appear separately on the day of arraignment, which seemed a bit bizarre to Carl Ingram especially if they were going to be together on the day of the trial proper.

Chris Tagoe was brought before the court, as if saved for the judge's dessert, wearing an orange tartan patterned shirt. He looked lean and, given the occasion, relaxed and composed. He had gone through the same red tape as Tuuro with the exception that the prosecution counsel now put to him two charges:

"Chris Tagoe, you're hereby charged under the United States Terrorist Act with count one: conspiracy to hijack Flight 675 and count two: conspiracy to cause grievous acts of terrorism. How do you plead?" the bailiff asked.

"Not guilty."

After the defendants' pleas, the final word went to the defence counsel. "Your Honour," Carl Ingram addressed the Judge, "I am submitting to you that the conditions my first client Tuuro Bondana is being held in are in breach of Article 6 of the European Convention of Human Rights which refers to adequate time and facilities to help prepare for a trial."

"What is the relevance of the European Convention on American soil?" the Judge asked. Everyone in the courtroom turned to look at Carl. Those who were in doubt as to where Carl's accent came from now knew as he stood there helplessly scratching his head while wondering why he had made such a fool of himself.

"I mean the Geneva Convention that applies internationally," Carl said, trying to regain his confidence. "Your Honour, I would also like to bring to your notice our intention to submit an application for judicial review in order to have Tuuro's conditions changed. He is being held at the Ohio State Prison which is some three hours drive from the court and assuming that the trial lasts up to three months then it would mean some six hours of Tuuro's time out of a 24-hour day will be spent travelling to and from court. Moreover the Ohio State Prison does not have the facilities to deal with category 'A' remand prisoners and given that it is the first time in its history that it has held a remand prisoner of category 'A' status it is not equipped to handle such a situation."

"Let it be known to defence counsel that it is not within my remit to intervene in such a matter. Besides, under the anti-terrorism legislation the trial should last for no more than seven days. The court is adjourned till nine tomorrow morning."

When the court resumed the next day a press representative made application on behalf of the press corps to the Honourable Judge for reporting restrictions to be lifted. When the application was read out to the court Carl Ingram objected, saying, "I find it strange that, unlike the UK, the United States allows the press in courtrooms, which I think could be prejudicial and could have an undue influence on the court."

"Objection upheld," the Judge said, "an order was passed that the trial should have reporting restrictions imposed and that order still stands."

Tuuro was brought into the dock and took his oath "... to tell the truth, the whole truth and nothing but the truth, so help me God."

Among the audience Rudolf Reinhardt sat listening to the proceedings. He was the only one in the courtroom who had experienced the failed hijack first hand and he felt as he listened to the arguments and counter arguments that no-one in the court really appreciated the feelings of the passengers as they went through their mental ordeal. As Rudolf watched the defence lawyer approach the dock he wondered whether lawyers understood that some things were either black or white and hoped that the insanity card would not be played.

"Mr. Tuuro Bondana, do you recognise this?" Carl asked, showing Tuuro a mobile phone.

"Yes, it's my phone."

"How did you get it?"

"My cousin Mike sent it to me."

"Why did you hijack the plane using the mobile phone," Carl asked.

"I didn't hijack any plane. I only used it to watch television," Tuuro replied.

"What did you see on the TV that night?"

"I saw an airport and a plane taking off. I couldn't see all the writings but I saw the letters LU."

"Lufthansa, I believe; nothing further."

Prosecution counsel Jane Hunter got up from her seat and made her way towards the dock. She looked at Tuuro for a few seconds. "Mr. Tuuro Bondana, you said you didn't hijack the plane. Are you in the habit of watching television at four a.m.?"

Tuuro looked down, unsure of what to say.

"Do you?" Jane persisted.

"No," Tuuro replied.

"Is it true that when you received the phone you also received a set of instructions?"

"Objection, your honour, counsel is trying to imply ..."

"Overruled," the Judge cut in, "I would like to know what happened."

"Yes," Tuuro answered.

"You received a mobile phone programmed to hijack an airline and with a set of instructions you went ahead and hijacked the plane. That's what you did."

"All I did was watch a TV programme," Tuuro objected with a raised voice.

"No more questions."

Carl reviewed his notes as Chris Tagoe was called into the dock. There was silence in the courtroom as the Judge waited for Carl to examine his client.

"Mr. Ingram?" the Judge prompted.

"No questions, your honour."

"Mr. Chris Tagoe, how many of you were involved in the hijack plot?" Jane Hunter asked.

"I don't know anything about that."

"Is it not true that you and Mike Zinbalan were undergraduate mates at the university?"

"Yes, we were mates, but …"

"Is it not also true that you were both involved in student demonstrations?"

Chris sat in the dock trying to recollect any such involvements. He thought about Kutini Bomanso – he was the one with the big ideas; the one who always came up with the right solutions. "I don't remember …"

"Of course you won't remember," Jane said, "but you do remember your elaborate deception plan involved sending the phone to Tuuro to avoid detection, don't you?"

"Objection your honour," Carl said, rising to his feet.

"Overruled; answer the question Mr. Tagoe."

"I had no idea of any such plan."

"Then tell me what you meant by *I know I could have stopped it* in your own admission to your wife," Jane said, nodding to his colleague, who pressed a button to replay Faiza's recording of the couple's conversation.

"I was referring to Mike's death."

"Mr. Tagoe, is it true that you are currently on bail for the brutal murder of an ex-military officer and his entire family?" Jane asked.

"Objection your honour," Carl said. May I approach?" he asked.

The Judge signalled for the two lawyers to approach him and after a brief consultation upheld Carl's objection and adjourned the court.

CHAPTER 36

As soon as Carl got to his hotel room the first thing he wanted to do was call Kutini and withdraw his services, but then he thought about Frank and decided against it. He swore and wished he had never taken up the case because no one had told him that Chris was also wanted for multiple murders. He pondered over the day's events for a brief moment and left for the office of his American partners.

As Carl approached the office, he had one thing on his mind: to find out the link between the murders and the plane hijack. Inside the office Carl opened his briefcase and removed a copy of the file he had obtained from the prosecution counsel detailing the deaths in Ghana and linking Chris Tagoe to the crime scene.

Carl read Chris' statement to the police and the alibi provided by Amankwa Amofa's surviving child and sighed with relief, but the relief did not last long for he saw something on the next page that made him sit up. He was reading a report compiled by Faiza Iddris and had come to a transcript of a conversation between Chris and Betty:

"I've told you I was accompanying my friend. What else would you like to know?"

"I didn't mean to upset you, honey. I just want to convince myself that you're innocent. I don't want anything bad to happen to you and our future. I know I could have stopped it, but . . ."

"I know I could have stopped it, but . . ." Carl repeated Chris' last statement aloud.

"You did the right thing, pal, that judge is very tough."

Carl turned round to face Alan, who had come behind him unnoticed. "I was reading from the file," he explained.

"Don't bother about the murder; the trial is about the plane hijack."

Carl nodded and continued to read. Not finding anything else incriminating, his tensed facial muscles began to relax as an idea started to take shape in his mind. Law is not about guilty or not guilty, it's about technicalities. The mechanics of it are shrouded in the logic of human thinking and to some extent the psychology of the mind and personal emotions.

"I know I could have stopped it, but . . ." Carl weighed the statement, decided that it was the only one that could make or unmake Chris' case and made a mental note.

"That statement could refer to anything and therefore is subject to interpretations," Carl responded finally.

"You've got a point, young man," said Nigel. "Take a look at this."

Carl took the file from Nigel and read the label: Shenley vs. Hiscock. As he read the case he noted how a judge had thrown out a witness statement according to which Shenley had said, "I shouldn't have done it," on the grounds that Shenley could have been talking about anything. The judge had upheld the defence objection on the basis that the prosecution's suggestion of guilt based on that statement was mere speculation.

As Carl read on he was surprised at the similarity with his own case. Shenley was alleged to have wilfully caused Hiscock's paralysis in an attempt to kill him by using a mobile phone to interfere with a critical operation. Though the prosecution had established that Shenley had the motive and the means to harm Hiscock there was no law under which Shenley could be charged and he was acquitted.

"That is a useful piece of information, Nigel. Any more information?"

"No," Nigel replied. "I want a favour, Alan. Please find out what the law says about a mobile phone or other item of electronic equipment accidentally interfering with satellite or navigation equipment."

Alan searched through copies of all the statute books and all the legislation going as far back as 1950 when electronics had started becoming part of American civilian life. He searched through all the useful internet sites but came up with nothing. Nigel had given Alan a couple more places to look before drawing the conclusion that no law on electronic interference existed.

By the time Carl left the office he had a clear idea of how he wanted to proceed with the case. He walked the few blocks to his hotel on 8th Street, stopped briefly at the reception to pick up his room keys and took the elevator to the 9th floor. As he inserted the keys to his door he had a strange feeling, then realised that his room number 89 had a link to the street name and his hotel room floor put together. He shook his head in disbelief as he said aloud: "I was born on 8th September, what a strange coincidence."

Inside the hotel room Carl called to place an order for room service, made a cup of coffee and sat down to read the program code used for the mobile phone. He had trained as a computer scientist and had practised for two years before going into law. It had been a discussion on the subject of how the law was lagging behind the quantum leaps in technology that had brought Carl and Franklin Williams together, first as friends and later as business partners.

As Carl went through the hundreds of pages of codes he realised how much he had been left behind in programming. He interrupted his concentration to eat when the room service arrived. It was well past midnight when he came to the end of the code, made some notes and went to sleep.

The next morning as Carl handed his key to the receptionist he said without thinking: "Can you give me a different room please?"

"Why, is there something wrong, Mr. Ingram?"

"No, err, never mind."

"We gave you a room to match your date of birth for good luck, but if you don't like it we can change it."

"Ah, is the street name and floor number also for good luck?"

"That was a coincidental double luck, Mr. Ingram."

"Thank you, I need all the luck that I can get," Carl said laughing as he walked out to the waiting taxi.

The smile that Carl left the hotel with followed him through his busy day as he visited each of his clients in prison. His first stop was at Tuuro's prison.

"What wrong have I done?" Tuuro asked as soon as he sat down with Carl.

Carl stifled a laugh at the young man's innocence that bordered on naivety. "That's what I'm here to talk about. Tell me what you used the mobile phone for."

"I only used it once to watch TV."

Carl couldn't hold himself any longer as he burst out laughing. He stopped as quickly and apologised. "What did you watch on the TV?"

"I didn't catch the start of the film. I only saw the part where a plane was taking off."

"I see," Carl said, thinking of how far technology would go. "Thanks, I'll see you tomorrow in court."

"When are they going to release me?" Tuuro asked as Carl rose to leave.

"I don't know, the judge will decide at the end of the trial."

"I haven't done anything."

Carl was gone. His next stop was at Chris' cell. "I'm here to help you, but I can only do that if you tell me the truth."

"Look, I had no part in this; my only crime was doing a favour for a friend, which landed me in this mess." Chris was hysterical.

"The police report says that you're also involved in suicide murders."

"That's the whole point, why would I use a phone to call the emergency services if I was involved in any of these plots? I lost my fiancée, now I'm going to lose my wife and injustice is going to take my life away from me."

"Calm down, I'll do what I can to help you."

"Please help me. I don't want to go to prison."

"Everything will be fine," Carl tried to assure him.

When Carl got back to the office he called Kutini. "Tell me why Mike did it"

"Did it?" Kutini asked in astonishment, "You mean trying to invent something that accidentally gets into the wrong hands is a crime?"

If Kutini was acting, he was a damn good actor, Carl thought. "I don't understand," he said.

"Mr. Ingram, in the programming world we experiment with a dozen things each day. That gives us a lot of ideas that we try out on our own. How else did Mike come up with all the patents that he holds?"

"What other things did he experiment with?"

"I don't know, but he should have records of them somewhere."

"He should have records of them somewhere," Carl repeated, almost to himself

"Good luck, Mr. Ingram," Kutini said.

"Bye," Carl said, without acknowledging Kutini's last statement. Kutini is smart, he thought, and that worried him even more as he couldn't trust him. He hated to be manipulated and that's what he felt Kutini was doing to him.

As he walked out of the office building that evening to his waiting cab Carl's face lit up and he smiled as a thought came to him: *you mean trying to invent something that accidentally gets into the wrong hands is a crime?* Kutini's question came back to him. "The guy was an inventor," Carl said aloud as he entered the cab.

"Could you stop at a shop where I can buy a ghetto blaster please?"

"If you love music you should get an ipod; better quality," the driver suggested.

"I'll stick to a ghetto blaster for now, thanks," Carl replied.

The next day in court Carl requested to have a look at Mike's computer and to be allowed to visit his apartment. The court granted both requests and provided a police escort. The only reason Carl wanted to see Mike's apartment was to have a sense of his feelings and frame of mind when he wrote his programs.

When Carl entered Mike's apartment he was looking for signs of seclusion or some level of privacy that might suggest that he was trying to hide something. Everything in the apartment seemed to be where it was expected to be. After fifteen minutes Carl left and made his way to the office. It was late afternoon. Carl locked himself in one of the meeting rooms and started to study the information on Mike's computer.

There were several programs, each one meticulously documented, none of which could possibly be used by the prosecution to advance their case. Unknown to Carl, Rudolf Reinhardt had removed every item on the computer relating to the poison. Carl concentrated on a mobile phone program which had the interesting title *The Flight Simulator.*

It was well past midnight and his other partners had long gone when Carl got up from his desk, called a cab and left for his hotel.

The next day in court Chris was recalled to the dock.

"Mr. Tagoe, you first used the mobile phone to make an emergency call?"

"Yes."

"Would you have used it if you knew it was meant for a plane hijack?"

"No."

"Before you met Mike Zinbalan in Accra, when was the last time you two had any contact?"

"When we graduated five years ago," Chris said.

"No further questions."

Jane Hunter approached Chris holding some documents. "Mr. Tagoe, how much are you gaining from all this?"

"How do I gain from something I'm not part of?"

"Answer the question, Mr. Tagoe."

"I'm not gaining anything."

"According to your pay slips," Hunter waved the documents in the air, "you do not earn enough to fund the luxury lifestyle you've displayed these last few weeks. What's your source of funds?"

"I've shares in my father's fishing business."

"Nothing further."

There were only two expert witnesses during the entire trial: the first was a computer specialist from the FBI and the second a university professor with expertise in West African culture.

Jane Hunter, the prosecution counsel, was the first to question the professor. "In your expert opinion did Tuuro Bondana know what he was doing when he used the mobile phone to hijack Flight 675?"

"No."

"No further questions."

"Your witness, Mr. Ingram."

"No questions."

The computer expert took the stand. He had studied the code used to program the mobile phone.

The prosecution counsel showed the witness a mobile phone and file. "Do you recognise these, Mr. Miller?"

"Yes."

"Is this the mobile phone with the code in this file used in hijacking Flight 675?"

"Yes."

"No further questions."

"Mr. Miller," Carl walked to the dock and placed a document in front of him, "are there any similarities between the code in front of you and the code you read earlier?"

Miller studied the new code in front of him. "Yes, there are similarities. Why?" he asked.

"That code comes from this remote control," Carl said, removing a ghetto blaster and its remote from a bag.

The judge called Carl. "What is all this drama about?"

"Your honour, there is an element of interoperability between all infrared equipment, which is one reason why mobile phone use is not currently permitted on flights and in hospitals."

"You'd better get through with this quickly," the Judge said.

"Mr. Miller, I have no further questions," Carl said as he walked to his seat.

There was one more witness to be called.

"You know the defendant Chris Tagoe from your on-going investigations in Ghana."

"Yes."

"Mr. Rudolf Reinhardt, you were on the plane when it was hijacked," Jane Hunter asked.

"Yes."

"You subsequently led the investigation that resulted in the arrest of the defendants?"

"Yes."

"Please tell the court how the two men on trial conspired to hijack Flight 675."

"The phone was programmed by Mike Zinbalan who took it to Ghana and gave it to Chris Tagoe before killing himself in what we believe to be a multiple murder by suicide. Chris then passed the phone to Tuuro Bondana who committed the final act."

"No further questions, your honour."

Carl approached Rudolf. "In your investigations, did you find any *direct* evidence that Chris Tagoe and Tuuro Bondana conspired with Mike Zinbalan to hijack Flight 675?"

"No."

"No further questions," Carl said.

"This court is adjourned till tomorrow morning," the Judge said.

From the court Carl Ingram went with his team to their chambers, where they spent the rest of the afternoon putting ideas together for the final session next day. Nigel Fletcher looked at his notes. "The prosecution has not been able to establish during the trial that a crime has actually been committed," he said.

"What about the hijack charge against Tuuro Bondana?" Alan Shawley asked.

"No demands were made and as far as I'm concerned this could simply be a technological glitch," Nigel replied.

Carl made his notes as they spoke. "Anything else we should consider for tomorrow?" he asked.

"One more thing," Alan said, "the direct involvement of Chris Tagoe could not be established."

In his hotel room Carl Ingram finalised his closing statement and printed a hard copy as a backup before going to sleep. He routinely made hard copies following a computer failure he had experienced during a trial that nearly cost him the case.

The next morning as he gave his hotel key to the receptionist he said, "Wish me luck."

"Good luck in whatever you're doing."

"Thank you," Carl replied, smiling as he walked to his waiting taxi.

CHAPTER 37

On this last day of the trial Carl Ingram, who was gaining fame with his distinctive English accent and notoriety for his style of defence, arrived at the court with his defence team and went through the daily routine of security checks before taking their seats in the courtroom. Carl switched on his laptop and opened two files, one containing his notes and the other his closing statement which he had revised the previous day.

When the court had started proceedings, the judge first called the prosecution counsel to give her closing statement.

The prosecution's summary stated that the Flight 675 hijack had all the hallmarks of Al Qaeda type terrorism and that Mike and his associates had planned and executed this act in order to terrorise America, the very nation providing them with a livelihood.

"It was only due to the efficient intervention of our intelligence and security forces that the crime was nipped in the bud and not by design, as the defence attorney might try to make you believe. These criminals deserve nothing short of a guilty verdict."

As Jane Hunter summed up Carl made a few changes to his closing statement on his laptop. He finished just as he was called to give it.

Carl Ingram stood in front of the jury as he addressed the court:

"The Prosecution says the hijacking has the hallmarks of Al-Qaeda type terrorism. Is it conceivable that these men were involved in international acts of terrorism? Is it also conceivable all the available evidence was not followed through?"

He paused as he looked beyond the bullet-proof glass to his clients, taking the gaze of the rest of the court with him. The expressionless faces of the jury and the silence in the room didn't give Carl any indication as to what impact his statement was having on his audience, but he continued, "It is claimed that Mike Zinbalan was the mastermind. Mike's credentials were no secret among his contemporaries. He was an innovator with a mind that was constantly looking for new ways of improving things. His only crime was that he was experimenting with a flight simulator and tested the potential of remote flight control. Think of the possibility of being able to remotely take control of flights that have been actually hijacked and we will all begin to appreciate the wisdom in the deceased's invention. Mike should be given a posthumous medal."

Carl could see a few heads nodding as he turned to face the people who had gathered on the final day of the trial.

"That guy was a hero," a voice shouted from the audience. The judge spotted the person and ordered for his removal. When silence had returned to the court the judge asked Carl Ingram to continue with his closing statement.

"I'm going to summarise," Carl resumed. "It's clear that Flight 675 was never in danger and any competent programmer would know that there was nothing in the code to put the flight in danger. It was unfortunate that Mike mistakenly sent that phone to Ghana where the mobile network is satellite dependent. The insecurity of America's own civilian satellites resulted in the phone accidentally locking onto Flight 675 causing inconvenience by changing its flight path.

As for Tuuro Bondana and Chris Tagoe, it is already evident that there is no case against them. I therefore implore this court to return not guilty verdicts. Thank you."

As the jury left the courtroom to decide their verdict Carl thought about the events of the last few days. He had embarked on mission impossible, so the wait for the verdict was stressful for him.

When the court resumed the verdict was read:

"In the case of Chris Tagoe versus the State, the jury finds the defendant not guilty."

"In the case of Tuuro Bondana versus the State the jury found the defendant guilty of assisting in the hijack of Flight 675."

Betty, who had been quiet throughout the trial, jumped up in her chair in jubilation. She met Chris as he walked towards her with tears of joy running down her cheeks. "I always knew you were innocent," she said wrapping her arms around his neck.

The joy at Chris Tagoe's acquittal was dampened by the guilty verdict on Tuuro. As Carl thought about it one of his American partners said to him: "That was excellent; you did it."

"Did what?" Carl asked, absent minded.

"You got Tuuro's charge changed from an act of terrorism to *unwittingly* putting Flight 675 in danger."

Carl patted his partner, "I couldn't have done it without your help."

The next day Tuuro was sentenced to five years' imprisonment and a three-year ban on the use of computers and mobile phones following his release.

Rudolf Reinhardt bit his lip as he left the courtroom. "Whose side is the law on?" he asked in response to a reporter and continued pushing his way through the press to a taxi.

The next morning the *New York Times* carried the judgement on its front page, describing it as a triumph on the war on terror. Other newspapers were less convinced and saw the five years' sentence as a let down on the war on terrorist. Across the bottom of the *New York Times* was the news item: *The inside story of an American Soldier's involvement with Flight 675 hijack: Read Chris Tagoe's own story starting tomorrow.*

Chris had been acquitted and discharged, and although his job as a soldier with the US Army was no longer tenable, he was glad for the one million dollar payment from the *New York Times* to serialise his story.

***

Carl Ingram arrived at Heathrow the morning following the sentencing of his clients to be greeted in the arrival hall by someone waving a piece of cardboard with his name on it. "This way, sir," the person said as Carl identified himself. "There is a car waiting to take you home."

As they approached the car, Carl saw Kutini behind the wheel. "How did you know I was coming?" Carl asked as he entered the car.

"My friend told me."

"I'm sorry I couldn't get your key person acquitted, it was a difficult case."

"Don't be silly, you did great. I wasn't expecting a miracle from you."

"Thanks."

Kutini passed a briefcase to Carl and said, "This is yours."

"What's in it?"

"It's money. It should be enough to cover your fees and any additional expenditure incurred."

Carl opened the briefcase and saw the pile of cash. "I think we should appeal against Tuuro's conviction," he said.

"Yes, we should, but there is some important business I

need to attend to first. I'll get back to you on that." But Kutini never did.

***

As Kutini took the exit from the M25 London Orbital onto the M40 towards Birmingham the South African Consul, Viktor Mamphele was going through the final details with Carlos, the hit man, inside the backroom of the Elm Tree Pub in North London. "We need to take out his son just to send a warning message to him."

Kutini had been under surveillance for a while and now they knew about his plan for his son's first birthday party. "This would be the perfect opportunity to put the fear of God into him," Viktor decided.

"Leave that to me," Carlos replied.

CHAPTER 38

The July morning sun was bright, but the breeze blowing across the cool Atlantic waters of the Gulf of Guinea held the hot sunrays in check.

Suma Williams walked down the driveway of her rented flat at Labone Estates in Accra, crossed the street and hailed a taxi. She was very excited, exuding confidence, and had every reason to be, having won a scholarship to study a course she cherished in Canada. She was already thinking beyond the two-year master's programme. Her mind went to the possibility of meeting with development workers from other countries and thought about how she would build a network to prepare her for her own venture.

Suma had always wanted to run her own non-governmental organisation to help other women. She had gone to work with an international NGO in Ghana soon after graduation, eventually setting up her own.

As a woman who grew up in a harsh climate, Suma was well aware of the economic hardships and deprivation of women from Northern Ghana and beyond. She counted herself lucky to have had a university education and often wondered how her parents had managed to bring them up and give her and her siblings a good education amid such deprivation. She would help bring hope and dignity to other women from this area.

The taxi stopped a few metres from the front gate of the Canadian High Commission. Suma paid the cab driver, got out and made her way to the consular section. She had letters from the University confirming her admission and funding together with her original transcripts from the University of Ghana. She presented her application, the accompanying documentation and the application fee and waited until she was called into an interview room.

"Why do you want to go to Canada?" the interviewer asked.

"I'm going to pursue a Master's programme," Suma answered, unsure why she was being asked questions she had already provided answers for on the application form.

"Do you have any relatives living abroad?"

"Yes, I have a brother in the UK," Suma answered, wondering about the relevance of the question.

"Why are you not going to study in the UK instead?" the interviewer continued.

"I like the course I have been offered in Canada; besides, that's where I have funding for."

"Are you pregnant?"

"No. Why?"

The interviewer ignored her question and stared at the computer screen. "Your brother is in Canada, not the UK," the interviewer stated.

"My brother has never been to Canada. I know he has been to the US on a number of occasions, but not to Canada," Suma explained.

At this point, the interviewer called a colleague and showed her something on the computer. The two officers laughed, but Suma had no idea what they were looking at.

"You are lying, Miss Williams," the interviewer insisted.

"I doubt if my brother has been to Canada," Suma replied, trying to conceal her anger.

"So you're not sure; how do we know that you're not lying about your qualifications as well?"

"Why would I lie about my qualifications when you can easily check their authenticity with the University?" she asked angrily. In her mind, she wanted to say, "You fat pig with the brains of a sheep."

"I am afraid I cannot grant you the visa. I'm not convinced that you will return to Ghana after your course," the interviewer concluded.

"But I ..."

The interviewer walked away from the window leaving Suma transfixed with her sentence hanging in mid air, not believing what was going on. This morning she had been agog with excitement but now she felt all her energy draining from her body and her whole world crumbling beneath her.

"This way, madam."

Suma turned round to face a security man and obediently followed him out of the building.

When she got home she called her brother in the UK. "Why didn't you tell me that you had been to Canada?" she screamed down the phone line.

It took a few seconds for him to recognise his sister's voice. "Suma, who said I've been to Canada?" he asked, confused. This was unlike his sister.

"I went to the Embassy for the student visa and I was refused because they believed you were in Canada and if I went there I wouldn't come back."

"I have never been to Canada, but even if I had what has that got to do with your student visa?"

"I don't know; I'm confused," she said.

"This is what I want you to do: talk to a solicitor about been labelled a liar; we can prove that I have never been to Canada and that your qualifications are genuine."

"They will deny it and I have no evidence to prove what they said," Suma replied.

"I guess you're right."

We are still slaves even in our own land, Frank thought, I'll do something about this. One day …

Frank put the phone down, still angry at the apparent injustice to his sister. "This is not fair," he heard himself saying. The world is unfair when thousands go hungry and vast quantities of food go to waste. He found himself thinking about his friend Kutini Bomanso and their university days. They used to have these sorts of conversations when they were not talking about women. A ring on his phone broke Frank's thoughts about Kutini and his recollection of their postgraduate days in the university.

"Frank, this is Kutini. I am staying the weekend in Stratford upon Avon, would you like to have a meal on Saturday afternoon?"

"I was literally just thinking about you," Frank replied. "It would be a good opportunity to see you and to visit Shakespeare's birthplace."

"Shall we meet by the canal next to the Royal Shakespeare Playhouse about midday?"

"That's fine by me."

Frank lived in Birmingham, thirty minutes drive from Stratford, but hadn't been to see this historic town and was looking forward to it.

Late on Saturday morning Kutini left his hotel close to Stratford train station and walked the fifteen minutes' distance past the shopping streets to the canals. He had been waiting eight minutes when Frank arrived. "I hope I haven't kept you waiting for long?" Frank asked, sounding apologetic.

"Just a few minutes; it's a beautiful day."

It was indeed a beautiful summer day and the streets of Stratford were full of tourists. Americans were particularly conspicuous, which reminded Kutini of a conversation with a colleague after he had been to see the movie *Shakespeare in Love.* "The Americans have only seen the movie and they claim to know more about Shakespeare than the British," his colleague had said. It was now clear to Kutini why the Americans would make that claim. The film had helped attract Americans to this part of the world. They followed every trail of Shakespeare and devoured every bit of the history with passion and so they went back home knowing more than the average Briton knew about Shakespeare.

"Are you hungry?" Kutini asked.

"Not really." Phyllis had insisted Frank had breakfast before leaving home and he had obliged.

"Let's wander around a bit before going for a meal," Kutini suggested.

They walked around the canal area, watching the swans and ducks floating in the lake nearby in tranquillity. "It's beautiful out here," Kutini said, admiring the landscape and the surroundings of the canal area.

"We should be able to create jobs back home with places like this," Frank said, looking at the tourists all around the place.

Frank's statement provided the perfect opening for Kutini. "A situation like that can only happen if Africa pools her resources together."

"I just wish it could happen." Frank had never given up his hope that one day Africa would be united.

They reached an empty bench and stopped but continued their conversation. A frail looking white guy with punk-like hair walked towards them. As he passed just feet away from them, he paused, spat on the grass in front of them and said, "Niggers, go home," then started to walk away.

Frank made a start after him. "Pig, stop right there," he said as he caught up with the guy and held him by his shirt.

Kutini was right beside Frank and noticed a tattoo of the Nazi symbol on the guy's right arm just below the sleeve of his T-shirt.

"Let go!" The guy snarled.

"Let him go," Kutini pleaded with Frank.

"Idiot," Frank said to the guy and pushed him away.

As the guy turned round to go Kutini noticed the initials on the back of his T-shirt – BNF. "Don't let these pranks get the better of you."

"I could have strangled him," Frank said, still boiling with rage as they started to walk.

"You would be the loser if you had," Kutini advised. "They are the frustrated minority calling themselves the British National Front. They have national branches all over Europe who stir up racial hatred."

"I just hate this country," Frank said with finality.

"Calm down and let's sit." Kutini said. He had seen this kind of racism repeatedly.

They had reached another empty bench. "The reason why I wanted us to meet is to talk about situations like this," Kutini said and sat down. Frank sat beside him.

When Kutini had invited him to meet in Stratford his initial thoughts were that he wanted to discuss something important. He thought Kutini was probably in financial difficulty and needed his help. This impression had changed when they met and started talking about general things. He had reasoned that might be because Kutini had some marriage difficulty and wanted to share it with him in the absence of his wife. Later he thought that maybe it was just for company. Whatever the reason, he was upset about the incident and wanted to leave.

"Situations like this?" Frank was surprised, but suddenly rejuvenated with energy and renewed enthusiasm.

"Not directly," Kutini explained, "more about how to make Africa a better place for us to live in." He was still considering the best way to approach this despite the several private rehearsals he had had.

"I will do anything to help make Africa a better place, I'm sick and tired of this place."

Frank's answer gave Kutini the confidence to put his request directly. "It's been a few years since Jubilee 2000 officially came to a close, yet their call for third world debt cancellation can hardly be said to have started. I was hoping you could help jump-start the debt cancellation process."

"How?" Frank was intrigued. How could he help to jump-start a process that was certainly in the domain of governments?

"If we can get into the computer systems of the US Treasury we could simply transfer money to the World Bank and the IMF to pay off the debts owed to them."

That was the bombshell. Kutini paused to assess the effect his statement had on Frank and held his breath as Frank stared beyond the canals, beyond the buildings across into wonderland. Kutini was silently waiting for his response.

"That is not impossible, but it's criminal," Frank responded after a long pause.

"Now who is talking morals and ethics?" Kutini asked with relief. "We can discuss the morality of this later, but if it will make you feel better let's look at it as reparations for slavery and resource exploitation." There was another long pause before Kutini finally said, "I'm starving, let's go and get some food."

They walked out of the canal area and crossed the bridge over the River Avon, which formed part of the canal network, onto Kendall Street, looking at menus in the entrances to the numerous restaurants lining the street and eventually settled on an Italian one.

During the meal, because Kutini wanted Frank to think about the proposition before committing himself, they agreed to meet a week later at Kew Gardens in London.

On the following Saturday the two friends met at the entrance to the Gardens and strolled down a well-trodden footpath leading to an open grass area. Kutini had settled for this area with few people about for their discussions. He had become paranoid over the years and never trusted enclosed spaces. He preferred to discuss sensitive issues directly without notes and in an open environment.

When Frank agreed to write the program that would hack into major banks in the US and into the US Treasury he knew it was a matter of security rather than skill. He had been into the computer systems of the US Defense Department and the US Treasury before. That wasn't a problem. The problem was what new security had been put in place since he last went in there.

***

Back home the first thing Frank did was to find out about the Department's networks. He checked their firewalls, networking software and operating systems in use and found out they hadn't changed, which was a good sign. He then checked for hotlists, usernames, network connections and sibling domains. He wondered what the security vulnerabilities were as he surfed through the internet to find out what new technology existed, since in the world of technology history was a matter of seconds rather than years.

After a few trials Frank decided that it was safe to use packet sniffing to go into the banks. He surreptitiously inserted the software program he had written into the host computer of Chase Manhattan, monitored it for specific identifications and passwords and sent the information back to himself. Using the Chase Manhattan computers he was able to go into the networks of other banks through the back door route. That wasn't new to Frank. He had gained access into NASA computers before by going through Lockheed.

Getting into the US Treasury's network required a lot more work, as he had to use internet protocol spoofing posing as a legitimate host. He had fabricated an internet protocol address that let his computer impersonate an offshore bank on the Cayman Islands. Using it as a springboard, he logged on to the Bank of England and finally onto the computers of the US Treasury, tricking the firewall in the process.

The firewall had first checked and confirmed his credentials as an insider. Frank smiled at the confirmation of his credentials. The computer geeks are not innovative, he thought. They had designed firewalls as an electronic analogue of the security guard at the entrance to a large office block or factory building; nothing to worry about for someone carrying a fake identity.

There were other encrypting and security measures, which Frank bypassed. He loved it. He was masquerading as a legitimate user throughout the system and by using this looping method his identity and location were inherently concealed. He couldn't be traced.

Frank then set out to write a program code that would do all the hacking with the click of a mouse. Again, his initial reference point was the internet.

CHAPTER 39

While Frank was busy writing the hacking program, Kutini and Laz were planning a big party for their son's first birthday. Laz had been responsible for arranging the birthday events. She had rung several Thames River cruises before settling for the Silver Fleet because they offered some of the most luxurious cruise boats in London and their Silver Barracuda Luncheon Club offered the finest season menus and wines throughout the year, providing a unique gastronomic experience of bespoke lunch and dinner cruises. It was their son's first birthday and she intended to celebrate it in style.

Kutini and Laz had just left home when a man who sat in the van across the street got out and crossed the road towards Kutini's house. Any passer-by would have mistaken the man for a telecom engineer as his transparent jacket carried the sign *Cable Connections.*

Kutini had connected to a cable telephone and television network a month earlier and the cable from the main duct to Kutini's property had been left lying overground. It was this cable that Carlos had aimed for and within ten minutes had fitted a miniature wireless router to Kutini's telephone line. The hassle-free bug was complete.

The couple had returned home and Kutini was holding and playing with his son when the phone rang.

"Kutini, it's Frank. Can we meet for a drink some time?" Kutini instantly knew that the 'project' was complete and ready for delivery.

"I've got news for you. My son's first birthday party is two weeks on Saturday and we are having it on a luxury boat cruise on River Thames. Why don't you get him a present?"

"Absolutely, I wouldn't miss it for anything. Where is the meeting point?"

"At the Tower Millennium pier. I'll send you the programme through the post."

Two kilometres down the road Carlos removed his headphones. I guess I've got to get busy and prepare for a big party, he thought. "I love parties," he said aloud.

***

Kutini and Laz sat in the Queen's Arms with a glass of orange juice each. They looked excited and expectant as they shared a personal joke about how they had first met. Amiga was smiling in his pram as though sharing his parent's joke.

Brian Gladstone was the first of their guests to arrive at the Queen's Arms. The pub stood across from the main entrance to the Tower of London and Brian found the couple seated to the right of the entrance to the pub. "Laz, you look gorgeous."

Laz acknowledged the compliment with a thank-you smile displaying an exquisite set of dazzling white teeth.

"Hey, Brian, it's good to see you," Kutini said rising. "What would you like to drink?"

"No, let me buy you drinks," Brian replied, made a gesture for Kutini to sit down and checked what they were drinking. "Orange juice!" he exclaimed.

"Yea man, Vitamin C gives more appetite than spirits," Kutini said with absolute conviction.

"Don't give me a lecture on vitamins. I eat better with rum," Brian countered and walked off to the bar. He returned with two glasses of orange juice and a glass of Morgans.

"You look smart, Brian."

"Just for you," Brian replied.

"I believe you," Kutini said, knowing how much Brian hated formal dress.

By midday forty-three of their guests who wanted to visit the Tower had arrived, so they bought a group ticket and made their way through the group entrance. They had just passed through Henry III's Watergate and Laz was flicking through an official guidebook she had bought when Kutini turned to her and asked, "Sweetheart, what would you like to see?"

Laz opened to page two of the guide, pointed and said, "that."

"The Crown Jewels." Kutini read from where her finger pointed. "Do you plan to wear them?"

"Not yet, only when I become the Queen."

"Of course, you are my Queen."

"Wow! Did you see that?" Laz asked turning to her husband as they listened to the history of the largest diamond ever found in Africa.

"What is it with women and diamonds?" Kutini asked rhetorically.

"We love them," Laz answered without taking her gaze from the TV screen.

They watched the entire footage of the coronation of Her Majesty Queen Elizabeth II in 1953 before going to the treasury holding the Crown Jewels.

"This is the real thing," Laz whispered. She felt the power of the single largest diamond as it sat at the strategic point in the Crown, surrounded by a thousand smaller diamonds.

As they left the fortress Kutini remarked to his wife, "Castles and forts remind me of imperialism, colonialism, oppression, suppression and exploitation."

"I think you just love them; remember the tour was your idea."

"I just wanted to see the Crown Jewels," Kutini replied, wondering how much the monarchy had paid for all these diamonds and gold. He had often thought about the amount of gold reserves held by Western governments and wondered how much of it was gained through exploitation by inciting and supporting conflicts and civil wars. Kutini shook his head as another more painful thought occurred to him – it was the same concept of inciting conflicts that had been used during the days of slavery, but as an African he feared that history was repeating itself with no lessons learned.

They arrived at the boat a few minutes before departure from the Tower Millennium pier but one more person was still expected. Five more minutes to the scheduled take off. Just as the boat was about to leave, Franklin Williams came running down the platform. He joined the rest and the boat took off in the direction of the Millennium Dome.

"Welcome aboard the Silver Barracuda Boat Cruise," the voice from the intercom announced, "we hope to make your cruise a memorable one." Three waiters opened and served wine around the tables followed by the starters. The classic music playing in the background provided a soothing, conducive atmosphere for conversation.

Later the gentle clatter of cutlery against real China amidst voices and music made people oblivious to the world outside. They heard the familiar sound as the waiters were clearing the tables to make way for the main course.

Outside on the river there was an unmistaken sound of police sirens, which suddenly put Franklin Williams on alert. He felt the tension build up inside him and became visibly nervous, wondering if the police knew about their clandestine activities and expecting that at any moment he would hear an order for the boat to stop. The sound of the siren drew closer and then next to the party boat. He couldn't resist watching the entire incident unfold. First, he saw a speedboat race towards them at top speed. For a couple of seconds that seemed like eternity to Frank the police boats were abreast with the party cruiser; then his nerves started to calm down as the sound of the siren faded away. He relaxed, took a deep breath and carried on with his meal.

***

Carlos heard the police boat speed past with full-blast sirens without turning his head. His speedboat lay idle on the river as the party makers continued their cruise. He had picked his precise location and timing and had positioned his boat a few metres away from where the party boat would finally dock. He still wasn't leaving anything to chance. He checked the explosives lying at the bottom of his boat, the detonator and the escape shaft beneath. I probably won't need them, he thought.

As Carlos waited for the return of the party boat, he fixed a tripod to the improvised hooks inside his boat and bolted the legs. He then shook it to ensure that it was firm, then placed on top of it a special gun that would appear to on-lookers as a professional camera and fixed the silencer to the space that would normally hold the camera's zoom lens. The gentle movement of the water below slowed down his progress, but he had time and there was no need for him to rush. When he had finished, he pressed a knob and the LCD screen came to life. He scanned the platform where he expected Kutini and his family would be to bid people farewell, then moved the camera round on the tripod to a different direction as though he was filming a documentary.

Carlos smiled as he played with his toy. He had conceptualised it as a member of the Special Forces during his time in the British Army and had been instrumental in its development. He had been able to get through security and pose as a news reporter with this piece of equipment, which could also function as a camera, at various operations throughout the world. What he liked most about this hi-tech gun was its two-way communication ability. He would send an infrared beam seeking his target whose unique skin-cell composition would be stored in the memory of the gun. When the gun was eventually fired the skin-cell-seeking bullet would follow a trajectory until the target was hit. As a superb marksman, Carlos hardly needed this sophisticated piece of equipment but when he had first used it he had been surprised at how close he got to his target without suspicion. He had used this gun many times with success, but this was the first time he was going to target his victim from a boat, and for the first time his victim was a baby. He reflected for a brief moment about his victim's age, but discarded the thought and waited.

***

The party boat sailed on enjoying her own romance with the river she loved so much, a river she had been married to right from her adolescence through a marriage that was prearranged, but for which she had no regrets. She had come to the Thames Flood Barrier and had started to make a u-turn just as the party makers finished their main course.

"Did you enjoy your meal?" Kutini asked his wife.

"It was wonderful, thanks," Laz replied.

"You're beautiful," Kutini told his wife for the sixth time since they left the house.

"Thanks for all this," Laz said in the most affectionate way Kutini could remember and kissed him. They held the kiss for a brief moment catching the attention of Brian who flashed a camera in their direction. Two other camera flashes followed before they detached their lips to the disappointment of a few others who had missed this unique moment. Brian instinctively looked in the direction of one of the camera flashes and spotted his friend Alex at the other end of the boat finishing his dessert.

"I didn't expect you here Alex, when did you come back?" Brian asked as he approached his friend.

"I got here this morning. I wasn't going to miss this party," Alex said.

"You promised to call me from Ghana, what happened to you?"

"The weather was hot when I arrived…"

"Yes," Brian said sarcastically, expecting Alex to come up with one of his usual excuses.

Alex ignored his sarcasm and continued, "We had rains the following day to everyone's relief, but the rainstorm took away the phone lines! Probably a reminder of how vulnerable man still is in spite of technological advancement."

"Stop being philosophical," Brian said.

"Why would I make up such a story?"

"I believe you Alex, I'm just wondering why we take life so seriously."

"You're right Brian. It's all the little trivial things we take for granted that make life worth living."

"Exactly, like sharing a room with a little mosquito on a hot night. It makes you realise that little things matter." They both laughed out loud as Brian remembered the mosquito bite experience when he first visited Ghana with Alex.

As though in response to the conversation the boat was suddenly quiet, the music stopped and a voice came over the intercom. "I hope you all enjoyed your meal. By courtesy of Mr. and Mrs. Bomanso we would now like to introduce to you a leading solo harpist from Dublin to give the show of a lifetime. Ladies and gentlemen, let's welcome on stage Sasha."

For a second nothing happened, then the tiny imperceptible lights set into the woodwork of the boat's floor came on dimly producing ghostly and shadowy figures inside the boat. From the centre of the floor two large planks of wood sprang to life, sliding in either direction to display an opening into a space below.

Another piece of woodwork, propelled by hydraulics, rose through the space about two metres above the boat floor. Sasha was sitting next to a huge harp standing almost three metres tall and one and a half wide. Amidst a loud welcoming applause, and almost unnoticed, Sasha started to play.

She had learnt her harp-playing skills while a medical student at Trinity College in Dublin and played the harp with her entire body, moving in rhythmic response to the pace of the music. Her hand movements were magical, almost angelic, as she played with passion beyond obsession. Underneath her, the stage spun slowly round and the spotlights hanging from the roof of the boat seemed to transform her into a goddess from a different era.

The audience was entranced not only with the melody of the music, but also with the sheer skill on display. For most of them this was the first time they had heard harp music being played live.

Sasha had been playing for about fifteen minutes, building the music into a crescendo. She finished her performance with a spectacular throwing of the hands in the air, her body bent backwards and her head looking up. She rose up to a deafening standing ovation, bowed several times to acknowledge the applause before settling into her chair.

The boat was just approaching the Festival Pier at Waterloo Bridge close to the I-MAX Cinema when Kutini's voice came over the loud speaker, interrupting the noisy chatter in the boat. "Friends and colleagues, on behalf of my wife, Amiga and myself I would like to thank you all for coming. I hope you had a good time. For those who are interested you can join us at the cinema for the rest of the evening."

People came off the boat and some stood on the pavement bidding farewell or just continuing with their conversations. Vicky was holding Amiga. She had agreed to take care of him for the rest of the evening as he was too young to be taken into the I-MAX. Frank walked up to Vicky, held Amiga's hand and said, "Happy birthday, Amiga. May you live to be a hundred." He then turned to Kutini and handed him a small gift-wrapped parcel.

"Where is Phyllis?" Kutini asked.

"She wanted to be here, but she was a little tired with her pregnancy."

"Congratulations. You kept that quiet, didn't you?"

"It was her preference."

"Are you coming to the cinema?" Kutini asked.

"No, I have seen it before," Frank replied, "I will speak to you soon."

Kutini was expecting 'the present' and his face was lit with excitement as he started thinking of the endless possibilities of things he could do with it.

***

On the river another boat rocked gently with the current. Kutini thought he saw the man behind the camera wave. Inside it Carlos checked that the silencer was tightly fixed to his gun and then looked at the LCD screen. Amiga's head was in target but he couldn't keep it in sight for long enough for the infrared to scan and store his skin-cell data due to the water beneath him. Carlos was concentrating and when the next chance came, he pressed a knob and waited a few seconds as the camera processed and stored Amiga's data in memory, then pressed a button that served as the trigger. He watched as the bullet made impact, then calmly he started the boat and sped away into the twilight.

Amiga was giggling in Vicky's arms when the single bullet tore through his right arm into his ribcage lifting the boy out of her arms and landing him on the pram below. For a brief moment time stood still…and then the place erupted. Vicky screamed just as the stunned Laz bent down and tried to pick up her son amidst repeated cries of "someone's shot my son!" For those few seconds dozens of the partygoers stood speechless in shock, then in a sight nearly as scary as the shooting itself, started running towards the boat. The resulting melee was a spectacle of screaming, shoving and trampling as people tried to take cover, the memories of the London bombing still fresh in their minds. All hell had broken loose on the platform. Laz threw her hands from her head into the sky back and forth as tears ran down her cheeks.

Kutini was reacting in a similar manner to the sheer surrealism of what had just occurred: reel and real life had switched places. "Someone please help, someone please call the ambulance," he screamed as he took Amiga away from Laz trying desperately to stop the bleeding with a blanket and hoping that he would live. "Who has done this to my son?" Kutini asked, unable to control his voice and instinctively looked out into the river, expecting to see the man with the camera, but the boat was gone. He looked to his left, his tear-filled eyes now barely able to see. Is that him standing over there? Could he be hiding around a corner? Maybe he is behind me…, he wondered as horrifying thoughts flashed through his confused mind.

Frank, who was recovering from his initial shock, removed his mobile phone and dialled 999, then tried to help Kutini stop the bleeding. Within seconds the police patrol boat that had passed the party boat earlier on, stopped at the pier. Their presence encouraged people to come to the scene and when they learnt the full impact of the incident, their reactions fluctuated from shock to anger to despair to bewilderment and back.

"What happened?" a police officer asked, as he tried to encourage Kutini to put the boy down in a resting position.

"I think the bullet came from a boat that was over there," Kutini said amid sobs, pointing to the spot where the boat had been moments ago.

The two policemen looked at each other. "That's the guy who seemed to have been filming," one policeman said, "I thought it looked a bit odd, let's go get him," he added, turned on his radio and called for help to the crime scene. As they rushed into their speedboat they saw the air ambulance lower itself onto the platform. "I hope the poor boy lives," a policeman said as they started the boat, turned on the siren and immediately gave chase to the mysterious boat.

Carlos heard the police siren approach, took a brief look behind him and judged the distance between them. He turned to full throttle, racing the boat towards the Docklands. The sudden change in the boat's speed drew the attention of the police. "That's him," an officer pointed, then spoke on his radio. Carlos took another quick glance behind him and saw the patrol boat gaining on him. He turned his concentration to his boat and for the next ten minutes maintained his distance, swerving to avoid other boats in his way. Then he saw the second police boat in front coming towards him. Carlos judged that within the next minute or so the police would catch up with him. He put on his oxygen mask and with a sudden movement spun the boat around to face the opposite direction, splattering water in the process. In that brief moment Carlos opened the escape tube and allowed the jet to suck him into the Thames water below. As he came out of the tube he felt the vibration of the water above as the second police boat sped over him. He felt in his pocket and pressed on the detonator.

A few hundred metres away an explosion rocked the empty boat lifting it above the river waters to form a fireball in mid air. The two police boats swerved on either side to avoid collision. As they slowed down to watch it burn, Carlos emerged at the side of another boat, climbed up and disappeared below the deck.

About the same time that Carlos' boat exploded, Amiga was rushed through the accident and emergency department of St. Mary's Hospital in London.

"Please God, don't let my son die," Laz prayed and cried as Amiga was pushed away on the hospital trolley.

"He will be alright," Vicky tried to reassure Laz, unable to hold back her own tears.

Kutini stood next to Frank at the hospital reception area anxiously watching the movements of the medical staff as they hurried back and forth.

Inside the operating room Amiga had been sedated. Two doctors and two nurses were monitoring his heart beat as they carried out an operation.

Laz was still in tears when a doctor approached and asked, "Are you Amiga's mother?"

"Is my son alright? Can I see him?"

"The operation was successful, but he is still in a critical condition. You will have to wait a little while," the doctor replied.

"Why, why would anyone want to kill a child?" Laz asked hysterically, staring into the blank wall and didn't notice a second doctor standing in front of her.

"Mrs. Kutini, I would like to see you and your husband," the doctor said.

"Doctor, doctor, is my son going to live? Can I see him now? Was he badly hurt? Who would want to harm a poor defenceless child? Please, please help me."

"Please come with me," the doctor said ignoring Laz's barrage of questions.

The couple followed him into his office leaving Frank and Vicky waiting outside.

"I'm sorry to ..."

Laz didn't wait for the doctor to finish. She rushed to Kutini and started beating and kicking him, and crying uncontrollably. "It's your fault. You wouldn't listen when I talk," she screamed. "You've killed my son."

"I'm sorry," the doctor repeated.

By the time they got home Laz had made up her mind. She had had enough of the marriage and couldn't stand the pressures anymore. She was leaving, and she would never forgive Kutini for her son's death. Laz started packing and despite Kutini's appeals was out of the house barely two hours after they got back.

CHAPTER 40

Kutini woke up the following day to the dazzling late spring morning sun, looked at the brilliance of the sun and thought this was unfair. How could the sun be smiling and the whole world be happy when there was so much sorrow in his life? The previous day's events had come flooding back like a river breaking its floodgates. He lay in bed feeling sorry for himself, wondering whether the bullet that killed his son hadn't been intended for him instead as he had been just inches away.

He finally got out of bed and called his relatives and friends to find out where his wife was without any success. He then called the hospital to arrange for his son's burial, but was told that he couldn't bury the child until the police murder investigation was complete. He put the phone down and went to his front door to pick up his mail. As he rose, he saw one letter sticking half way through his letter hole, so he pulled it out and realised there was no stamp on it and it had a curious fold. He opened it.

The brief handwritten note read: *Don't mess around with the mercenaries' case. Your son's death was just a warning.* Kutini almost passed out from the shock. So, his wife had been right, he thought. Kutini was too devastated even to go to work. He had decided that this was too high a price to pay for wanting the good of Africa and he would forget about his plans. He had passed the note from his son's killers to the police but for his own safety had contemplated asking for witness protection before testifying in the mercenaries' case against Tony Conrat.

In his confused state of mind, Kutini thought about his wife and wished she was with him. He had tried vainly to locate her.

He was sitting in his living room in front of the television when he noticed a DVD lying on the floor. He picked it up, and without thinking, put it into the player and pressed play. He saw his wife lying on a hospital bed surrounded by medical staff, then he was holding his son. He stopped the tape as he felt his wet cheeks.

Kutini got up and wiped his tears with the back of his hand; his mind was made up. He decided that it was exactly lack of action and intimidation like this that had left Africa in its current state. He would testify and continue with his plans. He would either live to achieve his goal or die trying. After all, he had already lost the two people who mattered most in his life. If he didn't fight for Africa's emancipation, his son's life would have been sacrificed in vain. What was his life worth when over fifty thousand people had died in Sierra Leone, half a million people in Angola and over three million people and still counting in the Democratic Republic of Congo?

With Kutini's new resolve he was surprised at his sudden surge of energy, then he felt the hunger that had been churning his stomach but which his brain hadn't registered. Kutini had not eaten properly since the death of his son. He left his apartment and went out for a pizza. While he was eating a thought occurred to him: to be able to beat his enemies at their own game he had to stay alive. They knew where he lived and the first thing they would do if they found out that he was going to testify would be to kill him.

Kutini discretely moved out of his plush apartment and took up a room in a council estate in the London suburb of Peckham. Once he was settled he made direct contact with the investigation team and offered to give his testimony, but only in recorded form. During the recording Kutini presented copies of the documents he had given to the Consul and the note he had received after the death of his son to the investigators on camera. He then kept to himself in his one bedroom flat.

***

One Sunday he returned from the convenience shop with the *Sunday Times* and sat down to read. As he turned the pages a headline caught his attention: *Tony Conrat Gets 24 Years in Prison.*

The main conduit for conflict minerals from southern Africa, Tony Conrat, has been incarcerated for 24 years for his involvement in the failed mercenaries' attempt to overthrow the government of Angola. In this landmark case, the High Court judge in South Africa sentenced the eight convicted people to a total of 240 years for their different roles in the crime. Ruling on their case the judge said that this would serve as a warning to people who cause civil wars on the continent just to satisfy their own personal greed...

Kutini put the paper down, heaved a sigh of relief and decided it was time. He then set out to execute the second phase of his plan, but first he had to find the parcel that Frank had presented at the party. He searched through the presents, which were still boxed, looking for Frank's parcel. When he didn't find it, he went through the contents again, carefully. It wasn't there.

Had those thugs come to search his house without his knowledge? What else did they know? As he tore open the wrappings on some of the parcels, his face lit up. He stopped his search, walked over to his wardrobe and removed the jacket he had worn on the party day. From the inside breast pocket he removed the parcel, unwrapped it and removed a disk.

Kutini went over to his computer and switched it on. As the computer booted, he removed an infrared mobile phone from a bag and turned it on; it was still fully charged. He had purchased the second-hand pay-as-you-go phone from a Sunday market so it wasn't registered to any name or address. The phone had a wireless access protocol with internet access. He logged on to the net through the mobile phone and inserted the disk.

Within minutes Kutini had accessed Chase Manhattan Bank's computer systems. From their accounts he transferred $20 million to an NGO account in the name of Women Empowerment and Development. The NGO had been founded and was run by Frank's sister Suma Williams with branches in five of the poorest countries in Africa; she had plans to expand to countries throughout the continent. Kutini put a note in the transaction line with the statement:

Approved by the board of directors of Chase Manhattan for women's economic enhancement in Africa.

Instructions were posted within the computer system authorising letters to be sent out to the organisations involved informing them of the donations.

From the Central National Bank in Waco, based in Texas, Kutini transferred $15 million into the account of Médecins Sans Frontières. As he made the transfer to MSF Kutini thought about the circumstances that had led to the creation of this international independent medical humanitarian organisation in 1971 by Bernard Kouchner and other French doctors: The Nigerian Civil War fought between July 1967 and January 1970 – a war that had claimed an estimated 3 million lives of which over 2 million were thought to be civilians. Kouchner who had worked in besieged Biafra as physician for the Red Cross during this time had set up the organisation as an aftermath of the war, which now provides free medical services throughout the developing world. Working through his list he also transferred various sums of money from corporate accounts held in the bank to the accounts of a list of NGOs operating throughout Africa.

Each transaction had a different note entered and when he was done he ripped open the mobile phone, smashed it and deposited the remnants in a rubbish bin.

Kutini had told Frank about the purpose of this operation and promised that none of the monetary transfers would be for personal gains. Frank knew Kutini was a man of his word and he believed in the course they were pursuing.

Next week, he would deal with Third World debts.

He prepared breakfast and brought it to bed. "Laz, breakfast is ready," he said to the empty space, remembering how he used to bring her breakfast in bed on Sundays. He ate in silence.

The following day at the Falcon Documents Center in Albuquerque, letters were mailed to women's organisations throughout Africa. At the Hummingbird Documents Center in Sacramento similar letters were sent out to different clients. During the week the headlines of most news media throughout Africa were on the subject of multinationals supporting women's empowerment in Africa.

On the Tuesday following the hacking, the Board of Directors of Chase Manhattan held an emergency meeting. In front of the board members were resignation letters from two of their most senior people: the President of the Bank and the Computer Systems Manager. The verdict was short and simple. Their resignations couldn't be accepted because the associated publicity could spell doom for the bank.

***

The following week Kutini sat in front of his computer and logged on to the internet using another pay-as-you-go mobile phone. The computer itself had been put together from components bought from various computer fairs because he didn't want it to be traced. He didn't want to leave anything to chance.

The seamless hacking into the computer systems of the International Monetary Fund, the World Bank and the US Treasury had taken him by surprise. He had known he could do it, but he hadn't realised how easy Frank had made the entire process.

On his desk was a list of African countries and the various sums of monies owed to the IMF and the World Bank. The first transactions involved the transfer from the Treasury to the two institutions of the total debt owed to each one by African countries. The transactions noted that the payments represented the cancellation of debts to these institutions owned by African countries. The second entry issued a directive from the institution's directors for letters to be sent out to the respective African governments notifying them of the cancellation of the debts.

Once he was done Kutini destroyed the disk and the mobile phone which had completed their tasks and were no longer required. Over the week he started taking the computer apart and disposing of the components in bits.

He called Frank.

"How was your weekend, Kutini?"

"It was fun," Kutini replied. That was all that Frank needed to hear to know that the operation had been successful. All his hard work had been rewarded. No details of the activities were discussed on the phone and the rest of the conversation centred on the war in Iraq.

The news headline dominating the week was the bulk cancellation of Third World debts owed to the World Bank and the IMF by America, starting with African countries.

CHAPTER 41

0900 hours. At FBI headquarters, Director Craig Brooks put down the receiver of his secured phone line and picked up that of the intercom. It automatically dialled his secretary. "Please cancel all my appointments for the afternoon."

At 1230 hours, the Secretary of the US Treasury was shown into his office.

Brooks was standing when Henry Price walked in looking stressed and tired. He looked ten years older than when Brooks had last seen him a week before.

"Thanks for making time to meet me at such a short notice," Price said with uneasiness.

"Please," Brooks said, pointing to the three-seater suite. "Was it snooping or stealing?" he asked as they sat down, continuing from where they had left off in their phone conversation.

"It's both and worse," Price started, "forty-five billion US dollars was transferred from the US Treasury to the World Bank and IMF accounts, representing the total amount owed to these two organisations by African countries."

"Let me get this right," Brooks cut in, "what you are saying is that the person responsible is an African."

"That's my first suspicion. The hacker had complete control of the system but we can't afford to make this public."

Price was more worried about his own job after this gargantuan security blunder.

"When did the hacking take place?"

"It was over the weekend and we didn't notice it until this morning."

Brooks picked up a notepad. "Are there any other organisations affected by this scam?" he asked.

"I am not aware of any," Price answered.

Brooks started to write. When he had finished he raised his head, cleared his throat and said to Price while reading from the notepad, "Henry, could you provide me with details of your computer system, the network architecture, the firewall and all other security measures. I would also like to know the people responsible for your network security and access control, and all those who have access to your system."

"That won't be a problem. I'll send the information to you as soon as I get back to the office."

"Here's what I would like us to do," Brooks said, "I'll arrange for us to meet the President to discuss this."

"It was going to be my next line of action."

"I'll have a plan of action ready for us to discuss," Brooks promised.

"I'd appreciate that," Price replied.

Brooks showed Price to the door and asked his secretary to arrange a meeting with Ian Clarke, the head of the FBI's Internet Fraud Unit.

At 1500 hours the two men sat facing each other at the rectangular glass-top table in Brooks' office. He passed a file to Clarke.

Clarke read the content of the file. "This is deep," he said when he finished.

"Young man, what you've just read sums up the gravity of the situation," Brooks said, taking the file back.

"The money transfer was internal, from the US Treasury to the IMF and the World Bank." Clarke paused, feeling the pressure and tension in the room while the silent anticipation persisted.

"What's the point?" Brooks asked with impatience.

"The two organisations can return the money and this never happened," Clarke concluded.

"It's not that simple," Brooks said. "What's missing in the report is that letters have been sent out to governments in Africa informing them about the cancellation of all debts."

"I believe we would be able to assist with identifying the security lapses in their systems," Clarke suggested, thinking: Only if I'm given the full picture. Aloud he said, "Certainly."

"Before we come to that I'd like you to do a random check on the financial institutions to see if there are any similar incidences elsewhere not being reported," Brooks said, "and could you provide me with that information by," he paused and looked at his watch, "five o'clock?"

It was an order and Clarke knew it. "Certainly," he said.

"Good, I will arrange a meeting with the President. Thanks for coming," Brooks said and got up.

At 1630 hours a FedEx delivery was taken to Brooks; it was from Price. An hour later Clarke delivered a report to Brooks containing a list of five banks that had been victims of computer hacking the week before. The report outlined the sums of money involved and went further – it stated that the President and the Computer Systems Manager of Chase Manhattan had tendered their resignations, but that the bank's board had rejected these. The report concluded there could be more financial institutions involved, but this couldn't be ascertained immediately.

Brooks studied the information from Price and the report from Clarke. They were frightening in their striking similarity – the recipients were all women's organisations in Africa.

The mention of Africa in the report brought Rudolf Reinhardt's name to Brooks' mind. He called him to his office.

After briefing Reinhardt on the hacking situation he showed him the action plan he had drawn up. Rudolf studied it together with the other pieces of information Brooks had given him and suggested a few changes which they included.

At 1750 hours a file marked 'top secret' was hand-delivered to the President. Brooks waited forty-five minutes to get a response.

The President could meet him and Price the next day at lunchtime, but would like to involve the CIA and the National Security Agency. Brooks could see the sense in involving the NSA which coordinated and planned activities to protect US information systems.

Brooks and Price were shown into the Oval Office the following day. The CIA boss and the head of the NSA were already with the President. "Shall we start?" the President asked.

They all sat down and the President passed a file around the table. "Brooks has prepared an action plan to combat the growing international terror. Our war on terror is becoming bigger and we will keep fighting and focusing the American people on those events until we root out evil. Without security we cannot build the strong economy that every American wants."

Price was the last to read the Brooks Report. "I didn't know other banks were involved," he said.

The President had read the report a few hours before the meeting. "I like Brooks' plan of action. What do you gentlemen think?" he asked.

"This seems like an act of international terrorism against the United States," the CIA head observed. "I think we should involve our international partners."

There was unanimous agreement from around the table.

"Gentlemen, you have my full authority to do whatever it takes to make our information systems secure and to bring these terrorists to justice." The President spoke with the authority of the leader of the most powerful nation in the world today. He knew he could have his way in the world's political system.

"We will do our best," Brooks assured him.

"This information should remain strictly confidential. We don't want the whole world to know the computer systems of our financial institutions have been compromised," Price cautioned.

After an hour of deliberations a working document was agreed on and with the approval of the President Operation Hackdown was born as a cross-border crackdown on hackers across the globe, a precedent taken from the crackdown in the 1990's.

Along with a change in legislation, there had also been a change in the US government's behaviour toward computer hacking - it had become much more pro-active, launching Operation Sundevil, which had cracked down on computer crime and hackers across the country, followed by operation Crackdown Redux, which had led to the seizure of computers, dealing a heavy blow to hackers.

Operation Hackdown was meant to be an international operation.

Brooks put Rudolf Reinhardt in charge of tracking down the source of the hacking and put together a team of two computer experts from his outfit to work with the FBI. Within two days they were able to trace the origin of the hacker to the United Kingdom.

Rudolf informed MI5 in London about Operation Hackdown and provided them with information regarding the use of two mobile phones in the biggest hacking to hit the United States.

At the MI5 office in London, Ray Ford was assigned to tracking the two mobile phone numbers the FBI had given them. He punched the first telephone number into his computer, pressed return to get into the search mode and waited a few seconds as the computer scanned through a series of cellular information before stopping on a highlighted text, displaying the cell identification of where the phone had been used. He typed the second phone number which displayed the same cell identification with the location in Peckham, London. Ray then printed the information including the day and time of the use of the two phones.

The MI5-led raid on the homes in the London suburb of Peckham was unprecedented, and led to the seizure of many computers. These were taken to the MI5 office for the information held on them to be studied and analysed. They labelled each piece of computer equipment taken with the name and address of the owner.

Despite the large scale nature of the operation, the seizure of the computers was the easy bit. Ray Ford and his colleagues now faced the task of going through each machine searching for clues to the hacking. After several days, Ray found one with encrypted files and when they were decrypted the first striking piece of information was the discovery of the name of Ramsey Yousef, who was a member of the international terrorist group responsible for bombing the World Trade Center in 1994 and a Manila Air airliner in late 1995. These files also contained the startling discovery, for the first time, of the full elaborate plan that led to September 11.

There was a third-level encrypted file that Ray and his team at the MI5 couldn't get access to. To be able to progress they had to get hold of the owner of the computer. The problem was when they raided that address the occupant, Malik Al Shaba, who possibly had many aliases, was not there and MI5 had to break in to gain access.

When the neighbours were asked about him no one recalled seeing anyone living there.

Malik Al Shaba used his Peckham address only for his underground activities and visited there infrequently only when he needed to. He fronted his terrorist role with an on-line business selling Arabian and Persian antiques and carpets and conducted his sales through encrypted e-mail. All his financial transactions were made via anonymous wire transfers using another address. He had, on only a couple of occasions, worked from the computer seized in the operation.

Unknown to most computer users, the America and British governments had secretly agreed with Microsoft that it would provide Data Interception by Remote Transmission (DIRT) as part of their standard operating system without making the product obvious. DIRT was designed to allow remote monitoring of a subject's personal computer by law-enforcement and other intelligence-gathering agencies.

Using the information decrypted from Malik Al Shaba's computer MI5 was monitoring for any internet use containing certain keywords and key phrases. While scanning the internet across the UK they picked up the phrase Persian Antiques from several sources. The intelligent agents were using custom-designed, top-of-the-range computers with high specification processor speeds not available commercially. To process and act on intelligence in real time was the main objective when the 'thinking computer' was first put on trial at the FBI's Computer Analysis Response Team intelligence processing and forensics laboratory in April 1998.

The FBI matched the phrase against the email address found on Malik Al Shaba's computer. Other pieces of information they had about him were verified and his identity was checked. They had Malik; he was on the net.

Meanwhile DIRT was surreptitiously logging his keystrokes. The information captured was simultaneously transmitted to a pre-determined internet address where DIRT decoded the information and relayed it back to the investigators within seconds.

Malik Al Shaba had walked right into an FBI sting and within thirty minutes of locating him, police had sealed off the entire B13 postcode area of Birmingham with two choppers hovering above. Police efforts were concentrated on one block within the area. Three officers knocked on the door of 499 Moor Green Lane.

Malik's arrest at his hideaway in Birmingham was swift and precise. He was taken to the MI5 office in London. After several days of interrogations, it appeared Malik Al Shaba was still withholding information the FBI believed would be on his computer and considered vital for the apprehension of his other colleagues.

Malik Al Shaba was offered a deal that if he cooperated his sentence would be lenient; otherwise he faced several life sentences or the death penalty if he was sent to America. He provided a paperback copy of Mario Puzo's *The Godfather,* which held the key to decrypting the data: the first letter of each sentence in the last paragraph on every page. It would have been impossible to decrypt anything without this.

The decryption of the information on Malik's computer gave details of several operations planned across Europe and North America. It provided names, locations and important events when the operations would be carried out. This information was passed to the intelligence agencies of the countries involved and an international manhunt led to the arrest of several terrorist operatives, nipping their planned terrorist operations in the bud. Malik Al Shaba's arrest gained front-page coverage throughout the international press.

CHAPTER 42

While the FBI's triumph in arresting Malik Al Shaba spurred them to continue with their main objective of finding the computer hacker Kutini was enjoying the way he was directing their attention away from his big scheme of things. The distraction provided him with enough time to plan.

At the FBI temporary headquarters set up in London for this operation, intelligence agents went through the details of the crime again. This time they were looking to narrow down the search. They analysed the information available beyond just the location. The list of the beneficiaries of the crime was revealing. Out of the twenty-eight non-governmental organisations that benefited from the crime twenty-one of them had their headquarters located in West Africa.

By inference, the FBI decided the hacker must be from one of these countries and would most likely be from an English speaking West African country. They agreed to work with the theory that the person was either a Nigerian or a Ghanaian.

All the computers they seized were categorised and labelled. All those seized from people of African origin were grouped together, from which they isolated those belonging to West Africans and then started detailed checks with computers belonging to Nigerians and Ghanaians.

The investigation was slow and laborious as most of the computers did not contain much beyond emails and student project works. On one computer they found child pornography and decided they would let the Metropolitan Police deal with that. It was neither their priority nor their responsibility.

At FBI headquarters in Washington DC Craig Brooks and his Internet Fraud Unit head, Ian Clarke, sat down to reassess the direction of the investigation based on the updates Brooks had received from their operational headquarters at Hackdown in London.

"We face an incredibly uphill task with this sort of hi-tech crime," Brooks said, inferring from the dead ends they had come to so far in this particular investigation.

"Quite right," Clarke agreed, "especially when little is needed other than knowledge, a computer and a phone connection – and that is going to be less traceable than state-sponsored terrorism. Besides, we're going to have more potential for hoaxes."

"Have we considered the possibility that the hacker could be a lone ranger?" Brooks asked.

They had been working on the premise that they would find an individual who was working within a network to carry out the crimes. This person they believed came from one of the countries that benefited from the monetary transfers.

"I don't believe this is the work of one individual who carries a grudge," Clarke said, thinking it was unlikely for one person to undertake such enormous responsibility alone. "Criminal hackers sometimes offer their services to countries the United States would categorise as rogue states."

"That is a possibility," Brooks stated, well aware some of these hackers had various schemes to undo vital US interests through computer intrusions. The possibility of an 'electronic Pearl Harbour' was now a real threat.

"Computer crime and other information security breaches are now the biggest threats to our economic competitiveness and the rule of law in cyberspace," Clarke observed, his frustration glaringly obvious. He also knew the financial cost was tangible and alarming – well over $100 million in losses annually.

Clarke was no novice in this type of crime. In the summer of 2004 Russian hackers led by Vladimir Levin had broken into Citibank's computers and made unauthorised transfers totalling more than $10 million from customers' accounts. Citibank had recovered all but $400,000. In order to lure the Russians to America Clarke had created fictitious California-based Cyber Securities Inc. and posted the following advert on its website:

COMPUTER SECURITY PERSONNEL WANTED

Top salaries paid plus benefits
US Nationality given
Whoever is able to decrypt the following code should apply:

Searching and searching in the darkness of the abyss
I saw the light in the zenith overcome the darkness
Instead of the light illuminating my path, it blinded me

Searching and searching for ways to get out of bondage
I found freedom in the land of dreams and opportunities
Instead of freedom, I became captive of fear of terrorists

Searching and searching, I came to the truth
Trust in the might of America given by the Almighty God
This great nation holds the responsibility for world peace

Searching and searching, I came to this realisation
That ultimate power ultimately corrupts
Instead of the realisation enlightening me, it frightened me

The truth is placed in our paths everyday
Which we stumble upon in our daily quests
Instead of recognising it, we simply continue as before.

Even for Vladimir Levin and his group this code proved to be quite a challenge. They set to work as soon as they saw the advert and started by looking at the structure of the text, which was made up of five three-line stanzas.

The first considerations were the possibilities offered by the digits: three and five, three times five, fifty-three, or three plus five. However, these possible combinations could provide them with no sensible clue to the code.

Next Levin and his colleagues looked at the word layout. The first word of each stanza started with *Searching*, except the last stanza which started with *The truth. Searching for the truth.* "What is the truth?" Levin asked but none of his colleagues could provide any answers.

They continued their work but after several days of unsuccessful attempts with the word layout approach one of Levin's guys said, "Let's get back to basics and use the good old graph paper."

A copy of the advert was made onto an A4 sheet of paper. A similar size graph sheet was copied onto a transparency. The two were superimposed one over the other. The first words that jumped out of the code were *Trust* and *God,* and both words were located at the opposite ends on the same line, right in the middle of the code.

We are on to cracking the code, Levin was thinking. "What is the significance of this to America?" he asked.

"That America is a Christian country?" a colleague asked.

"More than that," Levin replied, "on their currency they have the words *In God We Trust.*"

"I don't see how that could be the code," another member of the group said.

"It isn't the code, but it's part of it," Levin replied. "What is the symbol of Christianity?" he asked, while drawing a horizontal line through the middle of the code with a red marker to highlight the two words Trust and God.

"The Cross," the group chorused.

"That's correct," Levin confirmed and drew a vertical line down the middle of the sheet.

"Amazing," a colleague said.

The position of the words *In God We Trust* corresponded to the four edges of the Christian Cross with the name America at the heart of it.

"Bastards," Levin said.

"FBI here we come," another member added jubilantly.

***

Inside the office of Cyber Securities in California Clarke and his colleagues posing as Cyber Securities officials asked the Russians to demonstrate their prowess. Next door, Clarke sat behind his DIRT-outfitted computer and watched his computer screen as the software recorded every keystroke while the Russians worked their way through another computer code.

Clarke's elaborate ruse had led to their arrest and Levin and his men had pleaded guilty to illegally transferring money to a number of their personal accounts throughout the world. Court papers had described the men as kingpins of Russian computer crime who had hacked into the networks of at least forty US companies extorting money.

Ian Clarke was contemplating a similar sort of approach to attract the new bank hacker, but then he thought, if the culprit had not made any personal gain from the hacking it was unlikely any such approach would appeal to them. He had to rethink strategy.

Rudolf and his team had worked tirelessly from their London base and in addition to Malik's conviction and the penetration of the terrorist network Operation Hackdown had led to several arrests involving drugs, credit card fraud and other criminal activities. However, the identity of the computer hacker was still a mystery. He returned to the United States with the case still unsolved on the FBI files.

CHAPTER 43

Since Kutini and Yaro returned from their near-death experience in the Democratic Republic of Congo, they had been in touch planning to unite Africa. After Kutini's successful hacking to transfer money to pay off Africa's foreign debts Yaro had come from Boston to discuss the final phase of their plan. He was with Kutini at his Peckham flat when they heard a knock on the door. Kutini was surprised as he wasn't expecting anyone. He hesitated but there was a second, louder knock so he went and opened the door.

"Police," a uniform officer announced, showing his badge, "we have a warrant to search this property for computers." Two other armed police officers stood behind.

"I don't have a computer here," Kutini said as the policemen moved into his flat and started searching. After ten minutes of searching in the one-bedroom flat they left, leaving behind an awful mess.

"Sorry for the inconvenience," one police officer said as they left without finding anything.

As soon as the police left, Kutini and Yaro looked at each other without saying a word. "What time is your flight?" Kutini asked looking at his watch.

"It's an evening flight. Check-in is at seven."

"We have all afternoon. Let's go for a drive," Kutini suggested.

As they left the house they saw the heavy police presence around the area and they could hear a door being forced open a floor above them. When they reached the ground floor there were police patrolling the residents' car park but Kutini hadn't realised the reason until they got into his car.

An armed police officer came and knocked on the driver window. Kutini rolled down the glass and the police said, "Can we check your car?" After satisfying himself there was nothing in the car, the officer said, "Drive carefully."

"Thanks," Kutini said and they drove off.

No-one spoke for the next fifteen minutes until Kutini came to a stop and parked the car at an on-street parking area. "Where are we going?" Yaro asked.

"Come, I will tell you."

When they got out of the car Kutini went to the parking meter, slotted ten pound coins in and took a ticket. He didn't bother to check how long it allowed him to stay. He knew there would be enough credit long into the night.

"Let's go and get a rented car," Kutini said after he had displayed the parking ticket in the car and locked the doors, "I'm taking no chances of my car being bugged."

They walked the short distance to the local rental for a car and drove off. For the next three hours they were either driving or sitting in traffic around London talking about their plan. Kutini later drove Yaro to Heathrow for his flight back to the United States.

***

After Yaro had left, Kutini came back and followed the daily news about the police operation in Peckham. He waited for six weeks until the raid had ceased being headline news before making his ultimate move.

Kutini assembled another computer from components he had bought from visits to various car-boot sales. Using a second-hand pay-as-you-go mobile phone he had also bought from a Sunday market he connected to the internet and typed the phrase 'computer fairs in UK'. After a few seconds, the search engine spat out thousands of matches. Across the screen he read '1 to 15 out of 34,519 matches found'.

Kutini knew from experience that the first fifteen results would provide him with the information he was looking for. He scrolled down the screen, paused at the hypertext *UK's major computers fairs* and clicked on it. A couple of seconds later he was connected to a site displaying all major computer fairs throughout the UK. He made an entry in his diary.

Kutini then removed a PC magazine from the book shelf above his desk and went through it to reacquaint himself with the latest gadgets in the information computer world. He found the things he was interested in, took a pocket notebook and wrote down a list of items with their specifications. As he made the last entry the phone rang. Kutini picked it up. It was Yaro Tunde on the line.

"Kutini, how are you doing?" Yaro asked.

"I'm doing great."

"Beautiful," Yaro replied. "Listen, I've booked my flight for next week. I should see you then."

"I'm looking forward to it," Kutini replied with excitement.

***

Saturday morning. Kutini started his weekend trip to Newcastle upon Tyne. He arrived late in the afternoon and spent the rest of the evening going through the list of items he wanted to buy. The following day at the computer fair Kutini approached a table with a variety of motherboards. He chose a regular one, then a Pentium IV with 2.4GHz and a Samsung double data rate RAM with a data transfer rate of 500MHz.

At another stand Kutini bought a 40 gigabyte hard drive, a CD-RW and DVD drive, a video card and a sound card. He looked at his shopping list; there were three items left, one of which he would buy in Ghana. He bought the other two items, a modem and a mouse, and decided to wander round the fair grounds in case he had missed out something. As he passed an accessories stand he saw a set of screws and picked some in case he needed them. His shopping was complete.

***

Kutini met Yaro at Paddington Station in London at half past twelve the following Saturday afternoon and they drove to the Connaught Restaurant in Mayfair.

Kutini had pre-booked the place a week earlier when Yaro had rung to tell him he was coming. It was one of the most expensive restaurants in the city and Kutini had been lucky to get a place with just a week's notice. He had chosen it not because he wanted to impress Yaro, but he wanted them to have a good treat after what they had been through together.

"What would you like to drink, sir?" the waiter asked.

"Champagne," Kutini answered without waiting for Yaro's opinion. "If we are celebrating, we must celebrate in style," he said to Yaro.

The waiter came back with champagne. "What is the occasion sir?" he asked

"It's my friend's birthday," Yaro lied.

"Happy birthday sir," the waiter said, opened the bottle and took their orders.

"To Africa," Yaro said raising his glass

"To our success," Kutini added.

The fresh seafood had taken forty-five minutes to arrive but they had been so engrossed in their conversation they didn't notice the time pass.

"It's is delicious," Yaro remarked after swallowing his first bite.

"The Connaught is renowned for good food," Kutini added.

"May be you should become a 'Friend of the Connaught,'" Yaro joked, reading from a leaflet, "then you will qualify for their guaranteed twenty-four hour service, a special delivery to anywhere in London and limo pick up service."

A man, dressed smartly and differently to the waiters, stopped by their table. "How is your meal, Dr. Bomanso and Mr. Tunde?" he asked.

"Excellent food," Kutini replied, surprised he knew their names.

As the man moved on Yaro noticed he would stop at every table and chat to customers, addressing some of them by their first names. He seemed to be employed just for that role, Yaro thought.

Yaro and Kutini had finished their meal, paid the bill and were on their way out of the restaurant. As they approached the door, the man who had come to speak to them during the meal was at the door. "Thank you, Dr. Bomanso," he said, shaking hands with Kutini. "… and Mr. Tunde. It was a pleasure having you both here," he added with the politeness, but somehow informality, of a host at a house party.

"That's what I call service," Yaro said as they walked out of the door.

The two men walked the short distance to the car park. Kutini opened the back door and held it open for Yaro. He got in after Yaro, closed the door and said, "It'll be better to have our discussion here without any eavesdropping."

Yaro and Kutini sat in the car and for the next hour they discussed their plans in details. They did not write anything down. It was a foolproof plan. No one knew of it besides the two of them. They couldn't fail.

There was a knock on the car door, alarming Kutini. Had they been bugged? For an instant he couldn't think straight.

"What do you want?" he asked in a panic.

"I was wondering if you needed a quiet place for your meeting. We have such a place for you as a complimentary gesture." A member of staff from the restaurant had seen them on closed-circuit television.

"No thank you, we are fine," Kutini said harshly. The staff member turned to go without saying anything. "Err ... sorry for being rude, I thought you mistook us for carjackers."

"That's alright, sir, this place is well secured; thieves don't get in here," he answered with a smile and disappeared into the building.

"Let's get out of here," Yaro suggested.

They drove out of the restaurant car park and headed towards the Embankment area of the River Thames. They parked on a side road and walked along the river finalising their plans.

"Is there anything we have left out?" Yaro asked.

They went over the plan again and when they were sure they had considered all eventualities, they walked back to the car. Kutini opened the door and before they could get in, they heard the command, "Don't move." They froze. A thousand things went through Kutini's head. That son of a bitch had bugged their car, he thought. How could they have been so careless? Why would their car be bugged in the first place? No, something didn't seem right. Was Yaro a double agent?

"Hands on your heads," another command followed. They obeyed. Two policemen approached with their guns pointed at them. The police frisked them and after satisfying themselves they were clean, asked them to turn round.

"Open the boot," one policeman ordered. Kutini went round to open it. As he did so, he asked, "What is going on."

"Just open the boot," the policeman shouted, "we have information you two are dealing in drugs."

"For heaven's sake, us into drugs?" Kutini asked in exasperation, mixed with a sense of relief it wasn't to do with what he had feared.

"We have to search the whole car, I'm afraid."

The police searched the car looking through the glove compartment, under the seats, beneath the carpet and in every conceivable place that could conceal drugs. They found none.

"Sorry for inconveniencing you; you may go now," a policeman said, satisfied they were no hidden drugs. "Be careful," the policeman added.

CHAPTER 44

The following weekend Kutini packed his prized buys into his travelling case. The next day he was on a KLM flight to Amsterdam, from where he connected to Lagos and travelled by road to Ghana.

The morning sun with its bright intruding rays greeted Kutini on his first day in the Ghanaian capital, Accra. As he lay on his bed he could hear the waves from the sea. He loved the sound of the waves. He stretched out on his bed, feeling he could loll there all day, but decided he had business to attend to. As he turned on the bed his hand touched on one of the hotel flyers. He picked it up and looked at the various facilities the hotel offered. He laughed, resting his eyes on the swimming pool, wondering why people would want to be in a pool when the sea was just a step away.

He was about to put the flyer down when the words *professional masseurs* caught his attention. An idea came to his mind and he felt so excited. He would go for a massage and pick up a few skills he could surprise his wife with. If she came back that is, he thought. She used to love being massaged and he used to enjoy doing it for her; the only problem was he had never got it entirely right. Either he was pressing too hard and causing pain or he was not putting enough pressure at the points where it mattered. He had thought about taking some lessons for her sake, but never had the time to do it.

He got up from bed and took a shower. It was only eight in the morning, but the tropical heat was already announcing its presence outside the hotel's air-conditioned rooms. He came out of the shower, put on his swimming shorts and a T-shirt, picked up a towel and went out into the hotel swimming pool. He stayed in the pool for about an hour, mostly looking into the sky and just watching people go about their business. There were few people around the pool at this time of the day. Most people staying there were on business.

Just as he came out of the water he saw one of the hotel workers and asked for the massage room.

"I want to book a massage," he said, announcing his arrival to two sporty-dressed young women behind a desk.

"You can have it now if you want," one of the women answered.

"Sure, why not?" Kutini took up the offer.

"An hour or half an hour?" she asked, stating the longer time first. It always worked as most people would take the first offer without a thought.

"An hour will be just fine," he replied.

"This way, sir," the woman said leading Kutini to one of the private massage rooms.

"Please remove your clothes and hang them up," she said.

"Everything?" Kutini asked naively. He had never been to a professional masseur and felt uncomfortable with removing all his clothes.

"Yes, there is a towel on the bed," she replied as she left the room and closed the door behind her.

Kutini removed his clothes, tied a towel around his waist and laid face down on the metre-high bed in the single-bed massage room.

Kutini had been lying on the bed for about two minutes when the young woman opened the door without announcement, closed it behind her and asked, "Are you comfortable?"

Without waiting for an answer she said, "Let me make you comfortable." She loosened the towel around Kutini's waist, then poured some essential oils into an oil burner and lit a candle beneath.

"You made a wise choice of an hour, Mr. . . ."

"Donchebe," he lied.

"My name is Hilda."

"Why is an hour a better deal Hilda?" he asked.

"Because you get a special treat with these relaxation oils," she replied as she put together a mixture of delicately scented oils and started working on Kutini's right foot.

"Are you here on business or holiday?" she asked.

"I'm on a short holiday."

"How long for?"

"Oh, just a couple of weeks."

Hilda was working her way up Kutini's thighs, her delicate fingers moving up and down and intermittently digging a little deeper into his skin, giving him a relaxing sensual feeling.

"Do you live in America?" she asked presumptuously.

"No, I live mostly here in Ghana, but I spend some time on my business dealings in the UK," Kutini lied again.

Working both hands Hilda's expert fingers came up to the end of Kutini's thighs. She paused for a second or so and lifted the towel slightly to expose the base of his buttocks. She worked there for a brief moment before slipping to his thighs. The two hands moved in opposite directions making a semi-circle as her hands made contact with the bed around his groin.

"That feels so good," Kutini said.

"I am glad you're enjoying it."

"How long have you been doing this?"

"About a year now."

"You're very good at it." Kutini paid her the compliment only because he was enjoying it. He had no previous experience to tell an amateur from a pro.

"I took some courses in it," she explained and moved to the right side of Kutini when she had finished working on his legs.

Kutini's head was on the pillow facing right when she came to his right side to massage his back. Her tight shorts barely covered her bottom, displaying a beautiful set of legs that went all the way to her ankles where her mini socks guided her feet into a pair of immaculate white Nike trainers. Her belly-button blouse moved upwards to hold a pair of shapely good-sized breasts before covering her shoulders and her back, exposing the contrast between her paler stomach and the sun-tanned darker legs of her mixed-raced skin. She looked more like a tennis star at the Centre Court in Wimbledon.

"You're muscular," Hilda said as she massaged his shoulders and biceps.

She was now standing directly where Kutini's head was resting sideways on the pillow facing Hilda's stomach. She pressed her belly in his face as she stretched to massage his shoulders from her standing position. Kutini closed his eyes.

"Turn round please," Hilda said when she had finished with his back. As she helped Kutini to roll over, the towel came off. She saw his hardness and pulled the towel over it. The towel dangled above like a scarecrow sitting on a lanky pole waiting for the wind to blow. She swallowed hard as she rubbed a mixture of oils into her palm.

Hilda was amazed at what she saw. She had heard about size, but this was out of this world. She continued massaging her client, starting from his stomach towards his chest. There was a delicate touch and twist at his nipples. It was for a brief moment, but for Hilda the deliberate tickle of his nipple with her ring, arousing a sensual mixture of pain and pleasure, did the trick. She heard a slight moan of joy from Kutini. With a hand glide movement, she separated her hands as they came down his groin. His iron-hard penis stood still in its sheltered position like a monumental edifice waiting to be unveiled.

Again, the sound came, of pleasure; relaxation had long given way to a more powerful and potent force taking control over Kutini's body.

"Anything else you want me to do?" Hilda asked, knowing she had hit the very core of Kutini's vulnerability.

"No."

"Are you sure?" she asked, deliberately dragging her speech and looking directly into his eyes.

"Yes."

"You're sure you don't want to have sex?"

"No, I don't."

No? This son-of-a-bitch cannot get away with this, she thought. She was already wet inside and so desperately wanted him inside her.

"Why? Are you married?"

"Yes." Kutini was surprised at how quickly the answer had come. Although his wife had left him, he still hoped she would come back and had not considered dating anyone.

Hilda was expecting that answer. "How would you like to read the headlines with your photo: Man trying to rape a hotel masseur?"

He instantly felt trapped and could not believe how he had let himself into this situation. The edifice was slowly deflating.

"You better keep that thing as hard as you can get it." It was a command that was not obeyed.

"Don't be scared. I'm putting on a female condom," she said as she removed her shorts to reveal a G-String. She removed it and inserted the condom. She bent down and took him in her mouth, not wanting to waste any more time getting him up. They had already been in the room for forty-five minutes.

As soon as he was up again, she climbed onto the bed and lowered herself on him. Slowly she moved up and down.

"It feels so good," she moaned.

Kutini lay there with mixed feeling wondering whether he could sue her for raping him. No one would believe him, he reasoned. No one.

He was coming. Oh, it felt good after all. He felt her lift herself up and stop just at the tip, pull on his testicles and hold them for a couple of seconds. It stopped him from coming just yet and when she climaxed her whole body shook and shuddered like an electrically charged robot dancing to *agbagya* music. She let her full body fall on Kutini. At that moment, he came.

She lay on top of him for some seconds before rolling off to one side and stepped on the floor. Kutini was half asleep.

"Your hour is up, sir," Hilda said, almost a whisper and walked out of the room.

Kutini got up and dressed, and when he opened the door Hilda was waiting.

"This way sir," she said, pointing to the desk. She took his room number, wrote out the invoice and said, "If you would like to sign here please."

Kutini obliged.

"I hope you enjoyed the session?" Hilda's colleague asked innocently.

"It was good," Kutini replied.

"Come back anytime," Hilda called after him.

Kutini walked away, stopping at the reception to pick up a local newspaper, and went to his room. When he went in, there was a message waiting for him. He read the note and suddenly his mental ordeal and physical exhaustion turned into excitement.

Yaro had arrived and was staying in Room 407. He wanted to go to see him immediately, but decided he would have a shower first. No, he changed his mind. He was so tired he would have to see him later so he lay on the bed and slept soundly for two hours.

When Kutini woke up, he felt so hungry and hoped Yaro would be hungry too. He dialled the intercom to Yaro's room, but there was no response, so he decided to go and eat alone at the hotel restaurant.

Yaro was at the restaurant and saw Kutini as he entered. Kutini walked over to the table and just as he approached, Yaro stood up with his arms opened ready for a hug.

"I thought you were out chasing women," Yaro said as they sat down.

"I was in the pool. How was your flight?"

"It was smooth and there was this beautiful …"

"You and women, don't you ever think of your wife?"

"Listen brother, life is too short to waste it on one woman. Think of what could have happened to us in Congo."

"It still doesn't make it right," Kutini objected, but he was thinking maybe Yaro was right and perhaps he should stop feeling guilty about what happened.

"Hey, let's forget about morals and let me show you Accra," Kutini said. It was Yaro's first visit to the Ghanaian capital in several years.

"Excellent idea; take me where I can see real Ghanaian women."

"You'll have your fill tonight, for now let's go and do some business."

"What business?" Yaro asked.

"I still need to buy some computer accessories and we need transport."

"I brought a laptop, ready to go."

"I told you I'm not taking any risks of being traced. I'm assembling a computer."

"Relax this one was bought with a credit card that cannot be traced to anyone."

"It still doesn't make the system safe, besides it sounds like fraud."

"Look who's lecturing me about morals!"

"OK, I've already got all the accessories except a monitor and a keyboard, there is nothing wrong with two computers."

When they had finished their meal the two friends went into the city to a computer shop. They didn't waste time; Kutini found the type of monitor and keyboard he wanted and took them to the checkout point.

"Have you seen our offers on CPUs, sir?" the woman at the till tried her luck on selling, "we would also do the installation and provide you with support."

"I've got everything I want, thanks," Kutini replied.

"How are you paying, cash or credit card?" the cashier asked.

"Cash."

"Dollars or cedis?"

"Cedis, of course. Since when did dollars become the legal tender in this country?" Kutini asked, getting angry at the apparent arrogance of the cashier.

"You get a discount if you're paying in dollars," the cashier added, ignoring Kutini's agitation.

Kutini handed her the cash in cedis.

Their next stop was a used car market for four-wheel drives. There were cars mostly from continental Europe, but some from

America. The salesman was pitching his prices based on the age of the car, but Kutini and Yaro were looking at both the age and the mileage. In the end they decided to go by the age and the physical condition as they couldn't be sure whether the mileage had been tampered with. When they had decided on the car they wanted they found a mechanic who checked the vehicle and confirmed it was in good condition.

The next day they drove 500 kilometres to Kutini's ranch in seven hours, where they spent two days assembling solar power equipment, which had been brought earlier. On the third day Kutini assembled the computer and turned it on when he had finished. He installed software and was ready to go to work.

For four weeks Kutini busied himself with writing the code that would get him inside America's defence computers. He had stayed away from computer hacking for moral reasons and had resisted the temptation of using it for personal gains, but now he was embarking on a justified course in the fight against the economic depravation of the African people who had long been marginalised on the global scene.

Kutini was compiling one of the routines in his code one cool afternoon when Yaro, who had been watching the cattle drink from a pond nearby, came up to him and asked, "How many cows have you got on this ranch?"

"I don't know; a few thousand maybe."

"What if the herd man should sell some without your parents' knowledge?"

"No, he won't do that. Besides, it's easy to check."

"How?"

Kutini took out Yaro's notebook computer, connected it to his cell phone and logged onto the internet where he called up a satellite navigation system to get an exact fix on his location. He then fed his location to another satellite, which scanned the area in an extra-high-resolution photograph. He exported it to an image processing facility internet site. After a few minutes, he received an email response and printed out a full-colour report on his hi-tech miniaturised laser printer.

He turned to Yaro and said, "There are exactly 2,856 cows in the ranch."

"That's ingenious."

"That's technology," Kutini said.

"How soon do you expect to test the program?"

"I'm almost there. A few more hours and we'll be ready to test it," Kutini replied, looking past Yaro, "it's a cool pleasant afternoon. I need a break, should we take a walk?"

"It's beautiful out here," Yaro observed as they made their way out of the grass field into the savannah woodland.

"I love the serenity, the sound of the birds and the natural environment," Kutini replied.

"You're a computer expert, how did you come to the idea of farming?"

"I wanted to provide employment for my people and to show we have the resources."

"Lack of resources and capital has always been our major problem," Yaro said.

"That's the theory we were taught in school, which is the problem with our education."

"What do you mean?"

"We are taught that foreign aid is the solution to the capital problem. No wonder we have a donor mentality," Kutini answered, "there are a lot of things we could do differently."

"Like what?"

"No income tax and no corporate tax."

"That's taking things to the extreme. How can an economy survive without such taxes?"

"Simple, let employers pay a percentage of earnings per head of each employee and corporate bodies pay a percentage of dividends per share," Kutini explained.

"It's a brilliant idea," Yaro said, "what about being a professor of economics instead of a farmer?"

Kutini laughed at the apparent joke.

"I mean it. It's a brilliant theory," Yaro said with a stony face.

After walking for almost an hour Yaro noticed the sun wasn't bright anymore. "Where has the sun gone?" Yaro asked. Kutini looked up into the sky and saw the rain-bearing clouds gathering pace very fast – the sky was growing darker by the minute.

"Let's go back," Kutini suggested and they turned to go.

They had barely walked for two hundred metres when they saw the raindrops coming at them from a distance and started to run, but the rain was a better runner. It soon caught up with them and within seconds they were drenched with rainwater, but they kept running. It was a heavy downpour and like most tropical rains it lasted for just two minutes and stopped suddenly giving way to clear skies – the only evidence of rain was the wet ground and running water in gullies. Kutini and Yaro stopped running and started walking while wiping water from their faces with their hands.

"It's amazing how we could see the rain coming from a distance behind us," Yaro said.

"It makes you feel like you can run ahead of it, but it catches up with the speed of the wind," Kutini acknowledged.

When they got back a meal was ready for them. They removed their wet clothes, dried themselves and sat down to eat. The rumbling of thunder grew louder into an ear-shattering sound within seconds.

"I haven't heard the thunder for years," Yaro said.

"It's not something you experience in Europe often," Kutini added.

"I love the tropical rainstorm; it reminds me of my childhood days."

"Home sweet home," Kutini said, thrilled at the easy life in the Ghanaian countryside. He was enjoying every moment of it: the fresh air, the fresh natural organic foods and the natural water drawn mechanically from boreholes. He had been born and brought up in a city and had always lived in a city so he just couldn't have enough of it. He slept under the big *dawadawa* tree after the meal and didn't wake up for two hours.

***

Kutini went back to work on his program. By the end of their second month he had been through the compilation and testing of his program several times. When he was satisfied with his work he told Yaro they were ready to deploy.

Kutini and Yaro sat behind a table next to each other in the spacious living room of Kutini's ranch house. In front of Yaro lay a large-scale map of North America. On it were nine spots marked with red dots and another nine marked with yellow dots. Each red dot was mapped to a yellow dot and each of the dots was coded with a number.

To the untrained eye the dots represented some cities and towns of America. To Kutini and Yaro the red dots were the nuclear launch sites of the American ballistic launchers and the yellow dots were the target cities. All the dots were the same size except one yellow dot. The location was frighteningly familiar – Washington DC. What the map didn't reveal was the exact coordinates of the dot.

Kutini turned on his mobile phone, connected his computer to the internet through it and waited for a few seconds while it picked up the locations of US military satellites. The first thing he did was to make sure he had control of the satellites with no possibility of their being turned off.

The next thing was to gain control of the defence computers. He typed several combinations of codes at several stages and took about thirty minutes to by-pass the firewalls and security systems. Once Kutini had gained control he asked Yaro for the co-ordinates of the small yellow dot and entered into the system the co-ordinates matching the central point of the Pentagon. Kutini then entered the code of the nearest red dot – the nearest nuclear warhead. In a matter of minutes the Pentagon was directly under the fire line of the warhead.

One point after the other Kutini and Yaro went through the rest of the dots, programming the warhead of each red dot to match its corresponding nuclear warhead. When they had been through all the dots on the map Yaro brought out another map and laid it on top of the first one. It had blue circles over patches of the ocean. These were the relative positions of the submarines capable of launching ballistic missiles.

Kutini had decided that since the locations of these subs were not fixed, the best way to deal with them was to track them through the GPS and maintain control of their launchers.

When they had finished Kutini jumped out of his chair and held Yaro by his shoulders shouting, "We've done it." They jumped, hugged and laughed together.

Kutini laughed at the idea that it would take such a short time to destroy everything that had taken the entire human history to develop. The thought was absurd. Humanity had developed through the ages to the current level of space-age technology, yet he could hardly see it as being civilized. He wondered why development was associated with civilization, when nations were fighting against nations. To his mind civilisation could only be achieved when people had learnt to live in peace and harmony.

After thousands of years of human evolution and development we were still engaged in fighting and developing even more powerful weapons that would wipe out the entire human existence with the push of a button. He wondered why humans could not devote their energies to civilization.

Kutini allocated the digits one to nine on his computer to the nine sites and used the letters for the subs. He then went through the sequence of things with Yaro.

"We haven't seen the old people for two weeks, let's go over to the village tomorrow," Kutini suggested when they sat down to dinner.

"Good idea, but before we go we should have a copy of the program on the laptop as a back-up."

"Good thinking."

The next morning Kutini transferred the program onto the laptop and together they went through their plan of action. When they had finished they drove into the village and headed for Kutini's parents.

As they approached the village, Kutini noticed the sheep and the goats grazing near the houses and the chickens roaming freely around. Then something caught his eye. At the market place there were a few stalls with wares on display and just a distance away from a stall was a cow.

"This is paradise," Kutini said pointing at the cow, "see how the people and the animals are living together in harmony."

That's an interesting way of looking at it," Yaro remarked. "I've never thought about it that way."

CHAPTER 45

Rudolf Reinhardt got out of his car and stepped onto the sidewalk. The winter frost bit into his fingers as he put on his gloves. As a kid he used to love it when it snowed and would go out with his parents to the garden and throw snowballs. He could still remember the thrill he had when he made his first successful snowman in the park.

It had all changed when he had slipped on ice and fractured his elbow and had been hospitalised for several weeks. Since then, each time it snowed he would dread the icy conditions that might follow.

As he walked on the snow towards the front door of 16 Kensington Drive in Washington DC he was well aware of the impending icy conditions the weather forecast had given. The white sheet of snow covered almost every exposed surface.

He knocked on the door and waited. He heard the footsteps stop behind; there was a moment's hesitation. He knew he was being looked at through the peephole as he stood in the cold.

The door opened slowly, and was stopped by the tension of the security chain. He saw her face. It was the same woman and not even the towel tied around her head could obscure her beauty.

"How did you find me, Mr. Reinhardt?" Effie asked, surprised.

"I called your old apartment and I was told you had moved so I called your old landlord and got your new address," Rudolf replied. "Can I come in?"

"Of course, come in."

Rudolf entered and hung his coat on the hanger behind the front door.

"Any new development since we last met?" Effie asked.

"No, I was hoping you might have some new information for us."

"Why's that?" Effie asked, feeling suspicious.

"It's nothing; I was just wondering if you remember anyone else who was close to Mike Zinbalan?"

Effie was thinking; nothing immediately came to her mind. She went into the kitchen and brought the kettle to the boil. "Would you like a cup of coffee?" she asked from the kitchen entrance.

"No, thanks," Rudolf replied.

Effie returned from the kitchen with a cup of coffee and sat down. For a moment no one spoke as she searched her memories.

"Was there any occasion where you went out with him together with friends of his?" Rudolf asked.

"Yes."

Effie had just remembered that on his graduation day a friend of Mike Zinbalan had come from the UK to attend. They had been introduced briefly. He was staying for a few days and Mike had made an excuse of it not to see her while his friend was around.

"Do you remember his name?" Rudolf asked.

It was all coming back to her now. After the graduation they had gone for a meal. They had talked about Effie's work and his friend had shown an initial interest, but the conversation had turned to the politics of African leaders and they had talked about corrupt leaders and their brutal tendencies. Mike had been quiet for the rest of that conversation.

"Kutini was his name." The name came back to her in a flash.

"Any family names?" Rudolf pressed further, happy his journey through the snow was paying off.

"No, that's how he was introduced to me."

"Thank you very much, Effie; you've been most helpful."

"Anytime."

It had started to snow again as Rudolf stepped out of Effie's apartment and walked the few metres to his car. It was freezing cold and he wished he had left the engine running. Now it was going to take a while to heat the car. As he drove back to his office he repeated the name Kutini a few times – it all made sense.

Back at his office Rudolf stood in front of his desk and extracted a file from among the few folders in his action tray labelled *Mike Zinbalan*. He opened a few pages, closed the file and went round the table to sit in his chair. He reopened the folder, going through it carefully. As he turned the fourth page the name sprang out at him – Kutini D. Bomanso.

During the execution of Mike Zinbalan's will the bulk of his savings had been bequeathed to Kutini. That itself didn't mean anything, except Rudolf was forming a theory. Could Kutini be the brain behind the plane hijack? Rudolf wondered. It was just a thought lurking at the back of his mind, but after so many years in the intelligence service he had come to trust his instincts.

Rudolf contacted MI5, requested information on Kutini and within fifteen minutes, he had the information he needed. Kutini was the beneficiary of the estate of Mike Zinbalan. That Rudolf already knew.

What was startling was the revelation that Kutini was the anonymous person who had paid for the defence lawyer in the criminal case against Tuuro Bondana and Chris Tagoe. I knew it; someone was behind the plane hijack, Rudolf thought, but I will need more evidence to bring in this man.

Rudolf was grateful for the way technology had revolutionised the intelligence service and the world at large. When he had joined the service a request of that nature would have taken days.

The next day Rudolf had a meeting with the FBI chief and presented him with his new findings.

"You are not suggesting this man could be linked to the Flight 675 hijacking?" Brooks asked; the answer was already obvious to him.

"I can see a pattern developing, but I don't have a complete picture yet," Rudolf replied.

"Can you put together a complete picture of this guy soon, say by Monday?"

"Sure," Rudolf replied, knowing that was his weekend ruined. It was already Friday afternoon.

When he returned to his office he called MI5 in London and requested a complete profile of Kutini adding "I would appreciate it if you could put an immediate trace on his movements and contacts please." He sent a similar request to his Ghanaian counterparts.

Rudolf had come to the realisation that increasing international collaboration and intelligence sharing were the best ways to fight the war against terror.

The next morning Rudolf spent half the day putting together the information he had about Kutini. When he was done he got up from his chair and looked out of the window. The last of the snow was melting away and he was glad.

Christmas was approaching. He had planned to do some Christmas shopping this weekend, but that wasn't going to be.

No matter how much he had planned ahead in the past he had always fallen into the trap of shopping at the last minute.

He decided to go to the mall. He came down the escalator into the parking lot, got into his car and drove off, heading towards the shopping mall without even thinking about what presents he was going to buy. He decided he would just wander around to see if he would find something that would interest him.

He stopped in front of a travel centre, attracted by the advert. He stood there for a while looking at the winter offers, then made a decision: he would give his family a surprise Christmas vacation.

His wife had always held a fascination about Egypt, the land of the Pharaohs. The thought of it cheered him up. They would travel down on the Nile River, the longest river in the world. This year they would do something different from the traditional family activity. As he walked out of the shopping mall he stopped by a kiosk, bought a doughnut and continued.

***

When Rudolf walked into his office late on Sunday afternoon he expected information from MI5 but he was disappointed. He called London and was told the information was not authorised to be electronically transmitted and would be leaving London Heathrow within the next two hours.

"Bastard," Rudolf swore, after he had put the phone down, wondering who this old backward enemy of progress was. He checked the time difference and calculated he would have the information first thing the following morning.

***

An envelope marked 'highly confidential' bearing the seal of MI5 was waiting on Rudolf's desk when he came into his office on Monday morning. He opened it.

Kutini's profile was detailed and informative. He had lived in the UK for over fifteen years where he had obtained his Master's and PhD degrees in Computer Science, and had been living and working there legally for the past ten years. He had been separated from his wife after they lost their son in tragic circumstances and police investigations into the murder were still ongoing.

Kutini who was widely travelled with no criminal record, was also on the payroll of Ghana Government as one of its economic and information technology advisers. He was last reported travelling to Lagos in Nigeria.

Rudolf's request for a similar profile from his Ghanaian counterparts yielded sketchy information on everything else except Kutini's progress through college to university, and details about his parents. The profile ended when Kutini left to study in the UK.

Rudolf read with interest as he went through the comprehensive profile he had gathered on Kutini and couldn't help but be impressed by Kutini's academic and career achievements.

Rudolf focused his attention on the people he came into contact with, the places he visited, his expenditure pattern and the social groups he associated with. A pattern was developing that helped him to complete the report he had started. He was ready to go and meet his boss when the phone rang. He picked it up and said angrily to his secretary, "I told you I was unavailable this morning."

"It's from MI5," his secretary said calmly, knowing that pressure was mounting.

"Put it through."

"This is Rudolf Reinhardt," he said, as he answered the phone.

"We have some additional information on Kutini we thought might be useful," the guy from MI5 said.

"Ah, huh."

"Kutini had been with the team that brokered the peace process among the rebels and the government in the Democratic Republic of Congo."

"That's interesting," Rudolf said, "anything else?" he asked.

"Yes, we have dispatched a brief about each member to you."

"Thank you very much; I really appreciate your help."

Rudolf added a couple of lines to his report and hurried out of the office. His boss would be waiting.

Rudolf sat with a cup of coffee as Brooks read the report. As he went through it his grin blossomed into a full-blown smile and matured into a laugh. Rudolf looked at him.

"Let's go get him," Brooks decided.

"But we don't have enough evidence yet," Rudolf suggested.

"The man had a couple of meetings with Mike Zinbalan, one on American soil, the other in the UK to cause terror to America. He is closely associated with the perpetrator of the terror deaths in Ghana. Under the Terrorist Act we have the legal backing to effect his arrest and detain him without charge," Brooks replied triumphantly.

"May I suggest we first find the other members who were with him in the Congo and interview them?"

"Let's do that simultaneously," Brooks concluded.

Rudolf assigned his assistant, Amy Green, to find and interview the other team members. Alfred Xuma was the first of the members to be located at his Toronto address. Alfred's account of Kutini revealed characteristics of a natural leader and a people's magnet. His impression was that Kutini was outspoken with strong convictions and didn't easily give up, which eventually had seen the success of their mission in the Congo.

"I assume he got on well with every member of the team," Amy asked.

"Not quite; Rahim seemed to have a problem with him, but Kutini handled it well."

"Did you at any time discuss other problems in Africa?"

"No, all the time the focus was on the situation in the Congo."

"Which one of you was he closer to?"

"I would say James Nziza, the leader, because he subsequently let him do all the negotiation."

The next person on Amy's list was James Nziza but after several attempts at locating him had failed she turned her attention to Rahim Mubarik.

Amy knocked on Rahim's door and when he opened it Amy showed him her badge. "I need information on Kutini Bomanso," she said, "I believe you were with him in the Congo"

"Why, is he in some kind of trouble?"

"We don't know yet. I hope you might be able to give us some information about him."

"Please come in," Rahim invited and led the way into his living room. "What sort of information do you want from me?" he asked when they sat down.

"Can you tell me the sort of things he talked about while you were on the mission?" Amy asked.

"That guy had nothing useful to say. He was all talk but no substance. Things like getting the warring countries to become one. How can you say a thing like that when these countries are sovereign?"

"What did you think of Kutini?"

"What did I think of Kutini? I think he is an arrogant bastard who almost got us killed in the Congo."

After a while, Amy realised she couldn't get much of Rahim apart from getting him to display his dislike for Kutini without explaining why.

***

Yaro Tunde's phone had a message saying he had gone on a holiday and the caller should leave a message. Amy made a note to keep trying.

The hunt for Kutini had received the presidential nod and one of the FBI's biggest manhunts had begun. They traced his last known movement to Lagos, but hit a dead end there. There was no information about his whereabouts. He wasn't registered in any hotel in Lagos and he didn't have any known friends or relatives in Nigeria. When they contacted the security and intelligence bureau of Ghana, they had no information about Kutini coming into the country and there had been no contact with the government.

When the BNI agent working with the FBI approached the reception desk of the Palm Beach Hotel he didn't ask about the name Kutini. He knew it would not yield any results. He had been to other hotels and been through their registers without success. He simply described 'his friend' to the receptionist.

"You mean Mr. Donchebe?" the receptionist asked from memory. How could she forget the man who had given her a generous tip before leaving? He was the first person who had stayed in the hotel to have given her a tip in pounds sterling.

"Yes," the BNI guy answered, resisting giving a first name that might not march the phoney name.

"Is he around?"

"No, he left about two weeks ago," the receptionist replied.

"Did he say where he was going?"

"No, but he said he would be back in a month."

"When he comes, could you tell him his friend would like to see him," the BNI guy said and wrote down the name of one of Kutini's friends, but with his own private phone number and passed it to the receptionist.

"Certainly," the receptionist agreed.

"Thank you."

Back at the BNI office, preparations were going on with the SkyHawks team to arrest Kutini. They were almost certain he would be in his hometown with his parents. Once they had agreed on the operation the SkyHawks team went back to their office to organise the logistics.

CHAPTER 46

As the evening sun was kissing the zenith a huge transport-carrier helicopter dropped two military vehicles onto the savannah grasslands in a remote village in the north of Ghana. The vehicles, each containing five heavily armed military personal, drove the one-kilometre distance to the mud house in the middle of the open fields. Before the vehicles had come to a stop all eight military personnel were on the ground and had surrounded the house. The two drivers manoeuvred the vehicles into position and with military precision took their positions to support their colleagues. At that moment another chopper, a smaller one, was also just touching the ground a few metres away.

Inside the compound the family, made up of brothers, children, cousins, grandchildren and grandparents, had just gathered to have their evening meal. There were about twenty people sitting on mats in three separate groups – one female group and two male.

An old man asked one of his grandsons to go and find out what the noise outside the house was all about. The boy came back screaming in terror as other members of the family got up and rushed towards the two main exits leading into a maze of entrances and exits that brought together this sprawling compound house typical of medieval architecture.

"Nobody moves," came the first order.

The poor villagers who knew little about military activities and their language continued to run. The first sound of a bullet was deafening. Every one froze. The gun had been shot into the air.

"Move slowly into the compound," a soldier spoke to them in the local language. Slowly and silently they all started to move inside the compound. Two soldiers, each covering an entrance, followed them in while the rest burst into the rooms to ensure they didn't get any surprises.

As the soldiers got the people into the compound, another command was issued in the local language, "Hands on your head everyone." They all obeyed except one.

The old man was still sitting, ignoring what was going on. He had fought in the Second World War in Burma and had seen it all. Death was a necessary end and it came when it will come, he would always say. "We had no trouble with any country but as a soldier in the then Gold Coast Regiment I fought in someone's war and saw many of my friends die. Do whatever you believe in, life is too short to have regrets," he had once told his son, Kutini.

"I said, stand up and put your hands on your head," the soldier repeated his order directing it to the old man.

"What do you want? He is an old man, can't you see," Kutini addressed the soldier.

Just then, Kanbe stepped forward. He had arrived in the second chopper with Faiza Iddris. "We are looking for Kutini Bomanso."

There was a brief silence. "I am Kutini, what is the problem here?" he answered, stepping forward, still with his hands on his head.

"The game is up," Kanbe told him.

"What game? I don't know what you're talking about."

Even as Kutini spoke there were a million questions going through his head. Had they found out about what he had come to do at the village? Had they already taken over his installations? This couldn't be happening, not when everything had gone so precisely to plan. He looked for Yaro, using his peripheral vision. He couldn't see him and hoped he had managed to escape.

"You are under arrest for Federal crimes under the Terrorist ..." Kanbe repeated the rehearsed words as he handcuffed and led Kutini out of the compound into the waiting chopper.

It sounded absurd for Kutini to hear his fellow countryman arresting him "... for Federal crimes under the Terrorist Act," and he wondered how long Ghana had been part of the United States. As they went out of the house there was a sudden outburst of wailing and crying. His mother came crying and held her son. Just then, Kutini sneezed. "*Iwe, Ambanyu, Yezaanadi, Chemaala, Dobakoobie...*," his mother started to sing his praise names amidst sobs. She let go as one of the soldiers tried to pull him away. Kutini's entire family had already started mourning him. He was considered a living-dead.

The old man came out of the compound with a slight stoop and watched as the soldiers hauled his son into the chopper. Kutini turned round and saw his father standing at the entrance to his ancestral home. He thought he saw him wave as he got inside the chopper.

As the door closed, the old man stretched his blessing hand forward in the direction of the chopper and said in the local language, "You will prevail my son; I prevailed in Burma." He watched as the chopper lifted off into the shadows of darkness. The rest of the soldiers hurried back into their vehicles and drove off into the night leaving behind clouds of dust.

Yaro waited for about thirty minutes after all the noise had died down before struggling out of his hideaway. He had gone to pee when he heard the gunshot. Sensing danger he had entered the storeroom and forced himself into one of the traditional silos. He was lucky: when he opened the silo door it was empty and had been empty for several years. The harvest hadn't been good for the last three years so there wasn't much food to store.

"Are you alright, my son?" the old man asked in the local language as Yaro walked out of the storeroom covered in ash, the substance used traditionally to preserve grain in the silo.

"Where is Kutini?" Yaro asked, not understanding what the old man had said. He didn't speak the local language and the old man didn't speak English, but responded to Yaro with a hand gesture towards the sky. Yaro understood. "Kutini will be back," he said, and went into a consoling embrace with the old man.

***

The midnight flight leaving Kotoka International Airport in Accra carried Kutini under heavy security guard. Alari Kanbe and Faiza Iddris of the SkyHawks team escorted him.

Kutini couldn't sleep for most of the twelve-hour trans-Atlantic journey to New York. He was relieved, however, for the simple reason that the charges preferred against him did not include taking control of the American defence system. He held an ace and was thinking about how he would play it. During the course of his project, he had thought about how he would go about it when he finished, but he hadn't thought of being arrested. He had finally fallen asleep.

Kutini had been asleep for an hour when the pilot's voice woke him up. They were making the final descent into JFK.

CHAPTER 47

June 19, 2008. Brooks and Rudolf were waiting on the tarmac at JFK when the plane carrying the 'terrorist' landed. For Brooks it was his big day. He had trusted his boys to deliver and they had done exactly as he had expected. He was now certain to get the congressional approval for a budget increase for the FBI, a request of his that was long overdue. He needed to modernise the organisation to cope effectively with the new threats of international terrorism and he was the man for the job.

Kanbe and Faiza were the first to get out of the plane, holding Kutini. They were led into the waiting vehicle for the short-distance drive to the air force plane, which took them to Washington DC.

***

"We would like you to tell us your involvement in the Flight 675 hijacking and the poison deaths in Ghana," Brooks started the interrogation.

"Haven't I got any rights to a defence? Why hasn't anyone told me about my rights?" Kutini asked in quick succession.

"Let me be direct with you," Brooks started, "under the Terrorist Act, we can hold you indefinitely without bringing you to trial. You can talk now or talk later, the choice is yours."

"I've been to the edge of the abyss in the Congo and looked over, so your threats don't move me."

"On my orders alone you could find yourself in Guantanamo Bay in Cuba," Brooks continued with his threats.

"You wouldn't want to do that."

"Then you better start talking."

"I will only talk to the President of the United States of America."

Brooks laughed so loud his stomach muscles began to hurt. It was the best joke he had heard in many months.

"An apprehended terrorist wanting to speak directly to the President? Which planet do you come from? Tell me, how would you do that?" Brooks asked, unable to stop the flow of questions.

Rudolf was looking intently into Kutini's eyes. There was something he didn't like. Something that troubled him: the calm about Kutini; it was too good to be normal.

"You will take me to him," Kutini replied to Brook's last question, "and you know why?"

"Tell me why I would take you to the President?"

"Because, as we speak, the entire US defence network is under our control!"

"What?" Brooks asked, not sure he had heard Kutini right.

"You heard me."

"You couldn't manage that in your entire life time."

"Before you decide to call it a bluff, check the target positions of all your nuclear warheads," Kutini challenged.

Brooks asked Rudolf to keep Kutini busy while he made a few calls. He went into his office and made a call to the Pentagon asking them to check the validity of Kutini's claim. He was asked to hold the line while they did an initial check.

"Holy shit," Brooks swore as the confirmation came back to him.

"Are you crazy? Are you some kind of a lunatic?" Brooks asked as he stormed back into the room where Kutini was being interrogated, still with chains holding his legs and handcuffs on his hands. Kutini ignored him.

"If you try to dismantle anyone of the warheads, it will go off," Kutini warned.

"Let's talk to the President," Rudolf suggested to Brooks.

The President was expecting Brooks as he walked into the Oval Office. "Why would you want me to talk to a terrorist?" The President demanded.

"Mr. President, this is a lunatic in control of our nukes."

"Is this some kind of a joke?"

"I'm afraid it's been confirmed by the Pentagon." Brooks said in a panicked tone.

"If he wants to meet me go and bring him."

Kutini was taken to the White House blindfolded and led into the Oval Office. When his blindfold was taken off he was facing the President of the United States. For the first time he was meeting the most powerful man on the planet face to face and was going to get his personal attention. Hitherto, he had only seen him on television. He felt a deep sense of achievement although he hadn't planned it that way.

"What do you want?" the President asked.

"You damn well know what I want. I want to be out of here," Kutini demanded.

"That's impossible, we can't do that," the President responded.

"You know, Mr. President, I come from a family of nine and naturally we used to fight as kids..." Kutini started.

"We can help you, just tell us what is bothering you," the President said, in a calm and persuasive tone of voice.

Kutini continued as though no one had interrupted him: "My mother used to say to us each time we fought, 'if the older one is not *experienced* enough to handle a situation peacefully, the younger one must be *wise* enough to calm it'. To my mind, the wisdom in that saying is the embodiment of all of the world's philosophy on peace put together. Don't you agree Mr. President?"

"I'm sure your mother was a great woman, but let's get down to brass tacks." The President was getting frustrated that the captive wasn't forthcoming with his demands.

"The onus is on America as today's youngest developed democracy to show wisdom through leadership, not to bully and cow everyone into submission," Kutini concluded.

He had settled into a cool, calm and collected mood and exuded confidence as he watched the President struggle to hold back his anger.

"This is what I want," Kutini announced, and instantly had the attention of everyone in the room.

"I knew you had demands, all terrorists do," the President said, jubilantly.

"We are not a terrorist group, Mr. President," Kutini replied. "When we took control of American Banks," he continued as shock and awe was written over the faces of all present, "we were in a position to empty them, but we didn't, we took out only the chains that bound Africa – we wiped out the debts. And where did the monies go? They were just internal transfers from American Banks to the World Bank and IMF – all owned by Americans. Are these acts of terrorists?"

The silence was absolute, only the breathing of the individuals could be heard. Kutini's chilling revelation was as daunting as it was devastating. They had spent millions of dollars trying to track down this evasive criminal, now he was sitting right in front of them on a different charge confessing to his crimes as though it was a game of chess.

"When we took control of the American Airline Flight 675, we could have made many demands, but we didn't." The shock and awe had given way to panic and desperation.

The President was visibly shaken. The intelligence chiefs could not even look him in the eye.

So Mike Zinbalan was in the employ of this grotesque contortionist, the FBI chief thought. "You hijacked that plane and you call yourself a peaceful man. Why?" he asked, unable to control his frustration and anger. They had imprisoned the wrong person, while all the time the real criminal walked free.

Kutini replied, "We took control of the plane for two reasons: to test the technology we are using today and to divert your attention from our ultimate prize."

"You imbecile, you ..." the FBI chief said, going into uncontrollable rage and had to be held down by his colleagues.

"There is no need for insults, I believe we are all reasonable men," Kutini cautioned.

"What did you do to Mike Zinbalan?" the FBI chief asked, still furious. He remembered the unsolved case of the mysterious deaths in Ghana and believed this man must be responsible.

"My friend, Mike Zinbalan, has finally found peace in avenging his parent's deaths," Kutini replied, displaying visible facial emotions that betrayed his human side. If only he had known Mike harboured such deep thoughts, maybe he could have helped him.

"How can we help you?" the President asked with a shaky voice that spelt desperation.

"Thanks for your offer, now we are speaking the same language," Kutini responded, for the first time with a smile displaying a beautiful set of natural white teeth.

"I have only two demands," Kutini started, and this time the silence was ghastly, people held their breath. "First, I want Tuuro Bondana released unconditionally; he is an innocent man."

"We can arrange that," the President offered without a second thought, "what's your second demand?" he asked, eager to resolve this single most scary security situation America was facing in her entire history of existence.

"I would like to address your scientific advisors, defence contractors, generals, a section of American corporate heads and your cabinet," Kutini said, putting his final demand on the table.

"That is preposterous! I can't do that," the President said, scared of the prospects of putting this maniac in front of those people. He had started to sympathise with this guy, but these were lines he couldn't be allowed to cross.

"Why can't you? I thought you were President of the United States," he said, in a relaxed, laid back kind of way, almost mocking. "I'm hungry," he added.

"What would you like to eat?" the Security Advisor asked, finding his voice for the first time.

"A sandwich and a can of Red Bull will be fine. Don't poison the food because if I die the bombs will go off, every single one of them," Kutini added as someone left the room, apparently to go and get his food.

When the food came he opened the drink and took a sip. He then asked the Security Advisor to take a bite. The Advisor turned and looked at the President who gave him a nod; he bit the sandwich, chewed for a couple of seconds, and swallowed. "Good," Kutini said, took it and started to eat.

He took his time as though it was the most delicious food he had ever tasted. He ate in a slow, deliberate, somehow sophisticated manner as if to tell the people around him that "I am in charge and you can all wait."

When the President wanted to say something, Kutini stopped him saying, "I don't want my meal to be interrupted."

He was in charge and watched as their patience ran thin. Kutini had learnt that in negotiations the key thing to remember was never to get angry; anger, he had found out, would weaken one's defence and make one vulnerable.

"Thanks for the American hospitality," Kutini said when he had finished eating. "Can we continue now, Mr. President?"

"It would be impossible to put you in front of that group; tell us your other demand, we represent the American people," the President said.

"You're not listening! I said addressing them was my second and my last demand. I have no more and I hope I have made myself clear now," Kutini replied and looked down.

The room went quiet. They were all waiting for the President to make that all-important decision.

Kutini raised his head laughing. They all turned to look at him stunned, thinking at first that he was weeping, breaking up. He stopped, then looking dead serious and in the sternest voice, he uttered the famous phrase: "Time is running out, Mr. President. In six hours, if my people don't see me, they will set off the first nuclear warhead trained on the Pentagon. After that, every hour a city will go under." Kutini uttered those chilling words with a grin.

Of course, the President knew the entire country faced annihilation at the hands of this antichrist if they didn't find a way of stopping him. He had been briefed to the last detail. He had no choice.

"We will need time to get them together, Mr. Kut…i…ni," the President struggled to use his name.

"Twenty-four hours from the time I was taken if my people don't see me they will start. I've been away for nearly eighteen hours. It's your call, Mr. President."

"We will do our best to get the group together for you, but what do you want to tell them?" the President asked.

"I just want to talk with them," Kutini replied casually.

The President had been beginning to take this guy seriously, but now he had his doubts about his sanity. He still had no choice. The security and intelligence personnel were fully deployed at the heels of Kutini's accomplices, but until they were apprehended and their installations dismantled they had to meet Kutini's demands.

As the President gave the order for the group to be assembled the FBI chief was ready with another protest. "We can't concede to a terrorist's demands." Despite failing to pick up any intelligence on this he still had the foolhardy conviction his boys would get the rest of the group before any harm was done.

"I'm ultimately responsible to the American people for any decisions I make. I've made the decision and the American people will acknowledge I made the right decision in their interest," the President said, defending his position.

***

The security surrounding the White House was unprecedented and the limousines carrying the high profile persons arriving were not spared the rigorous security checks. In less than three hours a meeting room in the White House hosted America's top brass. Among them was the Secretary of Defense, Larry Holmes.

When Kutini was brought into the room containing his audience he was impressed. There were about twenty people all together.

As he walked in someone shouted, "What do you want?"

"I just want to have a chat with you, that's all," Kutini repeated.

"You're a terrorist, why should we negotiate with you?" the same voice persisted.

Kutini sat down where he was shown and answered, "Don't kid yourself; if I hadn't done it, maybe a crazy idiot would have done it. America's strength has also become her weakness – computer technology. It will soon be the real terrorist weapon of choice and where would that leave America?"

There were murmurs among the people who had grouped there. A few were beginning to agree with Kutini, the majority still thought he couldn't be trusted even if what he was saying was true. One person argued America had the technology, the security, the intelligence and the military might to protect her citizens and that was why Kutini had been arrested in the first place.

As if in response to their arguments, Kutini said, "Before 9/11, you thought your country was invincible and I sympathise with your short memory indeed. How long ago did the Japanese send unmanned flying balloons with explosives to America through the Jet Stream?" he asked and waited for a response; none was forth-coming.

He continued. "God has given power to America to be custodians and a protector of the earth, not to destroy it, but for America destruction is your ode to joy and world dominion is your delusion of grandeur."

"That's a lie," someone shouted.

"Tell me it is also a lie that, to the vast majority of Americans, America is the world, Latin Americans are the nuisance neighbours, Africa is a jungle, the Caribbeans are the plantation people, Europeans are the old backward cousins left behind during the great escape, the Aussies and the Kiwis are the battle-hardened criminal seafarers who were banished to an unknown destination. The rest are Asian and Muslim terrorists!"

Kutini delivered this message as though he had been rehearsing for this occasion. The silence was eerie. Kutini's mind went back to his friend Yaro. If these Washington bureaucrats didn't start playing ball soon his friend would be tempted to carry on with plan B. This is not how they had planned it, but now everything was changed and Yaro had absolute control.

"And just how do you propose to achieve this utopia?" the FBI chief asked, still bent on exacting his pound of flesh.

"America must be a development partner to the world, not an exploitative partner," Kutini answered simply.

"Africa is a poor continent and an economic drain-pipe, this has been proven over time," one of the economic advisors stated, beginning to look at the economic implication of a major shift in making Africa a major partner.

He had always thought about Africa as a place to go and get what you want as quickly as possible before another semi-starved, trigger-hungry military man took over the government and nationalised all foreign businesses.

"There are over 900 million people living in Africa; if their economies were right, think about how many computers you would sell; imagine the number of cars you would sell; consider how many more airline passengers you would carry and project how many more planes you would sell, the list is endless. Contrast that with the amount of arms you sell to promote the conflicts for precious stones that you could walk in during peace time and take and you can begin to see how America stands to benefit from the prosperity of Africa under one flag."

At this point the reality and seriousness of Kutini's cause was beginning to sink in. The man was proposing a united Africa and to achieve that he wanted America to give up her arsenal. Everyone in the room, including the President, was now scared.

The President could hardly ask what he thought was the obvious question: "You're not suggesting we dismantle our defence arsenal?"

"Precisely, my smart friend," Kutini answered in a patronising manner. "Dismantle your nuclear arsenal, which is expensive, but ineffective, and show the rest of the world that they should follow without America having to say so."

"That will make us vulnerable," Defense Secretary Larry Holmes cautioned. He had all along remained quiet as the debate went on. He secretly acknowledged the wisdom in what Kutini was saying but thought that for the sake of the unwritten policy of mutually assured destruction by nuclear nations America would have to maintain her nuclear arsenal.

"Whether you like it or not America is the world's leader and unfortunately this role comes with responsibility, the biggest of which is to lead by example," Kutini reminded them.

"What do you stand to gain in all this?" Larry Holmes asked. The question amused Kutini because now they were beginning to ask the right questions.

"All we aimed to achieve in our quest are two things. First, to build Africa with African resources without any adverse external interference except to help us in the building process in a peaceful environment; and secondly to let America know that even if we hadn't done it, it was a matter of time before someone else would – and then the consequences would be anyone's guess."

The full impact of the situation was now clear. One of the economic advisors was thinking. The issue was not just a crazy terrorist trying to exact a pound of flesh. There had been no killings of innocent civilians. It had nothing to do with hatred for America; it had nothing to do with religious fundamentalism. It had everything to do with the desire for his people to develop and grow in a world of global peace and prosperity. He had never come across an idealistic person like this before. This guy was on the brink of creating a new world order.

The President started to speak, cutting his thoughts short. "We will have to consider your proposition without you," the President said as he motioned for Kutini to be taken out of the room.

"Sure, Mr. President, remember we have shown the way, but the choice is yours. We have shown that even if we let go, which we will, someone else may still do it another time, another place, and it might not be the right person."

Alone with his advisors, the President asked, "What choices do we have?"

The room was silent for a moment, then Larry Holmes answered, "In my humble opinion, Mr. President, we don't have a choice. As long as our defence systems continue to rely on satellite communications and global positioning systems it's a matter of *will* before anyone can break into whatever security firewalls we build."

The whole room started to clap in approval. The President took the cue. They had no choice. Together with his top aides they came back to Kutini and asked, "If we agree to your proposals how are we going to start dismantling them when you still have control."

"We will give up the control," Kutini replied almost immediately with a definite promise.

"Then let's do it." The President gave the order.

"I have to be back at the installation first. We have five hours left before the first bomb goes," Kutini said causing a panic alarm in the room.

"Can we not communicate with your people?" the President asked.

"There are no communication links and any attempt to storm the location if it was mistakenly found will lead to several bombs going off at the same time," Kutini replied.

CHAPTER 48

A supersonic fighter jet took off from Seymour Johnson Air Base for the eight thousand-kilometre journey to Ghana. Accompanying Kutini in the three-seater jet was Ian Clarke from the Internet Fraud Unit of the FBI. The new $400 million Lockheed Martin/Boeing F-22B Raptor was the first supersonic jet designed for three people for special operations in highly sensitive locations: a pilot concentrated solely on flying, a second person was in charge of selecting the target and a third crew responsible for firing the weapons. This time the F-22B's other two passengers were not identifying targets for bombing.

Kutini sat in the plane hoping they would be able to win this race against time. It was a race to stop Yaro from launching missiles attacks and Kutini wondered why it had taken the President so long to see there was present danger in order to call for action. Had anyone ever listened to Africa? Did Africa even have a voice? He remembered attending a lecture on the topic, *Making Africa Matter on the World Scene.* The speaker had stated that while Africa's artificial boundaries existed and we did not have one voice there was no place for Africa on the global scene. Kutini felt his anger rise as he thought about the senseless civil wars, the poverty, the human suffering while the West plundered the continent's wealth. As long as Africans didn't have the muscle to pose any real threat to the West, Africa would never matter, he concluded.

An eerie sensation of motionlessness interrupted his thoughts. He tried to look out but there was no window view.

He felt as though the plane had stopped although he was sure they were still flying since they had taken off about an hour ago, then his stomach churned. An hour and a half later the jet started to loose altitude and speed. On the cockpit the speed dial was moving anti-clockwise away from Mach 2.5.

"Are we in trouble?" Kutini asked through his microphone.

"No, we're preparing to refuel," Ian Clark replied.

Outside, the tanker aircraft from the American Military Base in Germany carried the extra fuel for the supersonic to complete its journey to the Ghana. Flying above the jet the tanker aircraft pumped fuel through and for the next five minutes the two planes were engaged like lovers on a first date.

It was an hour and ten minutes to their destination.

***

The President had ordered the evacuation of the entire Pentagon and its immediate vicinity around the Arlington conurbation in Virginia.

At the Pentagon, all non-essential staff had left the building under the orders of Larry Holmes. Only the computer experts remained, struggling with the systems to regain control, but it was virtually impossible and they knew any attempt to overwrite the controls would trigger the bombs. Specially trained emergency personnel at various locations around Virginia, Baltimore and Washington DC were on standby.

***

At the isolated ranch sitting within the vast savannah, Yaro walked away armed with a fully charged laptop and satellite mobile phone. He would walk the two-kilometre distance on foot to the operations room; an obscure farm shelter, made of mud and stones, big enough to accommodate about four people sitting.

When he got there he sat down on the floor, wiped the sweat from his face and set up his laptop. He then turned on his mobile phone and looked at his watch. It was eight in the morning in Ghana, three at night in Nebraska. Sitting inside their improvised operations room, Yaro entered a sequence of keys on his computer, then pressed enter and came out of the shelter. "This should convince the Americans we mean business," he said to the wind.

Deep under the Nebraska desert the ignition of the solid-fuel booster motor in the first launch pressurized canister hurled the thin cylindrical missile horizontally out of the ground, leaving behind a trail of white vapour from its burnt propellant. The 1440-kilogram missile, 556-centimetre long and 52-centimetre in diameter seemed to hang momentarily in the air, standing on its tail; then began climbing, gathering speed. A second later, a pair of 267-centimetre stubby wings in the centre of the missile and four smaller tail-fins unfolded and locked into place. Underneath the missile, towards the rear, an air inlet swung out, allowing air into the Williams F107-WR-402 turbofan sustainer engine to start and run up to speed. The missile appeared to shake itself into life; its tactical GPS guidance system began to take over. The booster burned out and fell away. The Raytheon-made Block IV Tomahawk Land Attack Missile levelled off at two hundred and fifty metres and streaked off towards the north-west horizon on its pre-programmed course at a speed of nine hundred kilometres per hour.

Time of flight eighty-eight minutes. Target due at 0428 hours local time.

***

The Missile Warning Control Center at North American Air Defense Command Headquarters, buried deep underground in Cheyenne Mountain in Colorado, picked up the missile track within seconds of its launch. NORAD's warning was, however, ineffective in stopping the missile. The few experts left at the Pentagon saw the missile follow the trajectory, gave up their last minute attempt to divert it and followed an order to evacuate the building. Outside the Pentagon, traffic was thinning out as the last of the residents drove out of the city.

***

The BLK IV TLAM-D reached Omaha within ninety seconds of its launch, crossed into Iowa State, followed a course along the Interstate 80 Route and headed for Chicago. The thrust of the engines slowed momentarily as the missile dropped altitude to skim one fifty metres above the waters of Lake Michigan; five minutes later it reached the eastern shore of the sixty-kilometre-long stretch of the southern end of the lake. The TERCOM terrain-contour-matching program kicked in, scanned the area below and made a slight correction to the inertial navigation system, then the missile started to climb again, flying into Michigan State along the southern border towards Toledo.

***

The fighter jet carrying Kutini touched down at the Wa airstrip in the Upper West Region of Ghana fourteen kilometres away from the target position. A waiting car picked Kutini and Clark up to rendezvous with Yaro.

Oblivious to Yaro's action and hoping he would delay the missile launch, Kutini sat anxiously as the vehicle carrying him pushed desperately towards its final destination. As they got nearer a thought suddenly occurred to him: "Stop. Turn around," he said to the driver.

"What's the problem?" the driver asked, well aware of the desperation of the situation.

"We can't drive there." If Yaro were alarmed in any way, the consequences would be tragic. He had to go there alone.

The vehicle cruised down on the dirt road, made a stop and a u-turn in a single movement at 50kph and drove back to the village. Kutini got out as the vehicle pulled to a stop outside his father's house. The old man saw him and smiled. Kutini acknowledged with a slight bow, asked for a motorcycle and drove the one-kilometre journey in record time.

***

The cruise missile turned southeast after passing Toledo in the direction of Pittsburgh. The TERCOM guidance systems had had some minor problems with the unpredictable radar signatures of trees northeast of Columbus but correlations from its on-board GPS, providing a constant and precise updates of position, confirmed it was on track. Passing Pittsburgh thirty kilometres to the north, it headed unerringly towards the Pentagon. People who heard the missile passing in the night assumed mistakenly that it was US Air Force Plane on a routine sky patrol.

***

Yaro was just preparing the launch sequence for the next release when he heard his name outside the shelter. Recognising the voice, he came out to see Kutini gasping for breath. "I knew you would be back," Yaro said embracing him.

Kutini pulled away, dreading the next statement Yaro was going to make. He hoped against hope he hadn't launched the first missile.

"I was just preparing to launch the second missile," Yaro announced.

"Holy shit," Kutini said. He hadn't anticipated this situation in his planning, but somehow he had to stop the missile if it wasn't already too late. "What do we do now?" he asked in exasperation.

"What about the patriots?"

"I don't bloody know...," Kutini stopped, took out his phone and called Ian Clarke.

"We have a situation. A missile is just minutes away from the Pentagon. We need you here right away."

"Stay on the line, I'm on my way," Ian said as he signalled to the driver to move, "have you disabled the system?" he asked as the car started towards the ranch.

"In a moment," Kutini replied, his concentration on the sequence of complex procedures to disable the control. "It's done," Kutini said just as the Ian's car pulled to a stop.

"How much time do we have?"

"Ten minutes."

"Can we launch a patriot from here?" Ian asked.

"No, it wasn't part of the plan."

Ian Clark made a long distance call NORAD headquarters. "We have control," he said to the unseen face at the other end of the line, "patriot launch required immediately."

He held the phone, staring helplessly at the computer screen, unable to do anything. Missile launches were not his field. In his mind's eye he could see the mile-wide hole created by the missile where the Pentagon once stood.

***

The missile now headed almost due east, screaming over the greenbelt of Robinson Crusoe Island at low level towards the western border of Loudoun County, Virginia. It was just ninety kilometres from its target due to impact at 1922 hours, exactly six minutes away. It switched on its Digital Scene Matching Area Correlator DSMAC terminal guidance systems, studying the terrain ahead, and using its on-board two-way satellite link, compared it with the digital pictures programmed into its library. The FMU-148 fuses on the W80 nuclear warhead armed with 200 kiloton of TNT; the missile had nearly reached the end of its journey. It suddenly recognised its target and locked on.

***

Across the skies of Virginia, a Patriot tracked the incoming missile with the ferociousness of a predator. Above the woods of the greenbelt there was a sudden whoosh as something passed overhead in the dark travelling in the opposite direction to the missile; then they collided: the predator against the prey; the night suddenly turned into day and the whole world seemed to disintegrate. The explosion lit up the night skies like a supernova in a distant galaxy.

***

Ian Clark pressed the phone close to his ears and held his breath. He could feel the tension several thousand kilometers away; his own heart was pounding. Then he heard the words, "mission accomplished," at the other end, turned round to Kutini and said, "They've done it."

Kutini jumped up with joy, tears running down his cheeks. "Thank God they stopped it," he said embracing Ian, "thanks for your help."

As Kutini pulled away he thought about the events of the last few hours. A terrorist-controlled nuclear destruction of the

Pentagon and the surrounding conurbation would have made 9/11 seem like a picnic in the park. The consequence would have been too dire to contemplate and would have signalled the end of America's world domination. Washington had been spared because he wanted only to prove that building fortresses, whether with stone and concrete or with advanced missile technology, for the sake of providing security would remain an illusion. For global security to be achieved, Kutini thought, we had to live in a world of shared resources and responsibility.

Kutini wiped his tears with a handkerchief, helped Yaro to disconnect the equipment and handed them over to the American.

Ian Clark made a call to the President. "I have all the equipment," he told him, then turned to Kutini. "What made you do it?"

"There is a sinister and callous disregard by America for the rest of the international community," Kutini started, "the cold-blooded arrogance of Washington's foreign policy is intrusive, criminal at times, murderous and self-serving, even to the extent that acts of mass murder are committed."

"I think every government has the right to do what is in the best interest of its citizens."

"Don't you see Mr. Clark? This stance is neo-colonialist and neo-imperialist, which goes hand in hand with the desire to control the world's resources. Gone are the days when one could tame the wilderness with the gun and the bullet, civilizing savages and teaching them the power of the cross through acts of torture, rape and murder."

"You give me the impression you are a well-read man," Clark said. He had no interest in politics and knew little outside his main line of duty.

"How would I put it? I'm interested in poverty issues and the deprivation around me, and that's why in today's world there has to be a greater degree of balance in decision-making processes. To exclude less developed countries from the process is to tell us we do not have the same rights. It is unjust to delay such a process and even criminal to use the underhanded tool of filibustering to do so."

"I am sure the President would take your concerns seriously in the light of what just happened. You're a very brave man, Mr. Bomanso."

CHAPTER 49

Within minutes of briefing the President, he was on the airwaves. "We regret the events around the Pentagon and large parts of the Virginia and Arlington conurbation today involving a patriot destroying a bomb that targeted the Pentagon. Due to the hard work of our defense experts a tragedy was averted. Our emergency services rose up to the challenge ensuring that no human life was in danger. We commend their efforts. I want to assure Americans that there was no terrorist involved. A committee is being set up to investigate the real cause of this tragedy. At the same time the defence community is working hard on bold new strategies and measures to ensure that never again will such an incident happen in America. Thank you."

As soon as the President had given his speech to the press he went back into the Oval Office and sat down with his war cabinet and senior advisers. He still could not believe America's defence had been compromised to the extent of rendering them incapable of acting. The world must not know this, he thought, and decided America must lead a new world crusade to maintain its world dominance.

"I believe the Russians sold the technology to these terrorists. It's about time we redefine our strategy for the war on terror," the President said.

"What do you have in mind, Mr. President," Secretary of State Gordon Ramsden asked.

"We will have to redefine our foreign policy to focus on positive engagement and do away with confrontation."

Defense Secretary Larry Holmes felt uncomfortable with the direction he envisaged the President was going. "The economy stands to lose with this sort of arrangement. There would be many job losses and the economic consequences would be dire." At the back of his mind Holmes was thinking about his personal strategic interest in America's largest defence supplier and how much he would lose from company profits if the President's proposal went ahead.

"The policy will enable us to strengthen our detection and Patriot missile capabilities. We can then spend more on intelligence gathering through our constructive engagement with other countries," the President replied. Across the table in the Oval Office he could see Larry Holmes shaking his head in disagreement. "Do you have any objection, Secretary Holmes?"

"I think the whole idea is crazy. Just because an unknown quantity managed to control our defence doesn't mean we should leave ourselves defenceless for any rogue state to attack. In a week or so our experts will cover all the loopholes to make a similar event impossible."

"From what we witnessed today I think the policy of engagement is the most sensible thing to do to protect the American people. Is there any objection?" the President asked. He took the silence in the room to mean no objection. "I would like Secretary Holmes and his team to get together and work out a strategy towards the de-nuclearisation of America for consideration in the House of Congress."

***

The following month Defense Secretary Larry Holmes outlined America's new strategy to the UN Security Council at an extraordinary session. He was beginning to see his interest in the bigger scheme of things. What are missiles worth when the future lies in developing sophisticated Patriots? His business interests would be assured whichever way he looked at it. He announced a number of sweeping radical reforms on a broad spectrum of policies that shocked the entire world. It would become the foundation for a new age, an age that would transcend any other period in the history of the world.

America was going to unilaterally start dismantling its entire nuclear arsenal. This would start in the autumn and continue over the next two years. After the first year of the nuclear dismantling process it would start dismantling all major intercontinental ballistic missiles and all other weapons of mass destruction. It would seek to promote peace through dialogue and negotiation and urge all other countries around the world to do the same.

"As a start, an immediate embargo has been placed on all arm sales from the United States," Holmes concluded.

Larry Holmes came out of the Security Council plenary session to meet a sea of reporters with their gadgets, each trying to get ahead of the other amid flashes from cameras. He paused as the reporters thrust microphones towards him, bombarding him with a plethora of questions:

"Is America kowtowing to the Pentagon terrorist demands?"

"Is America going to renounce capitalism next?"

"What is the President going to . . .?"

Holmes could hardly make one question from the other as the barrage continued from all angles. He tried to shove his way through the reporters when he heard a question close by.

"Why should one single event force America to take such radical actions with uncertain future repercussions?" an unidentified reporter asked.

"Historically, the world has been shaped by radical new ideas pioneered by individuals like Einstein and by single historical events like 9/11. If the Pentagon scare will lead to a major radical change that would shape the world in a positive way, I say we should seize the opportunity."

"Mr. Secretary, are you now going to sign up to the Kyoto Protocol on the environment?" a CNN reporter asked.

"Let's take things one at a time. We would like to see the defence reforms take shape before moving on to other things."

"What happens now if Iran decides to attack our ally Israel?" a reporter from ABC news asked.

"The President has asked Secretary of State Gordon Ramsden to engage Israel and Palestine and to work out a peace process that would lead to a lasting solution to the conflict. Thank you," Larry Holmes said, working his way out of the reporters into his waiting car.

Inside the White House the President opened the file containing the new proposals for a fresh start of the Israeli-Palestinian peace process. The report was the culmination of several months of consultations and it represented a paradigm shift from his previous approach to solving the conflict. He had always perceived the solution to the conflict to be a peaceful co-existence of the two nations side by side in security, prosperity and peace.

When the President finished reading the report, he sat back and sighed. This is a figment of someone's imagination, he thought, wondering why it was not recommended in the Road Map if it was such a great idea. He called his secretary. "I want a meeting with Secretary Holmes."

"Can you explain how this proposal is going to work," the President said to Larry Holmes, who sat across the table from him in the Oval Office.

"Although the conflict has a historical perspective to it, it has become a 21st Century problem that requires a 21st Century solution. So the approach we adopted was to move away from the narrow consultation used in the Road Map to a much broader consultation that went beyond Russia, the European Union and other key countries within the United Nations including some Arab Nations."

"So now we are proposing a single state for Israel and Palestine?"

"That is correct, Mr. President."

"It's preposterous. How can anyone even contemplate such a solution? Neither side will ever accept it," the President lamented.

"That was precisely our argument. The crux of the crisis in the Middle East Region is widely acknowledged to be the Israeli-Palestinian conflict. We have all been focusing on a two-state solution with borders and land ownership. No one has ever contemplated a single state solution. We should at least propose it as an option to both parties."

The President sat quietly for some time, lost in thought. His policies to dismantle America's nuclear arsenal in favour of more Patriots and prevention had gone down well with the American people and had seen his ratings go from thirty percent to fifty-one percent. To propose a single state solution to the Israeli-Palestinian conflict would be pushing the extreme-left Israelis, who see Palestinians as terrorists, one step too far.

"Right, let's discuss this with Israel first," the President decided.

***

Secretary Ramsden sat with the Israeli Prime Minister, Hanon Mahler, in the Israeli capital Tel Aviv. Ramsden was well aware of the uphill task he faced. He could see clearly the political stakes and the many unanswered questions to this overly complex conflict that mixed politics, culture and deeply ingrained religious beliefs, but he hoped that at least the topic would provoke discussion. The expressionless face of Prime Minister Mahler gave Ramsden no clues as to his possible reaction.

"We have considered your proposal for a single state, but the consequences of such a solution go beyond Israel and Palestine. Palestinians are Muslims with ties to radical Muslim countries world-wide; their influence on a united Israel-Palestine would present more far-reaching security problems than we currently face," Hanon Mahler said.

"I see your point." Ramsden considered Mahler's analysis for a moment. "What if such a union brought exactly the desired outcome and Israel becomes a friend of all the Muslims? I think the main reason for the animosity is the view that Palestinian lands are being occupied and that view would gradually change with a single state."

"We have different cultures, different religions, different languages and different values. I can't possibly see how such a union would be sustainable," Mahler countered.

"While I am not trying to draw a parallel I believe the achievement of co-existence between the different cultures and religions among Blacks and Whites in South Africa is a clear demonstration that a single state solution should be given a chance."

"Islamic fundamentalists are promoting the return of the Caliphate that would wipe Israel from the map through Jihadist activities. I think the Palestinians would throw the idea out even before they have had the chance to hear it."

"Prime Minister Mahler, the US Government has consulted leading Islamic scholars and theologians on the call to the Caliphate. There is almost a unanimous agreement that the Caliphate is akin to the Vatican as the spiritual leaders of Muslims world-wide, not some kind of a superstate. Should we at least put it on the table and hear what they have to say?"

"Well, Israel is a democratic country; I'll consult my cabinet on the issue."

CHAPTER 50

March, 2010. In the West Bank a historic meeting was taking place between the Prime Ministers of the Palestinian Authority and the Prime Minister of Israel. This was the culmination of several months of diplomatic negotiations. The outcome of that meeting would shock the world and lead to a new realisation. The announcement would defy the die-hard sceptic – a blueprint for the establishment of a single nation of Israel and Palestine to be called Judo-Palestine.

As the final details of the type of government that would rule Judo-Palestine took shape, the President of the United States had another agenda: the dismantling of the global terror network, dubbed *Dining with the Terrorists.* It was his biggest challenge since his accession to office. He had thought long and hard about the enormity of the problem, given the faceless nature of international terrorism.

***

September, 2010. On board the US military aircraft carrier *USS Abraham Lincoln* the President launched his new policy on international terrorism: America would work through the United Nations to root out the cause of terrorism and to eliminate all terrorist activities around the world.

Dressed in full military outfit as the Commander-in-Chief of the US Army, the President addressed the whole world. "America is committed, and I am personally committed, to achieving global peace and security. We believe people of all nations deserve to have adequate security and to live in dignity free from fear, because in freedom lies the road to reconciliation and reconstruction that would subsequently lead to development. We would therefore provide the necessary logistics, military and financial support through the United Nations to achieve this goal. It will not be easy to reach that goal but *Operation Dining with the Terrorist* is a way forward."

The fierce opposition the President's policy had first met had given way to support, paving the way for the United Nations to take centre stage in negotiating peace with rebel groups and terrorist organisations world-wide.

In the Indonesian capital of Jakarta the Supreme Head of *Jamaat Islamia* was meeting for the first time with the United Nations Special Envoy on Global Peace, Sadiq Iqbal, and US Secretary of State Gordon Ramsden. Inside the Istiqlal Mosque Gordon Ramsden sat uncomfortably on the floor shifting his weight from one hand to the other. Bashir Ibn Mustafa, a name no one had ever heard before, sat in front of his two guests with the beads of his *Tasbih* moving between his right thumb and index finger. The movements of his lips were almost imperceptible as he recited the ninety-nine attributes of Allah. Bashir had agreed to meet his guest only because of his recognition of the world body as the ultimate global power. *"Bismilah Al Rahman Al Rahim,"* Bashir said as he lifted his hands to his face, finishing his supplications.

"We're here today in the name of global peace, but we need everyone's effort to be able to achieve this goal. It's for that reason we in the West would like to understand Islam a bit more," Ramsden said.

Bashir, a diminutive bespectacled man in his late fifties, smiled towards Ramsden and spoke in perfect English. "You Westerners have not been interested in understanding anything else but your own beliefs and values. You've been quick to find someone to blame for your own ill-conceived policies, then wield your big guns to bully everyone into submission. I'm glad America is now living up to its responsibility as the world's only superpower."

"One of the things that will help us achieve this goal of world peace is to know what makes people in your organisation undertake terrorist activities."

"I don't know what makes people do what they do because our movement was founded on the basis of promoting the understanding of Islam world-wide through *Jamaat,* what you might call missionary activities. This is what the Holy Prophet taught. Individuals make their own decisions to go on *Jamaat,* plan their own activities and fund their own trips. We provide the guidance, but what people do in their individual groups is beyond our control."

"Are you saying your organisation does not preach Jihad that leads to international terrorism?" Ramsden asked.

"I'm not ruling out bad nuts in our movement, just as there are some in every society and people misrepresent Jihad. What I'm saying is that we abhor terror and we reach out to people with a clear message: to encourage Muslims world-wide to practise Islam and to invite non-Muslims to join."

"What message would you like me to take back to the UN?" Sadiq Iqbal asked. He had been listening and taking notes all this while.

"Our movement supports the United Nations' efforts towards global peace and would provide all assistance needed to achieve this goal."

"On our part the UN would provide assistance in producing literature to explain our combined efforts to your followers," Iqbal explained. "Is there anything you would like to see the UN do?" he asked.

"I think you should consider having religious representations on the UN General Assembly if not on the Security Council," Bashir replied.

"Point noted."

The Friday following the meeting TV cameras looked over every angle of the Grand Istiqlal Mosque as Bashir Ibn Mustafa gave his weekly sermon before the *Jum'a* Prayer. "Henceforth," he said, "all Jihad activities will be restricted to the Holy Prophet's noble ideal of individual effort to bring people to accept Islam."

His statement was re-echoed in major mosques throughout the Muslim world.

***

At the United Nations General Assembly, Secretary Gordon Ramsden called for the world body to complement America's effort at eradicating poverty on the African continent. "America's policy is now geared towards engaging Africa as our strategic partners and we welcome any ideas from African countries on how we can help them to achieve their individual goals."

The Angolan Foreign Minister, Edivaldo de Alvares, addressed the Assembly: "Following the global campaign to eliminate landmines, Angola in the last few months has been undertaking small-scale detonations using diseased animals. The quickest way to eliminate the millions of landmines scattered around Angola and Congo over several decades of civil war would be to detonate them by releasing shiploads of cattle onto the minefields. I therefore call on the support of this House."

"Your suggestion is laudable and I agree we need to take a detailed look at the landmines issue, but it might spark off huge international campaign by animal's rights activists," Ramsden responded, looking invitingly around the room for support. He thought the President's policy on providing more aid to Africa would not benefit the people who needed it most, as the money would be recycled through corrupt government officials back into foreign accounts. He had suggested to the President that they should tackle corruption first, arguing that if all the money stashed away by African leaders was returned to their respective countries it would deter subsequent government officials from doing the same, but the President had been adamant, preferring to support the countries that were already practising democracy of a sort.

The Ghanaian Foreign Minister, Kofi Mensah, who had been listening to the debate on Africa, was trying to figure out what America's real agenda was. In his years as a Foreign Minister he had come to question the stated motives for the West's involvement in Africa. He wondered whether all the failed IMF and World Bank policies could be blamed on corruption and mismanagement. In his mind the Western model was like a farmer who gave only what was necessary to his cattle to produce milk. Once the cows were past their milk production stage they were expendable and became dead meat.

"Africa is no doubt beset with a myriad of challenges and I can spend the rest of the day enumerating them," Kofi Mensah started, "but the one thing in my mind that can make a big change on the continent is the utilisation of Africa brains on the African continent. As a start I would suggest all World Bank sponsored projects should require, as a minimum, the employment of Africans based abroad. Secondly, I think we should move away from negative labels like *poverty* reduction to more positive ones like *wealth* creation in our language to promote more positive results."

"May I suggest that the UN Commission on Africa presents to this House a draft plan of action with key targets and a clear timetable for consideration," Ramsden concluded.

CHAPTER 51

The wind of change was blowing across Africa and beyond.

It all started when Kutini was refused entry into the UK following his release from America, despite the fact that he was a permanent resident there. He had returned to Ghana to work full time on his farm.

Early one morning, Kutini was lying awake in his farm house thinking about his wife Laz when the phone rang. The caller display showed it was an international call from the United States. "What do the Americans want this time?" he heard himself asking, thinking it was from the intelligence agents. He hesitated before answering.

"I hope I didn't wake you up."

"Laz, where are you? Are you in Ghana?" Kutini asked in succession, recognising his wife's voice right away.

"I'm in Boston. I've been with my cousin since I left London."

"I'm sorry about what happened to Amiga."

"Kutini, I need to talk to you, but I can't discuss it over the phone. I am coming to Ghana next week. Where can I find you?"

"Right here at the ranch. When is your flight? I'll come and pick you up at the airport." Kutini still loved his wife and had been hoping that he would find her somehow and ask her to come back.

"Arrival time is next Sunday at six-forty in the evening," Laz replied.

Kutini had come to Accra the day before Laz's arrival and was at the airport an hour before her plane arrived. It was a long, anxious moment for Kutini between the landing of the plane and Laz's emergence from the arrival gate. He had been thinking of what she would want to talk to him about that warranted her travelling all the way from the United States to Ghana. Had she found another man and was coming with divorce papers for him to sign? Suddenly Kutini wasn't sure if he wanted to meet her, so when Laz finally emerged behind a group of travellers he wasn't sure how to welcome her.

As soon as Laz saw Kutini waiting, she couldn't hide her emotions and ran to him, put her arms round his neck. "Oh, it's so good to see you. I've missed you so much," she said and kissed him.

"I've missed you too," Kutini said after breaking the kiss. He went to collect Laz's trolley out of the way of arriving passengers.

"So, what have you come to talk about?" Kutini asked on their way to the hotel.

"I just wanted to be with you," Laz replied, unable to hold her feelings any longer.

"Welcome back."

Kutini and Laz returned to the farm the following day.

***

Over the next few months Kutini became an active member of the African Unification Front and took on the responsibility of Organising Secretary, in effect the body's official spokesperson. The first thing he did was to push for the ratification of the African Parliament by all governments recognised within the framework of the AUF policy on the Diaspora. He had limited success in his bid with some governments who were afraid to relinquish power for fear of their own iniquities visiting them and for fear of losing ties to their colonial masters.

As the AUF's spokesperson, Kutini embarked on one of the most ambitious programmes ever undertaken in the continent's history. He lobbied and mobilised the various governments to establish an African High Command – a programme that had been on the drawing board for decades.

With this body behind him Kutini started to venture into unchartered territories, becoming the de-facto chief negotiator in all conflict situations on the continent. He would be the first to go into rebel areas to discuss ceasefires and pave the way for subsequent negotiations and the eventual signing of a peace pact.

Kutini's first action when he had secured a ceasefire would be to ask the rebels to agree to put their arms under the supervision of the African High Command prior to their eventual decommissioning and the integration of the rebels into the country's regular army. He had been known in some circumstances to offer a place within the African High Command to some rebel leaders, a stand that drew opposition but which he was prepared to defend on the basis of peace.

Kutini's bold initiative had resulted in the eradication of rebel activities on the continent. The last military-turned-civilian government was due to retire and was not seeking another term of office. Kutini's fame among the diplomatic circles in Africa had become unparalleled and so when he was invited to take up the position as the Chairman of the African Commission on Conflict Resolution Kutini accepted it as an honour and as an acknowledgement of his efforts.

Kutini had been invited by the All-African Students' Union to address a conference on the theme, *United we Stand* on the campus of the University of Pretoria in South Africa.

The 3,000-capacity auditorium was packed mostly with students and a cross-section of the press corps with their state-of-the-art gadgets. As Kutini entered the entire audience stood up. "Kutini, Kutini, Kutini …" they shouted as he walked up to stage. He wasn't surprised. His name had spread widely in the continent.

"United," Kutini shouted.

"We stand," the audience responded.

"United…"

"We stand."

"Friends and colleagues …," Kutini started as the applause gradually died down.

He addressed his audience on the activities of the African Unification Front telling them that over the years the organisation had set up the process necessary for unification to begin. He elaborated on the composition of an African Parliament and its policies, stating that it was past members of the AASU who had first started the AUF. He ended his speech by calling upon the AASU to take an active part in the evolution of an African State – a state that would recognise her people as "one people, one heritage, and one destiny".

The floor was now opened to questions and the announcer said that questions would be taken from the students before the press corps. There was silence as they waited for the first student to ask a question. There was none.

"We would now take questions from the press," the announcer said, unsure why such an unusual silence had descended in the room.

"Dr. Bomanso, don't you think this whole idea of a united Africa is as utopian as waiting for the day the chicken will grow teeth?" a member of the press asked and instantly attracted a handful of clapping from the press corps.

"I do agree with you, honourable member of the fourth estate of the realm, it is as utopian as when man first dreamt of flying."

The applause greeting the answer was deafening, the resonance in the auditorium causing the whole building to vibrate.

"Any more questions?" the announcer asked after the noise had died down, noticing that the number of hands which were up the last time had reduced. What he hadn't noticed was the gradual decrease in the number of people in the auditorium; the students were gradually leaving the hall before the closing courtesies.

There were no more questions so the announcer thanked the audience and brought the event to a close.

As the students came out of the auditorium they formed into two lines.

Kutini was engaged in a conversation when this unusual event caught his attention outside the auditorium. He was wondering what was going on when the procession started to sing.

"What's going on outside?" Kutini asked one of the conference organisers.

"I have no idea, but whatever it is, it's not part of our plan," the organiser replied.

What happened that afternoon after the conference shocked even Kutini.

The lyrics were slowly becoming clearer: *All we are saying; give us African Unity; don't waste our time.* They kept on repeating the words, marching slowly in the direction of the city and gradually bringing the mile-long procession to the seat of the Pretoria Government.

They stopped in their tracks as they approached the main road leading to the government offices. Policemen, in full combat gear, stood facing them. The students stopped their advance, sat right where they were, and continued with their monotonous song. The police looked on helplessly as the students sat there causing major disruption to traffic.

The actions of the AASU in Pretoria, which were carried on TV channels worldwide, became a clarion call. All across Africa people were taking to the streets in mass demonstrations calling for African unity – in an unprecedented scale and diversity.

A hitherto conventional student activity had expanded beyond the narrow confines of their academic fortresses; it had blazed like wild fire, engulfing entire countries that were calling for their respective governments to sign the declaration of an African Federation and to ratify the African Parliament. They wanted to be united under one government.

***

As the Global Africa idea gained momentum a different kind of phenomenon was taking place in Europe: the idea had come under attack. It had started when Black militant activists began dying of mysterious sudden illnesses. Kutini had become aware of this strange phenomenon through the news media.

Laz had been cuddled cosily in Kutini's arms watching television. She held the remote control, flicking through the channels when the Flintstones came up. She let it show. She loved TV, but she could never bring herself to watch scheduled programmes. She would just flick through and watch whatever she liked at that moment.

They sat watching the programme and laughing. Kutini was waiting for his favourite part of the Flintstones. It came; it always did, when Fred came out to drop the milk bottles at the end of the show and Dino closed the door behind him. "Fantastic," Kutini said for the umpteenth time.

On the hour Laz routinely turned the TV to the main news channel. "Coping with the mystery illness," a headline stated.

"Following the mysterious illness that has claimed its ninth victim of African descent, the European Parliament has passed a new law ordering the repatriation of anyone who showed symptoms similar to this strange illness," the details of the news stated.

The television pictures went on to show victims being moved on trolleys from their deathbeds to the morgue.

"The victims are suddenly attacked by this mystery illness and they die within hours, some before reaching the hospital. So far, all the victims are known to have been in good health at the time of the attack. Medical experts have not been able to come up with any explanation of the cause of the disease," the newsreader ended.

Kutini watched with disdain the unfolding drama of the plight of brothers and sisters and his heart bled. "If they can't find the cause of this illness in Europe, what chance do these people have back in their respective home countries?" It was more of a statement to Laz than a question.

"I think it's just a prelude to more heinous and sinister moves that we are yet to see," Laz said.

Laz's statement turned out to be prophetic. Europe's repatriation policy had come to involve more than the disease; it was a grand scheme of mass expulsions from Greater Europe of non-Europeans with criminal records, mental or physical illness, 'radical' political views, and non-Christian, non-Jewish backgrounds. The prospects and consequences were simply horrifying to contemplate.

In the United States, the White House was also becoming increasingly alarmed at the political transformation taking place on the Africa continent. Mass rallies were taking place from country to country calling for their respective governments to join the bigger Africa unification process. During most of the rallies, people carried placards calling for an end to Western Imperialism.

One particular placard showed the map of Africa in the background with people breaking the chains that artificially divided the continent with the inscription:

Let's break the artificial barriers and pursue the African Agenda.

This particular placard provoked reactions at the White House and the President called for a meeting of his Foreign Policy and Intelligence advisors. "We have to stop this madness going on in Africa. We can't allow this unification nonsense to go on. The civilised world must act to stop this international terrorism," he told them.

"The masses seem to be supporting it, Mr. President," Secretary of State Larry Holmes noted.

"How can a continent with such vast diversity of cultures come together? Even the predominant Black people differ in their culture and languages." The President was adamant.

"I think a united Africa will be good for business for American companies. The Chinese are already there and if we are not seen to be supporting the unification process they will steal all our businesses," Holmes persisted.

"Forget China; as long as we control the world's oil and energy resources they will always be at our mercy. Africa is a different scenario. With their vast oil resources from Libya, Sudan and through Nigeria to Gabon and Angola, if they unite we will lose our grips and we will be doomed. Remember, one of the conditions that led our predecessors to enter into the First World War with Europe was access to African markets. It is our duty to make sure their past efforts and sacrifices are not wasted."

"What do we do, Mr. President?" Craig Brooks asked.

"The first thing is to get intelligence from our field agents in the various African countries and then set up a committee to counter the process. Can you see to that?"

"It shouldn't be a problem, we have the men on the ground and we can start by isolating the Arab north," Brooks stated.

"Let's do whatever it takes," the President concluded.

***

Oblivious to the counter-intelligence machine being hatched in the United States, the executive board of the AUF met to discuss the new development in Europe and to devise strategies to resolve the situation.

The first of the strategies was to lobby African governments to agree to negotiate the situation with the European governments. As the official spokesperson, Kutini was elected to head a three-man delegation to carry the message to the respective African governments.

Their first mission took them to the South African capital of Pretoria. After two hours of closed-door discussion with President Joseph Thebe and his top government officials, the South African government agreed to support AUF's cause.

In the Nigerian capital of Abuja Kutini and his team secured similar support from the Nigerian government.

When they had secured the support of a majority of the African governments the case against the compulsory repatriation law was put to the Europeans, but the answer was simple – the law was non-negotiable.

Unperturbed by the resistance from the Europeans the AUF President called a press conference calling for Africans everywhere to come home. "There is no place like home," he declared. The impact of the call was overwhelming. From Britain and the United States, Africans in the Diaspora were moving en-mass to Africa.

***

In the Jamaican capital of Kingston, a historic meeting was taking place. Since the signing of the Charter creating the African, Caribbean and Pacific Consultative Assembly on 15 April 2005, the forty-two countries had provided an institutional framework for the work of the ACP Parliament. Mrs. Wayne-Davies, the ACP President saw the act as a formal re-affirmation of the existing inter-parliamentary cooperation in Article 18 of the Georgetown Agreement. Taking her cue from the new paradigm in America's foreign policy, she had increased her efforts at fostering greater cooperation among the ACP countries which led to the formation of the Joint Parliamentary Assembly. In spite of her exemplary leadership, she did not foresee what would become a one country of Island-Africans.

Events taking place in continental Africa triggered by America's foreign policy shift had resulted in a change in relations among the Caribbean countries. What had existed for many years as a dormant economic cooperation, had suddenly gained momentum and in a rather spontaneous reaction to a suggestion from the ACP President the people had called for referendum that led to the establishment of one state in the Caribbean.

Kutini Bomanso sat, among African leaders, as the guest of honour in the extraordinary session of the Joint Parliamentary Assembly of the ACP countries as Mrs. Wayne-Davies addressed the Assembly. "What you're about to hear and witness today is the culmination of years of hard work and determination; a determination borne out of our desire as Island-Africans to take our destiny into our own hands. Our time in the wilderness is over as all the Caribbean countries have decided we are one people with one destiny and for that matter deserve to be one country." She paused as the audience erupted with applause. She waited until the applause had died down, then called on all leaders of the Caribbean countries to come forward for the short ceremony to swear their oath of allegiance to the first Prime Minister of the Caribbea who had been elected through an electoral college from among the existing leaders.

"You will all repeat after me," Wayne-Davies started, "I..."

The room was filled with clear voices, as they started, accompanied by the muffled sound of several names pronounced together.

"...of...," Wayne Davies continued, "do hereby solemnly swear an oath of allegiance to serve the Federation of Caribbean Islands as one country hereby called Caribbea with honesty and integrity, so help me God."

As the new state governors returned to their seats the audience stood clapping and cheering. Kutini stood among the audience, removed a handkerchief and wiped the tears from his eyes. He had embarked on a mission to create a better world for his people but he never thought he would, in his lifetime, see the unification of Africans. This singular event had renewed his hopes that the changes taking place on mainland Africa were real. Kutini was still in tears when he heard his name.

"Ladies and Gentlemen, let's welcome Dr. Bomanso," Wayne-Davies said.

"I really haven't got much to say," Kutini started, "I came here to learn and to understand a part of me I never knew. The one lesson I'll take away with me is that we should forgive but not forget the wrongs against us. To forgive is divine; it heals and cleanses the soul, but to forget is to provide a fertile ground for complacency that leads to the path of destruction. Thank you."

As Kutini returned to his seat his mind went to his friend Yaro and the political campaigns taking place throughout Africa itself. He hoped that soon he would see a repeat of Caribbea's example on the continent. The first all-African parliamentary candidates were winding up the final stages of their election campaigns and Kutini had promised he would campaign alongside Yaro.

CHAPTER 52

A week after returning from Jamaica, Kutini sat under the shade provided by the temporary tent in the Nigerian capital of Abuja. In front of the tent the platform extended forward into the open sun to accommodate a dais that held over a dozen different microphones. Behind the microphones stood Yaro Tunde, looking every inch a dignified African dressed in a spotless white traditional Nigerian outfit with gold embroidery around the neck and the end of the sleeves. His charm and charisma held the crowd spellbound as he addressed the huge gathering in the open park.

"Africa is now ready to start on a clean slate. The days of military interventions and rebel activities belong to history. As a people we have the right to misgovern ourselves, after all that's what democracy is all about – going with the majority even if the minority is right," Yaro said, ending his political campaign to the seat that would be at the centre of the future governing body of the Federal African Republic.

The date for the inaugural session of the first African Parliament had been set for 24 November, 2012. Preparations were underway.

***

Kutini arrived in the Angolan capital of Luanda accompanied by his wife, Laz. "Our people have finally made their way home," she said, referring to the representatives of the African Americans, African British, African Caribbean and other Africans in the Diaspora.

Kutini simply nodded his agreement as the master of ceremonies walked over to the dais and waited for silence. "Before I introduce our guest speaker for this historic event," he started, "I would like to announce that the timetable for the President's visit to each parliamentary constituency will be communicated to members of the house when it has been finalised next week." He then walked over to the table where the dignitaries were sitting and spoke to one of them – they were all ready. As he walked back towards the dais to make his introduction he noticed someone walking towards him from one side. He looked back and one of the dignitaries whispered into his ear. He nodded with a smile – he was about to make a serious oversight.

"Shall we all rise and sing the African anthem," the master of ceremony said, glad he had been reminded before he committed the omission.

Nkosi Sikelel' i Afrika
Malupakam' upondo Iwayo
Yiva imitandazo yetu
Usi – sikelele
Sikelel' amadol' asizwe
Sikelela kwa nomlisela
Ulitwal' ilizwe ngomonde
Uwusiki lele
Sikelel' amalinga etu
Awonanyana nokuzaka
Uwasikelele
Yihla Moya – Yihla Moya!
Yihla Moya Oyingcwele

When the song ended, a woman from the house restarted it – solo – in the most beautiful voice Kutini had ever heard. As she sang, she moved slowly through the spaces onto the front row where she stood like an orchestra conductor. Hers was a quintessentially African voice, with a compelling command of vocal dynamics and glissandos fit to penetrate the hearts of everyone in the room. Her long notes sent shivers down the spine.

When she was about to finish she used a hand gesture to get the people on their feet and together they sang the song one more time. She conducted the song with her entire body. The orchestra obeyed her commands with emotions that showed through their body movements to the rhythm of the song.

Kutini joined in, humming the song, conscious of his discordant singing voice. He had been taught this song during his school days, but he had never known the words. Yet he could feel the song deep inside him, beyond the physical. He asked a colleague sitting next to him who the woman was.

"She is a Parliamentary Member from South Africa," he was told.

"Her voice is enchanting," Kutini said.

"Absolutely," his colleague agreed, his eyes still fixed on the woman.

Laz who had been equally moved by the song, turned to Kutini. "What's the meaning of the song?" she asked.

"God bless Africa, bless the leaders, bless the young and bless our efforts, descend Holy Spirit."

"The Holy Spirit is already here with us," she said.

When silence had returned after a brief outpouring of emotions following the song the announcer was back on the dais.

"I would now like to present to you this illustrious son of Africa who needs no introduction. He was not only instrumental in bringing peace and stability to the Congo but was also at the forefront of negotiating peace in most conflicts across Africa, mostly under life-threatening situations. He was the man who made friends with lions inside their own den. Ladies and gentlemen, I present to you Dr. Kutini Dobakoobie Bomanso."

When the unassuming, almost innocent-looking bespectacled man took the centre-stage he was welcomed with a tumultuous ovation.

"I don't think I deserve all these accolades you've bestowed on me, but thank you," Kutini said to the person who introduced him, his words transmitted throughout the hall by the microphone.

His modesty drew more applause as he stood looking down on the bundle of papers containing his speech while waiting for the applause to die down. Most people in the hall had heard his name and what he had done to achieve such high profile status, but fewer people had seen him in person – today was the first time for many.

"Before I begin to share with you my joy on this historic day," he started, when the hall had gone quiet, "I would like us to pay a tribute to one of Africa's greatest sons who lived and died in the Diaspora calling for Africa to unite. Ladies and gentlemen, please rise up and join me in singing Bob Marley's *Africa Unite.*"

Africa unite:
"Cause we're moving right out of Babylon,
And we're going to our Father's land, yea-ea.

How good and how pleasant it would be before God
and man, yea-eah!
To see the unification of all Africans, yeah!
As it's been said a'ready, let it be done, yeah!

We are the children of the Rastaman;
We are the children of the Iyaman.

So-o, Africa unite:
"Cause the children (Africa unite) wanna come home.

"Thank you," Kutini said to the house.

The whole assembly started clapping after the song and Kutini joined in. "Please sit," he said twice before the frenzied assembly gradually calmed down to listen to what he had to say.

"Kwame Nkrumah has been described as a dreamer who was born before his time, but it is only by looking at the realities of the failed promises of independence, the tragic consequences of neo-colonialism and the contemporary attempts at re-colonising Africa, that we can truly say he was not born early enough. It was not by mere coincidence that this day was chosen to inaugurate the first parliament of the Federal African Republics. It is the least we could do to honour this venerable son of Africa. May his soul rest in perfect peace."

"In more than five decades since the end of the so-called second world war, a war that had nothing to do with Africa, but a war in which Africa played a significant role, when the victorious allied leaders uttered those fateful words 'never again', historians and politicians alike have called for the establishment of peace and stability in the world. Beyond the Cold War, which was itself part of a European conspiracy to fool the rest of the world, they pointed to the 'nuclear deterrent' – or was it detergent? They say that's why *we* have been at peace for so long. Of course, no one conspires these days and any person labelled a conspiracy theorist becomes an outright outlaw, and I make no apologies for being an outlaw."

By this time, Kutini had left the bundle of paper containing his speech and was standing away from the dais. He was not the one for formalities. He was a man of action and preferred to be where the action was. He continued without the written speech.

"After the Cold War, Russia and the Baltic states are now seen as part of Europe – the new Europe and the talk about the continuation of peace and a more secure and prosperous future for Europe and North America continues. The talk about building 'mini-nukes' to be used against 'rogue states' continues, but what is this peace they talk about? While the Europeans have been celebrating 'peace in our time' a third world war has been raging all around them. At one time there were over one hundred real wars in progress, fuelled by arms, ammunition, and 'advice' from the 'civilised world', not to mention the war against AIDS. In fact, more explosive power has been used up in the past fifty-eight years than in all the wars in the history of the world put together, including the first and second 'world wars' and the megatons of nuclear power dropped on Japan, a non-European nation. More people have died as a result of these wars than the total deaths of the first and second 'world wars'."

He moved to the dais and picked up a glass of water to drink. It was a deliberate pause for effect. Kutini was a well-spoken man who had mastered the art of public speaking. The room was silent, except for the mild humming of the air-conditioning. The sombre melancholy faces of his audience summed up their feelings.

He continued, this time maintaining his position behind the dais.

"But let's look on the bright side, the days of the division of Africa into dubious categories of Anglophone, Francophone, Lusophone and all the other 'phoney phones' that further divide us from our goal of unity are over. When we started on the road to unification, our European friends told us it was a utopian concept, citing all sorts of problems. However, when we look around today, what do we see? The same European countries that divided us into these dubious categories are united in one common European Union."

"The circumstances of neo-colonialism were antithetical to the advancement of African unity. They sought to reverse the course of African unity because those who have been exploiting and pillaging Africa's vast human and material resources know the significance of African unity. They know the day Africans unite will be the end of their rule as masters of the universe – and that end, a necessary one, has come and is here with us today."

Someone started to clap and the rest of the house picked up the clapping. The entire assembly stood up to give Kutini yet another ovation. The first President of the Federal African Republic would be the next person to address the assembly, but Kutini was really stealing the show.

Kutini used the pause to take another drink of water and allowed his eyes to sweep across the room. He was unmissable. Standing there, tall, handsome, and in his traditional Nigerian outfit was Yaro Tunde. He had stood for and won elections as the first African Member of Parliament for his area. He was part of history and he relished his new-found position.

Just before they came inside the conference room Yaro had remarked to Kutini that he should consider standing for president in the next general elections and Kutini had replied that he would be happy to be an African statesman.

The applause died down bringing Kutini's mind back to his speech.

"How many African countries are really important internationally? Angola exports more oil to America than Kuwait, yet Angola is no more relevant to America than the most deprived country on our dear land. Poverty, perpetuated by greed, has become the greatest source of insecurity on our land in the midst of abundance."

"We are currently dominated by a unipolar-hegemonic-hyperpower that has become the world's judge, jury and executioner, feeding the world with half-truths, lies and innuendos. The country with the largest stockpile of weapons of mass destruction is now the self-imposed police of the world for weapons of mass destruction. If America wants to rule the world it's simple: the whole world should take part in deciding who goes into the White House."

"That's right," someone shouted.

"Say it one more time," another voice from a different part of the room shouted.

"You're the one," came yet another shout.

"You'll be our next president." Kutini recognised that distinctive voice. It was the woman who had sung the anthem.

As Kutini waited for the voices to quieten down his eyes locked into those of Yaro and from the distance, Yaro seemed to be asking, "Are you still going to be a statesman?" Kutini ignored the voices and started wrapping up his speech.

"We have the resources to sustain and improve the well-being of our population. We have the skill to build the industries. How many Bill Gates does it take to produce Microsoft? We have decided enough is enough so:

Today we present to the world
The beacon of hope: A united Africa.
The chains of bondage have been broken

And there shall be no difference
Between the Arab north and the Bantu south
The Hausa from the west
Is united with the Masai from the east.

Today we're fulfilling the historic saying:
We can make music on black or white keys.
We're making music on both keys,
And we're achieving harmony to the glory of God.

Today we redefine the scramble for Africa:
Sharing in Africa's love, peace and prosperity.
Africa will no longer be divided and ruled,
We have regained our true identity.

Today we have shown that Africa is indeed one
We are united as one people with one goal;
The stone cut out not by human hands
Struck the statue on its feet of iron and clay
The giant has awakened in strength forever.

Today is the beginning of the African agenda.

Thank you."

Printed at Arabian Printing & Publishing House W.L.L.
Kingdom of Bahrain.

The African Agenda

ISBN: 1-4196-1898-9
ISBN-13: 978-1419618987
Library of Congress Control Number: 2007901375

Visit www.booksurge.com to order additional copies.